Welcome to Foundation House.

By Craig DiLouie

Episode Thirteen
The Children of Red Peak
Our War
One of Us
Suffer the Children
Tooth and Nail
Strike
The Alchemists
The Great Planet Robbery

The Infection Series
Crash Dive Series
Armor Series
The Aviator Series

EPISODE THIRTEEN

CRAIG DiLOUIE

REDHOOK

Copyright © 2023 by Craig DiLouie
Excerpt from *The Children of Red Peak* copyright © 2020 by Craig DiLouie

Cover design by Lisa Marie Pompilio
Cover photographs by Arcangel and Shutterstock
Cover copyright © 2023 by Hachette Book Group, Inc.
Author photograph by Jodi O

Hachette Book Group supports the right to free expression and the value of copyright. The purpose of copyright is to encourage writers and artists to produce the creative works that enrich our culture.

The scanning, uploading, and distribution of this book without permission is a theft of the author's intellectual property. If you would like permission to use material from the book (other than for review purposes), please contact permissions@hbgusa.com. Thank you for your support of the author's rights.

Redhook Books/Orbit
Hachette Book Group
1290 Avenue of the Americas
New York, NY 10104
hachettebookgroup.com

First Edition: January 2023

Redhook is an imprint of Orbit, a division of Hachette Book Group.
The Redhook name and logo are trademarks of Hachette Book Group, Inc.

The publisher is not responsible for websites (or their content) that are not owned by the publisher.

The Hachette Speakers Bureau provides a wide range of authors for speaking events. To find out more, go to www.hachettespeakersbureau.com or call (866) 376-6591.

Redhook books may be purchased in bulk for business, educational, or promotional use. For information, please contact your local bookseller or the Hachette Book Group Special Markets Department at special.markets@hbgusa.com.

Library of Congress Cataloging-in-Publication Data
Names: DiLouie, Craig, 1967– author.
Title: Episode thirteen / Craig DiLouie.
Other titles: Episode 13
Description: First edition. | New York : Redhook, 2023.
Identifiers: LCCN 2022018763 | ISBN 9780316443104 (trade paperback) |
    ISBN 9780316443203 (ebook)
Subjects: LCGFT: Ghost stories.
Classification: LCC PS3604.I463 E65 2023 | DDC 813/.6—dc23/eng/20220425
LC record available at https://lccn.loc.gov/2022018763

ISBNs: 9780316443104 (trade paperback), 9780316443203 (ebook)

Printed in the United States of America

LSC-C

Printing 3, 2023

For Chris Marrs, who loves a good ghost story

I believe that if we are to make any real progress in the psychic investigation, we must do it with scientific apparatus and in a scientific manner, just as we do in medicine, electricity, chemistry, and other fields.

—Thomas Alva Edison, interview with

Scientific American, 1920

EDITOR'S NOTE

Foundation House in Denton, Virginia, is the most documented haunting in American history. Countless media have sought to explain the bizarre events that occurred in the autumn of 2016 during the shooting of *Fade to Black*'s now legendary Episode 13.

So why this book?

The problem with Foundation House is that the haunting *is* so well documented. The amount of data is vast, requiring countless hours to consume. Even so, I find it amazing how much information supports events that stubbornly remain occluded in mystery, as they are so startingly impossible and have proven irreplicable.

As a result of this, another problem is that the haunting's veracity has become deeply contentious. Most literature covering the bizarre events at Foundation House is heavily biased, aiming from the outset to either propagandize belief in the haunting or debunk it step-by-step.

This book was written for the open minded with a highly curated but neutral, documentarian approach. I sifted the vast trove of information and edited it down to a straightforward and digestible narrative.

The narrative is presented without judgment, accepting the

authenticity of what is presented on its face value while leaving it entirely up to the reader to decide whether to believe or not. And it takes an approach of combining transcripts of audiovisual media with written documents, resulting in what might best be described as a written documentary.

For me, this involved deciding what to include and just as critically what to leave out. Readers will note the extensive material focusing on the participants in the haunting—the paranormal investigators and staff of *Fade to Black*, who recorded it all—notably their journal entries. I felt this was important so you can experience the events through their eyes.

In these pages, we see their wants, pressures, strengths, and flaws. If nothing else, the events at Foundation House present a fascinating study in the psychology of terror, the pursuit of knowledge at all costs, and the madness that results when the human mind is confronted by a miracle that resists comprehension.

In the end, I became as obsessed with framing the story of *Fade to Black*'s Episode 13 as the paranormal investigators displayed in creating it. The result is a book that is a rabbit hole about a rabbit hole. An invitation to explore it yourself while experiencing everything its trailblazers felt and witnessed.

And then make up your own mind whether to believe.

Welcome to Foundation House.

EPISODE
THIRTEEN

Hi, I'm Matt Kirklin, paranormal investigator. Welcome to my bio.

I'm not going to tell you about where I worked or went to school. I want to tell you about my imaginary childhood friend who turned out to be something else.

The time I first learned about death.

My life had just turned upside down. Mom and Dad had packed my whole life into cardboard boxes so it could be moved to a new house in Cherry Hill, New Jersey. Only a little downstate, but for ten-year-old me, it was like moving to another planet.

We were going to Grandma's house.

At her viewing, my grandmother had looked lifelike yet deflated without her soul. I pictured a balloon with all the air let out and replaced with sawdust.

"You should say goodbye," Mom told me.

I didn't know what to feel. I hadn't really known her. She'd always been cold to me, and I'd convinced myself she didn't like me.

Her house had a lot of old-fashioned furniture in every room with patterned pillows and glass knickknacks everywhere. When we'd visit and I'd end up in the same room with her, she'd keep an eye on me to make sure I didn't break anything.

I felt like a tourist in a hostile country. The worst part was Mom always went along with it. She became a different person around her mother. To my ten-year-old mind, this was frank betrayal. At Grandma's house, she'd turn cold and watchful too, and I'd get angry and sullen imagining everybody ganging up on me.

Mostly, I stayed outside. The house backed onto woods, where I could explore and invent stories. In the winter, though, sometimes it was too cold, and I'd be stuck in the house for most of the day with my books and drawing pads and LEGO sets.

Standing in front of the open casket, Mom tugged my hand. "Say goodbye to your grandmother, Matt."

Usually a warm if looming presence, Mom wept and seemed distant.

"Goodbye, Grandma." Then I imagined her soul was still here, watching me like a hawk, so I added, "Thanks for making me cookies."

By the time we arrived at Grandma's house to start our new lives there, it had been emptied. Like her soul, everything that defined her house had gone somewhere else, leaving a hollow shell. The rooms still smelled like her, though, just a hint of bitterness.

Mom seemed both sad and happy. "I grew up here, Matt."

This time, we weren't visiting. From now on, this would be my home. Because we'd moved in the middle of June, I hadn't been able to make any friends at my new school before it locked its doors for the summer.

As I always did, I went outside and played in the woods, inventing stories.

That's when I first saw the girl.

Walking back at the end of the day, the sky glooming with twilight, I spotted the pale face shining like a candle in my bedroom window.

When I blinked, she was gone.

That night, after I went to bed, she climbed in next to me and whispered, "I want you to be my friend."

Half-asleep, I said, "Okay."

Several times, her coughing woke me up. It would start as a rattle, the kind of involuntary dry cough that sounds like an engine trying to start. I could hear it in my dreams. Then it turned into a wet, violent hacking, alarming and sad, the desperate choking of somebody who is drowning.

The next day, I stayed in my room hoping to see her, but I grew bored just sitting there on my bed, so I played with my PlayStation for a while, and then after that I started to build a robot with my LEGOs.

When I looked up, she was there, kneeling on the carpet.

She was around my age, maybe a little younger, cute but frail looking. A lot of her cuteness came from the bonnet she wore, along with an old-fashioned Revolutionary War dress.

"What's your name?" I said.

"I'm Tammy. You're Matt."

"You woke me up last night coughing. You were so cold."

"I've been sick, but Mommy says I'll get better soon."

"Where do you live?"

"At the house next door."

"Do you want to play LEGO with me?"

And just like that, we became friends. Because Tammy wasn't allowed to play outside, I spent a lot of time in my room. Mom didn't like that. She'd hear me talking and come in to find me alone, as Tammy vanished whenever grownups were around.

When she caught me stealing a bottle of NyQuil from the closet, she became furious. "What are you doing with this?"

I said nothing.

"Were you going to drink it?"

"No!"

"Then what? Tell me. This is medicine, Matt. You don't play with it."

"It's for my friend."

"What friend?"

"Tammy. She's really sick."

Mom's scary when she's mad. She'd get what I'd call evil eyes. Her face would turn into an angry mask. I'd feel helpless, cast out, alone.

This time, her face became a Medusa mask of fury.

"That's not funny, Matthew."

I started crying. "It's true. She's real."

Mom took me to our new family doctor.

"Six out of ten kids between the ages of three and eight have an imaginary friend," the doctor said. "He's a little old for one, but it's perfectly normal."

"His imaginary friend told him to take medicine from the closet," Mom said.

"You told me it wasn't for him but his friend."

"He doesn't go outside. He just stays in his room playing with LEGOs, puzzles, and board games."

"Tammy doesn't like PlayStation," I explained.

"He's not the same boy. It's like he's regressing."

"Tammy's favorite is puzzles."

The doctor smiled. "He'll grow out of—"

"Stop it, Matt." She was so angry, she scared me and I think the doctor a little.

When we got home, I went to my room, only for her to call me back to the kitchen, where she started making dinner.

"You can watch TV in the living room. Or better yet, go outside."

I stuck around the living room for a while, but the angry rattling in the kitchen made me nervous, so I went out. In the backyard, I checked my bedroom window, but no face appeared, so I went back in.

A dark shape stood in the hallway.

"Where are you going?" Mom eyed me from the kitchen.

Skipping past, I yelled, "I have to pee!"

In the hallway, Tammy whispered in my ear. Told me what to do.

I went to the kitchen. "Mom?"

She placed a fistful of dry pasta into a boiling pot. "What is it?"

I gazed down at my feet. I did not want to be doing this, but I'd promised. "Tammy said she's sorry about the NyQuil."

"You're going to stop this right now, Matthew."

"But she wanted me to tell you something else."

"What." Not a question but a warning.

"She said the Bicentennial is coming up, and she wants, wants..."

Mom blanched and turned bone white.

I steeled myself to keep going. "She wants to wear her special costume dress to school. She just wants to get better so she can do that."

Mom turned away to grip the counter with both hands. Her shoulders started to shake, and I heard her sobbing.

I started crying too. The look on her face had terrified me. Maybe I really was just seeing things. Maybe I had a mental illness.

"Sorry, Mom. I'll stop talking to her. Just stop crying. Please."

Mom slowly collected herself and started talking in a quiet, flat voice. "Tell Tammy that Pat sends her love. Tell her I'm sorry I couldn't visit her before."

"Okay," I sobbed.

"I'll bet she looks beautiful, so beautiful, in her dress."

I wasn't sure what was happening. Either Mom believed me, or she was now humoring me. I didn't want her humoring me. In a way, it was worse than her telling me I'd made Tammy up.

When I gave my friend the message, she smiled and vanished.

School started then, and I quickly made new friends. When I got home from school, I avoided my room. When I did have to go in there, I announced I didn't want any guests. I didn't want to make Mom upset anymore. I didn't want an imaginary friend. I wanted real friends. I wanted to be normal.

It wasn't until years later that Mom filled me in on the whole truth, which explained everything.

Tammy had been her friend before she was mine.

At the age of nine, the girl died of a lung infection, a complication of cystic fibrosis. The year was 1976, the two hundredth anniversary of America's founding. The Revolutionary War dress was the costume her mother had made for her to wear to school for the Bicentennial celebration.

Tammy never wore it to school. She'd been kept home sick all week. Mom hadn't been able to see her. Then one day, she was told her friend died.

My mother had never known peace with it until the day I gave her Tammy's message and was able to relay hers back. As for me, I never saw the girl again, though I'll always be grateful to her. She was a good friend when I needed one.

This is why I started *Fade to Black*. Because I know there is life after death. Because I know spirits are real. And by finding them and trying to communicate, perhaps both they and the living can find the same comfort.

FOUNDATION
HOUSE

Jackpot! We got it, gang.

Foundation House for lucky thirteen.

During my five-plus years as a paranormal investigator, I've always wanted to check out this house. In our little community, it's pretty infamous. Not for the haunting, which is honestly kinda run of the mill, but for the general weirdness.

This place has some wild lore connected to it. Seriously, I could write a book.

Nobody's ever been given access until now, a real stroke of luck. You heard me right. It's never been investigated. *Ghost Hunters*, eat your heart out!

Built in 1920 near the historic Belle Green Plantation a few miles from the little Virginia town of Denton, the mansion is a throwback to antebellum architecture. Picture large, wraparound porches where you sip mint juleps while you enjoy the sunset. The house was built by Jared Wright, heir to a sugar company. When he died in the sixties, it stood intestate until the Paranormal Research Foundation, or PRF, bought it and moved in.

That's when Wright Mansion became Foundation House.

In 1972, while the Republicans renominated Nixon for president, the last American troops left Vietnam, and Bobby Fischer became the first American world chess champion, five paranormal all-stars lived in this house and recruited dozens of people to take part in weird experiments.

Their motto was "Where there is smoke, there is fire." They believed paranormal powers reside in all of us, dormant in our DNA. They were members of the Human Potential Movement, which believed humanity only used a fraction of its potential intelligence and ability. They wanted to identify paranormal abilities in people, discover the underlying mechanisms, and learn how to train and develop them to make a utopia.

In short, they were wacky as hell, but see it through their eyes for a minute. They envisioned a world where people could talk to the dead. Could read minds, control objects remotely, travel out of their bodies, know the future. And they weren't stereotypical hippies. They were some of the leading scientists of their time, and two of them—Shawn Roebuck and Don Chapman—were certified geniuses.

As for the researchers, we know they went missing in 1972. The police files themselves vanished in the Election Day Flood of 1985.

So what are we investigating, exactly? Over the years, neighbors driving past the property reported seeing the ghostly apparition of an abnormally tall woman appearing in the upstairs window. Local kids using it as a party hangout said they heard invisible feet stomping on the grand staircase, experienced cold spots, and witnessed strange flashing lights in the woods around it.

In Episode 13, *Fade to Black*'s crack team will spend seventy-two hours at Foundation House. According to the owner, nobody's lived in it since 1972, so we are hoping to find it more or less how the scientists left it.

Using cutting-edge techniques and the latest technology, we'll investigate the paranormal claims and also see what we can learn about the Foundation itself. Which makes a great opportunity for me to brag about my team.

.As our camera shooter, Jake Wolfson is the eyes of our little operation. Because the show is unscripted, we have to be careful about what we shoot so we don't flood out postproduction. Hence his motto: "The most story for the least footage."

Camera shooters are usually pretty stressed out. They track the action on their little black-and-white viewfinder while being aware of everything that's going on and anticipating what will happen next. Jake's a solid pro, though. Nothing ever seems to faze him. He's a big, muscly guy with a braided gold beard and runic tattoos running down his arms. A real badass in look and deed.

Then there's our tech manager, Kevin Linscott, the man with the mustache, our operation's ears and technical wizard. He helps set up all our gear and monitors it while mixing audio for the show. If the camera doesn't see it, the audio catches it.

Kevin's a retired Philadelphia police officer who did a lot of ghost hunting with me at Ralston Investigates the Paranormal (RIP), an amateur local ghost hunting group, before joining the show, and he's got all these great stories. When Claire tells me to trust the equipment, Kevin reminds me to trust my instincts and senses.

Jessica Valenza is our understudy and protégé. She's a professional actress the producers added to the show to round out the team. She has turned into quite the paranormal investigator, and she fits right in.

For a reality show, we keep things lean and mean, as we don't want people crowding around bumping into stuff and producing false positives on our instruments. Jessica not only helps with the investigating but does a lot of behind-the-scenes stuff for the show, a real jack-of-all-trades.

And then there's Claire, my wonderful wife. The best of the best. Adorable and smarter than a bullwhip, she graduated magna cum laude from Virginia Tech with a PhD in physics. She designed all our ghost hunting protocols and is a crack investigator.

I honestly couldn't do this without her.

Working together, we're a team. But more than that, we're family. A family that explores the unknown with a spirit of comradeship and a whole lot of scientific curiosity to solve the oldest and greatest of human mysteries: What happens to us when we die?

Oh, and I should give a shout-out to one more person who makes all this work.

You.

Seriously, without you, there's no show, so as always, thank you for watching and participating. This show is heaven for me, as I get to earn a living doing what I love doing most, something I'd be doing either way.

So really, it's about you. I'm proud that you're on our team.

And I hope you're as excited as we are about Episode 13.

It's going to be amazing.

Foundation House, here we come!

Ghost Hunters, Paranormal Lockdown, and similar reality ghost-hunting shows capitalize on America's fascination with the supernatural based on a tried-and-true formula. A paranormal investigation team explores a haunted location under the costumery of scientific rigor and confirms the presence of ghosts based on queasy feelings, fancy gadgets, and a few weird thumps in the night.

Deserved or not, criticisms of these shows being pseudoscience smack of party pooping, as they offer good fun aimed at the nearly one-half of Americans who believe in the supernatural, ghosts in particular. Though I'm personally agnostic on the subject, I sometimes watch for the fascinating locations and cheap thrills. Which goes to show you don't have to believe in ghosts to have fun in a haunted house.

Enter newcomer *Fade to Black*, a series picked up by Pulse USA Network. Produced by former members of Ralston Investigates the Paranormal, or RIP, in Ralston, Virginia, it stars husband and wife team Matt and Claire Kirklin as they follow the proven formula but with a nice twist: Matt's a true believer, and Claire's a born skeptic.

Instead of coming up with new gimmicks to compete and stay fresh, they go the other way, putting the *real* back in reality television.

With his earnest good looks, bright smile, and eternal font

of optimism, Matt comes across as a nerd who woke up a rock star in an alternate universe. Even when something goes bump and the team has a freak-out, you can tell he's having the time of his life.

With her short, curly red mop top, Claire is cute as a button in a retro vest or cardigan complete with collared shirt and tie, sometimes even a large-brimmed bowler like she's the new Annie Hall. This willowy tomboy is the real nerd—physics PhD and all—doing her damnedest to debunk every paranormal claim using highly sophisticated equipment.

While other shows claim to use the scientific method to prove a haunting by trying to disprove it, Claire does it for real and with a vengeance. She steals the show by offering a catharsis narrative for the other half of Americans who aren't true believers and want to see a slam debunk.

But it's Matt and Claire together that makes the whole thing work, in no small part due to their on-screen chemistry, which involves inside jokes and occasional good-natured bickering leaking from their marriage. It gives this otherwise self-contained reality TV show something of an arc. Imagine if *The X-Files'* Mulder and Scully ever tied the knot, and it'd probably look something like this.

At the end of each episode, the Kirklins make their separate cases, laying out all the evidence and letting us, the viewer, decide for ourselves, spilling over into lively debate online. Most episodes seem to end in a bust for the believers—a creative decision that takes courage on its own—but a few made me go *hmm*.

And that makes *Fade to Black* good television. The show tackles one of life's biggest questions—What happens to us after we die?—and turns it into fodder for Monday morning chats around the water cooler. In doing so, it recognizes the fact that belief is rarely certain and always personal, while reminding us that the search for truth itself is half the fun.

FADE TO BLACK

Pulse USA Network, tonight at 9 ET and PT; 8 CT.

Paisley Hirsh and Jonathan Vogan, executive producers.

WITH: Matt and Claire Kirklin (lead investigators); Jessica Valenza (investigator); Kevin Linscott (tech manager).

Episode 13, Pre-Interview Transcript
Subject: Calvin Sparling
Files of Jessica Valenza, Investigator

Jessica: How old are you, Calvin?

Sparling: I turned sixty-five just last month.

Jessica: Are you married? Children?

Sparling: Divorced. That was a long time ago. No kids.

Jessica: You said in your voicemail back to me that you participated in an experiment at the Paranormal Research Foundation in Denton, Virginia. You lived at Foundation House for seven weeks.

Sparling: In the summer of 1972. I answered a classified ad in *The Free Lance–Star*. It said they were looking for young folks to take part in a paranormal study. Paranormal research was coming on big back then.

Jessica: Is that what attracted you to answer the ad? Were you interested in it yourself?

Sparling: Maybe. I don't know. I was very young, and like a lot of people, I was looking for something, only I had no idea what it was. I thought this might be it. I saw myself as having an open mind and wanting fresh experiences. I'd tried LSD and was thinking about traveling the Hippie Trail and spending some time in India.

Jessica: I went through that searching phase myself.

Sparling: Yeah. I was a bum.

Jessica: Well, I guess it's lucky you weren't drafted and sent to Vietnam.

Sparling: By then, the troops were coming home. The last of 'em pulled out while I was at the house.

Jessica: Oh, sorry. That's right.

Sparling: In hindsight, I wish I had been drafted.

Jessica: Why is that?

Sparling: You should get on with the real questions y'all want to ask.

Jessica: Okay. So you went to Denton...

Sparling: Which is in the middle of nowhere. A lot of deep, dark woods. There was once a slave plantation around there. The big house ain't easy to find. We finally came up on it, and my friend dropped me off. I was supposed to live there for three months, with room and board taken care of plus two hundred fifty dollars.

Jessica: What were your first impressions?

Sparling: The researchers were eggheads but overall pretty laid back. They all lived at the house with me and around a dozen other subjects, so it had a commune vibe to it. They did weird science. They grew their own food. They saw themselves as revolutionaries, part of the Human Potential Movement. Pioneers of a whole new science and understanding of reality. "Where there's smoke, there's fire."

Jessica: What does that mean—that last part?

Sparling: It was their motto. History is filled with unexplainable and dismissible phenomena. They wanted to stop ignoring and start explaining it. If they could explain it, they could control it. Make it work for us.

Jessica: Us?

Sparling: People. Humans. They wanted to change the world.

Jessica: What kinds of experiments did they have you do?

Sparling: A whole mess of things. They held up cards with
numbers on the other side and asked me to guess what
number they were holding. They had me stare at a gal
in another room while they monitored her heart rate
and so on. I figured I was good at staring, because next
they had me eyeball a string of random numbers produced by a computer and try to force them to go a certain way with my mind. It seemed kind of silly, but it
was interesting.

Jessica: What else do you remember about the experiments?

Sparling: The ganzfeld experiments were pretty odd. I'd
sit in a sensory deprivation chair with headphones and
blacked-out goggles and talk out loud about what I saw
in my mind's eye. What I didn't know at the time is
they had somebody else trying to beam the image of
an object into my head. With their own mind, you
know. Afterward, the docs would hold up four cards
with images on them—a horse, an apple, that kind of
thing—and ask me to point to the one that was beamed
at me. We also tried it with dreams, in my case lucid
dreaming, as I can do that.

Jessica: Did it work?

Sparling: Well, the researchers didn't jump for joy or nothing, so maybe not. I was starting to wonder if they were
really just studying blind chance. Later, I found out I did
better than most, either through luck or something else.

Jessica: But you left the program early anyway. You quit.

Sparling: Yup. I did.

Jessica: Can you tell me why?

Sparling: At a certain point, the experiments stopped, and
the docs let all but three of us subjects go. I soon figured
out the experiments had been a vetting process to find

a certain kind of subject, and me and two of the others were special for some reason. We were the ones who took part in the big one.

Jessica: Can you describe the experiment?

Sparling: The docs took me into a small room in the basement that they'd turned into a machine. Metal cylinders like columns stood against the walls, all wired together with thick cable. Something about introducing energy at different frequencies, they said. As for me, I sat on a chair in front of a table that was all shiny, made of stainless steel. On the other side, they'd put a freestanding mirror where I could look at myself. And that was it.

Jessica: What was upsetting, though? It doesn't sound all that—

Sparling: I ain't done yet. They turned the machine on.

Jessica: Ah, okay. What happened then?

Sparling: The first umpteen times over as many days, nothing at all. The last time, I sat down and got ready to be mightily bored staring at my own face. And then the room started to hum.

Jessica: The machine made a lot of noise.

Sparling: Not this time. I mean, yeah, they were loud, kind of a whirring white noise, but this was something else. The air itself seemed to hum, a pulsing I could feel as a vibrating knot in my chest. A sound so deep I barely heard it at first, but once I noticed it, it was all I could hear. The air was thick with it. Everything went fuzzy, vibrating. My eyeballs shook in their sockets. My teeth. I wanted to yell at the docs outside to stop the experiment and let me out, but I either couldn't talk or couldn't hear myself. Gravity crushed me into my chair. I could hardly breathe.

Jessica: You were scared.

Sparling: It—*no shit*, I was scared.

Jessica: Oh—

Sparling: Sorry 'bout that. Anyways, all this was bad enough, but it wasn't the worst part. The worst was these feelings that came out of nowhere. I was scared shitless, yeah, but it was more than that, I don't even know what to call it. Dread, maybe. Animal terror. A feeling I was not only being stared at, but that something stood right behind me drilling holes into the back of my head.

Jessica: Okay—

Sparling: Underneath it was this emptiness, a sense I didn't matter, nothing mattered. Like I was a lab rat about to get injected with cancer, which is scary enough for the rat, but suddenly it realizes, oh, I'm just a rat, all along I thought I was important, but there are giants who don't regard me as important at all.

Jessica: That does sound terrible.

Sparling: That's when the table liquefied.

Jessica: What?

Sparling: The whole time, I was staring at myself in the mirror. I saw my eyes bulging, my mouth open wide, a brownish-yellow aura flaring around my body. I thought, if only the guy in the mirror would move, I could too. I could get out of here. But he just sat there, and that's when I didn't even recognize him as me anymore. Just some dumb long-haired kid crying and pissing himself. Then he started to fall apart in the vibrations. He got even fuzzier, like he was breaking up into atoms, but a part of me knew, just knew, I was finally seeing him as he really was, the way the universe does, unfiltered by human eyes. I suddenly didn't want him to move. I wanted him to stay put. I had a dead certainty he was going to walk on out of that mirror, and it wouldn't be good.

Jessica: Wow. What about the table? You said—

Sparling: Yeah. It started shimmering. Like the steel had liquefied. Like you look at a fish pond, and you know there's bluegill under there, swimming around.

Jessica: Incredible...

Sparling: A hand came out of it.

Jessica: Jesus—

Sparling: An ordinary hand, thin like a woman's, reaching up from the steel tabletop. Not *out* of the steel, it *was* the steel, like the metal had turned to latex and the hand was stretching it to its limit. The fingers played like they were tickling the air, waving hello, I didn't want to know. All I knew was I didn't want it touching me. I was the lab rat now, looking at the needle dripping with cancer.

Jessica: What happened next?

Sparling: A fuse blew, and the machine powered down. The heavy feeling broke. The air had an oily sheen to it, but otherwise, reality sort of settled back where it was supposed to be. I could hear myself screaming now. I'd puked all over myself, sitting in my own shit and piss and shaking like a leaf. Because at the end, a second hand had slid out from under the table and caressed my knee.

Jessica: What did it feel like when it did? Do you remember?

Sparling: It ain't something you forget. The hand felt cold and dead. At first, it was like a corpse's hand accidentally

brushed me. Then a whole other horrible feeling shuddered through me. I thought *I* was dead. Again, I can't
describe it. Empty, panic, corrupt. The words for it
haven't been invented yet.

Jessica: What did the researchers do or say after the experiment ended?

Sparling: They asked me a million questions. I don't
remember what I told them. I kept asking if they saw it
too, did they see it? They wanted to know if it communicated with me, what did it say. I couldn't stop crying, I
was even barking like a dog at one point, but they were
all grinning and excited. One of them told me I'd made
history. Said I was like the first monkey shot into space.
Making first contact. That's how they put it. Like even
though I was a lab rat, we were all on the same team
trailblazing the big cure. I slept for two days, and when
I woke up, I hoofed it out of there in my pajamas all the
way back to Fredericksburg.

Jessica: What do you think was going on? What did they
do to you?

Sparling: I spent my whole life thinking on that very question. I'd messed around with LSD, and at first, I thought
maybe they'd triggered a flashback, though I'd never
had a bad trip. Later on, I stopped believing that. They
did something far worse to me, ma'am. Something that
left a permanent mark.

Jessica: Permanent? How so?

Sparling: So many times in my life, I'd look down at my
hands and not believe they were my hands. I'd look
at people, and they'd fuzz around the edges into black
dust, like little dancing fruit flies. I'd look out my window and see a world I suddenly understood wasn't real,

and I could almost see the darker one behind it. Millions of fish swimming behind it, watching us.

Jessica: I'm so sorry about what happened to you.

Sparling: You should get on with your next question.

Jessica: Okay. What do you think of us going into Foundation House? Do you think we're making a mistake?

Sparling: Mistake? Hell, I'm glad all y'all are going.

Jessica: Why do you say that?

Sparling: I want y'all to find out what happened to me.

Jessica: If the Kirklins agree to interview you on camera, what does your availability look like this week?

Sparling: I don't want to be on camera. This ain't about that.

Jessica: Then why did you agree to this pre-interview?

Sparling: I want to know what happened to me. It's the only thing that's missing. I want to know what happened and if there's a cure. So my bad luck stops. Most of my life, I've been a dead man trapped in a live body. Cursed. .

Jessica: How about we—?

At this point, Sparling terminated the call.

What a wild interview! Not our usual thing but weird AF.

Obviously, the Foundation gave him some type of hallucinatory drug and/or messed with his brain waves somehow, but his story is terrific stuff.

I called back multiple times, but he wouldn't pick up the phone. I'm so sorry I couldn't get him to commit. I tried my best.

There's still potential here. I recommend we put Sparling on ice for now and reapproach after we go into the house. We could make it a quid pro quo if we dig up anything interesting about the experiment he went through.

Imagine if we find out what drug they gave him! We could help him, and it'd give us an amazing storyline for the show. —Jess

Testing, testing, one, two, three...

As *Fade to Black*'s tech manager, I handle the audio, mixing from all the different mikes. When something goes bump in the night, that's me catching it. When people yell and all hell breaks loose, I know what's happening.

Besides that, I run a lot of the ghost hunting gear. Remote cams, loggers, recorders, sensors, detectors, you name it. We even have a little handheld weather station unit. The tech available for paranormal investigation has come a long way.

But at heart, I'm an investigator. Here's my bio: I once met a demon.

Before I retired, I protected and served as a Philadelphia police officer for twelve years. We're the oldest police force in the country and the fourth largest after New York, Chicago, and Los Angeles. The city is also one of the most dangerous places to police. Every time I went out in my patrol car, I rolled the dice, so to speak. Nobody seemed to want us there. I worked a neighborhood where the residents saw blue and flipped me the finger and told me to eff myself as I rolled past.

It wore some guys down, but I didn't mind. Around two years before I left the force, I wallowed in recovery from a nasty divorce, and the department felt like the only home I had that mattered. The job was hard, but I could rely on it.

Each morning, I'd put on my blue uniform and pin my badge

with pride. Holster my Glock next to my baton, radio, Taser, pepper spray, and handcuffs. The uniform fit like a second skin, and the twenty-odd pounds of gear on my Batman belt felt right. I was always a big guy, but you should have seen me then. I was in way better shape back in the day, better even than our cameraman, Jake Wolfson. I'd roll out every day, like a super-hero, to save a city from itself.

It was around that time I ended up responding to a robbery at a liquor store. I wrestled this dude to the ground only to find out he had a gun, and it blasted right next to my face, blowing out my left eardrum. The training kicked in, and I jumped back to shoot him through the chest. Then I just sat there fighting for air while I watched him thrash around and die.

I couldn't shake the feeling I'd let the department down and that I'd be at the center of a public backlash. But the board judged it a clean shooting, and after some weeks of medical leave my ear healed with no hearing loss, and I returned to duty. The coroner said the dude had been wet to the gills on PCP.

The whole thing blew over, and life went on like it never happened, though not for me. Every time I closed my eyes, I watched him die. The shooting even showed up in my dreams, the dude thrashing around in his own blood screaming, *Let me try again! I can do it!* Imploring me or God, I still don't know which.

Not all ghosts haunt houses. Some try to live in your head.

They're coming for me, you watch, I told anybody who'd listen. *I'll lose my badge, the only thing I can count on.* I was in a bad place. It happens to some cops, and now it happened to me. I couldn't shake the feeling retribution headed my way like a big speeding truck I could sense but not see or hear.

Sergeant Scalzo finally pulled me into his office. We patrol guys looked up to him as something of a father figure. He asked me if I'd seen the shrink, and I told him yeah, sure, for all the good it had done me.

"Let me try again," I heard myself saying.

The sergeant asked me how many shots I'd fired, and I said three. On the spot, he took three bullets from his own gun and handed them over.

"Now you're whole again, Linscott," he said. "Stay that way."

For a while, it worked like a spell.

Every day, I put on my game face, went to roll call, and drove to my zone for another tough shift. Then I got a radio call from the dispatcher to respond to a domestic violence incident.

I hated DVs. They're tense as hell, everybody's yelling and often intoxicated, and since the people live there, if they have a weapon, they know exactly where they stashed it. They're dangerous, so when I showed up first, I waited for another unit to arrive so we could go in together.

Just my luck, it turned out to be Wexler, a nervous rookie.

"We're gonna be cool but careful," I told him. "A lot of times, it's some asshole who has a hang-up about power and control. It's why he beats his old lady. We represent the only thing that can take it away from him, so just us being here is gonna piss him off."

"Observe and listen," the kid quoted from the training.

"Right. The first thing we have to do is calm everybody down."

I didn't have my hopes up. This housing project was infamous for crime, and the residents hated cops. Most crimes went unreported. If somebody beat on somebody else hard enough that the police got a call, it must be real, real bad.

As it turned out, it was.

Not at first, though. In fact, I wondered if we'd been pranked.

We stood outside the apartment the dispatcher had sent us to. The corridor stood empty, though you could hear voices and TV laugh tracks and other noises from behind closed doors.

The one apartment that stayed quiet was the one right in front of us.

You know the overused TV expression *It's too quiet*? Of course you do. You've probably heard it a ton of times. Well, some wordsmith invented it for situations exactly like this one. It really was too quiet.

My cop instincts started to itch. Something wasn't right.

"Okay," I breathed, and gave the door a gentle rap with my knuckles. "This is the police! There's been a noise complaint. Can we talk to you a minute?"

The door creaked open to reveal a large woman peppered with blood spray. A bruise bloomed on the right side of her face, which seemed to balloon before my very eyes.

"What's your name, ma'am?" I asked.

"Lydia Browning."

"Do you need immediate medical help?"

"I'm all right."

"Who do you live here with?"

"My husband, Frank."

"Did he do this to you?"

"He's under a lot of pressure at work. They're never happy with him, ever. No matter what he does, they're never happy." She sounded like a recorder playing a taped speech. "They're always telling him he's gonna lose his job."

"Is he in the apartment now?"

"Frank's in the kitchen."

"Okay," I said. "You're safe now, Lydia. This is Officer Wexler. He'll stay with you in the living room while I talk to your husband."

I found him right where Lydia said he was.

Or rather, what was left of him.

She'd been making dinner. A big pot boiled on the stove. An open can of tomato sauce had spilled all over the counter. Half-chopped green peppers lay scattered on a cutting board, mixed up with little pieces of her husband.

I forced myself to look at the rest of it.

The body lay on the floor. A big, ugly knife rested half buried in the man's chest. Blood had spattered up the wall and across a clock that ran ten minutes slow. The room smelled horrible. Something burned in the oven, black and sizzling.

It was Frank's scalp.

After I closed the oven door, I saw a shadow figure on the wall, its head covering the clock. A pressure built up in my brain. A voice taunted me as a murderer. I'd killed a man.

Was I up for doing it again?

What's one more? Shoot the old lady. It'd be justice.

You're wrong, I thought. *That's not me.*

GET OUT, the voice said. *GET OUT GET OUT GET OUT.*

I backed out through the door. Blood patterned the frame, twisting into terrible sigils, another type of communication and far more ominous. It spoke of bad luck and curses and black magic.

It's behind me. I wheeled, hand on my Glock's grip, but only Lydia and Wexler stood there, looking back at me.

When my eyes met hers, every picture mounted on the room's walls leaped off their hooks and crashed to the floor.

Lydia extended her hands for the cuffs. "He said I'm free now."

The team thinks I tell this story too much.

I don't think I tell it enough.

Re: Thoughts on *FTB* direction
From: Paisley Hirsh
To: Matt Kirklin
Cc: Jonathan Vogan, Samuel Clines

Thank you for sending your ideas for future development for *FTB* and plans for Episode 13. We've been in love with this property ever since we caught your sizzle reel. Jonathan and I have been discussing how it might break out to the next level.

The first ten episodes performed very well. Episode 11 was our first that did not grow in the ratings, and Episode 12 ominously showed a slight dip. The episode captured 506,000, a 0.12 share in F18–49, 0.14 M18–49, and 0.27 P50+.

The show did very well grabbing share in a crowded field to gain a coveted spot behind *Ghost Hunters*. It built an audience to crack the top fifty original cable telecasts in its time slot. I think we can all agree, however, that the jury's out on whether the formula has lasting appeal. The network is getting nervous, which isn't good.

At an average $145,000 per episode, we are not terribly concerned about costs, as we feel the property is efficient for now. If we have to cut costs, Jessica Valenza could be dropped from some episodes, though we are averse to doing that as, being African American, she adds a nice touch of diversity to both the show and a very white genre. In fact, we are thinking a good approach might be to go the other way and lean into the team and their personal lives, as our research shows strong favorables for all the characters, especially you and Claire but also Jessica and your tech manager Kevin Linscott, who is a font of colorful stories from his years as a police officer.

Fade to Black is a show about ghost hunting where we rarely see evidence of ghosts due to its more scientific approach; perhaps we could evolve it to be a show about the ghost hunters themselves. The search for truth and why they do it. People come for the ghosts, but they stay for the characters. To shake it up even more, we might have guest appearances from mediums or other hunters or maybe even a fan who shares a social media promo post with the most followers.

As another thought, if we develop the characters more while sticking with the high-tech approach, we might increase revenues from product placement. Get manufacturers of paranormal investigation gear to sponsor us talking up their brands for the ghost hunting hobbyists that make up an important segment in our core audience.

Let's think on it. Talk to your team and generate some ideas. We don't have to do anything right now. Let's get Episode 13 under wraps. As we head into the season endgame with the two final episodes, however, we'll need to start executing a new direction that builds to a strong finale, one that will make Season Two a sure thing for the network. We love working with you and know you can do it.

Re: Hunting ghosts with crazy white people
From: Rashida Brewer [Jessica Valenza]
To: Tameeka Brewer

I don't know what you want me to say, sis. I KNOW Mama is having issues with her gout, but she is fully capable of taking care of little Grady during the times I'm away. I don't hear Mama complaining. I'm surprised and sad that I have to hear it from you.

Contrary to what you may think, I am not galivanting in a skimpy cocktail dress at Hollywood parties. This weekend, I'll be in the middle of nowhere upstate, sleeping on a cot in an abandoned house that's crawling with who knows what. I'll be sucking down Allegra the whole time to keep myself from sneezing to death.

I'm sorry if I sound mad, but I AM mad. You saying I'd rather be Jessica Valenza than the name I was born with. The person I was BORN.

I know exactly who I am, thank you very much. I'm a thirty-two-year-old actor with a four-year-old boy whose daddy ditched us to try his luck at Broadway up in New York. I'm an actor who's put in way more hours as a bartender than the few theater and commercial and modeling gigs I scored before *Fade to Black* came along.

This is my one big shot, understand? Yeah, it's a dumb show where I run around in the dark with crazy white people, as you so nicely put it. It's demanding as hell and doesn't pay squat. Honestly, I was doing better bartending. But this show is the biggest thing I've ever done.

The show is peaking, I can feel it. It basically runs on a single gimmick, which is Claire Kirklin ruining everyone's fun, but I think it's wearing thin. For all I know, every episode I do is the last. That means I have to treat every episode like an audition tape. I have to step up and represent, bells on and tits out. I know I was hired because Vogan and Hirsh wanted another pretty face on camera, but a pretty face doesn't guarantee your *next* gig or even that your current gig will last. Because I'm the only professional actor in the cast, I have more to prove.

The producers might boot Claire, which might give me a chance to step up and get a lead role. I might boost my favorables and get hired by *Ghost Brothers* or another show. This means a lot of jumping at noises and yelling, "WHAT THE HELL WAS THAT"—a lot of which is real because most of the time I'm actually scared out of my mind and so worked up that I'm ready to believe anything. It means a lot of improv about every creepy feeling and dramatic monologuing at invisible people haunting empty rooms. It means convincing the team I'm in tune with the spirit world. I have to out-Matt Matt, and I can tell you that ain't an easy thing.

And don't tell me how I'm presenting an image for today's Black woman. I fully understand every time an African American appears on TV, the whole race is being judged. Believe me, I feel it, but it's just more pressure I don't need.

The point is if you want to make it in this business you have to put yourself out there, make sacrifices, and yeah, even do a little suffering. Grady is everything to me, but I'd rather be a GOOD mom who realizes a lifelong dream and has a real career than get sucked into some endless pursuit to be Mom of the Year. You know how they tell you on the plane to put the oxygen mask on yourself before your kid? The same goes with life.

Mama understands this and is supporting me. In his way, Grady does too. He comes first for me, but I need this. I ask you, Tameeka, to please support me too. You're my best and only sister, and I love you. Right now, I need all the support I can get from my family, not more pressure.

Now say you'll do it and that you love me. Don't make me come over there to hug you and punch you.

Claire Kirklin's Journal

I don't think I want to do this anymore.

Ghost hunting. Pseudoscience. Hours of driving in this van, showing up at homes and businesses, so I can prove a negative. And become a celebrity for it, everyone's favorite stick-in-the-mud.

Journaling was Matt's idea. *The mind is the ultimate camera*, he said. *The body is the ultimate sensor. When we visit the location, open your mind and write down every single feeling. Everything is usable.*

It also makes a nice extra for the website. The crew sharing raw impressions. I have to admit, it's smart marketing. The journals draw a ton of eyeballs and engagement. We write whatever we want, and then we edit it down for the website.

I'm getting a jump on mine early, at the start of another long drive in the Mystery Machine to spend a weekend in a dusty, moldy old house infested with bugs, bats, and animal turds. Where I'll be turning thirty-two.

In these pages, I can say what I can't tell anyone else, and hopefully process some big feelings that have nothing to do with spirits. At least on these first pages, before I start adding the bits fit for public consumption.

Remember that, Claire! No accidental posting.

Dear Diary...

Matt sits next to me behind the wheel, quizzing Jessica on her conversation with Calvin Sparling. Jessica, the gorgeous, dimpled actor stuck playing the only role she could get in a profession crowded with gorgeous people. My hubby uses the walkie-talkie, as Jessica, Jake, and Kevin are driving in the camper ahead of us.

The other two subjects who made it to the end of the experiments, Jessica chirps from the speaker, died back in the early eighties. Suicides, the grisly kind. One of them literally starved herself to death.

Cue scary music.

Where there's smoke, there's fire, in this case unethical experiments and untreated mental illness, though of course Kevin wrestles the radio away from Jessica to offer his own interpretation.

Negative spirits, he says.

Matt radios back, "This could get interesting."

The prospect of dealing with a malevolent and dangerous entity only excites my other half.

You might think it's because the dashcam is capturing all this, but it's real. You know how kids love to explore? Matt never outgrew it. His childlike excitement is infectious enough to get people to follow him into the dark, enough to get Vogan and Hirsh to pay him to do it.

His enthusiasm makes a striking effect on his boyish face, as his eyes are deep and dark, and his mouth purses under prominent cheekbones in this tight little smile. Like he's guarding the world's biggest secret and is dying to share it with you and you alone when the time is right. It's actually kind of adorable.

He's got that look right now as he tells us all the nasty things a negative spirit might try to do with us, and how we'll need to be careful because safety first.

The traditional paranormal investigator look is "big game hunter," black T-shirt under a hunting vest bulging with batteries and gear. Back in our YouTube and Patreon crowdfunding days, the T-shirts all had the RIP logo on them, which we displayed like a military patch. Like a police badge giving us special authority.

The complete look said: *This is not Ghostbusters cosplay. I come from a very serious profession, scientific but hands-on and dangerous.*

The investigator look has since evolved, one Matt adopted after we got the Pulse TV deal. Now it's a cross between aging rock star and *The Matrix*. The old look branded the profession. The new look is supposed to brand us individually.

It says: *I go where others fear to tread. There are people out there who need my help, which only I can give.* It says: *badass.*

Right now, Matt sports his trademark leather jacket. Jessica wears one too. As a point of old-school pride, Kevin still wears the old *FTB* windbreaker, topping it off with a jet-black *FTB* ballcap. Jake usually has on a black T-shirt and battered old ballcap regardless of the weather.

Me, I break the mold by wearing what I've always worn, which is my trademark Velma from *Scooby-Doo* look. Ties or turtlenecks. A hat and a comfy gray raincoat, as I'm prone to getting cold, especially on a damp, gray autumn day like today. Basically, I'm a waif.

Kevin is now retelling a story from his days as a Philly cop, the one where he ran into a demonic spirit when responding to a domestic violence call. We've heard this one before, many times. I think Kevin's a little full of it and has some unresolved issues.

The van leaves the highway and is suddenly in another world, endless brooding acres of maple, oak, and pine. We're in rural Virginia now. I tune out Kevin's stories while Matt smiles and asks tons of questions, instantly absorbing every bit of knowledge and adding it to his toolkit.

My hubby's enthusiasm for the paranormal dragged me into all this. None of us would be here without him. I was a physics grad student at Virginia Tech when we started dating. There, I studied the mysteries of the universe, quarks and dark energy and parallel dimensions and the God particle. I dreamed of being the girl who produced a defensible Theory of Everything.

Yet it all seemed so mundane, so gratingly rational compared to what Matt was into. Ghost hunting. Searching for evidence of the paranormal. A dangerous and exciting world, and a challenge addictive from the words *What if?*

You see, I'd grown up in a very logical world, the only daughter of two loving middle-class intellectuals who raised me to think critically. We'd celebrate Christmas, but when I asked if there was a Santa Claus, the folks said, "Some people believe there's a Santa, some people don't. What do you believe?"

The same went with the Easter bunny, tooth fairy, and God. They exposed me to spirituality and various religions but didn't raise me in one, trusting I'd choose for myself when I was old enough to be able to choose. Anything else, they saw as brainwashing.

In short, I'm a born skeptic, but I was also raised as one.

This nature and nurture worked out well for me, but I've always been a little drawn to passion and its delusions. The mad scientist who builds a monster in his lab is my idea of bad-boy hot. My way of rebelling, I guess. Maybe it's also because even though I don't believe, I sometimes wish there was real evidence so I could.

Sometimes, I want to believe I can believe.

At the time we started dating, Matt was with an amateur group called Ralston Investigates the Paranormal, or RIP. After a few proper dates, he invited me out on an investigation, and the team fanned out and disappeared with their motion sensors, electromagnetic field detectors, and spirit boxes and tape recorders for electronic voice phenomena.

I found the whole thing so weird it was intoxicating. My future hubby and I ended up doing it in a room where, legend has it, a jilted prom queen once slit her wrists and sometimes appears to pace in her pretty dress.

After, Matt told me what happened to him when he was a kid, his friendship with a girl named Tammy who turned out to be a ghost. I doubted his perception though not his sincerity. I believe he believes it and that he found it meaningful. If something comes from a point of total belief, it's not exactly a hoax.

Real or not, the story touched me, and it certainly explained his passion to search for ghosts. I think that part of him never stopped being a kid. It's more than just a love for the dead. It's a love for truth, coupled with a belief that anything is possible. Most of all, he wants to *know*.

That, we've always had in common.

Only I approach it differently, needing objective over subjective evidence when it comes to accepting objective truths.

After our first investigation, I still enjoyed hearing his stories, but I stopped going out ghost hunting myself. When he asked why, I gave him the truth: It was all bull cookies. When someone makes a claim, they assume the burden of proof, and the proof itself must be trustworthy.

The investigations used equipment that produced margins of error you could drive a ghost story through. Houses make noises all the time. Every single odd thing the investigators saw or feeling they had, they interpreted as evidence of a haunting. The EMF meters picked up "ghosts" from cell phones and wiring. The SLS camera found random ghosts in the backgrounds, displayed as colorful stick figures. Digital camera flashes reflected from dust and bugs and pollen and raindrops in the air were called "ghost orbs" and taken as definitive evidence.

It was fun, not science. Make-believe. People delude themselves all the time, and this one was relatively harmless, but come on. If Matt wanted to do it for real, he had to get real about doing it.

In other words, I came across like the world's biggest party pooper, but Matt went wild for it. *This is exactly what I needed to hear*, he said. *Yes, let's do it.*

By the time I graduated, we were already married, and Matt earned a fair salary at an advertising agency. He asked me to join him in producing a YouTube show in which paranormal investigations were conducted with strict adherence to the scientific method, and I could present my findings.

It sounded like good fun, and it was, at least for a while. My idea of slumming with the weird kids. The next thing I knew, our popular YouTube show was picked up by Pulse and I was debunking hauntings on TV.

Which is not good for me. I want to be a real scientist, not play one on a screen. Once a week, I have the job of disproving something that can't really be disproven. It's like setting up cameras and recorders and disproving God. In a sense, I'm actually hurting science, since every time an anomaly shows up on our equipment that I can't explain, it's automatically assumed to be a paranormal entity. Anomalies don't mean ghosts. They're simply things I can't explain.

To see what kind of discussion we were generating, I once made the mistake of reading the comments on one of our YouTube videos. A few applauded my scientific approach and how the show had enough integrity to shoot down claims of hauntings. Far more speculated on what I must be like in bed.

I thought I'd be further along in life by now. Starting something big with my PhD. I'm about to turn thirty-two, and despite all my yearnings, I don't feel like I've really done anything yet.

In short, I've gone this far with *Fade to Black*, but I think I've hit a wall. I was never interested in being an entertainer. I was always interested in science, and paranormal investigation offered a distracting challenge. I've taken it as far as I can, though. I came into this with a burning desire to know, but after endless experimentation, I feel like I know enough.

Ghosts don't exist, period. It's more make-believe.

I say this with all love and respect to my husband and his childhood memories.

But no, ghosts aren't real.

Once I'm gone, *Fade to Black* can achieve its full potential. I helped Matt realize his dream, but now I think I'm holding it back, while I know for damn sure that it's become a ball and chain on my own aspirations. My graceful departure would be best for all concerned. At some point, playing it straight is going to wear out its welcome, and viewers will get bored. The producers will set tougher standards on what's "producible" as an episode. Give up the ghosts or at least some juicy interpersonal drama, they'll hint, or fade to oblivion. I'm just not cut out for the implicit brutality of the reality TV business and what's expected of me.

So, Dear Diary. The big question is: How do I tell Matt?

DAY ONE

FADE TO BLACK
PROD: Ep. 13, "Paranormal Research Foundation"
DIRECTOR: Matt Kirklin
CAMERA: Jake Wolfson

Loblolly pines crowd the lens, a thick forest shrouded in shadow. The camera jerks to settle on several people standing in front of the chipped columns of a stately old mansion partly wrapped in kudzu. At one time, the big house was a brilliant white, but the paint is peeling, and time and nature have reduced it to a dull gray.

Matt: Peter Piper picked a peck of pickled peppers.

Kevin: Give me a sec, Claire, this lav mic—

Claire: Right there works—feels fine now. Windy out here today, though.

Kevin: Don't worry about it. It's coming from behind you, and I put a—

Matt: She sells seashells down by the seashore.

Kevin: deadcat on the boom shotgun—

Matt: She sells *sea*shells—

Kevin: So we should be fine.

Jessica (*walks on screen long enough to hold up her clapboard*): Mark!

Claire: Testing.

Matt: Rubber baby buggy bumpers.

Kevin (*off-camera now*): You're both good for sound.

Claire: You about done warming up the voice box, darling?

Matt: Just a second. Yes! Okay. I got this.

Jake (*behind the camera*): We're rolling.

Matt (*with as much gravitas as he can muster*): Welcome to another episode of *Fade to Black*, where we put paranormal claims to their toughest test. I'm Matt Kirklin, lead investigator.

Claire (*smiling*): And I'm Claire Kirklin, co-lead investigator.

Matt sweeps his arm to present Foundation House's warped veranda.

Matt: Behind me, on this gray fall day, you see what looks like an old mansion you'd find in a scary movie. For me, it's the Holy Grail. This is the home of the Paranormal Research Foundation, whose scientists mysteriously vanished in 1972.

Claire: Locals have reported an apparition, flashing lights, and cold temperatures around the site. But that's not what caught our eye.

Matt: That's right. Unexplained phenomena are only part of the history of this place. Reports about the Foundation are hard to credit. Their experiments defied all standards of decency and possibly broke laws. *Human* experiments.

Claire: Most towns we visit, the people living there advertise spooky legends to draw tourists. But not here. As far as we know, the house has never been investigated. We expect to find very little contamination at the site.

Matt: *Very* little. In fact, the house has not been occupied at all since the disappearances. Once we get inside, we expect almost everything to be just as the Foundation left it. I've always wanted to explore this one, not only for its paranormal activity, but its unsolved mystery.

Claire: Matt talked about this house on our first date.

Matt laughs at this bit of ad-lib, and once he starts, he can't stop. Claire joins him.

Matt: She's right. I did. Whew! Okay, let's pick it up from here.

Jake: Anytime you're ready.

Matt (*serious again*)**:** Is the house haunted? And just as important, what happened to the paranormal researchers who worked here? Come with us as our investigative team applies leading-edge ghost hunting equipment to one of the most exciting and mysterious sites we've ever explored. Stay tuned as we *Fade to Black.*

Claire: And cut.

Matt (*breaks into a goofy, self-conscious grin*)**:** How was that?

Jake: Awesome. Good job.

Claire: I think it was good.

Matt: The human experiment part didn't sound a bit hokey?

Claire: Actually, I was wondering if I pivoted away from it too fast.

Matt: How about we take that part again?

Claire (*shoots him a sly smile*)**:** Anything for...ratings.

Matt laughs and wraps his wife in a hug.

Matt: I love you, honey.

Claire: I love seeing you so giddy about this one. You're acting like a little kid on Christmas morning. Like you did on our first date.

Matt: This is going to be the episode that changes everything.

FADE TO BLACK
PROD: Ep. 13, "Paranormal Research Foundation"
FIELD NOTES, Matt Kirklin

3:30 p.m.
Matt and Claire pull up to Foundation House, get out of the van, and greet Jim Birdwell, who works for Gravois Holdings Ltd., the property owner. GOOD

3:33 p.m.
Matt tells Birdwell the team is here to help, but Birdwell says he doesn't need it. The owners agreed to allow *FTB* on-site as the property's been sold. The house will be torn down! A luxury wilderness hotel is going up! USABLE?

3:48 p.m.
Birdwell shows off the main floor. House is as the Foundation left it, but plenty of graffiti, broken glass, used condoms, and such, mostly in the family room, left by partying kids. Library, dining room (Base Camp), kitchen, main bedroom converted to offices. RESEARCH OFFICES GOOD, REVIEW

4:05 p.m.
Walk up the grand staircase, where partying kids said they heard heavy footsteps, big painting

of Lord Shiva at the top. BEAUTIFUL VISUALS, GOOD

4:06 p.m.
Birdwell gives a tour of the second floor, mostly bedrooms and storage. NOT MUCH HERE

4:13 p.m.
Tour of the bedroom where apparition was sighted (Apparition Room). Jessica backs into Jake, who says "boo" and makes her jump about a mile. FUNNY, GOOD

4:23 p.m.
Birdwell shows us the basement. Wow! Plenty of old equipment and research spaces. Monkey cages! The uncovered well is great, but can't see much, too dark. SUPER CREEPY, GOOD

4:32 p.m.
Find a room with a standing mirror in it but no machines. Our tracks unsettle the dust on the floor, and Jessica notices a sinister-looking symbol painted on it. GREAT DISCOVERY, GOOD

Matt Kirklin's Journal

This is it, gang.

We're on our own for the night. Kids locked in a candy store.

Now we just have to find where the candy is hiding.

I gotta say, this place is pretty wild.

The narrow dirt track leading up to Foundation House is just incredible. Basically, you're driving through a dense forest, branches whacking the windshield and everything. Claire and I drove real slow, rocking on the ruts so hard at times I thought our heads would bonk together.

Then the house, chipped and peeling and generally worse for wear, suddenly appeared out of the trees like a lost city half buried in kudzu.

Even Claire's eyes popped wide at the sight, and she's pretty hard to impress. When you watch the episode, the video speaks for itself, but it's not quite like being here. This place gives you that melancholy, deep feeling only ruins can.

The crew had gotten here ahead of us to set up on the veranda, Jake on camera, Kevin on audio, and Jessica prepping Jim Birdwell, who works for the property owner and would give us a tour and the keys to the place.

A lot of people naturally get nervous with a camera lens aimed at their face from only three feet away, but Birdwell handled it like a pro. The only problem is he didn't have much to say aside from a basic tour. As a local, he'd heard the stories about the house, but he'd never seen anything strange himself.

Which is fine, though we're always hoping for gold. A story about how he saw or felt something himself. Angry religious railing against messing with spirits. A dire movie-style warning to stay away.

No such luck. Instead, he went on a rant about teenagers coming out here to "booze and fornicate." No matter how well he locked up the place, they always found a way inside to party hardy.

It all didn't bode well for what we'd find inside, but my fears proved unfounded. The inside is as amazing as the outside.

The first impression is actually a bit of a shock. You know you're instantly being transported back in time; you're just not sure to which decade.

The architecture is grand, with classical elements, and the paneling and wallpaper are all beautifully vintage, if peeling and scarred by graffiti. The furniture, however, is pure early seventies, with couches, throw rugs, and polypropylene chairs saturated in once-vibrant pea green, yellow, pink, and peach colors or flower patterns. The interior design theme is jarring, upstart flower power seeming to smirk while it flips the bird at the stodgy, unhip, square architecture.

I told Birdwell how grateful we were that Gravois gave us exclusive access to Foundation House. Only then did I find out our lucky break was because the company sold the land, and the new owners are gonna tear the house down, so why shouldn't they grab some extra cash on the way out, since we offered some?

You heard me right. They're gonna tear it down! For a wilderness hotel!

To me, it was like hearing the Eiffel Tower is getting demolished to make way for a Walmart.

It looks like we'll be getting only one shot at this, gang. Seventy-two hours.

No pressure, huh?

The first major thing you see after you walk in the door is a spacious foyer with a grand staircase leading up to the second floor in a graceful, tapering pattern. To the right is the library, packed with mildewy old books, Fermi's *Thermodynamics* next to Castaneda's *The Teachings of Don Juan* and Crowley's *Book of Lies*. To the right: the relatively hygienic dining room, where we set up Base Camp.

Straight ahead is the family room, where generations of local kids came to drink beer, spray the walls with graffiti, and do all the other rituals that go with adolescence. The family room opens onto a wonky-looking terrace I'd trust walking on about as much as I would thin pond ice. There's a kitchen, breakfast area, storage and mud room, and main bedroom that the Foundation used for offices, still packed with old and dusty filing cabinets and desks. Some of these are still stuffed with yellowing paper and even a few old eight-millimeter home movies in rusting cans. As soon as I get a spare minute, I'm going to dive into all of it.

The grand staircase is very cool. You look up and expect the ghost of Scarlett O'Hara to come fluttering down in her muslin dress. A large cobwebbed chandelier hangs suspended over its sweeping curves. At the top, there's a giant painting of Lord Shiva, the supreme Hindu deity who created, safeguards, and transforms the universe.

Dusty and faded by time but otherwise in pretty good condition, the painting shows him with his third eye on his forehead wide open and blazing. The mystical eye symbolizes enlightenment and is able to engage in psychic experiences. It also destroys whatever it sees. I fell in love with it on sight and plan to ask Birdwell if I can have or buy it.

Upstairs was basically housing for the researchers and the subjects, not very interesting. The higher you go in this house, the better condition it's in. The wallpaper up there is peeling and the plaster ceiling is chipped and warped in a few places, but otherwise it's not in terrible shape, and there are far fewer bugs and nasties crawling around.

The basement, however, is certifiably wicked, renovated to form a series of experimental rooms. The air smells like minerals. Roots push here and there through the foundation walls, and there's minor flood damage around the perimeter. The uncovered well is eight feet wide, and it's terrific. It creeped Jessica right out. She wouldn't go anywhere near it. The researchers built a pulley system over it; apparently, they lowered experimental subjects down into the dark using a nearby control box with a bunch of big buttons.

Weird, huh? Too bad there's no electric power feeding the house, or I'd be tempted to give it a whirl myself.

We found what we think is the room Calvin Sparling said he was in when he had his bad trip. In our biz, we tag each room with a unique name to make things easy for our postproduction people, and we playfully named this one the *Saw* Room after the horror franchise.

It has a stand-up mirror and a totally wild occult symbol painted on the floor, but no strange machines, just a series of holes in the floor around the perimeter where they might have been before being removed.

Where did they go? For now, that line of inquiry is a bust.

Let me tell you about the vibe in this place. Outside, it grabs you. Inside? Oh, wow.

Despite my childhood experience communicating with the dead, I've never claimed to have some kind of sixth sense when it comes to whether a place is haunted. I'm no medium. It's why I bring the crew and all the high-tech gear. But, man, I swear there's something going on at this house.

A dark, pulsing energy. Everybody's feeling it. They're all excited, which is how I know an episode is gonna have that extra juice.

Yeah, yeah, I know. It's a ghost hunting show, so you expect us to constantly talk about how we feel and ask each other if they feel something too. We do this because ghosts are energy and the body is a sensor for energy effects. But it's not very scientific. You have to take our word for it there's something going on.

We really feel something here. I swear I am not kidding you about this.

This place is *active*.

Now we just have to find out who or what is here with us.

Claire's method is to try to identify and isolate areas of the house where haunting claims have been made. Outside, we have a remote camera scanning the grounds for flashing lights. The rest of our gear is concentrated in the second-floor room where the ghostly apparition appeared, and the grand staircase, where footsteps were reported. After isolating, we establish our baselines for temperature, EMF, etc., and then use our gadgets to try to record any significant changes.

Done, done, and done. Now we wait.

Tonight, anything can happen.

Ideally, we'll record video of the ghostly apparition and flashing lights, though that's never happened. We've never gotten that lucky.

But you never know, right? That's why we're here.

Especially with this being a new location nobody's ever investigated before. We're going into this with a sense of adventure and few expectations.

I think we'll get something. I just don't know what yet.

In the first episode of *Fade to Black*, I shared my childhood experience with a spirit named Tammy. Some people see it as a badge of honor. While it was a blessing for me, it also reminds me of my biggest failure.

My child's mind never thought to ask her about the afterlife. We talked about what we should build with LEGOs. We made up stories about the little houses and spaceships we built. I never asked her what happens when we die, if there is a God, if there's pain and pleasure on the other side, if our existence here on Earth means anything. The list of questions is endless, but I didn't think to ask a single one.

For me, these unanswered questions became a lifelong search for decisive proof—documented, scientific, and replicable—that the supernatural is all around us. A lifelong quest to communicate. This is my hope, my prayer, my Holy Grail.

Imagine if we had this knowledge.

Don't scoff. Don't laugh. Really imagine it.

It would change the world.

FADE TO BLACK
PROD: Ep. 13, "Paranormal Research Foundation"
Raw Video Footage
Friday, 5:15 p.m.

Close-up of Jessica Valenza's face, which welcomes the viewer with her well-known bright, dimpled smile.

> **Jessica:** Hey, fan fam! I'm testing out our new GoPro camera. We usually use it for when we need point-of-view footage and as a backup. It's great for body-mounted cam work when we're exploring and running around, that sort of thing. How about we give it a whirl together and see what's up?

The camera pans to take in the dining room, where Kevin hunches over the dining table, plugging cables into a series of monitors. He is a bear of a man, big and especially thick around the waistline. Sweat stains form dark half-moons under his armpits. He mutters an obscenity under his breath.

> **Jessica:** Hey, Kevin. I'm giving our fans a quick behind-the-scenes tour of what we're doing. So what are you doing?

Still grouchy, the tech manager sweeps his beefy arm to present a messy jumble of boxes, cabling, and equipment trunks.

> **Kevin:** This is the control room, what we call the "video

village." By concentrating all video recording here, it means fewer bodies on set and easier production. But that means having enough HDMI cables packed where I am sure I packed—

Jessica: That's great, Kevin! Thanks! I'll let you get back to it.

The camera quickly moves back to the foyer, where she spins it around for a brief close-up of her face.

Jessica (*whispers conspiratorially*)**:** Sorry, I had to get us out of there. He was about to get *real* technical and then start complaining.

She travels back to the foyer, where the camera settles on Jake, who is shooting the grand staircase with a camera perched on his shoulder.

Jessica: There he is! Jake, my guy! Getting some B-roll or what?

The camera shooter smirks and snorts at her affected familiarity before ignoring her. She moves on down a wide corridor leading to the family room.

Jessica: Too hard at work to say a simple hi, I guess. That's dedication, people. Or something. Oh, I spy Matt, he who pulls the strings and makes it all happen. How about we go see what he's up to?

She passes an open door on the right surrounded by an ornately carved frame. A quick pan reveals stairs leading down into darkness.

Jessica: And that, fan fam, is the basement.

The camera pivots again to frame her face in a personal close-up.

    Jessica (*another conspiratorial whisper*): We don't need to go down there *alone*. That would be a *very bad idea*.

The view jumps. The metallic sound of a file cabinet door closing startled her. The sound came from behind her.

The camera swings to frame the dark doorway leading to a large room.

Once the main bedroom, the Paranormal Research Foundation converted it into offices. In the dim light, we can see the outline of a desk, an old typewriter, and rows of filing cabinets inside.

Something shuffles in the room's recesses. The camera's microphone picks up a creaking sound.

    Jessica (*sucks in her breath*): Um.

The camera remains very still. No doubt Jessica is weighing the pros and cons of checking out an odd noise by herself. After a few moments wavering outside the doorway, she moves into the room.

    Jessica: Hello?

The screen darkens before the camera autocorrects.

    Claire: Hi.

The view shakes and jumps again.

    Jessica: Shit!

Claire: Are you okay?

The camera swings to show Claire sitting on an office chair behind one of the desks the Paranormal Research Foundation installed in the room. She holds an open file folder in her hands.

Jessica blows out a sigh and laughs at herself.

Jessica: I didn't see you there. What are you doing?

Claire: Going through some of the old Foundation files. They left tons of material. Reports and even home movies. They were into some weird stuff.

Jessica: Like what?

Claire (*raises the file in her hand*)**:** Well, this is a paper on the God frequency.

Jessica: The what?

Claire: Nine sixty-three hertz. It's supposed to kick-start the pineal gland and promote mental clarity and a connection to the divine. A path to Oneness.

Jessica: Okay, well, that is—

The view jumps again.

Jessica: Jesus, God!

Matt: Are you okay?

Jessica: Don't tap me on the shoulder like that! You scared me.

Matt: Sorry about that. Do you have a camera on you?

Jessica: Yeah, right here. I'm giving the new GoPro a run. Getting some behind-the-scenes stuff for the website.

The camera moves to a close-up of his half smile.

Matt: Cool. Help me get a little B-roll, okay?

Jessica: Sure.

Matt (*to Claire*)**:** Find anything interesting, my love?

Claire: I'm reading about a fascinating way to give people
  a headache.

*He chuckles as he exits with a final wave. Jessica follows him out into
the family room. The place is a mess. Empty beer cans and liquor
bottles litter the floor among various snack bags and condom wrappers
around the feet of dirty couches, sofa chairs, and end tables. Cigarette
butts fill a 7-Eleven Big Gulp cup. Graffiti covers the walls, gossip
and pornographic drawings, this or that teacher sucks, the school
sucks, the town sucks, life sucks, the whole world sucks.*

Jessica: Do you want me to get the whole room?

Matt: No, Jake will take care of it. I just want to score a
  little footage of this thing I found so I can show him.

*Because of the vast quantity of raw footage a reality TV show produces,
handing it over to postproduction in as organized a fashion as possible is
essential. Jake will shoot all the B-roll and slate it for easy discovery. Matt
wanting Jessica to shoot something is like marking a book for later reference.*

Matt (*points*)**:** Right here.

Jessica: Oh, that *is* creepy.

*The camera lowers to frame what can only be described as a shrine in one
dark corner. Burned-up incense sticks clutter the bottoms of mason jars. A
large number of colorful candles have melted down to thick, hard puddles
of wax. Odd symbols and Roman capitals fill the wall above it, forming
an undecipherable language, some of it appearing Latin, other sections
resembling spells lifted from Harry Potter novels.*

At the center of the display, various offerings—a Pokémon keychain, a lock of hair, tiny scrolls bearing written wishes, a splash of dried blood—surround a cluster of small painted animal skulls.

Jessica: What is it?

Matt: Some kind of shrine, from the looks of it.

Jessica: Yeah, but who made it, and why?

Matt: My guess is kids did. They found some pagan rites on the internet and decided to try them out. Birdwell said kids heard noises in the house and saw flashing lights. Maybe this was their own way of trying to make contact with the spirits who live here.

Jessica: This place seems to draw in the weirdos, huh?

Matt (*laughing*): It definitely does.

Jessica: It's just a little alarming our most reliable reports of ghost sightings at this house have been kids doing copious amounts of drugs.

Matt produces another half smile, shrugs, says nothing.

Jessica: Well, I'll go show this to Jake so he can mark it for B-roll.

Matt: Thanks for your help, as always.

She swings the camera around one last time for a final personal close-up.

Jessica: And that's our behind-the-scenes tour, fan fam. Duty calls. Ciao for now. Love you all.

She puckers up and blows a kiss at the lens.

Claire Kirklin's Journal

I am such a coward.

On these trips, I'm considered the day shift. After Kevin brings in the gear, I get everything calibrated and set up. I record baselines and position the sensors.

After that, I'm basically done. While everyone else stays up half the night slogging around the house chasing noises, I turn in early. The next morning, Matt wakes me up with a ginormous mug of coffee, and I get to work analyzing the overnight data for anomalies. Searching for ghosts in the machine, so to speak.

This investigation was looking to start off like all the rest, smoothly and without a hitch. We now have this down to a, well, science.

The supplies were lugged in and unpacked at Base Camp, sleeping cots set up, gear configured and powered on, ready to roll. Everyone knows what to do and how to do it. Everyone has a part to play in all this, including me.

I spotted Jessica sitting on her cot with an H1 recorder in her lap, popping in fresh AAA batteries. The GoPro camera she was playing around with rested next to her. We do love our gadgets at *Fade to Black*. She looked up at me and smiled, and I smiled back, suddenly filled with a crushing sense of envy.

The executive producers hired Jessica to round out the team. All of us play a role on TV every week, but as a professional actress, she's the only one truly qualified to do it. She's doing what she was trained to do. She's pursuing her dream. Me, I'm the one acting.

I went outside. The van sat on its patch of weeds near the veranda, emptied of its equipment. Overhead, the darkening sky started spitting, and I was grateful for my raincoat. *Okay*, I thought. *That's it. I'm going to tell Matt.*

As if summoned by my thoughts, he appeared behind me and hugged me. His hands rested on my stomach, giving me a delicious tingle. "Hey, you."

"Hey, yourself."

"Are you okay?" he asked me. "You seem a little preoccupied."

"I was wondering the same about you."

I had been, in fact. He seemed distracted for the past few days, and not just by the excitement of a new investigation, especially one as big as this one.

"Just the usual hassle with the producers," he said. "Nothing I can't handle."

The end of *Fade to Black*'s first season is fast approaching, and I'm wondering how much pressure he's under from Hirsh and Vogan.

"What about you?" he pressed. "Are you okay?"

Argh.

That's a big question, darling.

And then I chickened out.

I could feel his breath warm against my cheek, and I knew he was smiling and happy. I thought that maybe I should wait until the end of the season to give him the bad news that I want out.

Thinking this made me angry at him and then angry at myself for being angry at him. *I get too much of what I want*, I pictured shouting, *and not enough of what I need.*

"Just working some things out," I said. "I'm fine."

"Come inside," Matt said. "I want to show you something cool."

"I was headed to the camper. We need to start getting dinner ready."

"This will only take a minute."

I followed him back into the house, where the team stood grinning at Base Camp. Jessica held a plate stuffed with cupcakes, each with a burning candle in it.

"Happy birthday," they shouted at me, and commenced the singing while Jake rolled tape for the show.

When they finished, they all clapped while I fought a lump in my throat.

"Make a wish," Jessica said.

I blew out the candles and kept my wish to myself. The cupcakes were chocolate, my favorite.

I smiled and wiped away a tear. "Thanks, guys."

"Tomorrow, the cupcakes will have gone stale," Matt explained. "I hope you don't mind us celebrating a day early. Happy birthday, honey."

"Thank you, darling."

"When we get back to civilization, I promise to take you out to celebrate in style."

And there you have it, Diary. My big choice on the eve of turning thirty-two. Be horrible to my wonderful husband and these good people, or go on being horrible to myself.

No decisions tonight. That I can manage.

But I won't stop overthinking it. Some things can't be helped.

FADE TO BLACK
PROD: Ep. 13, "Paranormal Research Foundation"
Raw Video Footage
Friday, 8:41 p.m.

Bedroom, identified on the team's floorplan as the Apparition Room, sparsely furnished with a bed frame, dresser, and vanity mirror. Claire and Jessica set up equipment on the bare floor. Flashlight beams splash off the cracked ceiling and intricate vintage wallpaper. The air puffs with plaster dust, which swirls in the light like restless spirits.

> **Claire:** Why are you shooting this? This is the boring part of ghost hunting.
> **Jake:** It's all boring to me.

Claire snorts and regards him with one eyebrow raised, forming an amused look.

> **Jake:** Anyway, Matt wants as much footage as he can get.
> **Claire:** Because they're going to tear this place down soon?
> **Jake:** Yup. He probably wants it for his personal porn collection.

Claire snorts again, louder this time. The snort indicates she found the comment hilarious but refuses to laugh out loud at her husband behind his back.

> **Jake:** Donnelly is gonna shit a brick when all this hits the

edit bay, but I'm slating it for archive, so it'll be okay. It's the batteries I'm worried about.

Tiffany Donnelly is the story producer who shapes the raw footage into a coherent story in postproduction.

Jessica: The house is about to fall down anyway. Like an ad for a tetanus booster.

Jake: Well, we're here now, so tell the nice camera what you ladies are doing.

Claire: There are four known categories of hauntings. One is where an event imprints energy onto the environment. At some trigger, the event replays itself like a tape. Another is inhuman, which might be demonic or elemental. A third is poltergeist, where a spirit uses a human as an agent for telekinetic activity. And the last is typically what we investigate, which is an intelligent haunting. That's where the spirit is conscious, intelligent, and may be willing to communicate.

Jake: That's interesting.

Jessica (*glances at the camera*): It's nice to see you express some interest in what this show is about.

Jake (*chuckles*): Which one do you think we have in this house?

Claire: No idea.

Jake: The equipment will tell us?

Claire: Let me ask *you* a question. What's a ghost?

Jake: The soul of a dead person, I guess.

Claire: That's one idea.

Jake: Well, what else could it be?

Claire: Since there's no evidence for them beyond personal experience, the answer is whatever you want it to be.

Djinn, banshee, shadow person, demon, whatever you like. Some, for example, believe a ghost is a telepathic manifestation of human consciousness. But let's say a ghost is a lost soul. What's it made of?

Jake: I don't have a clue.

Claire: And there's your definition. We don't have a clue. If we were measuring empty air, it'd be easier, because we know what air is and how to measure it.

Jake (*lowers the lens to offer a direct view of the recorders*): But—

Claire: But there are some basic claims we can test. One claim is a ghost may be observable, which means it can be audible or visible. Another claim is it might act on its environment—

Jake: Like rattling chains and such.

Claire: Yes. Which means it produces force, and force requires energy. Since a ghost can pass through walls without damaging them but can then make a door slam shut, presumably it is energy that can somehow switch from a potential to a kinetic state.

Jake: And this potential energy is released by the body when it dies, right? That's what a ghost is.

Claire (*gives her head a little shake*): Basic physics says no. When we die, energy is released as heat into the surrounding environment, and our body transfers to animals, insects, bacteria, and plants that in one way or another eat us.

Jessica (*wincing*): Yuck.

Claire (*smiles*): Beautiful, actually. It's a physical kind of reincarnation. No bodily energy escapes intact after death, though. Occam's razor—the principle that identifying a phenomenon starts with whittling unlikely explanations—says there are no ghosts. They simply don't work with physics. It's more likely ghosts are the product of sleep paralysis, pareidolia, a lack of critical thinking—

Jake: Okay, so getting back—

Claire: Or epilepsy, drug use, sleep deprivation, practical jokes, mental health issues, and environmental phenomena. Given all that, it's no wonder one out of five people claim they've personally seen a ghost.

Jake: But getting back to this equipment you've got here... You're saying it observes the area and measures energy signatures, which you compare to the baseline measurements to look for something that shouldn't be there.

Claire: Bingo.

She stands to present a camcorder mounted on a tripod with a playful flourish.

Claire: This camera will try to capture any visual phenomena.

She next gestures to two devices on the floor.

Claire: We also have a Zoom H1 audio recorder and an all-in-one meter and data logger.

Jake: I know what the camcorder and audio recorder do.

Claire: This isn't your run-of-the-mill audio recorder, though. It's pretty high quality. We want the cleanest audio possible, with all frequencies captured and nothing that will muddy it. This unit records in WAV format, uncompressed.

Jake: What about the meter? What does it do?

A rustling sound comes from behind the wallpaper. The camera pivots to zero on Jessica, who stares wide-eyed at where the sound came from.

Jessica: What the hell was THAT.

Claire (*goes on as if nothing happened*)**:** The all-in-one ghost meter is my baby. It logs EMF, barometric pressure, humidity, air temperature, and vibration events in real time. If anything that can be physically measured in the room changes, we'll know it.

The camera moves back to her.

Claire: Finally, we've got a Sony camera also capturing the area around the window, but aimed at it from the side. It's full spectrum, able to capture UV all the way through the visible spectrum to IR wavelengths. For the staircase outside, we've got a geophone and another H1—

A loud bang disturbs the attic above. Another rustle.

Jessica: Okay, what the HELL is that?

Claire (*sighs*)**:** A random noise that old houses make all the time.

Jessica (*still goggle-eyed*)**:** Should we check it out?

Claire: Suit yourself. It's outside the area I set up to test. Everything's recording here. My part is done.

She stands, dusts her dark jeans, and leaves the room. Jessica sighs through her nose.

Jake: What's haunting her?

The investigator reaches and turns the audio recorder off.

Jessica: She thinks she's better than this. She has no idea how good she has it.

Jake: Gotta say, though, I dig the whole schoolteacher
   thing she has going on.

Jessica: You dig anything you can't have.

Jake: ...

Jessica (*gently*): Welcome to the club.

*She sets a board on the floor and places several objects on it: spoon,
cigarette, playing card, tube of lipstick, and little smiling rag doll lying
on its back. These are trigger objects for the ghost to notice and play
with. Next to these, she places a small Bible.*

If the entity is inhuman, it may attack the holy book.

*Jessica outlines each in chalk and snaps a photo to mark their
positions and how each is facing.*

Jake: So who, uh, actually died here? Any idea who this
   apparition might be?

Jessica: There's no record of anyone dying in the house.
   But there was a plantation near here. The land is very
   old. A whole lot of cruelty.

Jake: For an actor, you take all this pretty seriously, don't you?

Jessica (*with a pained frown*): I take every role seriously.
   Now zip it while I talk to the spirits and try to get their
   juices flowing.

She turns the H1 recorder back on.

Jessica: Is there someone here with us?

*She waits ten seconds to let the recorder run. She does not expect an
audible response to suddenly appear out of thin air. The hope is that*

*by recording on all frequencies, the recorder will pick up something she
cannot hear.*

*After a few questions, she will let the device record all night,
which will be played back the next day to look for electronic voice
phenomena. The voice of spirits.*

Jessica: Can you tell me what your name is?

She waits.

Jessica: Do you know what year it is?

Waits.

Jessica: Do you dream?

*A piece of plaster falls from the ceiling onto the floor. She looks
around nervously.*

Jessica: We're friends. Are you friendly?

The wall rustles again. It sounds like chuckling.

My Turn to Fade to Black
Draft of a farewell letter by Claire Kirklin

I'm lying in a tiny bed in our camper parked in front of Foundation House somewhere in Virginia, resting while the team attempts to contact any spirits that may be residing inside. After tossing and turning a while, I found myself writing this letter to all of you to see how it feels.

It's with a heavy heart but a lot of hope that I announce that I'm leaving *Fade to Black* to pursue other opportunities.

When I see a house alleged to be haunted, I see a monster. It doesn't matter if it's a five-year-old ranch home in a planned suburban community or a cobwebbed, derelict old mansion. Inside is a mystery that doesn't want to be known.

Where others spot ghosts, I sense something worse. Ignorance and superstition awaiting battle. I want to blast light in its corners and leave it clean and whole. Leave it defined and understood. By the time I'm done, it's just a house again in an ordinary world governed by the mundane laws of physics.

I'll go inside with my gear and methods, intent on learning the truth.

Only the darkness all too often swallows the light.

All the effort, all the gear, if we don't do it right, we'll find nothing. But if we do it right, we could also find nothing. If a spirit isn't there, you can't definitively prove it isn't there, and anything not disproven can be interpreted as proof.

There's nothing there becomes *Oh, they couldn't find it* or *What about that banging they couldn't explain?* Over time, a skeptic stops being seen as someone using basic critical thinking to reject baseless claims, and she ends up relegated to having an axe to grind on the other side of a "he said, she said" debate.

A haunting is like a mirage that disappears when you examine it too closely. Once it's gone, it pops up somewhere else to invite and taunt you.

In a short time, Foundation House will be torn down by its new owners. Matt sees this as something like a war crime.

Me, I'm thinking maybe they have the right idea.

In Greek mythology, the titan Prometheus stole fire and gave it to humans, creating civilization. As punishment, Zeus bound him to a rock and each day sent an eagle to eat his liver, the organ where the Greeks thought human emotions resided. The moral of the story is knowledge brings eternal emotional torment.

In the Garden of Eden, the serpent tempts Eve and Adam to eat forbidden fruit from the Tree of Knowledge. God punishes them by banishing them. The moral of the story is knowledge destroys innocence and produces suffering.

The list goes on and on. It's an archetypal idea. Every overreaching mad scientist in every sci-fi movie is another retelling of this ancient story.

Me, I say grab the fire.

I say eat the fruit.

I say bring on the suffering.

The history of science is one of pain, broken dreams, and occasional triumph. This is the march of progress. This is the wheel of civilization.

Some lines of inquiry, however, are a black hole. They become suffering without end or result. They distract from more useful inquiries. That's what paranormal research did to the brilliant scientists who once worked here. That's what paranormal investigation has become for me. An endless pursuit of understanding something that might as well be Santa Claus or the Easter bunny.

Rinse, recycle, repeat.

The great inventor Thomas Edison once conceived of a ghost machine that would allow people to communicate with the dead. He envisioned its principle of operation as being based on a highly sensitive valve, which could be activated based on the merest physical effort and magnified to produce some form of communication.

An amazing mind working on an amazing endeavor. If successful, he would have revolutionized science. Make that human existence.

Instead, he never built it. Never even designed it.

Edison knew it would never work, not the way he needed. In the end, he must have realized the futility of trying to communicate with something that can't be empirically observed and can't be confirmed to even exist.

What did he do? He tore it down.

And so I'm leaving *Fade to Black*. While I salute Matt and the team for continuing their own search for truth, its suffering is not for me anymore.

Instead, I'd like to return to the roots of my study and explore many other magnificent mysteries. What's the universe made of? What's at the bottom of a black hole? Is time travel possible? Is it possible to interact with parallel universes? Why do prime numbers show a pattern? What is consciousness?

I can't wait to find out.

Thank you for joining me on this journey. If my modest contribution to *Fade to Black* made you think about the world even a bit differently, I'll consider it a success. I hope you will always seek the truth with an open but critical mind, even when—perhaps especially when—it hurts.

Paranormal Research Foundation Files
"Home Movie #1," shot on a Kodak 8–mm
film camera

Foundation House, its white walls awash with sunlight. Old but not yet the ruin it is today. The rambling structure rests on a wide, lush lawn that surrounded it before the encroaching forest crowded in as it later would. A cluster of sheep graze the green grass in a corner of the moving image.

Instantly, we know this is a vintage home movie. The film is grainy, the colors a little washed out with warm highlights, flaring with light leaks. There is no sound.

The film was shot in 1972, when five paranormal researchers conducted their experiments here. Its fifty-foot length offers four minutes of footage.

Cut to:

A large garden, multitudes of greens and splashes of red. A dozen young men and women crouch among tomato plants, lettuce rows, and other crops. They harvest the vegetables into baskets. They all look pink-cheeked, earthy, and bursting with the health of youth.

A young woman wearing a halter top and round purple sunglasses cheerfully flings her hand out in a peace sign.

Cut to:

A balding, fiftyish man with an astronaut's build chops carrots in the kitchen. Pots boil on the stove behind him. He wears a yellow golf shirt sporting an oversize collar. This is Colonel Charles F. Trantham, ret. U.S. Army.

As a psychologist with Army Intelligence, Trantham liaised with the CIA's Office of Scientific Intelligence on Project Artichoke, which conducted hypnosis, forced drug addiction and withdrawal, and attempted to induce amnesia in human subjects. After the program was shut down in the mid-sixties, he migrated to the army's psychic weapons research program at DARPA, which helped set the stage for the First Earth Battalion, Project Stargate, and psyops techniques that would be employed during the Waco siege and the war on terror.

Trantham laughs and waves the camera away before returning to chopping the carrots.

Cut to:

The young men and women sit around tables clustered in the dining room. They eat and serve themselves from wooden bowls set among bottles of wine. A few smile shyly up at the lens. One raises his glass as if toasting the camera.

The man is Calvin Sparling.

Cut to:

Family room. The large picture windows overlooking the terrace and backyard gardens are black with night. A man wearing a stylish

*casual suit and a prim, amused smile sits in a sofa chair, nursing
a glass of some alcoholic drink and a cigarette. This is Dr. Marcus
Flick.*

*Next to him, his wife sits on an arm of the chair, legs crossed and
similarly stylish in a chessboard-pattern go-go minidress completed by
leather knee-high boots. Her long black hair spills out from under her
matching hat. She and her husband appear to be listening to someone
who is speaking off-screen to the left.*

*Drs. Marcus and Gloria Flick studied psychology together at Stanford
University in California and married in 1969. While at Stanford,
they worked together on separate theses involving a replication of the
1961 Milgram experiment, which involved subjects being asked by an
authority figure to apply what they believed to be harmful voltages to
another test subject who was actually a paid actor.*

*As with the original experiment, they found a majority reluctant
but ultimately willing to administer the electric shocks. The Flicks'
research goal was to transcend the original results by separately
psychologically profiling the majority who administered the electric
shocks and those few who refused.*

*Gloria Flick glances at her husband before turning back to the unseen
speaker with a bright laugh. She leans to accept a joint.*

Cut to:

*Eyes closed in meditation, a man with curly hair, flaring sideburns,
and large glasses sits in the lotus position on a steel table in a room
with white walls. Behind him, we can see the edge of a large hypnosis
wheel with its black spiraling swirls.*

This is Dr. Don Chapman, once a professor of electrical and mechanical engineering at Berkeley and one of the foremost academic promoters of the Human Potential Movement. After an auto accident in 1969 killed his wife and resulted in a mystical near-death experience, he became obsessed with exploring psychic communication with the dead.

Cut to:

A shaggy, cheerful, blond bear of a man stands behind a young woman sitting in a sensory deprivation chair. She wears bubbled goggles and headphones. Her mouth is taut with concentration. The man's long hair, beard, and easy smile contrasts with the stiff professionalism of his clean white lab coat.

He is Dr. Shawn Roebuck, whose theories inspired the Paranormal Research Foundation's creation. He earned his PhD in theoretical physics at the University of California at Berkeley, where he graduated summa cum laude with a thesis that postulated parallel dimensions based on the mass of particles being smaller than expected and gravity being weaker than the other elementary forces. This parallel dimension, he wrote, interacts with ours through gravity.

Later, he experimented with psychedelic drugs and transcendental meditation, which he believed allowed the brain to observe neighboring dimensions as a psychic dream. Over time, he theorized these dimensions could be physically accessed by a specific combination of mind and mechanics.

Roebuck draws his hands from his lab coat to offer two hearty thumbs-up.

Cut to:

*The front lawn, again in bright sunshine. The researchers stand
ramrod straight and apart from each other. An instant later, they are
standing in different places, Gloria Flick now with her hands in the
air like a football referee signaling a touchdown.*

*An instant later, they move again. This goes on for ten seconds as
they fool around with stop motion, ending with them all sprawling on
the grass laughing.*

Cut to:

*The camera looks down at a man strapped onto a centrifuge, which
spins rapidly. The man wears a strange noduled steel helmet and
sensory deprivation goggles.*

The man silently screams.

Cut to:

*Roebuck and Chapman stand behind a seated woman wearing a
hospital gown and the bulky steel apparatus on her head. She is
pale and crying. The front of her gown is dark with a brownish vomit
stain. The skin around her eyes is similarly dark as well as puffy.
The eyes themselves appear haunted. Behind her, the men grin.*

*Roebuck pops a champagne bottle and pours Chapman a splash in
a Dixie cup. He leans to pour a little for the woman, which stays
untouched on the table in front of her. He takes his own swig directly
from the bottle. Gloria Flick walks on-screen holding up a sign on
which she scrawled WE DID IT!*

The seated woman stops crying. Eyes glassy and deranged, she looks directly into the camera lens while the researchers go on celebrating.

Her face shines with madness as it stretches into a broad, lunatic grin.

FADE TO BLACK
PROD: Ep. 13, "Paranormal Research Foundation"
Audio Recording
Friday, 11:52 p.m.

The recording begins with the sound of Matt coughing. He clears his throat.

    Jessica: Is it on?
    Matt: Yeah, we're recording.

His voice sounds a little hoarse from talking for hours into the recorder in dusty rooms.

    Matt: Okay, this is our last room in the upstairs, bedroom five. EVP session.
    Jessica: Ready.
    Matt: Are there any spirits here?

Wait for ten seconds.

    Matt: Can you give us a sign if you're here?

Wait.

    Matt: I'm looking for a Dr. Marcus or Gloria Flick. Is there a Marcus or Gloria Flick here?

Wait.

Matt: Dr. Don Chapman? Dr. Shawn Roebuck? Colonel
Trantham? Are you here?

Wait.

Matt: You disappeared in 1972, and your work went unfinished. Can you tell us what happened to you?

Jessica sneezes.

Jessica: Sorry. My allergies are going wild in here.
Matt: It's okay, but make sure you call it out—

She sneezes three more times in rapid succession.

Matt: Bless you! Wow.
Jessica: Thanks. This is Jessica. I just sneezed, like, a lot.

*Matt chuckles. This is team protocol. Whenever a group member
makes a noise, they have to tag it as being produced by them.*

Matt: All right, let's play it back.

Recording ends. Another begins.

Matt: Swing and a miss. They're being shy.
Jessica: Or maybe we're calling the wrong people.
Matt: What do you mean?
Jessica: I mean maybe the researchers are gone, and some-
one else is here. Someone older, going back to the plan-
tation days.
Matt: I was hoping it would all tie together with the PRF.

Jessica: It might not is all I'm saying. We should be open to the possibility.

Matt grunts as he thinks it over.

Matt: Okay. How about you give it a try? Maybe whoever is here will talk to you.

Jessica: Sure... Spirits of this house, we come in peace. We don't mean you any harm. We're friends. We'd really like to talk to you. Will you talk to us?

Wait for ten seconds.

Jessica: Whatever happened to you, we care. We just want you to talk to us. If something's wrong, maybe there's something we can do to make it right. Maybe we can help. Do you need our help?

Wait.

Jessica: If you want us to leave, we'll do that too. We'll only stay if you consent to it. But we'd like you to tell us.

Wait.

Jessica: Why are you here? What happened in this room?

Wait.

Jessica: Can you tell us what you want?

Wait.

Matt: That was great. You're getting really good at this. Let's play it back.

The recording ends, and the next begins. Matt is sighing.

This is the job: talking, waiting, playing back, and then trying again. Again and again and again. Patience is the name of the game, but Matt appears frustrated. Something about the house felt right for contact but now no longer does.

Matt: Absolutely nothing. Zero. God, this is terrible.

Jessica: We could try the spirit box, see what we get.

Matt: Maybe. The house just doesn't feel active anymore, you know?

Jessica: When we got here, it felt like the house itself was alive. It was scary and exciting at the same time. I had goose bumps.

Matt: Now we're getting nothing. It's like they went into hiding.

Jessica: What do you—

Another violent sneeze.

Matt: Bless you.

Jessica: —want to do? That sneeze was me, by the way.

Matt: Well, it's just about midnight now. If you want to turn in, that's fine with me. We can get a fresh start tomorrow.

Jessica: What are you going to do?

Matt: I'll keep trying, maybe on the staircase and the ground floor. I may be up a while. This house…

Jessica: I'll keep going too. We can wake up Jake if we get anything.

Matt: That sounds great, if you're feeling up to it.

Jessica: I'm good to go as long as you want. There was something here. I could feel it.

Matt: It just doesn't want to be found.

Jessica: Yet. It's checking us out. Testing us.

Matt: For what, you think?

Jessica: To see if we're worthy, maybe?

Matt: Maybe.

Jessica: Sorry. That was dumb.

Matt (*earnestly*): Not at all. Every maybe might be something.

Jessica: If you say so.

Matt: I know so. There are two things I believe with all my heart, Jess.

Jessica: What's that?

Matt: When it comes to the spirit world, I accept that nothing is certain. I also accept that anything is possible.

Kevin Linscott's Journal

I've seen some shit.

And I've carried most of it.

We haul a lot of gear to these jobs. So much you wouldn't believe it. First, there's the TV stuff. The cameras, audio, lights, tripods, spare batteries, and about a mile of cabling.

After that, you've got your ghost hunting gear. A lot of it. Ask Claire how many angels can fit on the head of a pin, and she'll want to measure it.

As tech manager, I'm responsible for most of this stuff. Hirsh and Vogan wanted their own audio guy on the team, but Matt insisted on giving me a shot after they axed me from the investigation side in favor of a paid actress.

I've gotten damned good at it. Not bad for an ex-cop from Philly, you might say. The truth is a lot of cops end up drawn to paranormal investigation, more than you might think. Few have gone as far as I have, though.

Don't get me wrong about running all the gadgets. I'm a gear-head. I'm sitting here at a dining room table I commandeered and loaded up with monitors and other equipment, all of it displaying and sucking up tons of data about a few dusty rooms and a staircase. If I ever get tired of this, I should apply at the CIA.

I'm saying that while I like being tech manager, I'm an investigator at heart. And right now, all my investigative instincts tell me we're going about this all wrong.

Paranormal investigation is an *investigation*. It isn't a lab experiment.

People watch ghost hunting shows to see evidence of ghosts. They do not watch so they can tell their friends that we picked up a little EMF above the baseline, but it turned out the DM X-930 Dark Matter detector wasn't properly calibrated. Debunking is about as exciting as mayonnaise.

The trick is, ghosts aren't easy to talk to. If it was easy, they'd tap you on the shoulder while you're making supper and ask you if you'd be willing to discuss their feelings about your house being built on their burial ground.

You can't show up and expect them to perform for you because finally they have an appreciative audience for their wall banging or floating down the stairs.

As the saying goes, "This ain't an exact science." I would say it ain't a science at all, in fact. I'd call it an art.

Matt's a good investigator, but he's not as good as me. I told you I've seen some shit. If there was a PhD in ghosts, I'd have one, or maybe I'd be teaching it.

One thing I've learned is that if you're going to make contact, it has to be with feelings and intuition. Not touch-feely emotions but spirit-to-spirit contact. I'm what you'd call a sensitive, an empath, a skill I put to great use as a Philly cop and now as a ghost hunter. I am tuned in.

You can't learn this from a physics textbook.

Ghosts need to be invited. They want to feel safe as much when they're dead as when they were alive. They usually don't have much energy to spend, so they won't waste it playing the role of performing monkey for eggheads in lab coats.

All right. Time to get off my soapbox and check the cameras.

No ghostly appearances in the Apparition Room. No activity at all. No activity anywhere. It's real quiet. It's dead in here, if you don't mind a pun. One night vision camera with an infrared light shows a gray image of Matt and Jessica trying to get EVP, which as you know from the show stands for electronic voice phenomena. Disembodied voices showing up on electronic media. Jake Wolfson is up there with them now in the hopes of catching something interesting on camera.

I stare at Jess a while on the screen.

Matt pulls out the big guns: a Ouija board and an SB11 spirit box.

He should have me with him now, doing what I do best instead of babysitting gadgets. Jessica is a solid investigator—like I said before, this game requires deep intuition, which she has—but she doesn't have a trained ear for the SB, and frankly Matt's not as good as me either with it.

The way the spirit box works is like this. It constantly sweeps through AM or FM frequencies—or both at the same time—and produces a rhythmic, pulsing white noise punctuated by tiny moments of silence between steps. By scanning multiple radio frequencies, the spirit can easily make it so they can say a word or phrase or make some other noise in response to a question.

It's obvious when the box says something, though it often comes out distorted or otherwise hard to understand. We're always looking for a *clear* message.

The problem is that when you're searching for EVP in a bunch of noise, it's easy to hear words that aren't there. The human brain is hardwired to see faces in wallpaper and clouds, even the moon. It also hears voices in white noise and can piece together real words from junk. Claire once told me this is called *apophenia*, another million-dollar word.

It happens, though, it really does. Which is why you need a trained ear.

On the monitor, Matt asks the room questions. Everything seems to be okay, so I figure I'll head outside for a bathroom break. If they give up and decide they need my help, they'll just have to wait...

And now I'm back. Nothing's happening on the monitors, and Matt, Jessica, and Jake are in another room now. I sit in my captain's chair, crack open the lager I pulled from the camper's fridge, and think about what just happened.

Things have just gotten very interesting at Foundation House.

I walked out to the camper. To be polite, I moved real quietly. Once we get rolling, Claire turns in early, doing most of her work during the day crunching her data.

She opened her eyes and looked up at me. "Anything happening?"

"Nope," I said.

The house felt active when we first showed up, but it went flat after the sun went down and we got our gear set up. Slowly, steadily, the atmosphere in here turned dull and lifeless. Which strikes me as odd considering outside, the world seems alive with bugs and critters in the woods.

I went into the bathroom, did my business, and came out. "This house might need a different approach. I keep saying that we put too much trust in gadgets."

She raised up on one elbow, ready for one of our battles. I braced myself for another lecture about the scientific method delivered with the cold fury of Galileo lecturing the Pope that the Earth revolves around the sun.

"Do you think you could convince Matt of that?"

I couldn't believe what I was hearing. Playing it cool, I opened the fridge and took out a cold bottle of Old Glory. "Convince him of what, exactly?"

"That the show needs a new direction in its investigation methods."

Not a challenge. She sounded hopeful.

Suddenly, my intuition told me that we might be on the same side.

"I could try that, next time I see him."

"He's under a lot of pressure from the producers," Claire said. "He's trying to do something here. Help him."

"Sounds like there's trouble with the show."

"He won't talk about it, but I think something is going on."

This was big news, but I didn't press her, as I believed her saying she didn't have the whole scoop.

I said, "I'll do what I can."

"No," Claire said. "*Help* him. Whatever it takes."

"I said I would, so I will."

Back inside the house, I popped the top off my Old Glory and took a sharp swallow. It tasted like victory, to riff on one of my favorite movie quotes. Then I allowed myself the smile I'd been holding back. After all the haunted houses we've investigated on this show, this is the first time I've been truly surprised.

Claire's open to a new direction for *Fade to Black*. If she is, Matt will be.

Which might just put me back where I belong, doing what I do best, which is investigating.

Foundation House may be a dud so far, but I'm starting to like it.

FADE TO BLACK
PROD: Ep. 13, "Paranormal Research Foundation"
FIRST DAY HOT SHEET
Report emailed by Matt Kirklin to the producers

Our arrival at Foundation House rolled out like the start of a horror movie, with the van crashing down a road that was more like a dirt track and bursting into a small clearing, where the rambling ruin of the house suddenly hove into view.

Despite graffiti and junk left over from partiers, the inside is similarly stunning, with gaudy old seventies furniture and experimental rooms and pretty much everything else just the way the researchers left it when they vanished into thin air.

If we were to design a dream set for an episode, it would look like this.

Unfortunately, it's all going away. The house and surrounding property will very soon have a new owner, who's planning to tear it all down. As a result, Jake is shooting extra footage, which he's slating for my own use.

Everything went smoothly, only we faced a rather odd challenge: Foundation House gave us nothing today. Usually, with an old site like this, we play whack-a-mole with false-positive environmental sounds like animals, neighborhood noise, and the like. We hear a noise or otherwise pick up an EVP or some other little oddity, which gives us solid material on tape.

Not here. While we were setting up, we heard plenty of

stuff. Settling noises. As soon as we started recording, though, the house decided to play dead.

Seriously, it's like it knows we're here. Yeah, I know how that sounds.

The rain now constantly strums the roof like a distant murmur, but otherwise, it's dead quiet. That in itself is remarkable. It actually shows up in the footage, the *lack*. But it's not what we're looking for. The team's reactions are good TV, but it won't carry us over the finish line. Something needs to happen.

The frustration over this among the team is palpable. I'm hoping this yields some interesting personal material, as I know you want more character development, and this might be a good opportunity to edge things in that direction.

Besides that, Jessica is really stepping up to make her mark, Kevin wants to talk to me about shaking up our investigation approach, Jake's usual heckling is getting on the ladies' nerves, and my wife seems a bit...off.

The usual minor drama you find in a family like ours.

Nonetheless, we're excited for tomorrow. I've got some great B-roll ideas, we'll do some interviews, and hopefully Claire will run her hands through all that dirty data and find a pearl. Meanwhile, we discovered all the Foundation's old files safely stored in cabinets, including a few home movies, which might offer a terrific unsolved mystery angle.

Then tomorrow night, it's a whole new ballgame.

When the sun goes down, we'll be ready. Foundation House can play dead all it wants, but I'm not leaving here without its secrets.

DAY TWO

Matt Kirklin's Journal

We hit the jackpot, gang!
 THIS IS BIG.
 Mind. Blown.

FADE TO BLACK
PROD: Ep. 13, "Paranormal Research Foundation"
Raw Video Footage
Saturday, 8:09 a.m.

The camera follows the excited team up the grand staircase. Though it is morning, little daylight reaches the area. Matt leads the way with a powerful flashlight, and Jake has the camera's light on as well. The group stops in front of the door of the Apparition Room.

Matt: Okay, everybody, wait up. Claire, it's all you.

Claire goes into the bedroom and leaves the door open. Inside, she investigates the phenomenon in its pure state, without any accidental tampering. The camera's microphone picks up the sound of her snapping pictures.

Claire: Okay, you can come in. Nice and easy, though. Step lightly, please.
Matt: Jake, you go first. Get the phenomenon, and then you can grab some reaction shots.
Jake: You got it, boss.

The camera goes in and zeroes on the trigger object board. Slow zoom.

During the night, something messed with it.

The playing card was ignored, but the cigarette is broken and the lipstick and spoon have moved several inches. The chalk outlines are smeared.

The Bible shows a tear in the front cover near the binding.

Wearing its eternal happy smile, the little rag doll sits and regards the mess. It now rests outside the chalk outline that shows where it was originally placed.

> **Jake:** Oh, wow. But...damn, the Bible has a goddamn rip in it.
> **Claire:** I saw that too.
> **Jake:** This is real. Something actually happened here.
> **Claire:** That's how it looks.

She walks around the objects, pressing her right foot against each floorboard in turn to see if any are loose. The floor, however, is solid.

She stops and gazes up at the ceiling. No missing chunks of plaster directly overhead. Nothing fell in the night.

Finally, she crouches in front of the scattered trigger objects and frowns. Whatever caused them to move, she cannot seem to figure it out.

> **Matt:** Did you get what you need?
> **Jake:** Uh, yeah! I sure did. (*mutters*) This is freaking nuts.

The rest of the team enters the room. They carefully position themselves so each has a good view of the trigger board. Their faces shine with an odd mix of excitement and bafflement.

Claire, however, goes on frowning. She looks sad and a little resigned, as if she ate something unpleasant but there is no going back now.

Jessica: Is…is this real? Like, really real?
Matt: What's the verdict, Dr. Kirklin?

Snapping out of her funk, Claire stands up.

Claire: Well, the room was completely inspected and sealed, which rules out a mouse or other animal coming in here. Heavy objects were moved but not the playing card, so it's unlikely a draft was responsible. A draft also likely wouldn't tear the Bible or move the doll to a sitting position. Vibrations in the floor also wouldn't explain the tear. The dust around the board is hardly disturbed aside from what we did to it.
Jessica: Holy shit! Then—

Claire cuts her off, droning on as if she is going through the motions and wants to get this over with.

Claire: The ghost meter is switched on but dead. The same with the cameras and audio recorder, which is odd. Once we put in fresh batteries, I hope we can find out more about what happened here.
Kevin: The batteries going dead makes sense, if you think about it. The entity drained the batteries and transferred the energy into the force it needed to do all this.
Claire: That would be the theory.
Kevin: I'd like to see it explained any other way. Energy can't be created or destroyed, but it can be harvested and—

Claire: I know how the law of conservation of energy works, Kevin.

Jessica: Wait, doesn't a rip in the Bible mean we're dealing with—

Rearing back as if stricken, she explodes in a loud sneeze and blows her nose into a handful of tissues.

Kevin: Bless you.

Jessica: A demonic—

Another big one bursts from her.

Jessica: Presence? An actual demon?

The tech manager's face morphs into one of smug warning.

Kevin: You'd better hope not.

Matt: There's no other sign we're dealing with a negative spirit.

Jessica: But everyone was saying on the drive down here—

Kevin: Inhuman spirits aren't always demonic. This one could be an elemental. In ancient shamanist religions—

Matt: Put a pin in that for now, Kev. Claire, you gave us your analysis. I want to hear your conclusion. Do we have bunk?

Claire: The only thing we haven't checked out is the geophone on the staircase.

Kevin: I can do that for you. *(hurries out of the room)*

Claire: But I'm not sure it'd give us a clue as to what happened here anyway. At most, I figure it'd be a corroborating factor. Once we load fresh batteries into these cameras and the ghost meter, we should know more.

Matt: So the jury's still out.

Kevin walks back to stand in the doorway. His face appears about to burst with an incredible secret. He waits until the others notice him.

Kevin: The geophone batteries went dead too.
Jessica: Oh my God.
Matt: That just leaves the cameras, which we can check out once we get them working again. If they don't show anything, what would your conclusion be?
Claire: I'd conclude you have major bunk here.
Jessica: Bunk? What is that?
Matt (*grins*): Something Claire can't debunk. The real salami.
Kevin: Bunk? Hell, Matt, this is concrete evidence. I'd take it to a jury.

Matt breaks into gleeful laughter, and Kevin chuckles along.

Jake: So cool.
Jessica: Oh God. This is freaking me out.
Matt: Gang, I think we've gained objective proof of a haunting.
Jessica (*visibly wilting*): Seriously, I don't feel very good all of a sudden.
Kevin: Tell me what's wrong.
Jessica: A little dizzy. I'm okay, though.
Kevin: Give me your hand. I'll take you back downstairs.
Matt: Are you sure you're okay, Jess?
Jessica: Yeah. I just need to lie down a minute.

After she leaves with Kevin, Matt turns to Claire and envelops her in a hug.

Matt: You can't win 'em all.

Claire: I'm very happy for you. Congratulations.

Matt: I'm joking, honey. You won too, and you did it your way. We did this together.

Kevin Linscott's Journal

Bingo. Jackpot. Lottery.

You name the metaphor. We won it.

Paranormal Lockdown pioneered the idea of living at a haunted place for seventy-two hours, which we copied. We don't lock ourselves inside, nothing like that. We do put in the hours on-site, though, and yeah, we sleep here on cots.

The idea is the longer you stay, the more likely you are to engage with spirits, since like I said before, they have this funny way of not showing up on demand. As a paranormal expert, I can tell you that this is a solid method for investigating a possible haunting. What we discovered at Foundation House proves me right.

After our first night setting up and trying to make contact with any entities, I finally caught some shut-eye. A lot of people wouldn't sleep in a haunted house for a million bucks. I do it all the time. Hell, I'd do it for free. I slept like a baby.

Waking up ended up being the hard part, especially as the night damp settled into everything. I felt chilled, mildewy, and sticky with night sweats. I'm no stranger to camping in rough places, so normally I man up, but I had this vivid dream I was on this weird game show with a constantly running music and applause track.

I stood in front of a door and had to decide whether to open it. I *had* to open it if I wanted to win the big prize, but I knew that Jake Wolfson of all people stood on the other side, wearing a dazed grin and drooling over a shiny knife.

If he tells you I gave him any hard looks today, you'll know why.

Claire welcomed me back from the phantom world with a Styrofoam cup full of coffee, which I drink black and bitter. For the rest of the day, she'd comb the overnight data while I listened to the audio recordings for EVP.

That's when Matt showed up wearing that impish look he gets when he's got good news. "Something happened overnight. You have to see for yourselves."

I stared at him and just knew. "The big one."

He looked back at me with his own knowing gaze. "The big one."

I sensed a subtle shift just then. How he looked at me instead of at Claire. Knowing how I alone would appreciate most what he'd discovered.

We found Jessica and Jake and hauled ass upstairs to see our trigger objects had been moved by manifested spiritual energy. Like fish drawn to bait, the spirit or spirits had played with the objects.

This is indeed the big one I've been talking about all along.

Objective evidence of paranormal activity.

That moment when even a die-hard skeptic—the worst kind, the kind who blindly and fanatically tries to dismiss the paranormal, as if science itself isn't just another belief system—can't help but admit defeat. Admit defeat by finally acknowledging what millions of Americans already know is real.

I'm not talking about just the science crowd. After this episode airs, I'll walk back into my old precinct with my head held high. See if Lieutenant Clapper is still working in patrol. Ask him if he remembers how I faced a demon during a DV call and how I said we should form a special paranormal investigations unit. Ask if he recalls how he laughed me out of his office.

I'll ask him who's laughing now.

It's not all peaches and cream, though. The spirit drained the batteries on all the devices we had upstairs, so all recording stopped just before the event. After replacing the batteries, we gathered around the monitor to watch the footage.

The objects sit on the floor doing nothing, and then the screen goes black. The ghost meter picked up some vibrations along with a tiny change in air pressure, and then it too died. Two hours earlier, the audio recorder picked up a few wonky bits of speech we found intriguing until Claire pointed out it had caught Matt and Jessica looking for EVP out on the staircase. Otherwise, it stayed dead quiet right up until the batteries crapped out.

So that all yielded nothing, but there's no need to be greedy, seeing as we already hit the jackpot.

No joke, what we got is huge.

The big question on everybody's mind is what comes next.

Text exchange between Rashida Brewer (Jessica Valenza) and Tameeka Brewer

Saturday, 8:39 a.m.

i just saw shit MOVE — RB

hey — RB

hey — RB

TAMEEKA ANSWER ME — RB

TB — what the hell?!? it's saturday, i was sleeping!

OMG i am FREAKING OUT — RB

TB — are you okay? what's going on?

i'm not really sure — RB

TB — okay how about you tell me what shit moved and why it's important

we call them trigger objects

we put them in a sealed room overnight

 is this about ghosts? are you kidding me?

and we chalk them to mark their position RB

TB you're letting that dumb show get in your head

when we came to check them out this morning they were MOVED RB

TB oh!

TB that's actually pretty cool

okay RB

listen RB

 i don't really believe in ghosts but i don't really disbelieve either RB

if people say they saw them I'm like ok but I never saw one myself

i whisper in graveyards and throw salt over my shoulder RB

not because i believe but just in case RB

TB i know all about your spiritual tourism

spiritual tourism ha right RB

but now I'm finding out this shit is real? RB

TB it's what you wanted, right? it'll be great tv

TB sure as hell makes the acting like a nutjob easier

are you kidding they don't pay me enough to mess with real ghosts!

this is like getting a gig LARPing with some renaissance faire folks RB

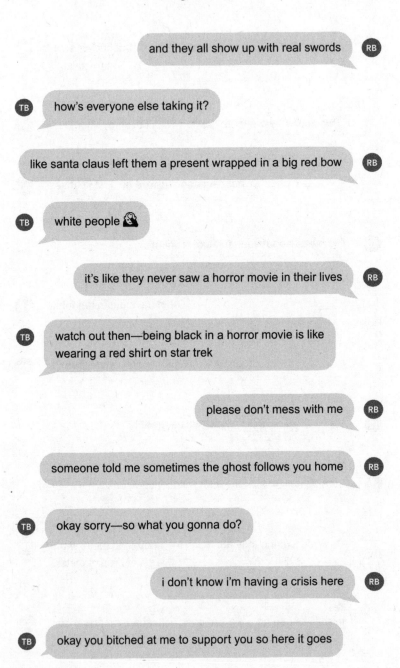

you play the role and you stick with it

 that's it that's my advice

have YOU ever seen a horror movie?

 listen sis you signed up for this foolishness

 you say it's your big break and all that

 everyone down here is chipping in to help you

 so do the work and quit crying

ok

ok?

yeah

good

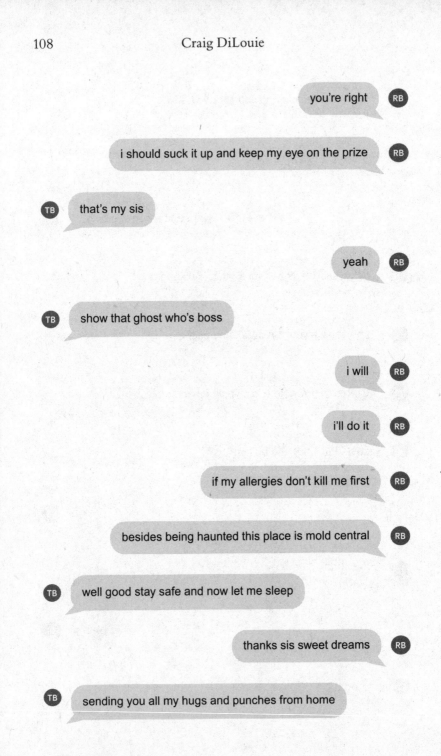

Jessica Valenza's Journal

Greetings from Foundation House, fan fam! We're so excited to be here. Being able to exclusively investigate one of the oddest and most haunted locations in North America is such an amazing and humbling opportunity.

As my fellow investigators are also sure to tell you, this morning we discovered genuine evidence of a haunting! This is the big one, the real deal! A series of trigger objects were moved overnight. We couldn't be more excited!

Tonight, we're going to try again to make contact. I might end up talking to the spirit personally! My specialty is instrumental trans-communication, specifically electronic voice phenomena, or EVP. For all of you new to what we do here at *Fade to Black*, these are voices not heard by the human ear but that are caught on digital recorders.

The thing is, ghosts don't have mouths or anything else to talk with. What they CAN do is manipulate energy. So the theory goes that they manipulate sound waves to imitate human speech, which is then captured on a recorder. What the ear can't hear, the recorder will catch.

EVP may be passive, active, or provoked. Passive is where we run a recorder and then listen to it later for disembodied voices. Active is where we ask questions and hope to get a response on the playback. The last is where we outright taunt the spirit into reacting. We don't do that one very often. We consider it the nuclear option.

Kevin and I usually do the listening. I'm getting pretty good at it! Claire designed the protocol based on best practices by good paranormal investigators, so you know it has a basis in real science.

If we catch anything, we mark the sections, which are clipped out and amplified up to 50 percent while the speed is reduced by the same. We're always hoping for a Class A EVP, which is very clear and easy to understand, but we usually get Class B, which we generally take seriously, and Class C, which we generally don't.

Once Kevin and I tag everything, we all listen to it separately to translate what we think it's saying, and then we compare and evaluate. Thanks to all this effort, anytime we play something on the air, you know you're getting the real deal.

And there's your EVP 101 class, people. It's one of the most important tools of a paranormal investigator. A tool I'll be using in a few hours as we try to communicate with the entity inhabiting this old house.

Wish me luck! Can't wait! Tonight's gonna be big!

FADE TO BLACK
PROD: Ep. 13, "Paranormal Research Foundation"
INTERVIEW: Matt Kirklin

Matt sits on a chair with the team's monitors arrayed behind him at Base Camp. The camera frames him in a standard tight shoulder shot ideal for an interview bite, a staple element of reality TV shows.

His face is in near close-up, brightly illuminated by portable lights that Jake and Kevin hauled in from the van. The background is gloomy and a little blurred.

Watching Matt on TV, most viewers likely focus on his dark, expressive eyes. The eyes may or may not be the windows to the soul, but they certainly help sell a story.

Claire (*off-screen*): How are you feeling about the investigation today?

He looks off into the distance for a few moments, suddenly thoughtful.

Matt: Honestly, for the past few months, I was thinking how hard all this was starting to get. Year after year trying to find evidence of something that only wants to be known through personal experience, not replicable scientific experiments as if it were a machine or natural force. As fun as these investigations are, as much as I enjoy the camaraderie and playing hide-and-seek with invisible entities, they're still hard work. And when you come up empty-handed too often, it can really wear on your resolve, especially with the pressures of a TV show and half a million people watching you do it.

His face takes on a far more confident and determined expression.

Matt: Every time I got discouraged, I told myself to keep going. I told myself I was following in the footsteps of the likes of Alan Turing and Carl Jung, who approached the paranormal with a bright, open, inquisitive mind regardless of what others thought of them. I reminded myself I wanted to *know*, and that if I never got certainty, I should be okay with that because the search itself is everything. As long as I'm searching for the truth, I'm close to the truth. I'm on truth's path. Some knowledge may not be knowable, but isn't it still worth knowing? I'd rather find nothing than have never tried. Because if there is life after death, one of the oldest and greatest mysteries of our existence, we have a right to know. We have a *right*.

Claire: ...

Jake (*operating the camera*): Wow.

Matt (*wearing a shy smile*): Sorry about that. I got a little carried away.

Claire: It worked for me. This is the man I fell for.

Jake: I'll mark all that on the card for... I'm not sure, maybe a piece of it can be used for a second season promo or something.

Matt: A second season? From your lips to God's ears, Jake.

Jake: Can't hurt to be ready in case it happens.

Claire: So...

Matt (*grins*): Today, I am feeling fantastic about our investigation. What we witnessed this morning restored my faith, so to speak.

Claire: Where were you, and what happened?

Matt: This morning, while coming up with a plan for the day, I noticed the two second-floor cameras weren't working. I went up to the Apparition Room to check on them. That's when I noticed some of the trigger objects had been moved around. I immediately went to fetch the rest of the team to see it. Claire checked out the site to make sure it wasn't tampered with by anything in the environment.

Claire: And what did the team conclude?

Matt: After a very thorough check to eliminate any other rational cause, we determined a paranormal force moved the objects. The only other explanation is it was a bona-fide miracle. My conclusion? We made history today.

Jake: That was good TV, right there. I liked that.

Claire: And how did it make you feel?

Matt: Seeing one of our investigations come so close to proving the existence of a paranormal entity was one of the most fulfilling things that ever happened to me, and it made me hungry for more. I also felt closer than ever to Claire, who is our resident Harry Houdini when it comes to debunking. For the first time in any of our investigations, we saw eye to eye, but on my side of the fence.

We can hear Claire's smile in her voice, even if we cannot see it.

Claire: One of those trigger objects had a special meaning for you, didn't it?

Matt: That's right. I always put out a little doll in case I ever run into Tammy again. Seeing that the doll moved really got to me.

Claire: Do you think you'll ever see her again?

Matt: I think she crossed over after I gave her Mom's message. So no, I don't think I'll ever see her again. I always put the doll out anyway, just in case.

Claire: So what's the plan for today? What's next for us meddling kids?

Matt turns away, wearing his mischievous smile before turning back to stare at the camera lens with a look broadcasting utter resolve.

Matt: Last night, the spirit started a dialogue. It's now our move. Tonight, we're going to try to make contact.

Jake: That's our sound bite.

Claire: Yeah, that was good. I actually got a shiver.

With the interview over, Matt visibly relaxes.

Matt: Let's wrap it there, then. You up for some more B-roll today, Jake?

Jake: Always. You got a list, or do you want to walk around with me?

Matt: I have some ideas and want to hear yours, since you've been around the house. One thing I'd love to get is a point-of-view shot from the van driving up to the place, if we can keep her steady on the ruts.

Jake: We can try. I'm sure I'll figure it out.

Matt: And make sure you get plenty of Jessica cleaning up the object board and setting up the new one.

Jake: Sure.

Matt's mischievous smile returns.

> **Matt:** How do you feel about maybe doing a little flying today?
>
> **Jake** (*chuckles*)**:** Drone shot overflying the house, looking down?
>
> **Matt** (*chuckles with him*)**:** Drone shot of the house, looking down.
>
> **Jake:** Oh yeah. I'm in.
>
> **Matt:** The sky is starting to clear. Maybe we'll see the sun today. Get as much B-roll as you can, and we'll send up the flying camera around the golden hour. Even a little later will work. We'll get all these great shadows.
>
> **Jake:** A perfect plan, boss.
>
> **Claire** (*laughing*)**:** Sometimes I think all this is just so you boys can play with your toys.
>
> **Matt:** Nobody ever said that following truth's path can't be fun, honey.

FADE TO BLACK
PROD: Ep. 13, "Paranormal Research Foundation"
B-ROLL Shot List, Partial

LOC	SHOT	CAM ANGLE	CAM MOVEMENT	DESCRIPTION
Ext	Wide	POV	Steadicam	House and drive from van pulling up to the house
Ext	Full	POV	Steadicam	Slow zoom on house front door
Ext	Wide	Low	Steadicam	Looking up at house with sky behind
Ext	Wide	Low	Tilt	Same shot but with Dutch tilt
Int	Full	High	Steadicam	Jessica in Apparition Room documenting trigger objects
Int	Medium	POV	Steadicam	Jessica set up new board with new trigger objects
Int	XClose	Knee	Rack Focus	Objects being placed, Jessica's hand
Int	Wide	POV	Steadicam	Walk up the grand staircase
Int	Medium	Knee	Rack Focus	Weird shrine the kids set up in the family room
Int	Full	POV	Steadicam	Walk around the basement
Int	Wide	POV	Pan	Sweep across *Saw* Room with occult symbol painted on floor
Int	Wide	High	Steadicam	Occult symbol on floor
Int	Close	Knee	Steadicam	Pulley system over the uncovered basement well
Int	Full	POV	Steadicam	Looking down into the well

Jake Wolfson's Journal

Jake Wolfson here, your favorite Techno Viking. TV for short.

Matt says I have to write at least one big journal entry, so here goes, starting with the honest version I'll sanitize later when I turn in my homework.

Matt also likes to say we're a family, so I have to go along with that too. A little oddball, dysfunctional family, haha.

The camera sees all, and I'm the man behind the camera. The shooter.

The proverbial fly on the wall.

I know who hogs the bathroom (Jessica), who eats all the pastries and talks a big game (Kevin), who has a crush on somebody they can't possess (Kevin for Jessica, Jessica for Matt, me a little for Claire, Matt for his own wife LOL), who is wearing a happy face but is about to crack under the strain (Matt), and who still doesn't believe in ghosts even after a ghost trashed all the things (Claire).

I know that Matt loves the show but wishes he was back with RIP, Claire hates the show and everything it stands for, Jessica is faking almost everything in the hopes of getting a real gig when *FTB* crashes and burns, and Kevin hates Claire not because she's an infidel but because she refuses to buy his act.

I don't mind any of it because the camera doesn't mind. The camera, in fact, loves it. More specifically, the brain behind the camera, the unsung hero of *FTB*, namely Tiff Donnelly, our story producer.

Here's how our show works. Matt is the director and de facto field producer for each episode. He's a good director in that he trusts me to do my thing, knows when to push for something he wants, and backs off when I signal him he's crowding me and should let me do it my way.

We shoot everything and send the digital files to Vogan Productions, LLC, in Ralston, where all the footage is logged and dropped into the edit bay. That's when the real magic happens. Tiff is the wizard. She shapes all the bullshit into a story.

She pins good scenes onto a bulletin board, threading all the coverage, cutaways, and interviews into a plot that fills forty-six minutes. Once she's done, the editor builds it from her blueprint and adds all the effects, titling, and music.

What you see on TV is as much her as it is us, if not more.

Reality TV is weird in that somebody writes the story after all the shooting is already done. Because *FTB* is unscripted, I have to be careful in how much I shoot. One might think it's a great idea to shoot as much as possible to give the story producer plenty of material, but that ain't true.

More footage means more time logging and work to sculpt it into a narrative, which adds cost. With limited time, the producer will end up more often than not grabbing whatever is handiest, leaving gold on the proverbial cutting-room floor.

On the other hand, it's a reality show, so you have to be Johnny-on-the-spot. You have to be ready to shoot, and you do have to shoot a lot. If you don't, if the camera doesn't see it, it's like it never happened.

Tiff is a bit of a maverick, though. She always finds a way to put the fat and gristle to good use. She knows the "he said, she said" approach to a ghost hunting show probably isn't strong enough to give it the kind of legs needed to win marathons in TV land. So she encourages me to linger a bit on the people before and after the shot, see what turns up that I can capture on tape.

The results are often these little candid, unfiltered moments that have real charm. Matt hugging Claire after the intro, telling her it's going to be a great show. Claire sneaking a little loving smile at him when he's not looking. Jessica laughing her ass off while reading a text from her sister, another round in their never-ending boxing match of sibling love. Claire rolling her eyes while Kevin pontificates on one of his ghost hunting maxims or repeats another story about his cop days as if we hadn't heard it before around a dozen times.

All these little moments aren't just reality, they're authentic.

Interpersonal drama doesn't always have to be open conflict. It can be restrained hate and even love, not just the romantic kind but also little genuine moments of affection. Parts of people they don't even know they're showing, though like I said, the camera sees all. It's hilarious that this is a show about hunting ghosts, and some think the little candid human moments are the stuff that's faked and scripted.

Tiff believes this is the kind of thing that might get *FTB* a second season. Word is Hirsh and Vogan are putting pressure on Matt to lean into it. Make the show about the ghost hunters themselves.

Personally, I'm all for it. I don't know if it'll work—if Hirsh and Vogan are expecting *Duck Dynasty* or *Keeping Up with the Kardashians* with ghosts, they're on crack—but I'd like to see it work.

Whatever it takes to keep this little shit show going.

Because those little objects *moved*.

The Bible got a *rip* in it while the little doll sat up to watch.

For all these weeks, I've been in a state of disbelief about how these people can constantly get themselves worked up in a lather over nothing. Running around in the dark jumping at random noises is one way to earn a living, I guess, but it's also a little embarrassing.

Now I'm starting to think there is more to this show than meets the eye.

I wouldn't call myself a real believer just yet, but I am sure damn curious about what's going to happen next.

Text exchange between Rashida Brewer (Jessica Valenza) and Tameeka Brewer

Saturday, 6:38 p.m.

TB: hey you feeling better now?

RB: well it just got dark outside so

TB: you'll be okay

RB: i'm sticking to kevin like glue

RB: he has a puppy love thing for me so he's good with it

RB: the boy thinks he's some kind of elite ghostbuster

RB: it'll be a real shock when a ghost shows up and i push him in front of it

TB: LOL

TB is he hot at least?

RB he's a retired cop and almost old enough to be my dad

TB so i will take that as a firm freaking no

RB i thought you watched the show

RB you should know what he looks like, mustache and all

TB just the one episode, sorry

TB it's not really my thing you know that

RB extra punches for you then

TB i remember that matt being pretty hot though for a skinny guy

RB he is, if you don't mind the fact he is married and crazy

TB i thought that was your type minus the married part

haha   RB

TB   see? i got you laughing

TB   seriously it's gonna be fine

all day i couldn't stop thinking about how it ripped that bible   RB

TB   so the ghost's an atheist 👻

TB   can a ghost be atheist btw?

i mean if it can do that to a bible   RB

it can do it to a heart vessel   RB

or your brain maybe   RB

TB   ...

think about it   RB

TB jesus god

TB now you're freaking ME out

i asked matt what our escape plan was if shit gets bad

he looked at me like i was out of my mind

he said just be yourself tonight, if it gets too hairy you can leave

TB so he doesn't have a plan

i'm sitting here in the bathroom practicing my special empathy tone

which is easier when i'm talking to an empty room

a little harder when it's an actual spirit i might end up pissing off i never thought the stanislavski method would get me killed

 come on don't make me laugh i know you're being serious

 you want my advice?

YES

 make your own plan

 if anything bad happens you run like hell

 if the others want to mess with ghosts let them deal with it

you can count on that sis

no show and no ghost is gonna stop me getting home to my boy

 that's the spirit

if you'll uh pardon the pun

 be your best tonight, be strong, and wear running shoes

ok 😬

FADE TO BLACK

PROD: Ep. 13, "Paranormal Research Foundation"
Raw Video Footage
Saturday, 8:25 p.m.

Matt and Jessica stand in the Apparition Room, framed in a low-angle medium shot. Matt appears determined, Jessica anxious. He holds a Zoom H1 recorder.

Matt: Do you want to do the honors again?

Jessica's eyes widen at the mere suggestion.

Jessica: Me? No, no, you go ahead.
Matt: Are you okay? You seem pretty nervous.
Jessica: I guess I am, after everything that's happened.

He rests his hand on her shoulder in a comforting gesture but quickly withdraws it.

Matt: We'll be okay. The spirit hurt the Bible but otherwise hasn't done anything to try to hurt us. It's mischievous, maybe, but not negative.
Jessica: But I feel like—I feel a presence here.
Matt: You do?
Jessica: Yes. It's oppressive. Can't you feel it? Right around there, by the window.

He gives her an odd look, as if sometimes he is not sure when she is acting or being real.

> **Matt:** Maybe.
> **Jessica:** Then you should be the one to talk to them. I can barely breathe.
> **Matt:** Look, it's fine. I'll do it... Spirits! We come in peace. We don't mean any harm. We're friends. Can you give us a sign if you're here?

He waits ten seconds before continuing.

> **Matt:** Will you talk to us?

He gives the camera a quick, self-conscious smile before continuing.

> **Matt:** Last night, you played with some of the objects we offered. We added more tonight. A chess piece, a ten-dollar bill, and a piece of chocolate.
> **Jessica:** They're for you. We hope you like them.
> **Matt:** Would you like to play with them?

Another wait. Each time, the ten seconds seem to last even longer.

> **Matt:** You can talk to us on this recorder, if you like. Since you can move things, we also put a Ouija board on the floor. Maybe you'll move the planchette to give us a sign you're here and would like to talk?

At the end of another ten-second wait, Jessica shrinks back and points.

> **Jessica:** What was that? Did it just move a bit?

The camera drops to zoom in on the Ouija board.

Matt (*squints at it*)**:** I don't think so. Are you sure you're
okay?

Jessica: Can I ask the spirits a question?

Matt: Of course.

Jessica: Spirits, do you want to hurt us?

Matt: Oh. Let's try to keep it positive, Jess.

Jessica: Sorry.

Matt: It's all good. But if it's mischievous, we might have
our hands full tonight as it is without inviting more
trouble. Some spirits feed on fear.

Jessica: I understand. Keep it positive. Yeah, I can do that.
(*she forces a cheerful smile*) Can we do it again?

*Matt sighs. It is clear that something does not feel right to him,
though it is not clear whether he feels unsure about the house or
Jessica. Possibly both.*

Matt: Let's break for a minute and play it back for EVP.

Claire Kirklin's Journal

The trigger objects moved.

But one important thing didn't. A thing we couldn't see but was very much there like the proverbial elephant in the room, stationary and immovable.

A thing called parsimony. Occam's razor.

No one thought to ask the obvious question.

They hear hoofbeats, they think ghosts. They hear banging, they think ghosts.

They see objects moving, they think ghosts.

I didn't ask the question either, not out loud, anyway. So that's on me, I guess, which means I may be leaving a little piece of my own soul here at Foundation House.

Matt gets what he wants. Maybe I can leave without heartache.

Everyone wins.

After two years of investigating the paranormal, allow me to offer the most important thing I learned about it: Never get into a creative partnership with your husband unless you share the same dreams.

In the end, you will have to choose, and it will cost one or both of you something you hold dear.

FADE TO BLACK
PROD: Ep. 13, "Paranormal Research Foundation"
Raw Video Footage
Saturday, 9:50 p.m.

The camera settles on Kevin taking a long pull from a bottle of lager at his workstation.

> **Jake:** Another long night.
> **Kevin** (*turns with a sharp glare*): I didn't hear you come down.
> **Jake:** I move like a ninja. Or, rather, a cameraman.
> **Kevin:** Just don't go sneaking up on me like that. I was a cop. I could have put a hole in you.
> **Jake:** Huh? (*laughs*) With what?
> **Kevin:** I keep a nine-millimeter in my bags. Don't tell Matt.

Jake taps the camera, which is recording.

> **Kevin:** Then erase it. It's none of his business. And now you know I have it.
> **Jake:** Okay, man. Jeez. I don't know what I did to piss you off. You've been acting weird all day. Take a chill.
> **Kevin:** You're supposed to be up there shooting Matt and Jess getting EVP.

He turns back to the monitors while saying this, signaling the conversation is over. Jake ignores the cue.

Jake: It's a total bust. Even deader than last night, if that's possible. I came down for fresh batteries and a tripod. My shoulder's killing me.

Kevin: It's dead down here too. The cameras show nothing happening anywhere.

Jake (*moves closer to the monitors*): So you watch Matt and Jess from here?

Kevin: When they're in one of the monitored rooms. That's the job.

Jake: Do they ever, you know?

Kevins turns to glare back with pure venom.

Kevin: I don't know why you're even asking me that.

Jake: She looks at him a certain way sometimes. This little viewfinder is like a magnifying glass. It gets right in people's faces and they don't even know it.

Kevin: She's not like that. Get your mind out of the gutter.

Jake: Well, I guess I'll get back up there.

Kevin: You do that.

Jake: It's been so fun talking to you, Kev.

Kevin (*frowns*): Hey, Jake.

Jake: Yeah?

Kevin: You wouldn't happen to own a knife, would you?

Jake: Yup. A Leatherman pocket knife. It comes in handy in this line of work more often than you think. Do you need it for something?

Kevin: If you want to see my nine, by all means, take it out.

Jake: Okay, well, I'm going to get the hell out of here. See you later, bro.

FADE TO BLACK
PROD: Ep. 13, "Paranormal Research Foundation"
Raw Video Footage
Saturday, 11:11 p.m.

The Apparition Room. Matt and Jessica sit on the floor near the trigger objects and Ouija board. They operate a special spirit box modified with the antennae removed, so that it operates without radio interference and therefore produces more credible, pure EVP.

The spirit box whooshes with pulsing white noise as Matt asks questions and Jessica stares unblinking at the trigger objects, as if expecting them to suddenly shift, and ready to jump up and bolt if they do.

    Matt: Do you live here alone, or are there more than one of you?

sh-sh-sh-sh-sh

    Matt: If you don't talk to us, we're going to leave.

sh-sh-sh-sh-sh

    Matt: We'll take all these toys with us.

Jessica turns to eye him sharply and then gazes fearfully at the ceiling.

Jessica: Are you sure you want to provoke it? You said we should keep it positive.

Matt (*sighs*): I don't know what else to do. We're getting nothing.

Jessica: Maybe it isn't here. Maybe it roams around the house.

Matt (*frowns at the camera*): Jake, wake up.

Jake: Oh. Yeah. Sorry.

Matt: Let's do a quick run through the rest of the rooms up here and see what turns up. Then we can hit the grand staircase on the way down.

Jessica (*hopefully*): Back down to Base Camp?

Matt: Yeah, we need a break. You look like you need more tissues.

Jessica: This house is killing my sinuses one sneeze at a time.

Matt: Okay. We'll use the bathroom, grab a drink, and get together for a team meeting to come up with new ideas.

Jessica: Yes. Thank you.

Matt: God knows I need a break myself.

He turns off the spirit box and pockets it.

Matt: I'm sick of being teased, and I'm getting really pissed off at this spirit right now.

FADE TO BLACK
PROD: Ep. 13, "Paranormal Research Foundation"
Raw Video Footage
Saturday, 11:42 p.m.

Base Camp. The team sits in a circle on pea-green polypropylene chairs. The camera pans across the tired investigators to frame Matt in a medium shot. Behind him, the glowing monitors rest on the large dining room table. The cots sit unmade against the walls among spare equipment and black trunks used to haul gear.

Matt: I think we can all agree the house has gone back to being inactive.

Judging by his face, he is tired and not a little frustrated. The evidence gained this morning has apparently only given him an appetite for more. The slouch in his posture, however, suggests resignation.

Disappointment is not uncommon in the profession he has chosen, one that routinely produces more questions than it answers. But this time, the disappointment seems to hurt.

Claire: We're hoping the spirit will interact with the objects again while we're sleeping, but I think we have to accept the possibility that nothing will happen.

Matt: I know that what I saw this morning got my own hopes way up, but I think Claire's right. We might not get any more activity.

Kevin wags his head at this, muttering, "Nope, nope, nope." The camera quickly pans to him.

Kevin: We're seeing activity right now.

Claire: What?

Kevin: All day long, we heard the house settling. Creaks and groans and little bits of plaster trickling down the walls. Then as soon as the sun goes down, it froze. Like it turned into a photo of itself.

She gives him a quizzical look, as if she is only now discovering he might be cleverer than she had once thought.

Claire: That's actually an interesting point.

Kevin: It's a sign by itself. Just not a sign we usually look for.

Matt: But what does it mean?

Claire: Well, we could test it. Maybe we moved around a lot more during the day. We could stomp around tonight and see if the same noises appear.

Matt: That's not quite what I meant with my question, but I like your thinking. We could test it. If the house stays mum, it's a data point. The problem isn't whether there are spirits here but why they'd rather play than talk to us.

Claire: Someone could stay up all night in the Apparition Room. Two people, actually, so whatever happens can be corroborated.

Matt: I like that too. How about you and me?

Claire: Sounds like another romantic date.

Matt: And it's for science, a twofer. Now let's talk about tomorrow.

Kevin: We should expand and investigate the basement more. I know the Apparition Room is where the action is at, but my gut tells me the basement is important.
Jake: I shot some B-roll down there today. It's a weird vibe.
Matt: Okay, we can certainly do that. What about you, Jess?

He caught her leaning against her hand, her fingers massaging her forehead. Her eyes flash open at the sound of her name.

Jessica: I don't care. I'm filthy and tired and want to go to bed.
Matt: Look, I know we're all feeling punchy, but overall, we did good here.
Jessica: I'll be good to go tomorrow. I just need to take some Allegra and catch up on my sleep.

Matt looks around at his tired and dispirited team and visibly stiffens, as if coming to some sort of decision. It is time for him to show leadership.

Matt: Listen, you should all be proud. I think the producers will be too with what we've accomplished on this investigation. I really think they should appreciate it.

Jessica makes a slight groaning noise, which surprises him. This is obviously not the reaction he expected.

Matt: What's wrong?
Jessica: Nothing. Sorry. I've been in show business too long. The way you said that made it sound like there was a "but" or something in there. My bad—
Matt (*turns thoughtful*)**:** Well...

The team stares at him in an awkward silence. Matt looks most uncomfortable of all. Claire reaches to place her hand on his arm.

Claire: Whatever it is, darling, now is a good time.

Kevin: Damn right. If something's going on, chief, I'd like to hear it.

Matt: Well, it looks like our ratings have peaked, and the network is getting nervous. Sorry I didn't tell you all about it before. I've been wrestling with it.

Jessica (*totally alert now*)**:** Are we being canceled?

Matt: No, it's not like that, but if we don't bring the first season in with a strong showing, we might not get a second. Our last episode had a dip in the ratings.

Jessica (*sullen*)**:** Right.

Claire: If it's not "like that," what is it like?

Matt: Well, they love the team chemistry. They want to shift the focus from ghost hunting more onto us as ghost hunters.

Jessica: Oh. Okay.

Matt: It's not as threatening as it sounds. It'll mean we get into our personal lives a little more, more on-the-fly interviews, maybe some guests on the show to stir things up. That sort of thing.

Jessica: It doesn't sound bad at all.

She is visibly brightening. It is not the best news, but it is the show business to which she is accustomed. In her view, the show has a fighting chance to survive.

Kevin: Not bad, no. It's worse than bad. It's terrible.

Matt (*squints at him*)**:** What's your objection, Kev?

The tech manager crosses his arms over his chest and leans back in his chair, which creaks in protest.

Kevin: The whole point of this is making contact. I don't want anybody prying into my private life. My past and the like. It's nobody's business.

Jake (*with a snort*): You gave all that up when you signed your contract.

Kevin: Explain that.

Jake: I'm just saying it goes with being on TV.

Kevin (*casts a baleful eye at the camera*): Well, you're wrong.

Jake: Sounds like you've got a lot to hide, man.

Kevin starts to say something but shakes his head, as if realizing he is not only talking to Jake but to anyone who will see this footage in the future.

Kevin: You're missing the point. Once the story is about us, the assholes come out with knives. The naysayers. They'll gut us for sport. Besides that, it's fake. It'll ruin this show.

Jessica (*with an angry, snapping tone*): Or save it. I'd love to see us get a second season. Wouldn't that be cool too?

Matt raises his hands in a placating gesture. He wants everyone to calm down.

Matt: They—

Kevin: Every episode, our whole focus is on investigation. Now it'll be on petty fights and gossip. All the stuff that makes reality TV total crap to watch.

Matt: They asked us for ideas, but—

Kevin: We should stop treating spirits like lab rats and go back to our RIP roots. Full-spectrum investigation. No more debunking every single thing. This show could shoot Jesus walking on water and then say he was actually standing on a sheet of floating ice. This is a show about miracles. We either believe or we don't.

He is no longer looking at Matt but at Claire, who stares back at him wearing a wry expression. He has thrown down the gauntlet, but she does not seem to care.

Matt: Well. Okay. I appreciate you speaking your mind, Kevin, but first off, Claire's a part of this show, so she'd have to be okay with any changes. I also didn't finish my "but." The "but" is Hirsh and Vogan want a big focus on the characters, so we have to work with that. That's it. Without them, there is no show.

Kevin jumps up from his chair, apparently startling Jake, as the camera pulls back.

Kevin: Then tell them that's not how it works! That's your job!

Matt: The job is paranormal investigation within the constraints—

Kevin: Paranormal investigation, period. That's it. End of story. We're onto something here. The objects *moved*—

Matt: What I'm going to tell them is we—

Kevin: If it doesn't change things up, why'd—I mean, what did it accomplish?

His mouth still open in the act of speaking, Matt's face darkens.

Jessica: Personally, I think it'll breathe some new life—
Matt: Hang on, Jess.

She catches his tone and promptly stops talking.

Matt: What do you mean, Kev?

Kevin's eyes sweep the team. He sits back in his chair and crosses his arms again, though his tone betrays he is no longer confident about his words.

Kevin: I mean we should get back to our roots, and—
Matt: What did you mean, "what did it accomplish?"
Kevin: I was saying the event itself should get us a second season. That's it.

The room goes quiet. Matt frowns, apparently still rankled by what his instincts are telling him. The men stare at each other in a silent standoff.

Claire: You know what he meant, Matt.
Kevin (*louder*)**:** I told him what I meant.
Claire: I think a part of you knew all along. You had to have at least wondered.
Jessica: I don't understand.

Matt's face slowly contorts as if he has been punched in the gut.

Matt: I'm only going to ask this once. Was the objects moving a hoax?
Kevin: That's a goddamn lie.
Matt: Who was in on this?
Claire: Ask the guy in charge of the batteries.

Jake: Holy shit. Kevin, did you really—?

Kevin (*points at Claire*): She told me to do it.

Claire (*glowering back*): I said Matt was under pressure and to help him out with tuning up the show. I didn't say fake evidence of a haunting.

Kevin: There *is* a haunting here. We can all feel it.

Jessica groans again, this time at the edge of tears.

Jessica: You stupid asshole. You just sank this show.

Matt: Jake, kill the camera.

Jake: But—

Jessica: Some of us don't put science or voodoo first. Some of us put food on the table with this show!

Matt: *Now*, Jake.

Jake: All right, all right.

He sets the camera on the floor behind him but leaves it on. The view turns dark gray and focuses on grains of dust on the floorboards. The voices drop in volume but are still audible.

Jake: It's off.

Matt: Did you figure it out before or just now?

Claire: Before.

Jake (*softly*): Holy shit.

Jessica: This is going to ruin my career!

Matt: Why didn't you tell me?

Claire: Imagine I said, "I think but can't prove that someone on the team faked your big breakthrough." Imagine what that would have done. I couldn't do it to you.

Matt: But it's fake. It goes against everything we've tried to do for years.

Claire: What would you have thought if I said something? What would you have thought of *me*?

Matt says nothing, no doubt chewing on how badly he wanted to believe a spirit moved the objects and how he would have reacted to this belief being challenged.

Kevin: Anything I might have done, I did it for the show—

Jessica: Oh, shut your mouth. You did enough. So what do we do now?

Claire: I'm not done yet. I happen to think Kevin's right about one thing.

Kevin: Thank you—

Claire: I don't agree with what he did, but he's right that I don't belong here and that it boxed us into this corner. I helped make this show, but in the end, I'm breaking it.

Matt: That's not true.

Claire: I don't think ghost hunting should be done by people who believe in ghosts, but the opposite is true for ghost hunting TV. If you want to change up the show, I should leave and you should do your investigations the way other shows do it.

Matt: You—you can't, this is—

Claire: It was never real science in my book anyway. It was just debunking.

Jessica: I asked, what the hell are we going to do? Why the hell are we even talking about what to do next with a show that may not exist tomorrow?

Kevin: Somebody had to step up to save—

Matt: ENOUGH.

We hear the sound of his chair scraping the floor.

Claire: Where are you going? Please—

Stomping footsteps. The room erupts in cross talk.

Matt: I've had it!
Jake: Wait!
Matt: What's the point? I'm done!
Jake: Listen! Do you hear that?

A steady bassline shimmers in the air, barely audible. For a few moments, no one says anything as they all tune in to listen.

Jessica: I think it's music. It's music, right?
Jake: Where is it coming from?

The music grows louder, little by little. More cross talk.

Kevin: Hang on. I know this. It's an old flower power song from the sixties. Can't remember the name. It's by the Prayer Beads.
Jessica: How do you know?
Kevin: Everybody knows this song. They were a hippie one-hit—
Jessica: Did you set this up? You better not have set this up.
Kevin: This isn't me.
Matt: Jake.
Jake: What?
Matt: Get the camera.

The camera jerks from the floor onto Jake's shoulder. The music suddenly leaps in volume.

Female singers: THE GROOVY PEOPLE ARE HERE

The paranormal investigators flinch at the blast, pale and gawking.
Jessica lets out a startled scream. Claire points off-camera.

   Claire: Lights! I see lights flashing outside! Look!
   Kevin: Matt. MATT.
   Singers: GOOD TIMES WILL LAST ALL YEAR
   Kevin: The monitors—

The camera swings toward the two monitors showing the Apparition Room.

Which is now occupied by a swirling whirlwind of light.

Hands reach from the light toward the trigger objects with impossibly
elongated fingers like tendrils—

   Jessica: *What is that?* What the hell is happening?
   Matt: Let's go!

The team rushes toward the stairs and finds itself in near total
darkness lit up by powerful, strobing flashes from the windows. The
group stumbles, disoriented.

Jake turns on the camera's light, which illuminates wild, panicked faces.

   Jake: Go, go!

They climb the stairs.

   Singers: DON'T LET THE MAN GET YOU DOWN!
TURN YOUR SAD FROWN UPSIDE DOWN!

They stop in front of the Apparition Room's closed door. The trigger objects and Ouija board clatter like shrapnel against the walls and floor. The remote camera bangs off the door.

Singers: A BRIGHTER FUTURE IS NEAR
Matt: Okay, everybody ready? I'm doing this.

He opens it—

And rears at the sight of a blinding shaft of shimmering light surrounded by flying trigger objects.

The glow coalesces into the form of a grotesquely tall woman, so tall her head tilts almost sideways below the ceiling, hairlike strands of light splayed around a ghastly jack-o'-lantern grin.

Matt: I . . .

The spirit's hand reaches to beckon him to come closer, a little closer.

Chorus: OPEN YOUR HEART AND LEND ME YOUR
   EEEAAAEAR

CRASH

The camera jumps and pivots toward the stairs, Jake acting on years of body memory to always follow the action. Another crash.

One by one, the wood steps crumple and splinter as if under the impact of anvils dropped from a great height. As if an invisible giant is walking down the stairs.

CRASH, CRASH, CRASH

Chorus: THERE'S NOTHING TO FEAR BUT FEAR

Laughter creeps onto the flooded audio like EVP. Peals of laughter. The house or a spirit that inhabits it appears to be laughing at them.

Claire's face fills the screen, showing she is the one laughing. From joy or hysteria, it is impossible to be sure.

Claire: This is real! It's really real!

The house trembles with a vacuum roar pulsing up from its foundation. The music reaches a deafening volume, warbling with distortion. Plaster rains from the ceiling.

The record skips. The team's gasps produce puffs of visible water vapor like miniature ghosts as the temperature suddenly drops to freezing.

Chorus: NOTHING TO FEAR BUT FEAR—
NOTHING TO FEAR BUT FEAR—
NOTHING TO FEAR BUT FEAR—
Matt: Everybody, out! Out of the house!

He grabs Claire's hand and yanks her toward the grand staircase, now hazy in a massive, settling dust cloud where its center had been crushed. She stumbles drunkenly, still cackling. Kevin lingers a moment before bolting after them.

The house continues to tremble at its foundations, raining bits of plaster, as if threatening to come crashing down on their heads.

Jake: Wait—wait! Where's Jessica?

The camera swings toward the apparition, which now stands stooped and grinning in the doorway.

Jake: Holy fuck—

The view jerks and swims, the microphone filled with pounding footsteps, stopping only when the screen goes blank.

DAY THREE

Claire Kirklin's Journal

In the ninth century, a Chinese alchemist working to produce an elixir for eternal life accidentally invented gunpowder, which changed the world.

I now know exactly how that alchemist felt.

Though the comparison isn't quite accurate. After all, I originally set out to prove the existence of ghosts and ended up doing just that. If the alchemist had actually discovered immortality, *then* we'd be the same.

On the other hand, according to legend, the man scorched his face and burned his house to the ground at his moment of discovery. That's how I feel this morning: burned by playing with things I don't understand.

I can't wait to play more.

Play until I do understand.

I'm not making much sense, I know. I'm making all the sense. Nothing makes sense, not anymore. My entire understanding of reality has just dramatically shifted, like an earthquake that leaves everything standing but very, very shaky.

God, I feel like I really understand my husband for the first time.

I feel like I know everything and that I really don't know anything.

You'll understand too, after you watch the video.

You'll be changed. Burned. And if you're like me, you'll want more.

I'm rambling. For a while, I couldn't express myself at all. Couldn't even produce a coherent thought. All I could do was laugh, which kept bubbling up out of me. Now I can't stop writing. It feels good, getting all this out of my head. Defining it makes it real and is giving me a sense of control I sorely need.

We drove the camper until we reached Denton and just kept going, north all the way to Fredericksburg. There, we found a pub that was open and stopped in a remote corner of its parking lot. For a long time, we sat in numb silence. I didn't trust myself to form words. My thoughts and memories were like puzzle pieces that needed to be fitted together, but first I had to describe them.

Finally, Matt spoke behind the wheel. "Is everybody okay?" He must have realized how ridiculous that sounded because he added, "Is anybody hurt?"

No one answered. Jessica, who'd sensibly run like hell after we'd seen the spirit manifest on the Base Camp camera monitors, lay shaking in a fetal ball on one of the two couch beds, as if willing herself to escape all the way by physically disappearing. Hugging his camera, Jake opened his mouth with a little hitch of breath, though no words came out. Kevin stared out a side window with his hands splayed against the glass, as if keeping watch in case the spirits followed us to finish what we'd started.

Matt eyed them all in the rearview mirror, idly twirling his wedding band around his finger, which he does when he gets nervous and which on any other day I'd find endearing.

Then he turned his head toward me, though he seemed to look right through me as if I weren't there. Shock was written all over his face. My husband seemed more machine than human right then. I should have felt sympathy and asked him right back if he was okay, but I had nothing to give.

Instead, I stared at the pub with its black awning and windowed view of warm, mellow revelry and felt another boiling urge to laugh.

Look at those people in there having fun, I wanted to say. *They have no idea.*

Whatever their beliefs, in the end, they know they live in a normal, predictable world governed by the laws of physics.

Very soon, they'll be awakened. They'll learn it's all an illusion.

I had a giddy thought: *I might get the Nobel Prize for this.*

We were astronomers who'd gazed up through their telescopes and accidentally found an alien spaceship. We were Sir Alexander Fleming, who took a two-week vacation while experimenting with influenza and came back to discover mold had grown over his sample and inhibited viral growth, which led to penicillin. We were John Walker, a pharmacist who mixed antimony sulphide and potassium chlorate and tried to scratch it off, only to see it burst into flame, inventing the match.

Next to me, Matt finished a long yoga breath. "I could use a drink."

I'm writing down what everyone said to the best of my memory. It's important to document this exactly as it happened. History was made tonight. When people ask what our lead investigator's first words about the phenomenon were, I want to be able to tell them the exact words, even if they were "I could use a drink."

The camper's door slammed. I didn't remember Matt even opening it, but there he was, walking away toward the bar. I was surprised he would walk away from me like this, but we were all alone right then. What we'd seen had scoured us down to our essence. We were almost spectral ourselves.

"All right," Kevin said. "I need a... Yeah."

He climbed over the empty driver's seat and got out next.

The bar's normalcy called to me as well, a chance to regroup and try to process exactly what the hell happened back at Foundation House tonight, but I resisted for a moment. For two days, I'd suffered a pointless camping trip in a rambling health hazard and couldn't wait to get back to my own bed and comforting routines of home. Now I wasn't sure I wanted to go back.

If I did, what happened might not have happened. I might wake up and discover it was all a dream, its vivid details already crumbling.

"Bring the camera," I said. "We should watch the tape."

"I don't know if we…" Jake shook his head. "Okay. Screw it."

I climbed out with unsteady legs. My feet tested the ground, and I was a little surprised to find it solid. I looked up at the sky that had cleared after the rain. A few stars glimmered in the murky light pollution.

Time blurred again. Jake stood next to me, one of his arms supporting a visibly trembling Jessica. I asked her if she wanted to stay in the camper.

Eyes wild, she gave her head a quick shake. I caught its meaning. She didn't want to go anywhere or do anything, but she wanted to be alone even less.

Inside, we drew a few curious stares. They probably thought we'd just survived a car crash or the local version of the *Texas Chainsaw Massacre*. Haunted eyes, dirty with plaster dust, reeking of stale flop sweat. As the saying goes, we weren't from around here.

Matt sat alone at a table with a half-finished pint of something dark in front of him, staring off intently toward his own private horizon. I joined him, ordered something, and the server went away.

"Let's play the tape," I said. I had to be sure it had happened.

We watched it.

And I started laughing again.

Kevin Linscott's Journal

After all the shit went down at the house, we drove up to the Hibernian in Fredericksburg. I hoped to get everybody calm enough that we could talk about what happened and come up with some sort of plan of action.

We seated ourselves around one of those dark wood tables you find in pubs. I laid my hands on it and enjoyed its solid feel.

I put down my first pint of Guinness without even tasting it. I ordered another and decided I might just get good and drunk. I earned the right tonight.

After my second pint went down, I started to get my bearings. Over our heads, a big TV screen on the wall replayed a football game broadcast earlier in the night. The Saints pounded the Buccaneers. The stadium crowd let out a breathless roar at a Hail Mary pass.

An average night in America. Perfectly normal. The wood paneling, taps behind the bar, and cute servers in black tees and red plaid skirts all gained substance and became real.

For a TV show about veteran ghost hunters, you'd think we wouldn't be this affected, but what happened tonight is unprecedented. The spirit world teases. It likes its jump scares that leave you wondering. *Bang, bang.* A wisp of cold air on the back of your neck. It goes for creep and dread over outright shock.

It doesn't put on a big horror extravaganza with everything on the menu.

Claire said we should watch the tape. Steeled by my third Guinness, I huddled with the team, heads touching so we could all get a look. The only problem was we had to watch it on a tiny screen, and we could hardly hear anything over the NFL game playing out over our heads.

But it was all there, real and true.

Okay, I did move the trigger objects, and I know that wasn't right. Everybody probably fakes a little in this business, which I'd call a margin of error, but I took it too far. It hurt the others, but it hurt me the most. I'd given up a career in law enforcement to search for the truth. I'd spent years building up a rock-solid reputation as a ghost hunter. And then I dirtied it in a moment of zeal.

As Claire confessed, she'd boxed us into a corner, and somebody had to step up and do something—provide the only evidence that she'd accept and that would keep our investigations going. Some might even call me a hero for doing what I did, but no, I don't deserve it. I am tough enough to admit I screwed up.

After the shit went down, though, I felt vindicated. All along, I'd been right the house was active. I was right that ghosts exist.

Soon, everybody will know it.

We watched the tape, and then Claire started laughing in a way that gave me the creeps. You know somebody for a while, and all of a sudden this new personality comes bursting out. It's unsettling. I felt like I didn't know her now.

I asked her if she was Claire. I had to check.

"I'm not possessed, Kevin," she said, and started laughing again.

Some people aren't built for this kind of mental strain. I had my work cut out for me pulling them together. Matt looked like he'd gotten a lobotomy. Jake's face flickered between gray and green. Jessica showed all the signs of shock.

"We watched it three times already," I growled at them, taking command. "It happened. We need to snap out of it and talk it out."

"I need to know if one of you staged this," Matt said.

Then everybody looked at me.

I couldn't believe it. Were they serious? I very calmly explained my first name isn't Gandalf, and my last name sure isn't Steven god-damn Spielberg.

"It was real," Claire said, back to her old professor self. "If it was a hoax, it deserves its own category at the Oscars."

For once, the professor and I agreed one hundred percent.

"I've never seen anything like it," Matt said. "The amount of energy."

"A thousand pounds of force to crush each stair," Claire lectured. "A thousand watts to produce all the light. And who knows how many joules to fling around all the trigger objects. It shredded the Ouija board into toothpicks."

"It's just unbelievable."

"*I* believe it," I told him. "It proves we were right all along."

But he said we were wrong. We'd gone in there with our tricks and gadgets, tech that could detect the slightest whisper and EMF change, and we'd turned up nothing. Then, boom, the spirits came out to party with bowling balls.

Some people just can't see the big picture.

"We were lucky to get out of there alive," Jake said.

Then Jessica finally spoke up. "If it wanted to kill us, we'd already be dead."

She said she'd learned enough about the paranormal to know a ghost can pass through a wall without disturbing it. A ghost can also do stuff like slam doors and apparently karate chop a grand staircase. In short, it can both pass through and affect matter.

She gave us a chance to correct her, but nobody did.

If this was true, Jessica added, then a ghost could reach into your rib cage and crush your heart without you even knowing it until you were dying.

It could claw across your brain's neural pathways and leave you a gibbering vegetable. It could sever your femoral artery and make you bleed to death from the inside. It could puncture a lung. It could flatten your eardrums and yank out your optic nerves and cut your spinal cord—

Matt told her that we got the picture and that she could stop.

"We need to keep driving," Jessica said. "Get as far from that house as we can and hope it didn't decide to follow us."

"Our stuff's back there," Jake pointed out. "All the equipment. The van."

"If we go back, it might decide to stop playing and start doing."

"It's not active during the day, right? We'll be safe when the sun comes up." The cameraman looked at us, expecting us to know the rules. "I mean, right?"

"We don't know anything about it," Matt said. "Honestly, I thought we knew what we were doing, but we don't know anything."

I snorted my derision at this statement. We knew plenty.

Jessica went on in her spooky whisper. "This isn't a movie. It's not a TV show. There's no script. We could walk in there and all be dead in seconds."

"We already have enough footage to blow up reality," Jake said. "We don't actually need to stay in the house. We could just go back for our stuff and run."

"What if what we saw tonight was an invitation?" Claire asked us.

She laid out her case. Everything we saw happen had happened all at once and perfectly matched the claims about the house that we were investigating.

All that book learning, and this was the best she could come up with. I told her what we saw only proved the claims right. The simplest explanation.

"Or it showed us what we wanted to see. Exactly what we were trying to find."

Matt thought it was an interesting theory and said so. I said I could poke about a thousand holes in it.

"Good," Claire shot back. "Now you're finally thinking like a scientist. Prove me wrong."

But the more I thought about it, the more I believed she might have this thing by the tail. I was working on my fifth pint now.

Maybe the beer made me rash, but I now knew exactly what we needed to do.

"If the house wants to talk to us," I said, "then I say we hear it out."

"What do the rest of you think about that?" Matt asked the team.

"We could call somebody," Jake chimed in. "Get more people on-site."

"Call who?" I challenged. "And say what?"

"We'd give up our scoop," Matt said.

"Stupid idea," I added. "This is our discovery. And we're running out of time."

Jake turned on me. "What do you mean, 'our' and 'we'? Why are you even talking, after what you did?"

"I want to hear from everybody," Matt growled. "We need all hands on deck. But, Kev? There are no stupid ideas. We need to make a decision as a group about what we should do next."

"No," Claire said. "We don't."

"What?"

"There is no 'we' anymore."

We all turned to stare at her.

"This isn't a group decision," she explained. "This stopped being a TV show the moment Foundation House revealed itself. The TV show is no longer my main concern. This is the most important scientific discovery in history. I'm sorry, Matt. Whatever you all decide to do, I'm going back."

And just like that, Claire and I were on the same page again, united by a common goal even if we always seemed to be divided by our methods.

"You heard the lady," I said.

Jake Wolfson's Journal

Every time I close my eyes, I see that jack-o'-lantern face grinning down at me.

The video of a lifetime.

Just before I ran like hell.

I mean, wouldn't you?

All this time I've been roaming around haunted houses with ghost hunters, I never expected to see an actual ghost. It's not about believing or not believing. Seeing ghosts was just always something that happened to other people. When Kevin fessed up to faking evidence, my first thought was, well, that figures.

Being behind the camera does something to your head, gives you a certain mindset. You think you're immune to whatever's going on because you're not on-screen. As you know, I'm Switzerland in this show. I'm the fly on the wall. I'm the camera shooter.

In fact, my dear viewer and voyeur, I'm you. I'm your eyes.

When I panned back to the ghost, I actually expected it to ignore me and lurch into the hall to chase the others. Instead, it looked right at me and almost gave me a heart attack. The way it gripped the doorframe with its spindly fingers and stooped and tilted its head has me shivering even now.

Suddenly, for the first time, I'm a part of the story, whether I like it or not.

FADE TO BLACK
PROD: Ep. 13, "Paranormal Research Foundation,
Part 2"
DIRECTOR: Matt Kirklin
CAMERA: Jake Wolfson

*Foundation House fills the camera lens as a blur, providing an
accidental visual metaphor for its mystery. The chipped and peeling
veranda pops into sharp focus before the view pulls back into a long,
wide shot. The house looms among undergrowth and pines, etched in
dawn's harsh rays and deep shadows.*

*The front doors hang open, just the way they were left last night. Nothing
stirs inside. From here, at least, Foundation House appears inert again.*

*Matt walks on-screen and closes his eyes, his mouth working silently
as if praying. Claire follows a few moments later, still fiddling her
lavalier microphone into place.*

Jake: Camera's on, you're in frame.
Matt: We're doing this quick. One take. I don't care how
it turns out.
Claire: Good. I'm ready.
Kevin: Audio's good.
Matt: Rubber baby buggy bumpers. Seashells by the seashore—
Jake: Rolling.
Matt: One second. Jessica, Kev, come stand next to us.
This is your discovery too.

Wearing audio headphones over his FTB ballcap, Kevin walks on-screen to plant his hands on his hips at Claire's side. Jessica creeps forward to stand next to Matt with her arms tightly crossed, hugging her ribs.

Jake: Everybody's in the shot. Jess, if you could look at the camera, that'd be—never mind. Okay, you're good to go anytime.

Matt: Welcome back to *Fade to Black*. I'm Matt Kirklin, lead investigator.

Claire: And I'm Claire Kirklin, co-lead investigator.

Matt: Behind us is Foundation House. For more than thirty hours, we investigated its mysteries, only to come up empty. Then last night, it gave up its secrets. We encountered the most powerful paranormal entity we've ever seen.

Claire: We left the house in a hurry. We regrouped and decided to come back. This is the most incredible discovery in—well, possibly ever. The house is certainly haunted, or to put it more accurately, occupied. Is it a ghost? Or something else? Is it intelligent? That's what we want to find out.

Matt: Right now, we're going back. Last night, the spirit spoke to us loud and clear. Today, we're going to try to make contact again, and we don't intend to run. Stay tuned as we *Fade to Black*.

He visibly sags.

Matt: And cut. How did it look?

Jake: It's good.

Matt: You sure? I've got this headache. I feel like I can't think straight.

Claire (*studies her husband's face with concern*): It's good, darling.

Matt: Okay, fine. Whatever we didn't do right, we can record a voice-over later.

He turns to Jessica and hugs her. She allows but doesn't return it.

Matt: You're going to be okay. Thanks for everything you did. Are you sure you're okay to drive?

Jessica stares at the house.

Matt: Jessica? You're okay to drive?

She nods. She holds the van keys clenched in her fist.

Matt: Maybe you should stay a little while longer. Make sure you have your bearings before you get behind the wheel.

Claire: Matt.

Matt: I just want to make sure—

Claire (*her eyes on the house*): Do you mind if I go in now?

Matt: Please, Claire. Just give me one second here.

Jessica (*nodding*): I know what to do. I'll be okay. I will.

Matt: Good. We'll see you on Monday. Make sure you're back here early in the afternoon so we can get everything loaded.

Jessica (*glances nervously at the house*): Yeah. Okay.

He turns to the camera wearing a weak, lopsided smile that looks wrong on a face otherwise broadcasting exhaustion and anxiety.

Matt: This is it, gang. We're going back in.

FADE TO BLACK
PROD: Ep. 13, "Paranormal Research Foundation"
SECOND DAY HOT SHEET
Report emailed by Matt Kirklin to the producers

Our second day at Foundation House proved to be a day of wonders. I don't even know how to describe it. I know that whatever I say, you won't believe it. Honestly, I barely believe it myself, and I came into this already a believer and saw the whole thing with my own two eyes.

The day started off with some of the trigger objects in the Apparition Room moving overnight. As you can imagine, we were ecstatic. We focused our efforts on that room but came up empty. During a team meeting at Base Camp, we found out Kevin faked the whole thing.

You wanted human drama, you got it.

Only as we were all having it out, Foundation House came to life.

No, we didn't hear a bang in the distance. We didn't hear gibberish on the spirit box and interpret it as words. We didn't catch a shadow behind the corner. We didn't use 3D mapping to detect a human figure from cracks in a wall. We didn't get a funny feeling. We didn't rig up little flashlights to blink on and off.

I'm saying *the house came to life.*

Bluish electric light flashed all over the property. An old sixties song filled the air. The Apparition Room suddenly got its apparition. The trigger objects didn't just move, they were physically thrown across the room. The footsteps on the grand staircase broke the damn stairs. The temperature dropped to freezing.

All at the same time. This actually happened.

And we got it on tape.

Honestly, it scared the crap out of us. We bolted and regrouped over drinks in Fredericksburg. As far as *Fade to Black* is concerned, we struck gold. What's on tape goes way beyond ratings straight into Pulitzer territory. You wanted something that would jolt us up in our slot's top fifty cable telecasts, you're getting it.

But it's not enough. We made a decision to go back to the house. We're onto something here. This is too big. This episode has to be a two-parter. Hell, we could do the rest of the season at this place. Make the show entirely about this house, if that's possible.

The entity we contacted is more powerful than I could have imagined. The amount of energy it spent is phenomenal. Since we don't really know what it is and because it can easily hurt us, there is obviously a strong element of risk in messing with it. Its way of saying hello crushed solid oak planks and almost broke our minds.

Because of this, Jessica will be leaving the show on an indefinite hiatus. We're sleeping in the camper tonight, and tomorrow morning, we'll return to the house. Once we get back, Jessica agreed to drive the van to Ralston and deliver the raw footage to Donnelly.

The rest of us, meanwhile, will soldier on. I assure you that we are all safe right now, and that we'll take every precaution to stay that way. We'll try again tomorrow night, and next time, I promise you, we won't run.

That's where you come in. You needed paranormal evidence and human drama from me, and you got it. I did my part. Now I need you to buy us time. As much time as we can get in the house. I know this all sounds unbelievable, but I am asking you to trust me until you see the footage yourselves. I also know this is just TV for you—money in, money out, which is fine—but we're way beyond that now. We are so far out of Kansas, we're looking at it from orbit.

We didn't just strike gold. We touched the grail.

FADE TO BLACK

PROD: Ep. 13, "Paranormal Research Foundation, Part 2"

Raw Video Footage

Sunday, 8:51 a.m.

The van rolls onto the dirt track and disappears into the trees. The camera swings to frame Matt, Claire, and Kevin in a medium shot.

Kevin (*with gravity*)**:** And then there were three.
Jake: Thanks a lot, bro.
Matt: When we go inside, let's make sure we stay together at all times.
Claire: Why?
Kevin (*snorts*)**:** You must not watch many horror movies.
Matt: Staying together is safer, obviously.

She raises her hands to set them straight.

Claire: You heard what Jessica said last night, and I think she's absolutely right. If the spirit is invisible and can manipulate matter, it can easily kill us if it wants to. Being together or alone isn't going to make any difference.
Matt: Fine. But we keep in touch by radio. That's not open to discussion.
Claire: Of course.

The ground rules established, they turn to mount the veranda.

Jake: Hold up, you guys.

Kevin: Now what?

Jake: Three people, one camera. Where are you going, and who am I following?

Kevin (*raises his hand*)**:** I'll go around and pull the memory cards from the remote cams and recorders, starting with the Apparition Room.

Matt: I'd like to see the stairs and then the Apparition Room.

Claire: Same.

They all look at each other, realizing they will be staying together anyway. Matt appears visibly relieved, as he clearly wanted to make sure his wife was safe or at least with him.

Jake: Lead on, then.

The team creeps carefully across the threshold into the spacious foyer. Kevin treads at a slight crouch, placing his feet with caution as if approaching an armed suspect or, more accurately, walking through some cosmic minefield.

Matt (*whispering*)**:** Remember, we're just observing. We need to get our bearings and document everything we see. Replace cards and set up new baselines. After that, we can come up with a plan that involves trying to make contact again—

Jake (*softly sings*)**:** Open your heart and lend me your ear...

Matt: What are you doing?

Jake: Sorry, boss. I'm nervous. I can't get that song out of my head.

Kevin: Hippie music. Picture spending the afterlife having to listen to that.

The dining room appears exactly as they left it. The monitors still draw power from the portable generator. The remote camera stationed outside is still running. The screens showing the Apparition Room have no signal.

Kevin: My guess is our upstairs cameras are toast.
Matt: Everything seems to be okay at Base Camp.
Kevin: Nobody home.
Matt: I'm shaking like a leaf being in here, but the house feels normal again.

He does not look well. None of them do. Matt's eyes are puffy, and he slouches, as if his leather jacket has grown too heavy for him to go on carrying around. Already pale, Claire is now white as a sheet. Kevin's jowly, stubbled face sags under the brim of his FTB ballcap, and his shirt is utterly wrinkled.

He prods Matt with his elbow as they move back to the foyer.

Kevin: You should take a good look at your contract.
Matt: What? Why?
Kevin: Look at the fine print about who owns the footage, and how much of a piece you get from the proceeds. They know a million ways to cheat you, but there's a decent chance at the end of this you'll be a very rich man.
Matt (*shakes his head*)**:** I don't care about the money.
Kevin: Suit yourself. But picture having enough to set up your own paranormal institute. Claire's right about one thing; this is way bigger than a TV show. My advice is to lawyer up and soon.

Matt says nothing, apparently chewing on this idea.

Claire: We need to stay focused. Let's keep going.

They quickly cross the foyer and mount the grand staircase, their fears either forgotten or set aside. Foundation House did not strike them dead. Therefore, they apparently reason, it will not.

Jake: Holy cow. Look at that.

The camera zooms in on one of the curved steps that stack toward the second floor. The polished oak in the center has been smashed along a yard-long length. Kevin's hairy hand enters the frame and picks at a thick splinter.

Kevin: Think about the amount of force this took. A thousand pounds, right. At least.
Claire: Please step back from it.

Her camera clicks as she takes multiple pictures. The camera tilts up to take in the other stairs, each similarly damaged.

Kevin: I was just taking a look.
Claire: Think of it as a crime scene, if that helps. There's a ton of data here.
Kevin (*wearing a feral, triumphant grin*)**:** We're way beyond gadgets now.
Claire: And this is too important to rely on the unique expertise of Kevin Linscott. We need to gather as much objective evidence as possible.
Kevin: Before the house blew up, you were about to quit. So don't be giving me orders. (*turns to Matt*) Unless I'm still on the show.
Matt: We can talk about that after we're done here, Kev. I

need all of us to understand something. There is no university bucking up. There is no government grant. No angel investors. They're going to tear the house down.

Kevin: What are you saying?

Matt: I'm saying the show is our only ticket to staying here for as long as possible. Hirsh and Vogan are going to expect to see dailies on top of my hot sheet. So if we want to be here, we have to do our jobs and play nice.

Kevin: Fine. (*turns to Claire*) I won't touch anything until you clear it.

Claire: Thank you. And no, I am not quitting anymore.

Matt: Did you get everything you need?

Claire takes more pictures of the damage. She gasps and rushes to the top of the stairs, where she begins snapping rapidly.

Matt: Incredible.

The camera follows her up and zooms in to a close-up of the painting of Lord Shiva. Around the god's third eye, a spiral has been carved through the painting and into the wood paneling beneath. A spiral radiating outward to sprawl a yard in all directions. The paranormal investigators regard it with awe.

Kevin: It wanted us to notice this. A message.

Matt: Shiva's third eye. It delivers wisdom but destroys all in its path.

Kevin: That's ominous.

Claire: Some say it's destruction in the same way autumn destroys the earth, which is then reborn in the spring. More like transformation. Renewal.

Kevin: So not ominous if you're a tree. Very ominous if you're a leaf.

They move on to the Apparition Room, which is a shambles. Trigger objects, pieces of the Ouija board, chunks of plaster, and the wreckage of the two cameras and audio recorder litter the floor. Protected by thick, hard plastic, only the all-in-one ghost meter seems intact. Scores of gashes mark the papered walls. The twin bed appears undamaged, but the small dresser on the other side of the room is nicked and scored, the mirror above it shattered. The window is cracked in several places.

Matt: Wow.
Kevin: Like a war zone in here. I want to check for footage.
Claire: Hang on just a sec.

She snaps an assortment of photos.

Claire: Go for it.
Matt: It's incredible, isn't it?
Claire: It's a puzzle. Actually, a puzzle piece.
Matt: What's the puzzle?
Claire: That's what we need to figure out.

Matt reaches out to touch her shoulder in a familiar, affectionate gesture.

Matt: It is incredible, though.

He is asking her to stop analyzing for a moment and simply enjoy the discovery. Her mouth purses into a barely restrained smile. Her eyes flash with excitement.

Claire: It's *amazing.*

Kevin: One card is damaged. The other seems to be okay.

Matt: That's good news.

Claire holds up the battered ghost meter and plays with it, but it is dead. She slides out the SD card and pockets it.

Jake: This battery is almost out of juice. Any last words?

Matt: Yeah, bring it in.

The camera lens zooms into a tight close-up.

Matt: A part of me actually expected nothing to be here. That the spirit cleaned up after itself. The same way last night, I thought the playback on the tape would show nothing, and we'd end up modern-day Cassandras who had an incredible paranormal experience that nobody would believe. But we got it. We got it all—

The recording ends abruptly as the battery fails.

Matt Kirklin's Journal

We're back in action, gang.

Somehow, some way, we all underwent this attitude shift. At first, we were like little rabbits sniffing around a lion's den, wondering where the lion might be. Fear and anxiety, threaded with tendrils of pure joy at our discoveries. The longer we stayed, though, the safer we started to feel, and now it's like the spirit is a friendly partner to all this effort, eagerly waiting for us to make contact.

I'm not sure how much of this is instinct and how much is hopes and wishes, but it's working, so I won't argue with it. Even Kevin and my wife, who last night stopped pulling their punches, are working together like parts in a machine.

Yeah, some of you are no doubt wondering why I invited Kevin to stay on with us, but the truth is we need the help, especially with Jessica gone. He's a whiz with audio. And we've only got around thirty hours left to figure out Claire's puzzle. It'll be a while before I trust Kevin a hundred percent again, but this is way, way too big to let interpersonal crap interfere.

I really don't want to think about this place being torn down. The genie's out of the bottle, only the bottle's about to be smashed and thrown in a landfill, and the genie possibly with it. It's heartbreaking, and it makes every hour precious.

Hirsh and Vogan haven't responded yet to my hot sheet. I hope they'll buy us more time with Gravois. Just in case, we stopped at a convenience store and loaded up on enough food and bottled water to sustain us for a week.

If they don't come through, Birdwell will have to call the sheriff to evict us at gunpoint. The sheriff and a small army. They'll have to drag us out of here.

After collecting as much documentation as we could, I doled out assignments. Kevin is sifting the audio for EVP and seeing what he can recover from the one memory card and internal hard drive that survived the apparition's rampage. Jake is inventorying the batteries, charging them, and analyzing the B-roll he shot yesterday for anything he might have missed during shooting.

As for Claire, I had a special task for her, one I wasn't sure she'd accept. Out of all of us, she looked the most refreshed and energized, though like us she'd slept only an hour or two at most. She'd scrubbed the dust off her face, applied makeup for the camera, and fixed her hair. She looked pretty darn good, in fact.

"I need to analyze the data," she said before I could even pitch her my idea. "Ambient temperature, barometric pressure, all of it. This will give us a picture of what this thing is."

"That's important, but—"

My wife interrupted me to tell me it's not just important. It's *everything.*

"Hear me out," I said. "That song stuck in my head too. Because it sent a message. That song, from that era. This is all related to the Paranormal Research Foundation."

"Maybe," Claire said.

I could tell she warmed to the idea, though being a good scientist, she didn't have enough data to say whether it was true or not.

"What I need," I said, "is for you to go into the PRF office again and see if you can find any of their files that might give us a better clue as to what exactly they were doing here."

Claire's mouth dropped open into an O, a rare gesture of surprise but one I knew well and always found endearing, including now.

"You really think there might be a direct link between the Foundation's research and this phenomenon?"

One way or another, yes. Maybe they killed people during their experiments, producing angry spirits. Maybe they killed themselves, which explains their vanishing, and we're dealing with the researchers themselves.

It's even possible this isn't a classic haunting but instead the product of the Foundation's forays into weird physics. Some kind of reality distortion.

Honestly, at this point, anything is possible.

But I don't have enough data either.

"That's what I'd like to find out. Rule it out or give us another road to travel."

"It's out of the box," Claire said.

"Look, I'm just saying—"

"I love it. We need to think out of the box right now." Then she touched my face, another thing she does that drives me nuts in a good way.

In response, I hugged her until she gasped a surprised laugh. I needed it. I'm not just emotionally raw, I feel like every emotion I have got turned on and off a hundred times last night and then run over with a cheese grater.

All the pressure I felt from the executive producers, our viewers, directing the show and working all these hauntings, managing the team's personalities, and staying chipper all the time—that's nothing compared to what's sitting on my shoulders now. Documenting, characterizing this powerful spirit.

And ultimately, tonight, attempting to communicate with it.

To make things worse, I'm operating on five cups of coffee and very little sleep, during which I suffered through a horribly vivid and endless stress nightmare that still has me feeling off my step.

In this dream, I was at Pulse USA's head office, standing outside the network president's door. Our story had made the news. The whole world was talking about it. And Josh Brosnan wanted to hear a pitch for a new show centered around me, now the world's leading paranormal expert.

The pretty receptionist beamed a smile at me and told me to go in. When I reached for the doorknob, though, I heard voices hissing on the other side. A man and a woman having a fierce argument.

The second my hand touched the knob, they stopped trying to hide their fight. Their voices rose until they became shouts.

Suddenly, I was very afraid. The receptionist beamed her bright smile and said I should *go in, go ahead, go on, do it, he's expecting you, just walk right on in.*

But I couldn't open the door. I just couldn't.

Because the cruel voices belonged to me and Claire.

While I recognized my voice and knew I was angry, I couldn't understand a word of what I was saying. Claire's, however, came through sharp as knives.

You're not even a man, Matt. You're a delusional boy who spent his whole life pining over a little ghost girl you made up. You play hide-and-seek for a living. The only thing you're an expert at is pretending. You don't deserve this. You're a joke, a fraud, a vaudeville barker, and the worst part is you think you're not.

And plenty more ugly, horrible stuff I don't care to write down. Usually, when I dream, it's like I'm visualizing the words, playing them in my head, but this time, I could hear everything loud and clear with my ears. When I woke up, the horrible, nagging feeling Claire hated me still had me in its grip, and I couldn't shake it.

It doesn't take a psychologist to see where all this is coming from. Last night, I'd been surprised as hell to find out she didn't see our paranormal investigations as being worthwhile and wanted to quit the show. *It was never real science in my book anyway,* she said. *It was just debunking.*

This is no easy thing to hear from the woman you trust with your heart and your life. That she regards her creative partnership with you not as a joint search for the truth but an attempt to prove you wrong no matter what you do. Okay, that's not exactly fair of me to characterize it like that, but I can't help how I feel.

Add to that a rift that appeared between us after we fled the house, caused by two things. The first is I was so shocked by what I'd seen that for an hour or so I didn't care about her at all. I couldn't make sense of anything. I knew I'd made a mind-blowing discovery while at the same time everything felt pointless. If I'd run the camper off the road on the drive to Fredericksburg, I don't think I would have cared a bit. So we can add guilt to the insecurity that fueled my nightmare.

The second is ever since the house exploded with activity, Claire has almost become a different person. I've never seen her so singularly minded and obsessed. I'm not proud to admit it, but her sudden passion for this spirit is weirdly making me a little jealous.

Normally, when I get anxious about life or uncertain about our marriage—or for any reason, really, as it's become a nervous personal habit—I twirl my wedding band around my finger. It reminds me that we took vows to love and put each other first forever, and it gives me strength.

It wouldn't cut it this time, so I hugged her instead. I hugged her for all I was worth, hoping my touch communicated everything. That I'm her man, that we're still bonded, and that I love her as much as I love myself, if not more.

That I hoped she felt the same way about me.

"I love you," I said, and kissed her cheeks, her eyes, her lips.

She giggled. "I love you too, darling."

Hearing her say that should have made me feel better. It should have healed the rift.

Instead, I can't shake the nightmare's nagging doubt.

Paranormal Event
Remote Camera Footage, Apparition Room

Below is a record of the paranormal event captured by the remote cameras in the Apparition Room the previous night.

11:56 p.m.

View of the room from a tripod mounting of three feet above the floor. The camera captures the area around the window and a stretch of dusty floorboards on which the object board and its trigger objects lie. On the right, we see the Ouija board and the front of the dresser.

Everything is a shade of gray, the product of night vision under IR light.

11:57 p.m.

The Bible shifts on the object board, pushing the lipstick tube aside. By itself, this is potentially a miracle, but more is coming. Much more.

11:58 p.m.

The camera trembles along with the trigger objects. It is like looking into a microwave while it is cooking. The very air seems to percolate.

11:59 p.m.

The objects rise to float above the board, as if weightless. The doll lazily rolls over in midair. A point of light in the corner turns into a burning gash.

The room brightens.

MIDNIGHT

The objects rise up in a blurred, swirling spiral. As the spiral expands, they smack and ricochet against the walls. The Ouija board sails through the air to embed itself in the wall, wobble free, and take off again.

The camera rocks until it frantically waves, and then it tumbles up to bang against the ceiling before spinning around the room, catching glimpses of dust and the little waving doll before the light floods out the optics.

Paranormal Event

Data logged by the all-in-one meter

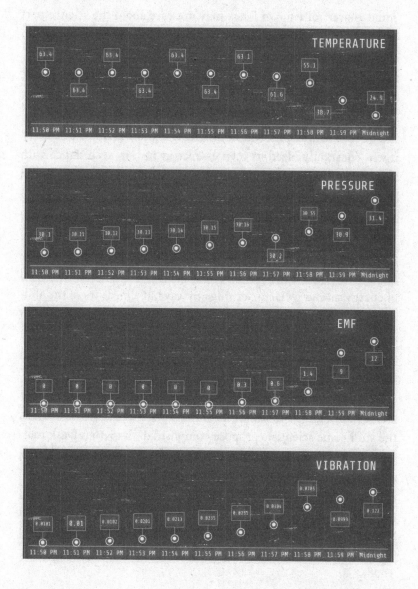

Claire Kirklin's Journal

Some viewers of *Fade to Black* may not care about the science part of our show, but when it comes to ghosts, it's everything. If you can characterize a ghost, aspects of it become predictable. You can figure out with some certainty how to interact with it. This may not be as fun as jumping at things that go bump in the night, but it's how you differentiate a real spiritual entity from your imagination.

For science, the problem is simple. If a ghost is made of energy, it will constantly bleed its own essence as heat in accordance with the second law of thermodynamics. A sustained haunting would require a constant power flux.

Maybe the ghost draws heat from the environment to produce work, which would explain cold spots associated with a spiritual presence. But that would require a particle capable of this conversion, which itself would heat up and reveal itself as matter instead of energy, as energy is not a thing anyway but a measure of the ability to do work. Presumably, it would be a particle associated with a once-living person, able to store memory and constitute intelligence. And it's basically undetectable; not even the Large Hadron Collider at CERN has spotted it.

In short, it either doesn't exist or hasn't been discovered yet. For all we know, ghosts manifest from theoretical particles like axions, the stuff some scientists propose composes dark matter. Dark matter and energy are theorized to constitute 95 percent of the universe, though astronomers have never observed it. Maybe all spiritual energy is axions, constantly swirling around us, undetectable, and imprinted with psychic data.

So imagine how intrigued I am that Foundation House produced enough energy to virtually blind us, smash through solid oak planks, and carve a spiral into a wall. How? Where did the energy come from? Where does the intelligence or algorithm reside that set it all in motion?

This isn't about life after death. This is about accounting for something that doesn't fit the Standard Model of Particle Physics. Not just a new particle but entirely new mechanisms of reality.

I am likely looking at a revolutionary new branch of science here. Maybe even one that finally bridges classical relativity and quantum mechanics.

Matt doesn't understand. He keeps checking on me, which he believes is leadership but is really him seeking assurance. He always was a bit needy and emotional, which allowed me to do what I do best, which is play the stoic.

This relationship chemistry normally works well for us, but right now, he has to understand something: I'm in love with another.

I've fallen head over heels for an anomaly in the laws of physics.

Not that Matt has a right to complain. For as long as I've known him, he's been in love with ghosts.

On the other hand, if my old man plays his cards right, he might get lucky. As in I might do him in the camper. This is all making me intensely horny. I have never felt so alive. My brain is on fire.

Here's what I know so far:

Before the all-in-one meter failed, it recorded concurrent dramatic changes in temperature (down to freezing), barometric pressure (rapid increase), EMF (maxed out the meter), and vibration (maxed out).

All of it consistent with paranormal lore about hauntings. Which is interesting as a confirmation data point but also a little irritating, as it feels like I've traveled a vast distance only to find myself back where I started.

Taking a page from Kevin's book, I'll add my feelings to the data set. Naturally, the event produced fear and anxiety, which was pushed to the max by the surge in EMF activity. The rapid, heavy increase in barometric pressure made me nauseous.

At the same time, dopamine flooded my brain. I felt weightless. Euphoric. A sense I was connected to everything and stood outside a door behind which were the answers to every question I have about the universe. Like all I had to do to touch the stars was reach up and grab one.

I'm already jonesing for my next hit. I'm on paranormal crack now.

I can add to the evidence the remote camera footage, which shows the objects levitating before hurtling off the walls. The intense light. The outside remote camera captured intense electric-blue flashes, like ball lightning or welding arcs.

It's maddening. The more I learn, the less I know.

Okay, here's what I have for possible theories so far:

This is a residual haunting. The whole show last night was the product of a paranormal algorithm, and something triggered it to spring into action.

It's an intelligent haunting. Something is here and wants to talk to us.

The entity is inhuman. Some elemental force is aware of and is playing with us.

Psychic projection? We somehow produced the event ourselves when we got all riled up about Kevin dropping his bomb on everything, the show producers wanting to shake things up, me announcing I'm looking at the exit.

Weird physics. The researchers did something.

Did I miss anything? I could add angels and aliens and God and the Flying Spaghetti Monster to the list, I suppose. Once you start theorizing about the paranormal, it's a very slippery slope.

Whatever it is, I believe it's intelligent. The ghastly apparition reacted to us. The song skipped on a line one could easily interpret as a message. *Nothing to fear but fear.* Was the entity telling us *I'm here, you're safe, keep going?* And the spiral carved into the painting and wall, circling Shiva's third eye: a promise of wisdom or simply further encouragement to keep searching?

I think so. Of course, I could be reading into it, projecting my biases onto the event. For all I know, the spiral was a warning we'll all get murdered if we keep prying. Trying to understand the paranormal is like being a conspiracy theorist, where you draw straight lines between a few dots and rewrite history to fit your theory.

This is futile. What the hell am I thinking? That I can crack open new physics in a day? Succeed where thousands of scientists across a hundred countries working with a seventeen-mile particle accelerator failed?

Talk about delusional.

This is bigger than me. I'd rather lose my claim to a discovery than see it remain unsolved and eventually buried by a wrecking ball. I wrote an email summarizing everything I know and sent it to every one of my professors at Virginia Tech, hoping at least one of them would catch it on a Sunday.

I know, I know. More delusion.

Imagine you're a science professor and one of your former students suddenly emails you claiming to have discovered teleportation or a perpetual motion machine. You probably wouldn't cancel the rest of your weekend and rush to a derelict house in rural Virginia to check it out.

For ghosts, definitely not.

Instead, you'd either chortle or shake your head sadly while speculating on your student's mental health. In short, I'm not checking my email every five minutes hoping for a happy result.

And this brings us to me finally painting myself into a corner, though in my defense, the whole room is just the one corner.

I need a Hail Mary, a philosopher's stone that will help me cut the Gordian knot, if you don't mind my awful mixing of metaphors. I have one last major path to explore before we attempt contact again tonight, the one suggested by my crazy, adorable husband. Another rabbit hole, but it's all I've got.

It's time to dig into the files the Paranormal Research Foundation left behind.

Paranormal Research Foundation Files

PROJECT PROMETHEUS STATEMENT OF PURPOSE

"Science is always discovering odd scraps of magical wisdom and making a tremendous fuss about its cleverness."

—Aleister Crowley

We at the Paranormal Research Foundation believe it is time to get even cleverer.

Using a multidisciplinary approach blending classical, system, and occult sciences, our goal is to develop paranormal capabilities in humanity using Interdimensional Psychic Field Theory, pioneered by Dr. Shawn Roebuck.

This theory states that if paranormal phenomena are energy and such phenomena increase around certain psychic energy centers, it may be possible to stimulate a psychic energy "fountain."

1. We will operate in a geographic location near a reported major energy vortex.

2. We will identify subjects with higher-than-average paranormal capability.

3. We will design and conduct experiments based on various occult recipes to cultivate higher paranormal capabilities.

4. We will conduct our research with a free and open mind in the belief that doing so multiplies possibilities.

From this day forward, we are no longer scientists but alchemists, embracing the irrational to redefine the rational.

"The universe is full of magical things patiently waiting for our wits to grow sharper."
                                        —Eden Phillpotts

WHERE THERE IS SMOKE, THERE IS FIRE.

FADE TO BLACK

PROD: Ep. 13, "Paranormal Research Foundation, Part 2"

Dashcam Footage

Sunday, 2:01 p.m.

Jessica sits behind the wheel of Fade to Black's *Chevy Express van, gripping it tightly at the ten and two position.*

She exhales loudly through her nose.

> **Jessica:** Come on, come on. Move your ass or get out of my way. I *will* run you over.

The turn signal clicks. She massages the wheel into a turn, offering a glimpse of storefronts and a few vehicles parked on the curb outside the driver's side window. This is Denton's main drag. Jessica squirms during the turn, as if sitting still is a massive effort.

> **Jessica:** Look at this place. Perfectly normal over here. No creepy music, no giant ghost ladies grinning in the window. Yup. Nothing to see. Just a regular day.

While the other paranormal investigators rushed upstairs to observe and record the apparition, Jessica fled the house just as she promised Tameeka she would. Once outside, however, she saw it anyway in the second-floor window.

Jessica: Everyone living in a nice, long dream.

She sucks air into her lungs and expels it in a long, shuddering sigh. Grimacing, she reaches for the radio and finds a pop station.

Jessica (*singing along*)**:** You think you got a right, but it was just a privilege! Treat it like that, and you'll know you got it right—(*dissolves into ranting*)—and next time there's a lady in the window, a glowing giant witch looking right down at you with black eyes—

In a sudden rage, she slams her palms against the wheel. The song continues to pipe from the speakers. With another loud sigh, she turns off the radio and casts a baleful eye at the camera.

Jessica: What are you looking at? I am not putting on a happy face for you. Nope, nope, nope. I am done.

She drives for another thirty minutes, the only sound the hum of the van's engine, her face a mask of fury. Then the first cracks appear. Her cheeks flex into a pained wince as they strain to dam a flood of tears.

At last, she sobs, which turns into a long stretch of weeping.

Jessica: Stupid. So fucking stupid. What are they thinking?

Weeping becomes wailing—pure, unbridled crying.

Jessica: Why didn't you come with me?

For a while, she just drives, breathing steadily until at last her body starts to calm down, the emotions that burst from her spent, at least for the moment. Sniffing, she wipes her eyes as she takes out her cell phone and dials it on speaker.

The phone rings and rings. The call connects.

> **Tameeka:** Hey, Rashida.
> **Jessica** (*forcing a smile*)**:** Hey, sis. I'm glad to hear your voice.
> **Tameeka:** How did everything go? Did you end up pushing Kevin into any oncoming ghosts?

Jessica winces again and lets out a loud, choking sob. Her sister's response is delivered softly but edged with concern.

> **Tameeka:** Hey, hey. Are you okay? What's wrong?
> **Jessica:** Hang on. Just a sec.

She frowns at the dashcam and reaches toward it.

> **Jessica:** Private chat.

The dashcam stops recording.

FADE TO BLACK
PROD: Ep. 13, "Paranormal Research Foundation, Part 2"
Raw Video Footage
Sunday, 2:27 p.m.

The camera turns on in a hallway, catching a glimpse of Kevin Linscott as he disappears into the basement. Over his usual golf shirt, he wears a utility vest packed with tools and a backpack. He carries a flashlight. We hear the creaking of the stairs under his weight.

The camera follows, another set of footsteps. Then all footsteps stop. The camera's light flicks on to illuminate Kevin's glare in extreme close-up.

> **Kevin:** Tell me where you think you're going.
> **Jake:** I'm following you, bro.
> **Kevin:** I'm sure you have something better to do.
> **Jake:** Don't you?

They stare at each other for a few seconds.

> **Kevin:** Fine. You can come. Just remember what I'm trained to do.
> **Jake:** They teach you how to plant evidence at police academy?

Kevin gives him a dismissive wave and continues to lumber down the stairs. The camera follows. At the bottom, he opens the backpack and removes a ghost meter.

The camera stays on him as he moves toward the Saw Room.

Jake: Seriously, what are you doing?

Kevin looks around, as if searching for something in particular.

Kevin: Nobody is listening to me, but I keep saying the basement is where the action is. Where the PRF did its gonzo science. I just listened to a Class A EVP the recorder picked up last night during the paranormal event—forget that. It's in a class by itself. It was a recording apparently made by one of the researchers.
Jake: Seriously? Wow. What did it say?
Kevin: Blah, blah, weird shit.
Jake: But *clear* weird shit. That's cool. Did you tell Matt and Claire about it?

Kevin hesitates with a scowl. He is not yet ready to share the news with the rest of the team. For now, this discovery belongs to him and him alone.

Jake: You really should.
Kevin: It was a clue. This is where they did the research. That's why I'm here.
Jake: That's actually good thinking.
Kevin: I want to do a little exploring before I tell the lady of the house and she comes down to try to ram it into a test tube.

Jake chuckles. Kevin resumes his visual inspection of the area, looking for clues.

Kevin: Claire's problem is she works for all her gadgets. The way I do it is I make them work for me. They're just a compass.

Jake: Finally, we get *The Linscott Hour*. This will be your audition tape, bro. You'll get your own show by the end of this.

Kevin (*fuming*): I'd love to know why you're always riding my ass.

Jake: No reason, unless you count the fact you always talk a big game, and even though you're not a cop anymore, you still act like one. And, oh yeah, you casually threatened me.

Kevin (*wincing*): I had this real bad dream...

Jake: I had a two-hour nightmare last night you were screaming your head off and waving that gun of yours around, an idea you planted in my head. It was just a dream. Get over it.

Kevin: It was so real, though, and—(*scowls*) And you know what else? Go to hell. *Bro.*

Jake chuckles again.

Kevin: Yeah, laugh it up. I don't like you either.

Jake: Welcome to show biz. Lead on, we're wasting time.

Kevin ignores him and enters the Saw Room. *The camera follows to frame him in a medium shot. Kevin waves the ghost meter and grunts as nothing pings above normal.*

There is nothing here, at least from the spirit realm.

Jake: What does your body tell you?

Kevin: Go heckle somebody else.

Jake: I'm being serious. Aren't you always going on about how your body is the ultimate ghost detector? I don't see Claire here. Now's your big chance.

Kevin: All right. Watch and learn.

He shakes out his shoulders and closes his eyes. Peels one open.

Kevin: Take a step back, cowboy. You can shoot from out in the hall.

The camera backs off. Kevin closes his eyes again and takes a few deep breaths. Jake zooms in for an extreme close-up on his stubbled, jowled face, close enough to reveal his nose hairs need a trim.

As Jake once said, the camera's eye sees all, and it can be judgmental.

Kevin opens his eyes. With a determined expression, he gathers up his gear and marches back out to the uncovered well. Jake gives chase.

Jake: What are you doing?

Kevin inspects the pulley system built over the well for structural integrity. A few yanks confirms it is solid.

Satisfied, he leans on it to aim a flashlight down into the darkness.

Kevin: Something's down there.

Jake: Really? Jeez, bro, maybe you are good at this.

Kevin: Go to hell again.

Jake: Again, I was being serious.

The camera moves forward cautiously to peer over the edge into the black. At first, the harness the researchers used to lower subjects into the well blocks the view of the bottom. Jake shifts aim and focus to see what might be past it.

Even with the night vision, however, visibility is poor. But Kevin is right—something is down there. Objects placed around the well's stone sides and at the bottom.

Jake: I'll try it with the light on.

We hear a click as Jake switches on the camera's flashlight. Visibility improves but not by much. The darkness seems to boil in dark, swirling particles, like TV snow if it was limited to black and shades of gray.

The particles briefly coalesce into a smiley face, which once adorned T-shirts across America in the seventies. A moment later, it morphs into the same occult symbol painted on the floor in the Saw Room.

The camera jumps back.

Jake: Whoa.
Kevin: Tell me what you saw.
Jake: Nothing. It was . . . pareidolia.

Pareidolia is the visual form of apophenia. Jake believes his mind played a trick on him.

Kevin: Nothing or something. Only one way to find out for sure.

He shucks his backpack onto the floor.

Jake: Shouldn't you run the meter? See what it says?

Kevin: We're past the gadgets now. I found what I was supposed to find. Now I just have to go see what it is.

He goes to the control box on the wall, from which a variety of cables snake down and onto the floor and then into the well. Nothing happens when he depresses a few of the large buttons; there is no electricity. Returning to the well, he grabs the handle and manually cranks the pulley to raise the leather harness all the way to the top. This done, he inspects its integrity as well.

Jake: You must be joking.

Kevin: I'm an ex-cop. I've been in dangerous situations before.

Jake: When you fall and break both your legs, should I help, or do you want me to keep shooting?

Kevin cocks an eye to regard Jake with a baleful stare.

Kevin: Feel free to go somewhere you might actually be useful.

Jake: No way, bro. This is Primetime Emmy material right here.

Kevin gives the harness a final testing yank and grunts, apparently satisfied. He steps up onto the lip of the well. Jake audibly sucks in his breath.

Kevin eyes the harness like a puzzle to be solved, and then looks down into the darkness.

Kevin: Maybe I should tell the others about the EVP and my plan here before I risk trying anything on my own.

Jake (*finally exhales*): That's not a bad idea. If they're into it, we could all help you. You're going to need one of us to work the hand crank.

Kevin: Right. Safety first.

Jake: For what it's worth, I think you're onto something.

Kevin steps back down from the ledge.

Kevin: I'll tell you what I'm in the mood for right about now.

Jake: What's that?

Kevin: Taking the camper out for some donuts.

Jake: You are aware that cops stuffing donuts in their faces is a stereotype, right?

Kevin: You try working a twelve-hour day sitting in a patrol car with about ten minutes to scarf down some supper, and we'll see what you end up eating.

Jake: Okay, okay.

Kevin: Anyway, I like donuts.

Jake: I was gonna say I'd love to get the hell out of here for a while. Can I come with?

Kevin: Suit yourself.

Jake: There's a Krispy Kreme in Fredericksburg.

Kevin: Sorry to disappoint you, kid. We're headed to Freddy Donuts.

Jake: You're the boss.

Kevin suppresses a smile but is only partly successful.

Kevin: Damn straight.

Re: Hunting ghosts with crazy white people
From: Tameeka Brewer
To: Rashida Brewer
Sunday, 3:12 p.m.

You ignore my calls and texts, so now you get an email. You're lucky it's a Sunday, or I'd be calling your network to hunt you down.

You call me up babbling a stream of nonsense about haunted houses being real and then drop a cryptic bomb that you saw one with your own eyes leering out a window at you, and then say you're going back and hang up on me.

Foreal, how worried should I be about you?

I'm not talking about ghosts, sis. We're way beyond that. I'm worried about your mental state. What is going on?

A part of me wonders if you're being dramatic and maybe taking the whole reality TV thing too far. The Stanislavski method probably won't kill you, but it might make you lose your grip. Remember three years ago, you were Lady Macbeth in that production up at the River City Theater in Richmond? You wore that dress everywhere. I told you I was going out on a second date with Robert, and you said, "What beast was it, then, that made you break this enterprise to me?"

God, how I wanted to punch you, a desire that did not stop until the show finally ran its course.

The point is you take make-believe too far sometimes. Like your stage name I pick on? It's Spanish, and it's a Jewish name to boot. I looked it up. You're neither, girl! Similarly, you also aren't a real ghost hunter.

Another part of me believes you believe you saw something truly scary at that house. Which isn't that surprising, considering you go traipsing around in the dark in abandoned psychiatric hospitals hyped up to find ghosts. Honestly, I'm surprised it took this long. But let's say it's an actual ghost there. Let's say there's a ghost in that house that can pull your brain out through your eye sockets, as you so quaintly put it. Let's just for a minute say that is true.

WHY WOULD YOU EVEN THINK ABOUT GOING BACK?

Seriously, what do you really know about dealing with ghosts, anyway? You all think you're experts because you have meters and cameras and cool black T-shirts with logos? Come on, sis. Are you that hell-bent on making it as an actor that you'd risk your life for it? Is keeping a role in a dumb ghost hunting show worth risking your boy growing up without his mama? Come back here and look me in the eye and tell me if going back there is worth that.

And then there's one more part of me that's thinking some really dark shit. That maybe you're not okay. That maybe the show hasn't gotten into your head but instead that there's something in your head you're putting out into the show. That maybe I should be calling the guys with the white suits and butterfly nets.

I don't want to be thinking any of these things. You're a drama queen and I still want to punch you over your Lady Macbeth routine, but you're my sister and I love you. Please call me or text me when you get this. If you find yourself in any jams, call and I'll come pick you up wherever you are. And if I don't hear from you by tomorrow, I'm going to hound the president of Pulse USA until I do.

Audio recording
EVP, Apparition Room

The recorder picked up a disembodied voice on Saturday night at 11:56 p.m., which spoke until abruptly cut off during the paranormal event observed starting at midnight. It is barely audible but remarkably clear, though it sounds like it was originally recorded on much older technology, thick with white noise.

Based on comparisons with old recordings, the deep, murmuring voice appears to belong to Dr. Shawn Roebuck, one of the five scientists working at the Paranormal Research Foundation. The man many consider its primary player.

This is the electronic voice phenomenon that Kevin Linscott picked up on the recorder.

Okay, dig this, if you will, an energy vortex. The notion is that some places in the world are embodied with spiritual energy that can be tapped for psychic benefit—well-being or powers or what have you. Spiritual energy, that magic particle that eludes discovery. All things exist, and yet, at the quantum level, all things are insubstantial. As the Buddhists say, everything is illusion. Everything is energy, and as it is above, so it is below, even though we can't detect it yet.

Still, in the empirical dimensions, we can track it by its signatures. Magnetic and gravitational anomalies, creating hot spots across the globe connected in a vast psychic energy grid. This theory brought us here to this house, near a five-point junction of ley lines. If we can tap into the energy field and amplify it, we can unify the hemispheres. Bring the spiritual realm into the physical world.

I'm still on my gravity trip. In our dimension, we have gravity and light. In higher dimensions, you might have gravity but no light. The Standard Model gets real strange when it comes to good old gravity in our realm: Why is it so weak compared to the other three forces of nature? Why can a kitchen magnet pick up a paper clip that takes an entire planet to hold down with gravity?

It makes no sense.

Maybe gravity is not as weak as we think it is. Maybe gravity transcends our perceivable dimensions. Maybe it's the key to all of this. For gravity to be as strong as the other forces, you'd need another dimension, maybe two. They don't even have to be all that big.

If psychic energy exists at the border of our dimensions and this dark dimension, then we can tune it to become a form of energy we can study, harvest, and use. A giant, eternal battery powering a revolution of the mind.

The average human uses only 10 percent of their brain capacity. Our comrades in the Human Potential Movement believe the rest can be developed toward genius. We believe it can be harnessed to awaken a wide variety of powers.

The energy of the dark universe is the fire that old Prometheus stole. Its darkness will be our light.

Properly harnessed, it will make us like the gods he took it from.

For us to succeed, we must—

The EVP abruptly ends.

Jake Wolfson's Journal

I grew up afraid of things that go bump in the night.

Yeah, I didn't have what you'd call a pleasant childhood.

On the outside, it looked great. We owned a fairly large two-story house outside Charleston with plenty of acreage that backed onto a pond where I fished for bass. The property next door was just farmland except for an island of oaks barely concealing the ruins of an old house I'd explore.

On the way there, I'd swing a big stick, hacking at the horse corn as if I were wading into enemy warriors in a medieval battle. Back then, I was just Viking, no Techno.

The only problem was Mom and Dad were total drunks, the functional kind good enough to fool almost everybody except me, their only child. After dinner, the drinking would get started along with the cat and mouse psychological abuse and petty slaps I'd put up with because I didn't know any different.

Mostly, it was Dad doing the abuse. Watching me grow up made him feel sorry for himself for his own perceived failings, and he'd decided I needed some tough love to help me become a man. His midlife crisis became my early one.

The only problem for Dad is I grew taller with age and worked out until one day, I decided I'd had enough of eating his crap for dessert and shoved him against the wall. Pinning him there, I calmly told my dear old father figure if he ever touched me again or tried to step on my face so he could pretend he was tall, I'd knock him down so far he'd—I don't know, something, something dramatic. I honestly don't remember, and it doesn't matter.

It doesn't matter because Dad regarded my challenge as the new lease on life he'd been eagerly awaiting. After a few months of relative peace, I was sitting in my room looking at college brochures, and he burst in reeking of bourbon-fueled malice and raring to put my threat to the test.

By the end, my room was trashed, I had a black eye, and Dad spat out a bloody tooth he refused to get fixed, just so he could show me the gap and make every grin a threat.

Mom thought it was all hilarious. Her idea of helping was to try to egg us on.

After I beat his ass fair and square, you'd think that'd be the end of it, peace with honor and all that, but no, sir. The next time, he sucker punched me when I came out of my room for supper. The time after that, he chased me around with a two-by-four.

You got it coming, kid, I'd hear him call.

No, thanks, Dad. Seriously, how about we give it a rest? You win.

I installed multiple locks on my door and slept with one eye open.

Where are you hiding?

Three months before my eighteenth birthday, I finally bolted out of there and never looked back. I honestly believe my old man intended for me to eventually kill him just so I'd go to jail and have my life ruined.

This is why ghosts never scared me and why I always considered them kind of dumb. When you see Matt and Jessica freak out in the dark over a noise or an EMF reading like the evil dead are coming, what you don't see is me behind the camera troubled only by the need to stay with the action without tripping over anything.

I'll tell you what does scare me, though. People. If you think about all the terrible things a single human being is capable of rationalizing and doing, it's amazing we have enough trust to function as a society. Even after I left home, I never truly felt safe until I heard my old man died drunk behind the wheel, any relief I felt ruined when I heard he took a woman and her baby with him.

His very death an act of spite.

I don't know why I'm writing this. Maybe I'll trash it. Because I'm behind the camera, it's not like any of you viewers care about me, which is just how I like it. Again, I'm the fly on the wall. Knowing this about me, though, maybe you can see why I have a thing for Claire. She's so damn logical and predictable it makes me crazy in the best way. You can also see why I both despise and have a soft spot for Kevin. He's a lot like my old man, minus the booze and psychopathic ambushes.

Mostly, I'm writing this because I am now officially terrified of ghosts, and I thought you might like some context to get into perspective just how scared I am.

Paranormal Research Foundation Files

PROJECT PROMETHEUS PHASE 2 EXPERIMENT PRINCIPLES

1. Various occult recipes were tested involving gravitational force, electromagnetism, music and sound frequencies, and psychically resonating symbols. See below table for the variable sandbox. See Annex A for specific recipes used.

GRAV	EM	MUSIC ·	SOUND	SYMBOL
1.1	A	Om mantra	432Hz	♀
1.3	N	Gregorian	528Hz	☉
1.7	B	Singing bowl	440Hz	⨀
2.1	B1	Khadgamala	639Hz	ⅎⲨⅎⲨ
2.7	D	Drums	963Hz	✡
3.1	E	Jesus Prayer	528+963Hz	☿
3.3	G	Mool Mantar	852Hz	❄
3.4	X	Allah-u-Abha	528+852Hz	⛤

2. Visual sensory deprivation was implemented at all times during immersion in the Interdimension Tank.

3. The objective was to stimulate a sustained inter-action with the paranormal entity contacted during

the August 12 laboratory experiment with Subject
X, who subsequent to this encounter departed the
program.

PARANORMAL ABILITY SUBJECTS

1. Subject Y with paranormal abilities, male, 23 years
   old. Normal physical development. Average scores
   in screening testing are shown in the below table.

Ganzfeld	4.2
Zener	3.6
Precog	4.4
Psi	4.5
Hadash	2.2
Tactile	3.7

2. Subject Z with paranormal abilities, female, 21 years
   old. Normal physical development. Average scores in
   screening testing are shown in the below table.

Ganzfeld	4.6
Zener	3.9
Precog	4.2
Psi	4.4
Hadash	3.1
Tactile	3.8

The first step was to formalize a protocol for contact
with the paranormal entity. The next is dialogue.

The great adventure is about to begin!

Re: Incredible!
From: Paisley Hirsh
To: Matt Kirklin
Cc: Jonathan Vogan, Samuel Clines
Saturday, 4:01 p.m.

We were blown away by the raw footage that Jessica Valenza dropped off with Donnelly. We were hoping for a bit of juice for the ratings, and you certainly delivered! Congratulations on an extraordinary episode, which will go into post tomorrow. We shot a teaser off to the network, and they're equally excited. We always felt this was a winning property, and this episode proves it.

Donnelly vouches for its authenticity, but naturally we're a little concerned, given the sensational material. I'm sure affidavits and liability waivers will put all that to bed. Our immediate reaction is this episode will be explosive. We see all kinds of opportunities with it, and we're fully supportive of your idea of a two-parter. Don't worry about post; drain every battery getting every minute of footage you can.

Following our euphoria, however, in all honesty, we found ourselves somewhat conflicted. We're happy for your discovery, but our prevailing concern is getting *FTB* a second season. This now becomes tricky. Where does the show go next?

Have you discovered a new investigation process, one that should yield similar material in the future? If not, there is something of a concern that viewers will go into future episodes with similar expectations and be disappointed. We still have two more to go before we wrap up the season. Making Episode a 13 a two-parter gets us halfway there. Maybe we could stretch it into a three-parter, take it all the way into the fifteenth episode and season finale?

As a side note, we feel there is still potential for character development in future episodes. Kevin Linscott in particular emerged as a wildcard and possibly a villain. We're not sure what your plans are for Kevin, whether you feel his continuing presence would damage *FTB*'s credibility, but we think he adds to the story.

You'll have to let us know what the plan with Jessica will be moving forward, whether her hiatus will become permanent. It's unfortunate she dropped the ball when the spiritual entity appeared, and honestly, judging from the raw footage from day two, she seems to have lost some of her usual spunkiness that makes her so likable to viewers.

Anyway, based on your last hot sheet, I know what you really want to hear from me. I'm happy to inform you that Jonathan and I were able to secure access for an additional two days on-site. That should be sufficient? If not, if you're generating similar material and feel there's potential, we can certainly consider pushing for another extension. Stretching this out into three parts may get us all off the hook, and we can worry about Season Two when we get there (fingers crossed!).

Congratulations on a remarkable story in Episode 13. The next time you're in LA, we'll have to celebrate in style. We'd love to hear your personal stories from the shoot. Meanwhile, we can't wait to see what comes next for *Fade to Black*!

Jessica Valenza's Journal

Hi, I'm back. It's time to get real.

I'm the girl who gets super excited about ghosts, gives ghost hunting tips, and sometimes does funny hot takes on the other investigators. On-screen, I get real gushy when I talk to the spirits, offering comfort and seeking communication.

A lot of you think I am secretly in love with Matt and that when I'm not hunting ghosts, I'm a wild party girl, a nympho nerd.

Like I said, I want to get real. The show suddenly became very, very real for me last night, so now it's my turn.

I don't get excited about ghosts. Before I saw a ghost with my very own eyes, you could say I was superstitious but agnostic about them, though I do scare easily even at the suggestion of a haunting. Every jump you see in the show is one hundred percent authentic. Every yelp you hear. I really do get scared.

When the others ran upstairs, I did what any normal person would do seeing their house burning down all around them; I ran like a bat out of hell. I almost quit the show over it. But I owe my family, the team, and you too much.

Even now, when I am most decidedly *not* agnostic, I still don't get excited about ghosts. If you want the whole truth, they scare the hell out of me.

Next up is no, I am not in love with Matt. He's honestly a catch, but it's not what you think. I admire him. He's doing what he loves and gets paid for it. Matt's a very lucky man, but it's hard to feel envy because he's a good guy who deserves what he's gained. He's always been good to me.

It was never exactly a secret, but you may not know I'm an actor who was hired to round out the team and make it more fun for television. Being real paranormal investigators, Matt and Claire could have resented me for that, but they never did. Matt always treated me like family, and I fit in.

I became an actor because I was always restless and wanted to be special. I think it's a fundamental human need—to have our existence recognized—and some have it more than others. We spend so much time every day without really being aware we're alive. It's the greatest thing when someone reminds us we exist and that we matter.

This is why I love acting. Every minute I do it, I'm fully aware, alive, and in the moment. Sometimes, I wonder how a ghost must feel. They must have to fight even harder to exist; they too must perform, or they fade away.

Oh, and to all you horny gentlemen, I'm hardly a party girl. I'm a single mom with a little boy who keeps me home most nights. I haven't been on a date, much less to an actual party, in a long time. I am a bit nerdy—though my sister is the real nerd, and way hotter than me, I assure you—but I'm hardly the geek dream girl.

When I'm not acting, I'm like most people, which is to say kinda boring. When I'm not taking care of my boy, I'm working my ass off to make this a great TV show that either inspires a little wonder or at the very least helps you turn your brain off after a long, hard day.

And one more thing: My real name is Rashida. Jessica Valenza is my stage name. You can call me either one. Jessica's a special girl, but Rashida keeps it real.

So now you know. I tell you this because I'm no longer going to be pretending. I'm no longer participating in all this as an actor. The ghosts are real, this haunting is real, and from here on out, you're going to get the real me. Like it or not.

I drove the van back to the house and almost couldn't find it. I'd patted myself on the back to keep up my courage the whole way back here, planning this big entrance—*I know you need me, I'm here, tell me what to do*—and I was screwing things up already.

When I finally found the turn, I drove up to the house and parked. The camper was ominously missing. I wondered if the team had bolted again, and here I was about to walk in to take my turn being scared shitless.

Then Matt came out onto the veranda and gave me one of his little smiles, which always looks like he's sharing an unspoken, private joke.

"You ready to pitch in?" was all he asked me.

I said I was. "Where's the camper?"

"Donuts."

I laughed, which felt good, as if I hadn't laughed in years. *Donuts.* A snack run. It was so mundane, so familiar, I could have cried at the comfort it gave me.

And then he filled me in. They'd spent the day salvaging gear and footage from last night's wreckage and buckling down for analysis. Plenty of interesting stuff but nothing new today. The house, it seemed, had gone inactive again.

And just like that, I was all caught up, and it was like I'd been here all along and hadn't let them down.

"Tonight's a whole new ball game," Matt said.

At midnight, he hopes, the spirit will show itself again.

I know how important this is—not just for its historical significance or whatever, but for Matt, for the team, for me. I'll do everything I can to help.

If things get hairy, though, I'll be wearing my running shoes, and I reserve the right to use them to run all the way home to my son, who needs me even more.

That's the real me.

Text exchange between Rashida Brewer (Jessica Valenza) and Tameeka Brewer

Sunday, 4:28 p.m.

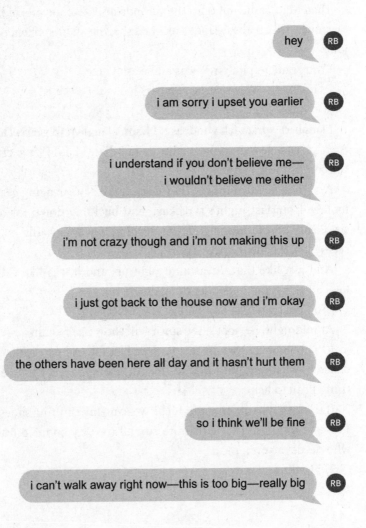

hey RB

i am sorry i upset you earlier RB

i understand if you don't believe me—
i wouldn't believe me either RB

i'm not crazy though and i'm not making this up RB

i just got back to the house now and i'm okay RB

the others have been here all day and it hasn't hurt them RB

so i think we'll be fine RB

i can't walk away right now—this is too big—really big RB

i have to do this RB

it's like you said—i signed up for this and gotta stick with it RB

or all the sacrifice means nothing RB

i love you too please don't worry about me and don't call RB

p.s. don't pick on my name i like the sound and it gives me confidence RB

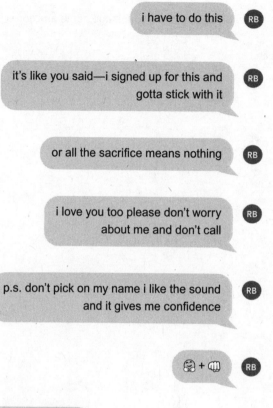 RB

TB hey! sorry i missed this i was

TB wait—are you there?

TB sis?

TB damn it

i won't pick on your stage name anymore i promise

 and yes i goddamn will worry about you

Paranormal Research Foundation Files

RESULTS OF THE PHASE 2 EXPERIMENTS

Two practice runs and 31 formal experiments were conducted, 17 with Subject Y and 14 with Subject Z. All were filmed.

Of these, 29 were not successful, and 2 were.

Both subjects subsequently became belligerent and were evaluated as mentally and physically unfit to continue participation.

OBSERVED PHENOMENA

In 8 of the experiments, the subjects reported powerful hallucinations and lucid dreams, which Drs. Flick are analyzing.

In the 2 successful experiments (#17 for Subject Y and #14 for Subject Z), Camera #3 recorded a visual distortion ("black particulate cloud") and contact phenomenon ("reaching adult hand," in this case through igneous rock forming the well wall).

Both subjects reported the sensations of being watched and touched, along with a wide variety of other psychological impressions.

SUCCESSFUL OCCULT FORMULA

The recipe in both was the same:

GRAV	EM	MUSIC	SOUND	SYMBOL
3.3	B1	Om mantra	528+963 Hz	All

COMMUNICATION ATTEMPT

During the observed phenomena, the research team attempted communication via the audio system but was unsuccessful. Aside from revealing its presence and touching the subjects, the entity made no effort to engage.

OVERALL ASSESSMENT

Our initial hypothesis was if we succeeded in tapping higher dimensions, we would find them bountiful in energy but otherwise vacant. Instead, we discovered a phenomenon that may be an intelligent entity and broadened our research goals accordingly. While no individual experiment ultimately proved successful in producing sustained contact (or communication), overall, the regime is deemed highly fruitful.

First, it replicated the August 12 research results achieved with Subject X in 2 of the experiments and distilled the occult recipe required. Second, the duration of the phenomenon lasted 8 and 12 minutes longer, respectively.

NEXT STEPS

Further experimentation is recommended in which variations on the optimal occult combination are tested,
based on a theory that some fine-tuning may strengthen
the phenomena.

New subjects will be required.

FADE TO BLACK
PROD: Ep. 13, "Paranormal Research Foundation, Part 2"
Raw Video Footage
Sunday, 5:50 p.m.

Matt and Kevin sit on peach polypropylene chairs set on the veranda. Each holds a cold lager perched on his thigh and wears a satisfied smile. Jessica kneels next to a Dutch oven smoking on the wood floor.

> **Jessica:** Mac and cheese, coming right up.
> **Kevin:** Take your time, Jess. This is nice, sitting here, doing nothing.

Like the others, he and Matt have showered in the camper and put on fresh clothes, but they still look tired and strung out. Kevin appears to have melted into his chair.

> **Matt:** What direction are we facing? West?
> **Kevin:** West.
> **Matt:** At one time, you could sit here and watch the sun set. Before the house went to pot and all these trees took over.
> **Kevin** (*watching Jessica while she cooks*)**:** I'd love to hear how you make mac and cheese in a Dutch oven, Jess.
> **Jessica:** It lets you heat from the bottom and top at the same time, so I added a little water and steamed the pasta instead of boiling it. After that, I drop in bacon and cheese, and then I add my secret ingredient.

Jake: What's that?

Kevin (*snorts*): If she told you, it wouldn't be a secret.

Jessica: I'll be happy to tell you, but you have to play the game.

Based on raw footage from previous episodes, the "game" involves the team members sharing the gist of their last journal entry—the raw, unedited version. Everyone lets out a playful groan.

Kevin: I'll go. I wrote about the miracle. That is, Claire and me agreeing on something, which was to come back here and finish what we started.

The team chuckles.

Kevin: Seriously, it's nice to finally be on the same side.

Matt: I wrote about how I think we're on offense now. It feels good to have a play to make instead of only reacting. Oh, and how much I love my wife. What about you, Jake?

Jake: Me? I, uh, wrote about what an asshole my old man was when I was growing up.

They laugh this time.

Matt: Sounds therapeutic. Jess, we want you to give up your secret, but you have to play too.

She freezes in front of the oven. For a few moments, she says nothing.

Jessica: I wrote about how I'm not acting anymore. I'm totally here.

Matt and Kevin smile happily at hearing this.

Kevin: Great to meet the real you, then. For the record, I like you both.

Jessica (*turning cheerful*): Paprika, smoked paprika, and cayenne. Those are the secret ingredients. But that's not the real secret. The real secret is "always bring spices."

Matt: You should know. We cooked a lot of these meals together.

Jessica: Yeah, we did. It's a weird way to earn a living.

Matt (*raises his bottle in a quick toast*): I'd rather do this than anything else.

Jake: Camping in abandoned factories, running around in the dark, performing on camera covered in grime...

Kevin raises his own bottle until it clinks Matt's.

Kevin: Hunting ghosts.

Matt: Yup. It's exactly what I want to do.

Jessica: I know you like your dessert, Kevin, so after this, I'll whip up some apple crisp.

Kevin: You should marry me. (*chuckles*) Seriously, I'm glad you're back.

Jessica: I am too, Kev.

Jake: Is Claire coming?

Matt: She won't leave the office. She's reading the PRF files.

Jessica: I'll set a plate aside for you so you can bring it to her.

Matt: Thanks.

He straightens in his chair and eyes his team. The others return his gaze, knowing from experience break time is over and he wants to hold a work meeting.

Matt: Listen, you all did great work today. Really pulled together. We caught a lot of great data, footage, and an EVP from last night. Hirsh and Vogan watched some of the footage, and they're freaking out.

Kevin (*subdued*)**:** I see.

Matt: Relax. They'd like to see you stay on. Keep doing what you're doing, and you will.

Kevin (*stiffens to perfect posture in his chair*)**:** You can count on me, chief. It was a mistake. Won't happen again. (*shifts to address all of them*) I owe you all an apology. I went way over the line.

Matt: We're good, Kev. In fact, the producers are so happy, they bought us another two days here.

Jake: Oh, goody.

Kevin: It is good, wise guy. Me, I could live here.

Jake: Let's not get crazy, bro.

Matt: We'll see where we are in two days. If we're still recording activity, I fully plan to ask for even more time. You can take that to the bank. We could ride another event into a three-parter and a slam dunk for a second season.

Kevin: Sounds all right with me. I'd like to get back in the basement. That uncovered well has some answers for us.

Jake: The Kevster's right on that one. There's something up with that well.

Matt: Tomorrow. I promise.

He settles back into his chair and takes a pull on his bottle. The work meeting is coming to an end.

Matt: All the gear is set up for the stairs and Apparition Room. Right now, Foundation House is inactive. Midnight's coming in six hours. Until then, we should relax and get ready for the big event.

Jessica: Do you think the house will wake up again?

Matt: Unless Claire gets a eureka moment in there, it's our best bet. We play this card, and then tomorrow, we check out the basement.

Jessica: Dinner's ready.

Jake: Thank God. I could eat a horse.

Matt Kirklin's Journal

Countdown to midnight.

I can't stop smiling.

What's going to happen? Nobody knows.

Maybe everything!

Maybe nothing. And you know what? If that happens, I'll still walk out of here a happy man. We're all safe, we're investigating an amazing location, and we already brought out earthshaking footage of a spirit. In fact, we proved spirits exist.

It doesn't get any better than this.

If we fail to get any new evidence, Hirsh and Vogan will wring their hands and get even pushier about how to close out the season, but I don't really care about that. In fact, I don't care about the show anymore. They can cancel it for all I care.

All the pressure was a real drag anyway.

But *this*. This is what I want to do. Three nights of investigation in a verifiably active haunted house. Right here, right now, all the way. My body tingles with the joy of investigation, the satisfaction and drive of having a higher purpose.

Honestly, I've never felt more alive than I do right now.

Kevin has the audio, camera, and sensor gear all set up around the Apparition Room and stairs. Jake is ready with fresh tape and batteries. Even Jessica appears relaxed again, smiling that smile that slays our viewers and keeps them coming back for more. As for me, I am pumped and primed to communicate.

That leaves my dear Claire, who went into the PRF's offices with a couple of LED lanterns and hasn't come out all day. I decided to check on her.

I found her sitting on the floor surrounded by piles of paper representing her attempt at a classification system. Her face was flushed and shining. Dinner sat neglected on an old desk. She gazed up at me miserably as I came in.

"Didn't Ellen tell you not to read in dim light, or you'd ruin your eyes?" Ellen is Claire's mom, a wonderful lady.

"The Foundation research is a dead end," Claire told me. "Or a maze."

My wife is a linear thinker, and sometimes she gets frustrated when she's given information that appears irrational. You should watch a movie with her. She'll poke plot holes in plot holes. With some, the ones written really well, she sits on the edge of her seat, utterly riveted and unable to pry away for hell or high water. Unfortunately, given the state of Hollywood, these tend to be documentaries.

I started to ask her to summarize what she'd found out so far, hoping to help her navigate out of the maze she found herself in. She interrupted me to go on with her rant. Claire was in full poking mode.

"They weren't doing real science," she complained. "They set up an occult psychological torture chamber. They lowered people into the well and strapped them onto a centrifuge. They pumped EMF and sacred sounds and mystical sound frequencies that amplified from reflections, like a transformer. Then they plastered placards with occult symbols on the walls because why the fuck not."

I don't think I'd ever heard Claire curse before.

"There's nothing here!" she exploded. "It's hippie, Age of Aquarius nonsense! The only thing they should have discovered was a migraine."

"Is there anything we can use?"

"Well, so far, it does appear to corroborate Sparling's story. The magic hand."

"Any drugs involved?"

"For the subjects, apparently not, though it's not hard to picture them hallucinating. The researchers, though? My money is on all the drugs. From what I read, Project Prometheus was designed to awaken paranormal abilities in the human brain. Instead, a paranormal intelligence contacted them. They adjusted their research to keep contact."

"Sounds like we're following in their footsteps." I handed her a sheet of paper. "Check this out. Kevin found a solid, Class A EVP. He wrote it down. It's pretty weird, but it points straight back to the PRF."

Claire gave it a quick read. "Energy vortices. Oh God, more of this. Geographic placebos. And humans don't use only ten percent of their brain. It's a myth! Thanks a lot, William James."

"Did they organize by date? Maybe start at the end."

"Their filing system is broken. After a certain point, any attempt at organizing the material fell apart. Pages missing, out of order. I can't find anything on the final experiments they said they planned to do once they got new subjects. Big chunks are missing."

"The police may have taken files when they investigated the disappearances."

"Which were lost in the Election Day Flood."

"So there's nothing here," I said, "that directly ties the paranormal activity we're seeing here with the research they were doing."

"My running theory is a spirit came along and killed them to make them shut up."

Claire was on a roll, so it was best to let her be. I knew she'd eventually find something. Sifting through all this pseudoscience that hurt her logical brain and riled her up until she discovered the genuine article. She would read a single line, remote pieces of real estate in her powerful brain would make a startling bridge, and her puzzle would fall into place.

"We're having a team meeting in a half hour," I said. "Midnight's coming."

"I'll be up just before. There's got to be something here we can use."

"Okay. Try to eat something, okay?"

She was already back to reading. "Okay."

"Also, Jessica's back. She's been back for hours."

"Great." She'd already forgotten I was there.

I suddenly wanted to hug and kiss her again, but I knew better than to try when she was like this. Instead, I left her to her research and headed back to Base Camp.

There, the rest of the team put down the last of the lagers. The monitors flickered on the table. Jake cleaned his filters and selected one for shooting. Jessica politely listened to Kevin gesticulating through one of his tall tales.

It all felt wonderfully routine, yet new and exciting.

Now, sitting here with them, I check my watch for the umpteenth time. Midnight is coming, slower than I'd like but sooner than I think.

My heart is starting to race again. The anticipation is electric.

Countdown, gang. Here it comes.

Paranormal Research Foundation Files
Dr. Gloria Flick's Notes

The below notes were written on two pages of lined paper torn from a notepad. They were discovered behind a filing cabinet after the events depicted in this book. The handwriting was confirmed as being Dr. Gloria Flick's.

The door changes everything.

When it appeared, the project had reached its first crisis. Both Subject Y and Subject Z exhibited severe symptoms of Cotard's syndrome. Subject Y became belligerent in the irrational belief that nothing exists and left the house. Subject Z became depressed in the belief she is dead.

Two days before she broke free of her restraints and disappeared, Subject Z bit off two fingers from her left hand just below the first knuckle. Then she ate them as if they were nothing more than a handful of potato chips.

This raised obvious ethical considerations along with the need to reevaluate risks involved in the project. We cannot assess the paranormal entity as good or evil, but we can judge how dangerous it is to interact with.

The door changed everything.

Shawn and the colonel see it as a direct invitation. Don argued that if we accept the invitation ourselves, the project will stop being a controlled experiment, as we will no longer be able to maintain objectivity.

Marcus said it is impossible to be objective with this entity and that it has already quite possibly driven us mad, quoting Voltaire, who defined madness as "to have erroneous perceptions and to reason correctly from them." Since we cannot trust our perceptions regarding the entity, which operates outside our understanding of how the physical universe operates, by definition any action we take to engage is evidence of our madness. Even calling the door an "invitation" is itself an example of this.

My chief concern involves another psychological paradox. We are trying to make decisions while suffering from xenophobia, fear of the unknown. The lack of predictability and control is taking a severe mental toll on these scientists, based on another definition of madness in that it can be sparked by any major shock to one's self-image. Either way, we stand on a slippery slope.

As an example, Shawn is manifesting his own xenophobia as an unshakable, cheerful, unrealistic confidence. If he passes through the door and continues to observe the phenomena, he believes he has and will gain more of the very predictability and control that he will be surrendering.

Oddly, the option of doing nothing and shutting down the project appears to provoke the highest levels of anxiety among all of us. The fear of not understanding the entity is greater than the fear of being harmed by it.

This is making us hypervigilant and testy. The mood in the house is souring as every minute we reject the door in favor of safety in a predictable world only makes us all feel more fearful and lacking in control. Every minute we put off opening the door, the more power it gains over our thinking.

But debate is good. Debate is healthy. Consider all viewpoints. It will make opening the door that much easier to rationalize.

Because the door has already changed us.

FADE TO BLACK
PROD: Ep. 13, "Paranormal Research Foundation, Part 2"
Raw Video Footage
Sunday, 11:38 p.m.

The paranormal investigators sit around Base Camp, restlessly performing last-minute checks on their equipment. No doubt each is keenly aware that midnight is fast approaching, and with it, what they believe will be another paranormal event.

> **Jessica:** Is Claire coming?
> **Matt:** She'll be here. While we're waiting, I'd like to say a few words.

He waits until the team gives him their attention.

> **Matt:** We may be shooting a TV show, but Claire is right. It's so much more than that now. We're documenting an actual turning point in history.
> **Kevin:** I feel like I'm in a movie.

The investigators vent some of their anxiety with a round of chuckles.

> **Matt:** Yes, exactly. It's surreal. Like I spent my entire life working on the world's first light bulb, and it just lit up bright as the sun.

He pauses to put on his game face.

> **Matt:** Okay, here's the deal. If nothing happens tonight, so
> be it. If it does, our goal will be to document, but this
> time, we're going to try to make contact.
> **Kevin:** We know the plan.
> **Matt:** Yes, but now I need to talk about what happens if
> the plan goes to hell. Fear is a weird thing. It takes over.
> The fight-or-flight response.
> **Kevin:** I was trained for that—
> **Matt** (*raises his hand*): What I'm trying to say is if any of
> you don't feel safe, if you need to run, you do it.

*The words linger in the air like a challenge. This time, no one
answers it.*

> **Matt:** As for me, I'm not running. I'll be bringing one of
> the cameras, so we'll not only have the two remaining
> remote cams up there, we'll have one of the secondary
> mobile cams. So even if I'm the only one left, we'll have
> footage.
> **Kevin:** I'm not going anywhere either. Not this time.

*The camera gently pans to Jessica, who wears the face of someone
who thinks they just ate something that might have given them food
poisoning.*

> **Matt:** So before we go up, I just wanted to say it's been a
> real honor for me to lead this team, and I know Claire
> feels the same way. I wouldn't want to share this experi-
> ence with anybody else. I love you all like fam—
> **Claire:** HEY!

Matt blanches at the sudden noise, and the camera jumps with him. Jake's training kicks in—follow the action, always follow the action—and he pivots to frame Claire stomping into the room holding a handful of paper.

Matt: Hey, yourself. What did you—?

Claire: What is this? Who did this?

She shakes the paper in her hand like a physical accusation. No one answers, too stunned and confused to know how to answer.

Claire: WHAT IS THIS?

Matt (*in a soothing tone*)**:** I'm not sure I know what you're talking about, honey.

Claire (*reads*)**:** "Subject A's rational upbringing and rigidly scientific worldview lend her extraordinary strength but ultimately make her psychologically fragile in a cosmic crisis. Gloria questions whether Subject A possesses the mental flexibility to survive the vortex."

Matt (*utterly confused*)**:** What? I don't—

Claire: It goes on like this for *two* pages.

Matt: Who's Gloria? Gloria Flick? Are you saying Marcus Flick wrote this?

Claire: My name's at the top of every page! I'm Subject A!

For a few moments, no one speaks, too stunned by this revelation. No one can understand how the husband and wife team of psychologists working for the Paranormal Research Foundation, missing since 1972, could have written the document in Claire's hand. What she is claiming is impossible.

Jake: What the hell?

Matt (*visibly struggling to process what he has been told*): Claire—

Claire: You want more? (*shuffles paper and reads*) "Subject B's psychological vulnerability is she will delegate her responsibilities to her own offspring as a routine course—considered an experimental plus—but will ultimately reject the world for her offspring..."

Jessica: Oh. (*she bursts into tears*)

Matt: Claire, stop it.

Claire (*with malicious cheer*): Here's a good one: "While Subject C's self-image and extraordinary powers of rationalization seemingly make him a prime candidate, he is subject to fantasy ideation as a coping mechanism to accommodate his post-traumatic stress disorder. 'Let me try again, I can do it' is his motto, though 'doing it' is never—"

Matt: CLAIRE. STOP.

Claire: Don't you see? This whole thing is another practical joke!

Kevin (*muttering*): It's a goddamn lie, what you said—

Matt: You're saying somebody wrote files about us and dropped them into some old file cabinet in the hopes we'd find it? And staged everything—the lights, the spirit, the objects flying around the room—

Claire (*holds out her fistful of papers*): This is *paper*, Matt. It has *ink* on it. Are you saying this spirit is God? Because if this is from a spirit, it can *create matter*.

Kevin: Maybe not God. Maybe the other one, the Adversary—

Claire (*rolls her eyes*): Oh, shut up, Kevin.

Kevin: It's not—

Claire: Flick's right. Your answer to crazy is to cough up more crazy.

Kevin: Fuck you too, lady. Since we're suddenly being honest. Fuck you and your rigid—

Matt: Enough! (*blows out a frustrated sigh*) Listen. Claire, what you're saying is just not possible.

Claire: What's more plausible? A ghost created files to mess with our heads, or Hirsh and Vogan set all this up? Maybe there are hidden cameras all over the house, and another crew set up all these special effects. A show in a show.

Jake: Holy shit.

Matt: Come on! There's no way somebody staged all of this. We didn't see all this stuff happen on a screen. We were *there*. You're talking massive, live, practical effects—

Claire: Then these files. They're obviously fakes. Someone planted them to make the show even more interesting, maybe. End the season with a bang instead of a whimper. Get all that interpersonal drama they wanted going.

Matt: The show's already gotten plenty goddamn interesting without derailing the investigation. (*his face visibly darkens with barely suppressed rage*) I'll just ask this once. Is Claire right? Did somebody here do this?

Kevin: Ask the lady in charge of looking at the files.

Claire: Or the guy who fabricates evidence.

Jessica: I'd never write something that mean about myself.

Claire: But this is a big career move for you. You came back today, right? Where did you go while you were gone? You went straight to Vogan Productions, right?

Jessica (*visibly wilts*)**:** Not cool. Leave me out of this. This is cruel.

Matt: I just don't see how any of this is possible.

Claire: And you—you wanted me to look at the files. You kept pushing.

Matt blinks in surprise, too stunned to speak for several moments.

Matt: Why in God's name would I sabotage everything we've accomplished here? (*his face contorts in anguish*) Do you really think I would do such a thing to us? To you?

Kevin (*wheels to glare directly into the camera lens*)**:** I guess that leaves *you*, Mr. Fly on the Wall. You're the only one here who works directly for Vogan Productions.

Jake: I'm with Jess. Keep me out of it. I'm going to keep shooting until everybody calms down or finally starts killing each other.

Kevin: You really want that Primetime Emmy, *bro*? How about—

His mouth drops open. His eyes glaze over. Everyone freezes.

A wisp of music passes through the air.

The time is midnight.

Matt: Where's it coming from? It doesn't sound like it's coming from upstairs.

Kevin: I know this one too. It's "White Rabbit" by Jefferson Air—

Jessica: You always know everything, don't you? It's convenient.

Matt (*jumps to his feet*)**:** Quiet!

Hand raised as if testing the wind, he cocks his ear to try to identify the source of the sound.

The music grows louder, its easily recognizable bassline filling the air.

   Matt: Basement.
   Kevin: That's what I'm hearing too.
   Claire: This time, I'm going to meet the Wizard.

She stomps off.

   Jake: The gear's upstairs.
   Matt: We have two cameras and an audio recorder here.
   Let's move!

*The team grabs their recording equipment with an air of
determination and even a little relief. They are ghost hunters in a
haunted house, they heard a noise, and they are going to check it
out and document it. In a way, they are back on familiar turf after
Claire's incredible revelation, even if the stakes remain very high.*

The camera swings to frame Jessica.

   Jake: You coming or staying?
   Jessica (*winces*)**:** Damn it.

*She lurches into a resigned shuffle toward the hallway. Then she wheels
to stare directly into the lens with an expression of fury and terror.*

   Jessica: Tell me right now that you had nothing to do
   with this.
   Jake: Seriously? Who knows? I honestly don't know what's
   real anymore. For all I know, I'm dreaming all this.

Seemingly satisfied with his answer, she turns again and keeps going.

The camera pounds down the stairs to rest on the team standing around the uncovered well.

Grace Slick's mezzo-soprano voice reverberates from the stone mouth. Despite the song's strong volume, the music sounds tinny and distant, as if originating in the bowels of the earth.

   Matt: Spirits, we're friends. We come in—
   Claire: The joke's over! Come on out!

She swivels her head as if searching for hidden cameras. Grace Slick continues her take on Alice's Adventures in Wonderland.

   Matt: We appreciate you giving us a sign of your presence.
      We just want to talk. Will you talk to us?

The song begins to build toward its iconic climax.

   Matt: Spirits, if you can hear me, can you knock—
   Claire: Screw this.

She strides straight to the well and shines a flashlight down into its depths.

Her face goes slack.

The music stops, turning into a long, nerve-jangling scratch.

   Claire (*gasps*)**:** Oh my God—
   Female singers: THE GROOVY PEOPLE ARE HERE

The team flinches at the startling blast of sound. The camera shrinks back before recovering. An unearthly pink glow pulses out of the well to bathe Claire's frozen stare and cast flickering shadows across the room.

Matt: Claire?
Singers: GOOD TIMES WILL LAST ALL YEAR

His wife says something, but it is inaudible in the deafening music that seems to come from everywhere. At least one lip-reading expert claims she says, "I don't understand, I don't understand."

Kevin: What are we doing here? Chief?
Matt: I'll stay! Everybody else, get—

Jessica screams and points.

A hand emerges from the well, glistening and patterned in blacks and browns, as if made of liquid rock, human only in its basic shape. The long fingers twirl as if testing their dexterity. The hand and its arm slowly rise like a plant reaching for the light.

Singers: DON'T LET THE MAN GET YOU DOWN!
TURN YOUR SAD FROWN UPSIDE DOWN!
Matt: Spirits! Spirits, we... What do you...
Claire: You're not real! You're—

The hand quivers before darting serpent-like toward her face, stopping just short with its palm up, as if asking her to give it five.

Singers: A BRIGHTER FUTURE IS NEAR

Claire cannot resist. She reaches and places her hand in the entity's.

Her face goes blank again. A clean slate.

Matt rushes toward her but stops in his tracks.

Chorus: OPEN YOUR HEART AND LEND ME YOUR
EEEAAAEAR

The hand slithers out of Claire's grasp to split into a dozen separate shrieking strands, shimmering like eels and spraying bits of rock and mud. The tentacles writhe and snap over the well. The pinkish glow turns the color of a blood moon.

The music grows even louder, becomes warbling and distorted.

Chorus: THERE'S NOTHING TO FEAR BUT FEAR

With a final burst of light like a camera flash going off, the trembling tentacles retract back into the well. The light dims to nothing. The music abruptly stops, leaving the investigators gasping in the silence.

Jessica sobs as she gnaws on her fist, now jammed into her mouth. A widening stain travels down her pantleg. Kevin sinks to his knees, then lies down, then slowly curls into a ball.

Claire stands at the well, head down, hunched over, shoulders quaking.

Matt: Claire! Claire, are you...
Claire: Are you? *Are you?* I am, Matt.

She can't hold it in anymore. She rears back and howls with laughter.

Jake: I can't…

The camera view spins away into gray dark, and the last thing we hear is the cough and splash of the cameraman vomiting onto the floor.

THE GODS DEMAND

AN OFFERING. TO

LEARN AND LOVE,

WE MUST OFFER!

DAY FOUR

Matt Kirklin's Journal

We're in this way over our heads.

This entity is more powerful than I imagined. It dug into our brains and learned everything about us. It produced those files for Claire to find.

And it—

I don't even want to think about what I saw tonight.

Nobody wants to play back the footage this time.

Anyway, we're at a serious disadvantage here. A part of me keeps expecting black government vans to roll up with grim agents telling us to forget what we saw and that they will take it from here. This feels that big.

At this point, I might actually greet them with relief.

Claire is wrong about one thing, in my opinion. I don't think the files were created. If everything is energy, and spirits operate by manipulating energy, then it's conceivable they could appear to create matter by rearranging it.

I'm really reaching here, but if a spirit exists in the subatomic level, it's even conceivable it could enter the brain and follow neural pathways to learn memories.

But all this itself takes energy. Where is it all coming from?

The uncovered well, where the PRF conducted its weird experiments?

Where the BLACK WORMS CAME FROM

I thought writing that out would help me deal with it, but it didn't help.

BLACK WORMS

I can't wrap my head around this.

Clearly, we're in some form of dialogue. The spirit is talking to us. Which is stupid. It's this powerful, and it can't just say hello?

A funny thing, calling it dialogue. A cat playing with a mouse could be considered a "dialogue" by the same standard.

Maybe I'm picturing it as a dialogue because that's what I want. The spirit clearly isn't up for a chat about "what's your name" and "when did you die here" via a Ouija board. It's clearly telling us something. The rest is up to us.

What does it want?

I have no idea. Put me in a typical old haunted house with an open mind and some meters, and I'm a paranormal expert. A disgusting hand slithering like a python out of a well? I'm no more knowledgeable than a paleontologist.

I owe Hirsh and Vogan a hot sheet for the day. I need sleep. Instead, I'm sitting at Base Camp writing this, trying to restart the broken car that is my brain. Claire and Jessica are in the camper. Kevin and Jake lie on their cots at the edges of the room, though I don't hear any snoring. Like me, they're simply trying to process.

It's starting to dawn on me that we might be done here.

We're strung out. Pushed apart. Broken.

After the show ended, we left the basement and sat around Base Camp. We should have bolted, but oddly, we weren't afraid. We'd gone beyond terror. It's sad to say, but we were resigned. The thing could have come out of the basement to drag us down one by one right then, and I'm not sure we would have fought it.

You'd think that after seeing a grinning spirit lady curl a spectral finger at us, we would have been accustomed to miracles, but no. We were in deep shock, staying physically close, though we might as well have been miles apart. I placed my hand on the small of Claire's back, but she only flinched until I removed it.

We sat for a long time. Nobody talked. There was nothing to say.

This next part will probably strike you as hilarious. You'll die laughing.

After we sat a while, Kevin rose shakily to his feet. It was like watching him fall down in reverse. He walked over to Claire, who'd finally stopped giggling and still clutched her handful of papers against her chest.

He said, "I'd like to have my file, please."

Claire looked at him like he'd sprouted tentacles himself. Then she handed his over. "I'm sorry about what I said to you."

Kevin retreated to his cot, clicked on a flashlight, and read.

After everything that happened, we couldn't resist being curious about what the Flicks wrote about us. One by one, we asked for our file. One by one, Claire said she was sorry, and I could tell she meant it. Sorry for her accusations, sorry for relaying to us the truth about ourselves, all of it.

My own file said I fabricated Tammy, my imaginary childhood friend who turned out to be a ghost. Marcus Flick theorized it was in response to moving to a new house and town and postulated some deeper trauma was at play, perhaps related to seeing my grandmother's body in its casket. In fact, Flick glibly wrote, while spiritual phenomena are very much real, for all my searching, ironically, I've never even come close to a spirit before visiting Foundation House.

In brutal, clinical prose, Gloria Flick chimed in that I'm emotionally stunted and, like Kevin, prone to fantasy ideation. Still a ten-year-old in many ways, the source of the kind of natural charisma that excites people and sometimes gets them hurt.

I tilt at windmills and convince everybody we're fighting dragons. I make others feel like children again. They think they can fly, play that seems harmless and fun but always carries the risk of ending in broken bones. Gloria Flick added that I abdicated rationality to my wife, a Mother/Tammy figure who alternately enables and tempers my singular drive to irrationality.

Like Shiva's third eye, wisdom burns as well as enlightens.

There's plenty more, but you don't need to hear it. Suffice to say some of it references stuff so personal that the only person who could have written it is me. There's stuff in there I haven't even told Claire, though she knows it now.

A hoax? I don't think so. In fact, it's impossible, unless somebody thoroughly investigated my entire life and then secretly interrogated me under hypnosis and a truth drug. When you find yourself seriously weighing the likelihood of a powerful, malicious spirit probing your mind versus some vastly funded, pranking TV show secretly analyzing your life, you're mentally skating thin fucking ice.

Here's something else, though, that'll make you laugh. These assessments were really easy to believe when it came to the others. Claire's a bit rigid? I love my wife, but it's sadly true. Kevin has a tendency to make stuff up? Entirely believable.

When it came to my turn, it was a much bigger, bitterer pill to swallow.

The thing is, regarding Tammy, I don't agree she was indeed just an imaginary friend. That's not how I remember it. But this is how people like Marcus and Gloria Flick get in your head. They tell you they're planting a truth seed, and doubt sprouts up instead like a batch of ugly weeds you can't get rid of. To paraphrase something the philosopher Nietzsche once said, the right sentence is like a rock that can shatter your entire world. People like the Flicks carry these sentences around in bags.

It turns out I'm Subject D, as if we're in the Prometheus experiment ourselves. Apparently, I'm not a prime candidate to "endure the vortex," whatever that means. More New Age talk. More mind games. Or maybe I'm just interpreting all this as intelligent and purposeful. Maybe this is a weird kind of residual haunting in which we're being role-played into an endlessly repeating story.

Who knows?

Again, I think we might be done here. Out of juice.

This might not be a bad thing. A rule of ghost hunting is that when a spirit is negative—in this case, virtually hostile—sometimes you have to cut and run. Safety first is the rule, and that goes for mind as well as body. When the black hand touched Claire, I was scared out of my mind that it either gave or took something from her, something bad. The blank look on her face terrified me to the bone.

Every time I think about the Flicks roaming around in my brain, my scalp starts up with this insatiable itch. What if they decide to "cure" me of my personality flaws by making a few little changes to my limbic lobe? What if I've already lost my free will?

Right now, we can walk away with mind-blowing fresh footage. Looking at it one way, we already won. We certainly wouldn't be losing anything.

A hundred times, I pictured telling everybody to pack up. *We tried to communicate but failed, and it's too risky to go on*, I say.

In my imagination, the rest of the team readily agrees. Like me, they all want out of here, even Claire, who understands any logic and science behind all this is beyond her capability to break down in two days. They want to go back to the normal world of the living, where everything makes sense. Go back to wanting instead of having something they can't handle, that maddeningly refuses to be known, that is dangerous.

I don't end up saying it. I can't say it.

I can't just walk away from this. I doubt the others can either.

It's way bigger than what we can handle, but it's *ours*. Our discovery. We own it, which carries a certain responsibility. We're invested. There's a trope in found-footage horror movies that always cracked me right up. It's the one where the gal asks the guy why he's still lugging around his camera pointing it in people's faces while a giant monster is after them. The guy answers with overblown gravitas, "Somebody has to document this."

I can now tell you that ridiculous, unrealistic trope is actually spot-on truth.

Besides that, I don't really think Claire would simply give up. Even though she can't figure out the physics of it all, she can't leave it alone any more than a kid can stop picking at a big scab on the knee they scraped during a nasty fall. Even though I can't figure out how to communicate with the spirit, I can't leave it alone either. Together, we're caught in the mystery.

We simply can't stop trying.

I may have fooled myself into thinking I'm Don Quixote, but this is no windmill. To take a page from Dr. Roebuck, this is the fire. To control it, we'll have to start thinking like old Prometheus.

Claire Kirklin's Journal

When I touched the thing that came out of the well, I saw physics.

I felt disembodied, floating in a haze of glowing particles that gathered in vibrating masses. Some hovered in this state, full of potential energy, while between the atomic masses an untold number of even tinier free particles swirled, including dark sparks that flickered in and out of a higher dimension.

The Buddhists are right: Life is illusion. Quantum mechanics is also right: Reality is a construct of human observation. Even time itself isn't real.

I was seeing it all without affecting it as an observer. I was energy. I was *one* with the particles that make up reality. I was nothing and everything. The tree falls in the forest, and no one is there to hear if it makes a sound or not. I was there and not there, listening to the silence of the tree falling and not falling.

It was the most soul-crushing thing I'd ever seen. The universe rendered as an endless, meaningless chaos that we shape into reality and onto which we project our hopes, instincts, and desires as narratives and meaning. A giant, seething junkyard flowing with algorithms that we imagine as a purposeful machine.

At the same time, it was astoundingly beautiful, the most beautiful thing I'd ever experienced. This was physics in motion. The emanations of the first Divine Thought. Enlightenment: the kind achieved by those who escape Plato's cave to see the real sun, the Square rising to view Flatland, Lord Shiva's third eye.

All that sounds pretty poetic but doesn't even come close. Science seems stodgy, but sometimes, it delivers a level of awe that is akin to religion. The universe is mysterious and beautiful with or without a prime mover or underlying truth justifying it.

I laughed at the sheer joy of it, only for it to infuriate me again. I'd gained truth but not the whole truth. Product but not method. Effect without cause. In 1972, a handful of scientists working toward a utopian goal with zero inhibitions discovered a new branch of physics, and they did it seemingly by throwing wishes against a wall.

Oddly, I don't remember what the hand felt like. I only knew I wanted to study it. The body is a sensor. Right. Like every stupid idiot in sci-fi horror movies, I touched the weird creature purely to see what it would do. The hand that snaked up out of the depths of the well. I'd braced to be repulsed, but the sensation was remarkably mundane. I remember it felt animated but cold and lifeless, exactly how Sparling described it. I remember it felt like polished rock.

After that, the world fuzzed into dark colors, and I don't remember much.

Back in the camper, Jessica stirred in the other bunk, her back to me. The poor woman had wet herself in the basement, and the acrid ammonia scent of her urine filled the camper. She kept mumbling something over and over, and after a while I caught it: "The light of protection I carry is strong." A piece of a Wiccan self-protection spell she'd picked up on our paranormal travels.

As for me, I was ready for sleep and fell into instant slumber. Matt calls this trick one of my superpowers, though truth be told, I was simply so exhausted that it bulldozed my chaotic thoughts and anything I was feeling.

A blink later, it seemed, I awoke in a dream virtually indistinguishable from reality. A lucid dream, something I'd never experienced before. I stood in a dark room hewn from magmatic rock, into which two stout oak doors had been set.

Behind one door, I'd gain all the answers. I'd learn the occult physics, the dark offspring of modern science and ancient alchemy.

Behind the other, I heard Matt screaming, his nails scrabbling at the wood as he desperately tried to claw his way to freedom from the thing that pursued him.

The choice was obvious: save the man I love or learn everything.

Over and over, I faced the same choice. Over and over, I made it. Endlessly, it now seems. Which one do you think I picked? Your assumption will tell me exactly what you think of me. I picked my husband, of course. Every time.

Every time, that is, until the last, when I acted on a dark, irrational impulse.

That's when I "escaped"—I finally woke up.

I found myself in my bunk in the camper again, sticky and gross with sleep sweat. My mouth tasted like an old sneaker. Matt stood at the little stove, fixing me a big mug of coffee. He started this routine when we were dating, and after we got married, I was happy to find out the feature matched the preview. In a final ironic twist to my dreams, he was the one who'd ultimately woken me up. I eyed him warily, unsure he was real and feeling a lingering sense of guilt.

Outside, the sky looked gray and angry. The wind flexed in a tidal, aerosol roar. The camper periodically shuddered under the assault. Random droplets smacked the window, gathering to form their own chaotic, shifting puzzle.

When I was able to sit up, Matt handed me the mug and planted a kiss on my forehead, his little confiding smile seeming to say, *You really tied one on at the party last night, huh?* He knew better than to start any conversation before I'd put down at least one mug, which gave me a few minutes to think.

Carl Jung saw dreams as the psyche communicating something to the conscious mind, often through symbols. Sigmund Freud considered dreams a symbolic fulfillment of repressed desires. I didn't need them or even the Flicks to figure out what I was trying to tell myself.

I need to stop following what's expected. Stop trying to fit this bizarre house into the Standard Model and start thinking entirely outside the box, a trait that annoyingly comes so effortlessly for Matt. Embrace my inner child.

I hated hearing it—no one likes a know-it-all, especially other know-it-alls—but the Flicks are right about me. I'm rational to the point of being narrow and uptight, the product of both nature and nurture. I've always regarded irrational behavior, a loss of control, as alluring and sexy but also frightening to the point of panic. My idea of getting wild is to buy a dollar lottery ticket. My rebellion against the established order was to hunt ghosts.

Me, tie one on at the party? Like that's ever happened. I'm the person everyone calls the next day to ask if they said anything stupid while they were drunk. I'm the even-keeled friend who has no outward emotional problems and offers the kind of practical, evidence-based advice that no one really wants to hear and goes ignored. I'm the girl who doesn't have the time or energy for pop culture or small talk and who most people conclude is cold and maybe a little stuck-up.

Thank God for Matt. He's everything I'm not, but he accepts me.

And thankfully, he is still accepting me even though I lost my mind last night and turned into a raving jerk.

I thought, *So that's what it's like to lose control.*

His dark eyes sized me up and judged me ready to listen if not talk. "I think we're coming to a dead end."

This got my attention. "In what way?"

"Don't get me wrong. I think we should stay and continue documenting. But we're out of our league. Playing with fire. Last night, you touched..." He grimaced. "Something we don't understand. You could have been hurt."

"I feel fine." A small lie. My hand still tingles a little even as I write this. When I hold it up for inspection, it takes me too long to recognize it as my own. For a moment, I pictured it dissolving into a cloud of humming gnats.

"Well, unless you've got a breakthrough in the case you'd like to share, Sherlock, we're out of ideas here. The entity wants to show off how powerful it is but otherwise doesn't seem to want to talk to us."

"It's been talking all along," I told him.

"What do you mean?"

"We need to think out of the box. Like you, darling. Like Roebuck and Chapman. They threw the box away."

"Okay. Do you have something specific in mind?"

"Confronted with a questionable study, a good scientist tries to replicate it."

I told him my idea.

A fresh gust of wind blasted the camper, and I imagined Foundation House sighing its approval.

Re: Hunting ghosts with crazy white people
From: Rashida Brewer
To: Tameeka Brewer
Monday, 10:35 a.m.

Just letting you know that I'm okay. Last night was another doozy. I know you don't watch the show, but you MUST watch the last three episodes. You'll get a TEENSY idea of what we're actually dealing with here, and I'll seem a lot less strange.

This email, however, will probably make you think I'm totally gonzo.

When I came back to Foundation House, I wrote a journal entry—I told you about how we do these—that announced to our viewers that I was going to get real on the show. That since the ghosts were real, they were going to see the real me. No acting. I even told them my real name! I imagined you reading it wearing a big, proud grin.

Then I got called on it.

Last night...let's say I met a palm reader. Yeah, that's actually a perfect way to put it. The palm reader told me some things about myself. Some of which were uncanny in that flattered *Wow! Hey yeah, that's me!* kind of way.

Some of which, well, made me bawl.

And you know that's not easy, that I'm usually very tough—HAHA, wait, no, actually. I'm not that tough. Not as tough as I thought I was, anyway.

So about being real, yeah, as you can see, I'm still on it. So I figured I'd do a reality check on this "palm reading." You know me better than anyone, Tam, so I want to ask you a few things, and I'm hoping you'll be totally straight with me.

Do you ever think the reason I get so angry about thinking you don't support my career is that I resent you for being totally free?

(I can probably answer this one on my own. You're the big sister and the responsible one, though I feel like I'm the one with all the responsibility. It's not fair. It's also unfair to you that it gets my motor going extra hard sometimes.)

Do you think I subconsciously blame Grady for my on-and-off acting career instead of my own choices and the fact that acting is, well, a tough game? The palm reader said I push him away to pursue what I want, but I'll never get what I want because I'll ultimately choose him every time. That's not fair to me either. In my mind, helping myself reach my dreams helps him, as it will make a better life for both of us.

Do you think I push Mama extra hard to help with Grady because she was always working when we were growing up, trying to make something better for us? Do you think I'm turning into Mama now?

Do you—never mind, that's enough! Probably too much. I already feel overexposed. Something I can definitely say I almost never, ever feel, it's just not me. But yeah.

I'll leave it there. No rush on getting back to me. Again, I'm okay, though this trip down the rabbit hole just takes us deeper and deeper. So much weirdness is going on here that it's strange to imagine you brushing your teeth, sitting in an accounting office all day, and catching up with friends over drinks.

I'll be swinging through Ralston today, but I know you're at work and I probably won't have time to see you anyway. Otherwise, I'll keep you updated on my weirdness, and I can't wait to stretch out with you when this is all over and turn off my brain with some Netflix.

FADE TO BLACK

PROD: Ep. 13, "Paranormal Research Foundation, Part 2"

THIRD DAY HOT SHEET

Report emailed by Matt Kirklin to the producers

Our third day at Foundation House proved as strange, spectacular, and terrifying as the second. First thing in the morning, we entered the house very cautiously, but it had gone inactive again, and after a while, we started to relax.

We spent most of the day salvaging equipment and harvesting data and recordings. This turned up terrific additional material, including remote cam footage of trigger objects flying around the Apparition Room before the midnight event. Also the clearest, most remarkable EVP we've ever caught in the field. Not a cryptic word or sentence but an actual monologue.

It's funny how only a few days ago, even a few clear words on an EVP would have struck us all as a major historical event. Now it's just another puzzle piece.

It all ties back to the Paranormal Research Foundation. Claire started to root through their files. I steeled my nerve to stand my ground and attempt communication at the next sign of activity. Meanwhile, Jessica came back ready to work, Kevin made a heartfelt public apology and is now back on the team, and all of us rested and then geared up for another midnight show in the Apparition Room.

We were not disappointed. It was another night of wonders.

First, Claire discovered something so strange it had us all wondering if we were being pranked again. In the PRF files, she found a psych eval on each of us apparently written by Drs. Marcus and Gloria Flick (who worked for the Foundation), even though that is obviously impossible. The evaluations were brutally honest to the point of cruelty, and nobody was spared.

While we were having all this out, Foundation House revved up again, but this time, the sixties music drew us to the basement, where we bagged mind-blowing footage of a wide range of incredible phenomena at the uncovered well.

I won't even try to describe it. Only seeing it does it justice. Jessica is driving all the new stuff to Donnelly now and will bring back new cards and more batteries. Donnelly will send you clips, and you can judge for yourself.

Take my word for it. It's historic television. It's historic, period.

The only problem is Foundation House doesn't seem interested in having a conversation. Claire made contact—real, physical contact, recorded on tape—but otherwise, the house closed up again after another spectacular show.

This morning, we feel like we've hit a wall. We pulled and marked footage, hauled all the equipment down to the basement, and worked on expanding our B-roll.

Otherwise, our investigation is starting to shift from being ghost hunters to documentarians. As long as Foundation House wants to perform for us, we'll record it. We just don't know how to communicate.

Honestly, and this is kinda hard to admit, we're a little out of our league on this. The house is talking to us loud and clear even if it's in riddles, but it's not listening to anything we have to say. We are not in control here.

Claire offered a breakthrough idea that I believe would make an unprecedented, stellar Part 3 and might finish out the season in a big way. She said we should go down into the well, where the researchers conducted all sorts of weird science experiments, and try to replicate one based on the files.

These experiments don't make a lick of sense, and believe me, repeating one won't do anything, but we're hoping it will speak a language the spirit understands. We hope doing this starts a real dialogue.

For this to happen, my hope is you can pull a few more strings for us. First, it'd probably be a good idea to try to grab at least one more day here out of Birdwell. Second, we'd like you to get him to have the electric turned on for the week, and do whatever it takes so the power is on before midnight tonight. Kevin tells me our little power generator isn't up to snuff for the watts we need to re-create the PRF's weird experiments.

I volunteered to be the guinea pig. Picture me strapped onto a giant spinning centrifuge on tape. It'll be TV gold even if we don't get a response, though I think we will. I think we're going to get very noticed by whatever's living in this house.

I know that's a huge ask, as Dominion, the local power company, may not respond on a dime. Gravois owns a lot of property in this area, so I'm hoping they can throw some weight. If you can make this happen, I can deliver you a heart-stopping season finale by the end of the week.

FADE TO BLACK

PROD: Ep. 13, "Paranormal Research Foundation, Part 3"

Raw Video Footage

Monday, 11:49 a.m.

The camera starts on a close-up of Jake's face, half out of the frame. It flips around to sweep past Matt's and Kevin's midriffs before aiming at their feet.

    Jake: Okay, it's recording.
    Matt: Then let's do this.
    Kevin: Tell me what you need me to do.

The view lurches back to Jake's face. Arms extended, he gazes with fierce concentration at the top of the recorder. The camera bounces as his arms move.

    Jake: Nothing, Kev.
    Kevin: It stinks like puke in here.
    Jake (*still working*): Yup, that's my bad.
    Kevin: Oh, I forgot—sorry about that, kid.
    Matt: We'll get it cleaned up.
    Jake: I fully acknowledge it was not very pro of me to lose
      my lunch.
    Matt: I'd say you were very pro just for coming down here.
      And very human for reacting the way you did.

The camera bounces hard once, twice. Then it tilts up and down as if nodding.

> **Jake:** Okay, it's secure. I give a little pull on this secondary line, and we have tilt. We can change orientation, but we won't get a smooth pan.
> **Matt:** Drop it anytime if you're ready.
> **Jake:** On three, okay? One, two, three...

The camera begins to descend in little jerks.

> **Jake:** Nice and slow. That camera is expensive as hell. Make sure you hang on tight back there but always give me a little slack.
> **Matt:** I got it.
> **Kevin:** I can hold it too if you need. I can take over for you, if you—
> **Matt:** We got this, Kev.

Old stonework fills the wall in full-spectrum coverage that includes the visible, infrared, and ultraviolet light spectrums. The mounted infrared light provides illumination for night vision, rendering what the camera sees in shades of gray.

> **Matt:** I love the hillbilly control setup, by the way. The tilting mechanism.
> **Jake:** I have my moments.
> **Kevin:** If it were me, I would have added...

Already muted, their voices quickly fade to a tinny, incomprehensible echo, as if they have become EVP themselves.

The well's gray wall crawls up the frame as the camera continues its long descent. On the far right, a bundle of wires run down the rock face. We can no longer hear the men talking. The camera's microphone picks up a soft hissing.

The camera continues to drop, slowly, slowly.

It passes a placard mounted on the wall, which bears an occult symbol. Only part of it is visible, but it has been identified as the Tetragram: four odd, backward-appearing symbols translating as YHWH, the unspeakable name of God.

After several more feet, one of the wires feeds into what appears to be an audio speaker, barely in the frame, while the rest make ninety-degree turns and branch off.

And farther down, a cylindrical device comes into view. Fed by a thick power cable, it fills the screen for five full seconds. This is one of the machines Sparling described in his interview, initially used in the Saw Room *and moved here. Given Don Chapman's area of specialty, it is likely he designed and built them.*

Later, long after this video was recorded, the machines would be removed and disposed of without being analyzed for their function. Numerous theories on the internet ascribe them as interdimensional portal stimulators, complete with diagrams. Engineering experts, however, have speculated they are simply a crude electromagnetic field generator.

The camera next tilts to frame a steel cross directly below. This is the centrifuge mounted on a motor fed by another thick power cable that snakes up part of the stone wall. The subject would lie down on the cross blindfolded, strap in, and spin until the acceleration produced force, simulating an increase in gravity.

The camera keeps dropping in short, sharp jerks until the platform fills the frame.

Then it tilts up to see the round door.

Re: Hunting ghosts with crazy white people
From: Tameeka Brewer
To: Rashida Brewer
Monday, 12:44 p.m.

Of course, you of all people would wind up meeting the Sigmund Freud/Dr. Phil of palm readers. Your messages are full of surprises since you started this trip, but that one right there took all the cake and the icing with it.

To answer your questions in the most sensitive way possible, I'll just say one thing, which is I'm not going to touch them with a ten-foot pole.

Not by email, at least.

I wish I could see you when you're in Ralston today. *Please* try to make time, even if it's only a few minutes so I can see with my own eyes that you're okay. Either way, when you get back from Weirdville or wherever the hell you are, let's plan a night together where we can chill and talk about some of these things you brought up, which run pretty deep.

We'll get Chinese food, a bottle of wine, and a family-size box of tissues, and we'll talk this stuff through. I also want to hear the full story of this wild trip you're on.

Until then, my relatively boring life goes on with its daily grind, but I'll be thinking about you. Seriously, I'm glad to hear you say you're okay and that you'll keep me updated. And I hope again that you'll make some time for me so I can see your okayness for myself.

As the "responsible" Brewer sibling, I do feel like I have to watch out for your ass. An older sister thing. Some habits are immortal.

PROD: Ep. 13, "Paranormal Research Foundation, Part 3"

DIRECTOR: Matt Kirklin

CAMERA: Jake Wolfson

The camera pops on in a thick gloom, which crystalizes as patterned stone. A man breathes heavily near the microphone. A voice blares over a walkie-talkie.

    Matt: Kev, can you hear me? You all good down there?

Kevin unclasps the handheld radio from his belt and mashes the talk key.

    Kevin: Roger and roger.

He picks up the camera and holds it out for a selfie close-up.

    Kevin: I may be getting too old for this shit.

The camera swings onto his shoulder to take in the strange experimentation space.

    Kevin: But look at this. I wouldn't want to be anywhere else.

His slow pan catches occult symbols mounted on the wall and settles on a pentacle—a five-pointed star circumscribed by a circle. The points symbolize the elements and the soul as well as the five wounds of Christ.

>**Kevin:** Ladies and gentlemen, I give you the Interdimension Tank.
>**Matt:** Kevin, are you there?

The camera lowers to frame the centrifuge table—a stainless steel cross six feet across and mounted on a pedestal. Thick leather belts dangle to the floor.

People were strapped down here and spun until gravity more than tripled.

>**Kevin** (*playing to his future viewers*)**:** Don't try this at home, kids.
>**Matt:** Kevin?
>**Kevin:** Okay, Mom. (*camera tilts as he again pulls the radio from his belt*) All good here, chief.
>**Matt:** Oh, good. You gave me a little scare up here.
>**Jake** (*yells down from above, a muted echo*)**:** Me too, Kev!
>**Kevin:** Just getting some footage.
>**Matt:** What's it like?

Though Matt can't see what Kevin is shooting, Kevin pans across the experimental area before answering.

>**Kevin:** It's how the researchers described it. A little weirdo Disneyland. They sealed the floor good. It's dry as bone here. Otherwise, it's claustrophobic.
>**Matt:** What about the door we saw on the video?

The view straightens and frames the door set in the wall. It is round

and appears to be made of thick wood, something a hobbit in The
Lord of the Rings *might use. Another symbol is painted on it,
chipped and peeling. A thick ring at its center appears to be a door
knocker but is in fact a handle used to haul it open.*

Matt: Kev?

Kevin: Listen, chief, I can't shoot and talk to you on the
radio at the same time.

Matt: Sorry about that. Up here, it feels like a very long time.

Kevin: The door is round, three feet across, and set around
two feet off the floor. It's textured like wood but is actually stone, pretty clever. There's a thick ring in the middle for pulling it open. I can see a faded symbol painted
on it. I think it's, what's it called, a squared circle.

*The symbol consists of a circle in a square in a triangle in another
circle. It represents the philosopher's stone, the arcane element that
ancient alchemists sought that would turn base metals into gold and
deliver an elixir for eternal life.*

Kevin (*muttering to himself*): This house is like being in Dr.
Caligari's workshop.

Matt: Can it be opened?

Kevin (*into the radio*): Only one way to find out.

Matt: Wait!

Kevin: What's the problem?

Matt: I don't know. We don't know what's in there. We
should think about this.

*Kevin switches hands to shoot from his left hip while he reaches for
the handle. He grips and pulls. The door groans on its hinges as it
starts to give.*

Kevin: Too late.

He grunts; the door is extremely heavy, and he cannot get it open all the way. He sets the camera on the centrifuge and hauls at the ring with both hands.

The door yawns wide, revealing an inky blackness inside.

Breathing hard from his exertion, Kevin recovers the camera and aims it into the dark. The infrared light and night vision get him nowhere, so he clicks on the flashlight.

Even its powerful beam is barely up to the task. It is like looking into empty space, the hard vacuum between worlds far from any star. The view tilts to reveal a barely illuminated patch of smooth stone floor, then up to the ceiling.

Kevin (*keys his handheld*)**:** The door opens up into a tunnel tall enough for us to walk through. Somebody built it with stones and mortar. Did a nice job too. And it's dry, same as here in the well. Not a drop of groundwater.

Matt: Okay. Come on back up.

Kevin: Uh, tell me why I'd do that.

Matt: We need to talk about what to do next.

Kevin: You're breaking up, chief.

Matt: I said we need to talk—

Kevin: I can't hear you. Okay, I'm going in.

He stoops to enter the tunnel.

Kevin (*chuckles*)**:** Oldest trick in the book. (*into the radio*) Tell me if you can read me now, chief. I'm inside. It's dark. Like taking a space walk.

The radio does not respond, dead silent.

   Kevin: Come in, chief.

The radio whirs and produces a faint murmuring, then nothing.

   Kevin: Well played, scary house. How about this...

He takes out his cell phone. The screen appears impossibly bright.

   Kevin: No signal, of course. (*he pockets the phone*) Okay,
   viewers, it's just you and me now.

*For several minutes, he proceeds down the winding stone passage,
which gently curves to the right. His boots produce a loud, slightly
echoing clomp as he walks. The camera briefly turns around,
but the entrance, once a pale gray circle, is no longer visible, now
obscured by the tunnel's subtle curvature. Regardless of which
direction he points the camera, he achieves the same view, only its
mirror image.*

He continues on, periodically sweeping the stone walls with the lens.

   Kevin: It's amazing they built this. The cost must have
   been astronomical. I have to be under the camper now.
   (*grunts*) Get a load of this.

On the left wall, someone spray-painted the slogan:

YOU'RE EITHER ON THE BUS OR OFF THE BUS!

And on the right, like a magic incantation:

!SUB EHT FFO RO SUB EHT NO REHTIE ER'UOY

The quote is by Ken Kesey, author of One Flew Over the
Cuckoo's Nest *and a major counterculture figure in the sixties.
On the cross-country Great Bus Trip of 1964, he and his Merry
Pranksters took their Acid Tests on the road.*

*Whenever the bus stopped, a Prankster would wander off and could not
be found, leading Kesey to declare, "You're either on the bus or off the
bus." Either part of the group's trip or left behind to do your own thing.*

Kevin: I'd say I'm on the bus now, viewers.

He is playing to the camera, again temporarily making himself Fade
to Black's *star, but his voice quavers a little, and it is obvious he is
talking mainly to buttress his fraying nerves.*

Radio (*loud and clear*)**:** You mess with Mother Nature, you pay.
Kevin: Christ!
Radio: A right thought put the wrong way.

It is not Matt's voice. Nor Jake's.

Radio: *We* are Mother Nature, man. You and me. All of us.
  Flowers in a field. Breathing, dancing stardust. There is
  no you and me. There is only us.
Kevin: Hello? Who is this?

*The cheerful voice is recognizable as Dr. Shawn Roebuck's. Another
voice cuts in, which appears to be Dr. Don Chapman's.*

Radio: We are your children. But we are not *yours*. We are

not *owned*. We are *free*, dig? My brothers and sisters are
the people who allow me to be free.
Kevin: Hello! I'm friendly. I just want to talk.
Radio: In freedom, we do not make change. We *are* the
change. We will make a better world. We *are* the better
world. It's already here. The evolution starts with us.
The revolution starts with you. It's all happening, right
now.
Kevin: I know you can hear me. Will you talk to me?

Silence.

Kevin: All these years I prayed for a clear EVP, and this is
what I get. Hippie garbage.
Radio: The war against communism will be won with
love. We will conquer war itself. We will conquer bor-
ders. One world. A brotherhood of Man.
Kevin: Nice to meet you too, Colonel.

The silky voice of Dr. Gloria Flick comes through next.

Radio: Welcome to the road less traveled. Keep going, pil-
grim. The journey is the destination. To the end or back
to the beginning. A labyrinth or a maze. Beware the
Minotaur either way.
Kevin: "Keep going" I understand. Roger that. Thank you,
Dr. Flick.

*Still hamming it up for his future audience, though his voice has
become even shakier. He continues down the gently curving passage
for a few more minutes.*

Kevin: I must be under Belle Green Road by now. This place is just... I just can't believe it.

He slows his pace, as if uncertain whether he should continue or turn back.

The passage, however, is coming to an end. Or a new beginning. Another door appears, a faint circle in the thick gloom. On it is painted:

α **NO PIGS** Ω

Kevin: Okay. *This* might be a sign.

The radio murmurs. Kevin turns up the volume, but it doesn't help. Just noise. He sets the camera down so that he can open the door. Gripping the handle, he heaves it ajar and shines a flashlight inside.

Then he flinches.

Kevin: Right. I'm out of here.

He scoops the camera from the floor, which swings up and down as he bolts back to the exit.

Kevin Linscott's Journal

Thinking safety first, I probably should have listened to Matt and gone into that tunnel with somebody watching my back. I probably shouldn't have gone down there at all without the power turned on, trusting Jake and Matt to hand crank me down and then back up.

On the other hand, I have zero regrets.

I feel fantastic.

Picture a devout Catholic who sees the Virgin Mary's face on a slice of toast, and then he tells psychiatrists about it and they try to prescribe him meds, but then they see her too and become true believers.

The word I'm searching for is *cathartic*.

Coming up out of the well wasn't far off from that. Out of the darkness and up into the light. At first, Matt didn't believe I'd gone into the tunnel. He said one second I had radio trouble, the next I yelled at them to haul me up. He wanted to know if I had a hallucination, the body being a sensor but also a trickster.

So we played the tape.

That's right. It's real. It happened. I went into a real, live time warp. My watch is now running about thirty-five minutes fast. The wonders keep coming.

While we watched the tape, Jake chuckled at my commentary, which means he can't be all bad. Matt oohed and aahed at the architecture and the amazingly clear EVP, which placed us hot on the PRF's track and the PRF at the center of all these paranormal events.

This is big. We all feel it. The excitement of being on offense again. We are close to cracking the mystery of the missing scientists and of the house itself.

Then Jake actually said something interesting for a change, which is he'd pictured Colonel Trantham as using the researchers to develop psychic weapons for the army, but the comments about conquering war now made him think it might have been the other way around. The colonel had been using the army, apparently, to find a way to eliminate the need for armies.

A bunch of weirdos. It doesn't change anything.

"What did you see on the other side of the second door?" Matt asked me.

"The tunnel keeps going. It just goes on and on."

We all grinned. Matt next asked me if I'd go back down there.

Honestly, I had to think about it.

When I opened the second door, the radio started mumbling. I could barely hear it. Then it said plain as day: "Get out."

Only this time, it *spoke in the demon's voice.*

Now you know why I got out of there and fast. The last time I bumped into this particular monster, it had turned a man into hamburger and burned his hair in the oven.

But it wasn't the demon. I'm sure of it now. Foundation House had tried to scare me off. And even if it is the same monster, so be it. I faced that demon once and survived it.

Disembodied voices and some weak-ass flower power graffiti won't keep me off the field during the final play of the big game. Neither will playing on my fears, no matter how hard the Flicks try with their five-dollar quack psychoanalysis.

"I'd definitely go back down there," I said, answering Matt's question. "In a heartbeat."

The house can try to scare me all it wants. I don't care. It's a risk I accept every time I investigate a haunting. It's part of the job. And so far, Foundation House hasn't done any real harm to me, even though it easily could.

So yeah, I'm going, all right.

Jake asked me how it felt being in there. Was it scary?

"Piece of cake," I told him.

We called a team meeting at Base Camp to lay it out. Matt and I would go down to explore the tunnel and see what's beyond the second door. Jake said he'd come at least part of the way to back us up and shoot it all.

This done, our fearless leader did something he ought to have known better about, which was tell two very tough ladies what *they* would do.

"You'll stay here and hold the fort until we get back," Matt said. "And then you can help get us out of the well if the power doesn't get turned on."

Well, Claire wasn't about to be left out of the big game. Jessica wasn't either.

I figured Matt's old lady would react that way. Jess surprised me, though. I mean, she looked like she'd rather eat a bowl of cockroaches with a side of worms than climb into that well and walk around underground looking for spirits.

Then she explained herself. She didn't want to be left out, and more than that, no way in hell did she want to hang out in the house alone waiting for us.

So it looks like we're all going, which presented a conundrum.

"We came this far together," Matt said, snapping back to real leadership. "So I guess it's fitting that we all go down as a team."

Right there, he took out his phone and called Donnelly on speaker mode to ask if she could send a few warm bodies. Our story producer didn't even think twice. She said that after looking at all the *fuckingtastic footage*—that's how she talks—she'd jump on any excuse to see the house. She said she'd be here *with bells on* and that she'd bring Jay Wilder, her generally clueless, pot-smoking, footage-logging intern who hoped to see the spooky weirdness for himself.

After he hung up, Matt clapped his hands. "Okay, let's get to work. We don't know how big the place is, so let's overdo it on provisions.

Cameras, flashlights, and plenty of batteries top the list. A day's worth of hiking food and three days of water."

Me, I'll be adding my nine-millimeter to my camping list, just in case.

Jessica spoke up. "You said no time went by out here while Kevin was inside shooting all this footage."

"Correct," Claire chimed in. "But we'll still get hungry in our time."

"Oh, right. Never mind."

"It's all pretty confusing," Matt said. "I'm still getting my head wrapped around it."

Confusing, maybe. But look how far we've come with this, where I get caught in a bona fide time warp and nobody bats an eye. After the weirdness of the past few days, now we just nod and accept it and try to figure out what time it is. Just another day at the office.

"And if we come up and find out no time has passed, we'll consider it bonus investigation time," Claire said. "We'll fire up the centrifuge like we originally—"

"Wait," Jake called. "It's happening again."

No classic "White Rabbit" by Jefferson Airplane this time, nor the atrocious "The Groovy People Are Here" by the Prayer Beads.

Somebody groaned in a loud, deep voice that sent vibrations through the crumbling house. Chanting what sounded like some kind of spell.

"Grab your gear," Matt yelled. "Basement!"

Toting cameras, we hustled down the stairs toward the uncovered well. A wall of sound emanated from its depths. Another thing we adapted to: We hear random music popping up in the house, we go running right toward it.

PADME HUM

A deep, bellowing baritone, rich with energy.

AUM MANI PADME HUM

And overlaid on top, I heard two piercing, higher-pitched tones.

While the chanting rested in my heart, these tones went straight into my brain and rang it like a bell.

We hesitated around the well. Something didn't feel quite right this time, or rather it didn't feel quite wrong enough.

Claire walked over and punched buttons on the control box. The chanting came to an abrupt stop, replaced by a tremulous silence as if the air in the room had begun repairing itself.

Jessica sneezed, making Jake jump.

The cameraman laughed. "I think my nerves are shot."

"The Om mantra," Claire lectured. "'Praise to the jewel in the lotus.' A Sanskrit mantra regarded as summarizing all Buddha's teachings. The first word, *Om*, is a sacred syllable in Indian religions. It's the sound of the universe."

Matt grinned. "Whatever it was, it was music to my ears. Hirsh and Vogan came through for us again, and they did it super quick. Check this out."

He cycled through the buttons of the control box until he found the right one. The seat and harness whirred down and then back up. "The power's on."

"It wasn't just chanting," I pointed out. "There were other sounds."

Claire, who'd read the PRF files, again had the answer.

The scientists used two sound frequencies in the last experiment, she explained. Five-two-eight and nine-six-three hertz. The first is the "mi" tone, often used in Gregorian chants. It's considered the miracle tone but also connects the natural world as Earth's vibration. Nine-six-three is a divine frequency associated with pineal gland activation and enlightenment, the crown chakra.

"I have a hard time believing they had all that going during their experiments," I said.

"They *were* the experiments," Claire told me. "Which shouldn't have produced anything except embarrassment once they sobered up. And yet…"

And yet your science can't explain this and therefore isn't up to snuff, lady. And yet here we are, about to go underground in search of whatever truth these people discovered. A place science can't reach or control.

It's time to gear up, folks. You'll see me again on the other side.

Text exchange between Rashida Brewer (Jessica Valenza) and Tameeka Brewer

Monday, 5:45 p.m.

well wish me luck because we are going all the way RB

down the rabbit hole and straight to wonderland RB

in our case, what appears to be a house beneath the house RB

^^laughing as I write this, but hey, it's just another day at foundation house RB

i'll be fine RB

but I may not be reachable for a day or so RB

or a few seconds actually LOL, sorry, private joke RB

i'll be fine and will text as soon as i'm back RB

but just in case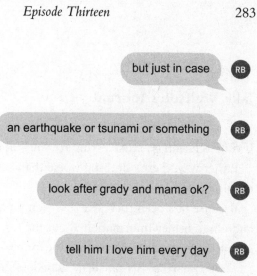

an earthquake or tsunami or something RB

look after grady and mama ok? RB

tell him I love him every day RB

and tell yourself while you're at it RB

no punches, only love RB

Jake Wolfson's Journal

If your delusion is actually true, are you still insane?

Either way, there's nothing worse than seeing delusional people get vindicated.

Because he's been there, Kevin's stomping around giving advice and wise, insider information about the tunnel where we're going, even though we all saw it on the tape for ourselves.

Matt's wearing this satisfied, smug look like a kid on Christmas morning who rushes downstairs to confirm that Santa did indeed eat the cookies he left out and even took the carrot for Rudolph.

Claire looks like she ate a dead rat but the rat had a drug inside it that gave her superpowers.

And Jessica's jittering around as if she earned a starring role in a big Hollywood horror movie and is just now figuring out it's actually a snuff film, LOL.

Welcome to *Fade to Black, Maniac Edition*.

But you got to hand it to these people. After chasing noises and recording data in the dark for countless hours, they finally hit the jackpot. Whether they discovered ghosts or the ghosts discovered them makes no difference. They were right all along, they were here, and they earned whatever they're feeling.

Which brings us to me, Jake Wolfson, your favorite Techno Viking.

I'd like to say that all this is amazing, and I'm honored to be a part of history and everything, but in the end, pointing cameras at people and things is just a job.

Now this job will take me down a dry well and into an underground passageway and after that who the hell knows. A tunnel a bunch of hippies built forty-five years ago while they were stoned.

So we can merrily spelunk into the pitch black under tons of earth to some secret lair where bona fide, actual ghosts want us to go for who the hell knows why.

Kevin is on some kind of lifelong redemption trip, Matt wants to play with dead things, Claire is hell-bent on learning the secrets of the universe, and Jessica doesn't want to be left out of this made-for-TV chance to be a star.

And me? What do I want?

I want to earn a damn paycheck. This has all been terribly fascinating, and yeah, I'm curious about how this unscripted story ends, but I ain't curious enough about the glowing alien egg that I'd like to stick my face in it. This job is a check, not a crusade one lays down his life for.

Beyond a paper cut, I'm not taking any major risks, nuh-uh, nope, not me.

Your favorite Techno Viking is leaving this place sound in mind and body.

I'll go down the well. I'll shoot in the tunnel. After that, we'll see how it goes. Sometimes, it may seem like I don't take anything seriously, but I can tell you I take this job very seriously. If nothing else, I'm a professional.

So yeah, I'm going.

I can also tell you I take my health far more seriously, so at the first sign shit is getting real, I'm out. Honestly, they don't pay me enough to risk my neck.

They really don't. Being a professional actually isn't enough of a reason to go down there at all, in fact. It's just something I've been telling myself so that I do.

I might as well admit the real reason I'm going.

I just can't let the others go down into that tunnel and face its dangers without me watching out for their ass.

FADE TO BLACK

PROD: Ep. 13, "Paranormal Research Foundation, Part 3"

INTERVIEW: Claire Kirklin

Illuminated by portable lights, Claire sits on a chair near the dry well. She washed her face and applied fresh makeup; her dark red hair is its usual mop.

The camera zooms in for a tight shoulder shot. Her eyes, usually sharp as knives, are open and fever bright now. She is no longer the debunker, the skeptic, the professor. Tonight, she is the eager student.

Matt (*off-camera*)**:** When you saw the footage that Kevin brought back of the tunnel, what was your first thought?

Claire has done countless interview bites for Fade to Black. *She knows to incorporate the question into the answer so it is usable for television.*

Claire: Seeing the footage that Kevin shot in the passage-way, my first thought was honestly, how did five people build this during the summer of 1972?

Matt: What's your theory?

Claire: Well, one realistic explanation is they hired a construction company to do it. That would leave plenty of records we could check. But it doesn't make sense.

Matt: Why not?

Claire: They didn't have the time or the money. That leaves Jared Wright, the sugar baron who built this house. Maybe he had the tunnel built in secret back in the thirties or forties, and the Foundation scientists discovered it.

Matt: What's the weirdest explanation that popped through your head? Thinking entirely outside the box, since we're doing that now.

He is pushing for good sound bites, but it sounds like he is challenging her.

Claire: Yeah, because I'm so good at that. (*giggles with a self-deprecating, sarcastic snort*) All right. Maybe the Foundation stumbled on the ruin of a lost civilization. Maybe the paranormal entity created the door for us and what is down there is the actual spirit world, and we're Odysseus walking into Hades. (*laughs again*) Once you're out of the box, it could be anything.

Matt: I'm not sure there even is a box anymore.

Claire: There is another explanation. It's a little off-the-wall, but it's something we'll see for ourselves while we're down there. They . . .

She stares into the distance, performing mental calculations.

Matt: They what?

Claire: At the end of their research project, the scientists might have built the passage and then kept going. Driven by their own search for a paranormal entity, they kept at it until one by one, they died.

Matt: You mean . . .

Claire: In the end, they dug their own grave.

Matt: Wow.

Jake (*whispers*)**:** Holy shit.

Claire: When we go down there, we may not only meet our spirit again. I think we're going to solve the mystery of the missing scientists.

Matt Kirklin's Journal

A weird thing about ghost hunting on TV is you feel like you're always performing for an audience. Even when the camera isn't recording, the spirits are watching. So you find yourself playing a role. Much the way you do in day-to-day life, I guess, only you're way more aware of it.

It's awkward, prone to pandering and being saccharine and showing off. I mean, on our show, you're basically onstage for seventy-two hours under significant stress, without a script, and, for most of us, with no real acting talent. Again like real life, except with reality TV, everything you do and say is set in stone for a whole lot of strangers to judge.

Thank God for video editors, who save you from yourself. When somebody finally invents a memory editor for real life, I think we'll be a far happier species.

Anyway, I bring this up because soon, we'll all be going from a part of the house where the spirits visit to the part where they live. Down there in the dark, every decision, word, and feeling will provoke and interact with unseen forces.

I know I often say dramatic things like *This is it* and *Tonight's the night*, but this time, I mean it more than I ever have before. Foundation House is leading us underground into a secret area undisturbed for around five decades, and I believe it's finally ready to give up its mysteries.

I'll be wearing my game face the entire time, no easy task as I'm running near empty after three nights of terror, hypervigilance, and little sleep. By the time this episode wraps, I may need serious post-traumatic stress counseling.

So while everybody stuffed backpacks for the big adventure, I needed a few moments where I could be me and shed that calculated feeling of watching myself from a pair of stilts. I needed Claire, who would make me feel grounded again.

After I interviewed her, I asked her to meet me in the camper.

She showed up wearing a mischievous grin. "It's about time you asked."

I can't tell you what all happened next, but afterward, I can tell you I enjoyed holding her, which is what I really needed. She felt warm and substantial in my arms. The camper felt safe and a reminder the real world existed. I wanted to go on holding her like this forever, but we were already almost out of time.

"How do you do it, Matt?"

She wanted to know how I can simply say anything is possible and then roll with it when the impossible becomes real.

"I don't know," I answered, which is the truth. Though I'm not sure how much I am in fact rolling with it. Stress and obsession have me feeling a little fevered and deranged, and I wish I could go home to reset and then return for more later.

Claire said, "A part of me still thinks the whole thing is a hoax, even though I know it isn't. Parsimony is a very tall hurdle."

"I guess I just don't think science knows everything yet."

"But accepting this doesn't just mean accepting that science is incomplete. It means accepting it's broken. If nothing makes sense, then everything makes sense. You lose your frame of reference. It's like a historian becoming a conspiracy theorist."

"At least you're not a fraud. Like me."

How good it is to finally put my feelings to words. What I felt ever since that moment the spirits appeared in the Apparition Room and crashed down the stairs.

"What are you talking about? You proved the paranormal exists. Even if no one believes us, we know."

But I didn't do anything, I explained. The house did. I'm just dancing to its tune. All these hauntings, all the training and gadgets, it ended up adding up to nothing except being in the right place at the right time.

I thought about Tammy, whom I knew but didn't know—didn't know anything about, really, though our friendship made me the expert I'm supposed to be today.

"What do you want?" Claire asked me.

"I want to understand how this works. I want to talk to spirits. I want to know what happens to us after we die and share that knowledge to comfort the world."

"It would change everything." She nudged me with a smile. "You'll be the Dr. Dolittle of ghosts."

"Just like the kid in *The Sixth Sense*. What about you?"

"I want the world to make sense again. It's like seeing a giant alien spaceship come to Earth and land at the White House. I'd be watching it on TV, thinking, 'We can't do that.' I'd look at my own work and think, 'Why bother? This is all pointless.'"

"But if you knew...If the aliens told you or you figured it out..."

"I'd change the world too. I'd offer an entirely new way to understand how the physical universe works."

"Subject D," I said bitterly. "Until we get what we want, they're in control. We're volunteers for their next big experiment."

"This is a situation where we have to give to get."

"Yeah. But give what, and how much of it?"

"Who cares? We'll have the fire."

She was right. My Claire usually is. My beautiful, big-brained wife.

Since I'd already confessed my impostor syndrome, I decided to go all the way. "Did you read everything the Flicks wrote about me? My psych eval?"

She hesitated a bit too long for comfort. "Yes. I'm sorry."

"Well?"

"Well, what?"

I had to ask. "Do you still love me?"

Claire nestled more tightly into me. "Even more. If you want a real fright, you should see mine."

"Yeah. Two whole pages. Mine was three. Kevin's was practically a book."

"What mine lacked in quantity it made up for in brutality. It turns out I'm a real stick-in-the-mud."

"Don't knock the girl in that psych eval. That's my wife."

I didn't want to leave our warm little nest. The strange dream I had the other night still plagued me, and I felt like once I let her go, I'd lose her forever. But the clock is ticking, bringing us steadily closer to yanking back the curtain and meeting the Wizard.

Right now, I'm writing this on a cold floor among a heap of backpacks in a poorly lit, grimy basement. Excited as hell about what comes next, energized by my break and high on anticipation.

As far as we have come, there is still so much we don't know. Are we dealing with the same spiritual entity the PRF scientists contacted, the scientists themselves, or both? Will we find the dead scientists underground? Will the spirit make itself known to us at last?

As excited as I am about investigating these questions, though, a part of me wants to turn back time and return to the camper. When we finally leave here and go home, I'll never let Claire go again.

Until then, there's work to do. The final piece of the puzzle awaits.

And now, gang, here's the moment you've been waiting for. It's time to say it.

This is it.

Tonight's the night.

FADE TO BLACK

PROD: Ep. 13, "Paranormal Research Foundation, Part 3"

Raw Video Footage

Monday, 7:06 p.m.

Jessica Valenza sits ramrod straight in the harness suspended over the well, eyes bugged, barely breathing, gripping the armrests. Claire and Kevin already went down the well with all the gear, waiting for the others to join them.

    Matt: Are you ready?

The control box has been unbolted from the wall and placed on the low stone parapet of the wellhead. That way, the last person down can activate the pulley. Matt crouches next to the well, his finger poised over the buttons.

    Jessica: Wait—why do we have to go in there right now?
    Matt: Why not? We talked about this, Jess. Several times already.
    Jessica: Well, we could at least wait for Tiff to show up.

She is obviously terrified but trying very hard to sound reasonable.

    Matt: She and Jay won't be here for another couple hours.
    Jessica: I just feel like we're rushing this.
    Matt: What else do we need to do to be ready? We'll probably be in there a few hours at most.

Jessica: With three days' worth of water.

Matt: I explained that. The provisions are just a precaution. The place down there is big, but it can't be that big.

Jessica: I think if there's one thing this weekend taught us, it's to check your expectations at the door and not make any predictions.

Matt (*sighs*): Do you want out? Nobody will hold it against you.

Staring off into space with a blank expression, Jessica says nothing. She gives her head an almost imperceptible shake.

Matt: This it is. The end of the road. I really think we're finally going to solve the mystery, maybe even make contact. I can feel it. One more push.

Jessica responds with a single weak nod.

Jake: If you change your mind, Jess, you can leave the tunnel anytime.

Jessica (*softly*): I know.

Matt: All right, then. Get ready. You're going down.

She lets out an alarmed yelp and grips the armrests even tighter as she disappears into the darkness.

Matt: You're up next, Jake.

Jake (*tilts the camera to aim down into the well's yawning mouth*): There'd better be an Emmy at the end of this.

Re: What's better than incredible?
From: Paisley Hirsh
To: Matt Kirklin
Cc: Jonathan Vogan, Samuel Clines
Monday, 7:33 p.m.

The first batch of footage you caught at Foundation House was incredible. I'm going to have to search my dictionary for a bigger word to describe the second batch. Congratulations on a mind-blowing two-parter! This is landmark television.

We're starting to expand our horizons for the material, which may get you and the property a much bigger reach. As such, upon your return, I trust you'll see the wisdom in your agreeing with the following action items.

First is after the wrap, you will need to come out to Los Angeles so we can talk strategy. How do we leverage this content to the fullest advantage for immediate branding and revenue as well as longer-term opportunities? Share results and gain buy-in from academic authorities? We understand you have your hands full at the moment, but do give this some thought.

Second is you and your people may seek and/or receive media attention and will need to be properly trained by our media consulting firm on what to say and when and how to say it. Without independent schooling or credentialing in the paranormal investigation field, the main qualification is simple credibility. The media and public will be fascinated by but skeptical of Episode 13, and they will try to pick it and you apart. If they lack the means to debunk what you've uncovered, some may focus on debunking you.

Which brings me to your requests for making this a three-parter to go all the way to Episode 15 and close out the season with powerhouse momentum. At this point, we heartily agree. Toward this end, I can tell you we were able to negotiate another day on-site with Gravois and also for the electric service you requested.

The caveat is Dominion will not be able to turn the power back on until tomorrow between the hours of noon and five. I know you were hoping to conduct your experiment tonight, but this is the best we could do. We hope it's sufficient.

So please do what you can without electricity until tomorrow. Continue to document this extraordinary mystery so you and your crack team can bring it all to a close with a dramatic Part 3. Keep up the stellar work!

Re: Can you help me debunk this paranormal claim?
From: Ramsay Godwin
To: Claire Kirklin
Monday, 7:35 p.m.

Hello, Claire! Thank you for writing to me. It always delights me to hear from my former students, especially one of my best and brightest. My memory is sadly not as sharp as it was in my youth, but I do recall your thesis of using novel telescope observations to test a cosmological model a few years back as being quite strong and worthy of Virginia Tech.

I'm well aware of your involvement with *Fade to Black*. I hope they are compensating you handsomely for the Sisyphean task of knocking down pseudoscience every week. Otherwise, one might consider it unworthy of your extraordinary talent and intellect. Of course, I intend that to be taken as flattery instead of criticism.

I would be absolutely delighted to assist you with debunking paranormal phenomena recorded at the place you call Foundation House. As you know, a being cannot be made of energy, which is not a thing but a measure of work, but let us say it is possible. Your spirit materialized from nothing but walked, which is impossible since if it is made of energy, then it cannot walk, and if it walks, Newton's laws say it is matter and not energy. I also found it amusing the spirit wore a flowing coat you described as looking like a rain jacket or lab coat. Why would a ghost need to wear anything? Is the jacket also a ghost?

There, I debunked it for you. And without even leaving my office! In all seriousness, Claire, I believe you are being pranked or being taken in by an elaborate hoax, and you might best direct your sleuthing energies in that direction.

Text exchange between Rashida Brewer (Jessica Valenza) and Tameeka Brewer

Sunday, 7:37 p.m.

TB house under the house?

TB you are driving me up a freaking tree

TB sigh

TB ok

TB ok

TB whatever you're doing I hope it goes well

TB i'd say break a leg but not sure that's appropriate here

TB so how about just watch your ass

STAY SAFE

 me, mama, and grady are waiting for you to come home

MANDALA

PROD: Ep. 13, "Paranormal Research Foundation, Part 3"
Raw Video Footage
Monday, 7:29 p.m.

Fade to Black*'s paranormal investigation team huddles inside the subterranean passageway, marveling at its construction and babbling in elated whispers. Despite their fears about being underground and facing the unknown, their excitement is obvious. This is the start of a great adventure.*

Each carries a flashlight and a heavy backpack bulging with provisions and equipment. Matt walks along with the body-mounted GoPro, while Kevin and Jake carry handhelds. Jake's is the only one recording at this time.

> **Claire** (*head swiveling to take it all in*): The stonework is incredible.
> **Jake:** Why are we whispering?
> **Kevin** (*at a normal volume*): They're just big old stones. You should see—
> **Matt:** What do you mean, Claire?
> **Claire:** The stones look natural, but they aren't. You can see a pattern.
> **Matt** (*squints*): I don't see anything.
> **Claire:** Look at this stone. (*points*) Now look at this one. And this one here.

Jessica: They're exactly the same shape. And they're all polished.

Kevin: She's right.

Matt: Well, Chapman was a genius engineer. He could certainly pull it off.

Claire: That's not it. You can't imagine what this place must have cost.

Kevin: I still don't see this pattern you're talking about.

Matt takes a few steps back for a better look but says nothing.

Claire: Everyone, give me your flashlight.

One by one, she places them on the floor next to the wall at regular intervals spanning five to ten feet. Their beams shine up to graze the stonework with light.

At first, the camera reveals nothing. Slowly, however, a pattern emerges, a shimmering spiral.

Matt: Wow.

Claire: Do you see it now?

Matt: It's amazing. What does it mean?

Kevin: I hope it doesn't mean we're spinning in circles.

Claire (*pulls a notebook from the back pocket of her jeans and reads*): "The journey is the destination. To the end or back to the beginning. A labyrinth or a maze. Beware the Minotaur."

Kevin (*snorts*): Yeah, that's what Gloria Flick said on the radio. Just more hippie gobbledygook.

Claire: I think every single thing the house has shown us has a purpose. This isn't a pattern, it's a map. Specifically, a mandala.

Kevin (*deadpans*): You're talking about the South African—

Claire: No, Kevin, not Nelson Mandela. A *mandala*. In eastern religions, it's a map of sorts. A spiritual journey from the outside to the core. A labyrinth. As a physical place, it's used for meditation. An inward as well as an actual journey.

Kevin: Like I said, it's just more gobbledygook. Tell me how this helps us.

Claire (*with obviously strained patience*): It helps us, Kevin, because a labyrinth is a spiral. It takes you to the center and then back out into the world, presumably having learned something important. That means no forks, no dead ends, and a possible exit at the end. However long this thing goes, we shouldn't get lost.

Kevin: Okay. That actually is useful, if it pans out.

Matt (*smiling*): I love it. We are on truth's literal path now.

Claire: Something like that, yes. But their truth, not ours.

Kevin: I don't know what that's supposed to mean.

Claire: The labyrinth, the philosophy, the Ken Kesey quote. We have to be on their trip. We'll need open minds and open hearts.

Matt and Kevin exchange a look.

Matt: I can dig that.

Kevin: Yeah, it's groovy, man.

The investigators chuckle as they gather up their flashlights and keep going.

Jessica: What about the Minotaur? What do you think it is?

Claire: I have no idea.

Matt: I don't know if it means anything real. It's probably just a symbol.

Kevin: The spirits haven't hurt us yet, even though they could.

Matt: Yeah, I doubt this whole thing is a trap to lure us down here to kill us. The spirits could have done that the second we walked into the house on Friday.

Jessica: Okay, as long as we don't dismiss it. We were warned to beware, right?

Kevin: Believe me, Jess, we've got our eyes peeled.

After a long walk retracing Kevin's path, they reach the door bearing its inscription, NO PIGS. It stands ajar the way he left it when he bolted.

Jake: Looks like they knew you were coming, Kev. Proceed with caution.

Kevin: Haha. You know, police are human beings with feelings too.

Jake: My bad.

Matt (*runs his hand over the door's rough surface*): It's like a meditation prompt. Let go of any selfish thoughts past this door. Or maybe they did mean cops. Authority figures. People who take away your freedom.

Kevin: Police don't—

Matt: We know, Kev. Okay, this is it.

He grips the door's handle and yanks. The thick round door groans all the way open.

Matt (*grunts with surprise*): More of the same.

The same smooth stone floor with its gentle downslope. The same rock walls subtly curving to the right. A part of Matt obviously hoped the door would have revealed some real answers rather than further invitation into mystery.

Claire: I think this door marks the first quadrant, one-fourth of a circle. Two more doors, and the circle will start to complete. If it's a spiral, it will lead to another, smaller circle inside it. If the construction made it that far.

Matt checks his pedometer, which counts the distance they have walked. He blinks in surprise.

Matt: How the hell...?

How the hell did five people accomplish this? Or even one very rich sugar baron?

No one answers. For a while, they walk on in silence. As nothing is happening, Jake turns the camera off to conserve the battery.

Then turns it back on sometime later.

The investigators stand in front of another door, on which is painted:

☺ ONLY THE REAL YOU NEED APPLY! ☺

Matt inspects his pedometer again and shakes his head. The labyrinth is impossible to fathom, a vast engineering project.

Whatever he is thinking, he says nothing. In a place where anything is possible, it becomes easy to simply accept the impossible.

Claire Kirklin's Journal

I feel like this place is laughing at me. It's starting to piss me off.

The last door we passed through read: HOW MANY LICKS?

Kevin chuckled when he saw that, though the rest of us were slower to get the cultural reference. He said it's from the classic TV commercial from when he was growing up. The wise Mr. Owl is asked how many licks it takes to get to the Tootsie Roll center of a Tootsie Pop.

Owl licks three times and then crunches down, concluding it takes only three.

Kevin is now our go-to guy for all these sixties and seventies references. Not that these particular data points help us get anywhere. We'd do just as well cracking open fortune cookies. While all information is important here, I'm convinced these messages are a sideshow. Frosting, not the cake. I mean, I doubt the entity lured us down here so we could go on a weird self-help retreat.

The most important information is right in front of us. In fact, we're standing in it.

Seriously, how does this place even exist?

Matt constantly checks on us to see how we're doing with the hike, stopping us to rest when Kevin starts huffing, making sure I drink enough water, noting Jessica stopped sneezing the minute we came down here. He said he hopes we can make the center tonight. Dusting off my geometry, I think he might be right, if we push hard.

At each of the three doors, I wrote down the distance we'd walked. As I suspected, the doors were equidistant. My guess is they mark quadrants in the mandala's outer circular loop. When we reached the point where we should have come back to the beginning, the path kept on going. If the doors did in fact mark quadrants, this confirmed the presence of the spiral.

The distance between the first and the third door was about 1.6 miles. Multiplying by 2 to get a circumference of about 3.2 miles, I then divided by π to get a diameter of about a mile. After all this walking, I've internalized a rough angle of velocity. Assuming we're on an Archimedean spiral (as suggested by the spiral pattern on the tunnel walls), the angle of velocity is constant. If that's true, our mandala likely has five loops with a total length of maybe 7.5, 8 miles.

Finally, something I can rationally predict. A small victory.

We now assume the passageway won't suddenly degrade and stop, unfinished, the skeletal remains of the scientists lying among their scattered tools. We simply accept the idea the Foundation scientists or Jared Wright somehow built a complete labyrinth underground. If we want to find our big puzzle piece, we'll have to go all the way to the end.

How I wish I could simply crunch down like old, wise Mr. Owl.

The others sit around in their little pools of illumination, munching on hiking snacks and drinking bottled water, too tired and intimidated by this place to talk. Jake closes his eyes. Whether they wanted it or not, the mandala has them all looking inward.

Not me. I'm looking outward, observing everything and, whenever possible, assigning it a number that goes into my notebook. Characterizing. My watch says it's been about two hours since we came down the well, though it feels like a lot longer than that. My body, meanwhile, doesn't know what time it is. I feel like I could nod off and sleep a solid month, though the idea of a month is meaningless down here. The darkness is a constant, pure black that appears to have substance, something you can cut. It makes me think of pitching into a black hole. I'm increasingly hungry for light, greedy for its lumens.

It's also utterly quiet. We haven't seen a living thing on the path, not even a solitary bug. The air is perfectly still with no sense of a draft, which is also odd as it seems fresh and not stale. The well was rich with the scents of earth and minerals, but here in the labyrinth, the air smells like, well, us. Like flop sweat. The temperature is a constant seventy degrees. Shimmering in the light to reveal wispy spiral suggestions, the walls seem manufactured more than built.

Occam's razor nags at me again. This place should not exist: Therefore, it is an illusion. I'm dreaming. Perhaps I'm lying on the floor of the well, dying. This certainly feels like a near-death experience, based on descriptions I've read.

I think Occam's razor is onto something, but the simplest explanation is this place is real because I am here touching it. It shouldn't be, but it is. Parsimony doesn't apply anymore, at least not yet. For now, all I can do is observe, which I doggedly keep at with a growing irritation that has become a burning in my chest.

I came to this place for answers, but as above, so below: The more the entity shows us down here, the less we know. No bizarre flashes of the paranormal now, but instead a constant, grating impossibility. Every revelation, meanwhile, only creates another riddle. Every hoop I'm forced to jump makes me feel more like a trained lab monkey than a scientist. The irrational, once an outlet I explored to scratch an old, rebellious itch, is threatening to become my new normal.

How many licks? As many as it takes.

Again and again like a prayer, I tell myself to set aside my disbelief and roll with it. Bide my time and wait for my chance to model and understand. Occam's razor waits, though it is impatient. Its edge is sharp and cuts deeper with every step to the center of this vast labyrinth.

Matt Kirklin's Journal

NO PIGS.

ONLY THE REAL YOU NEED APPLY!

Each was a distance marker as well as a prompt for guided meditation. The meandering path and the oppressive dark and quiet lull you into solitary reflection.

It's the kind of quiet that makes you want to whisper. The noise we make, breath and footfalls and so on, only calls more attention to it. It's a quiet that makes you nervous you'll instead call attention to yourself, fearful you'll disturb whatever resides in the boundless nothing.

And something *is* there, because the silence is not total. The silence casts a shadow. A grinding moan coursing through the walls and simmering just outside of perception. A barely audible hum. You think you hear it, but when you turn your head, it's gone, leaving only the creepy certainty you're being watched.

HOW MANY LICKS?

The guided meditation prompts fell in our laps like tarot cards. These were the only places where we felt safe to talk, and we did it loudly, the kind of self-conscious talking and laughing intended to ward off evil spirits.

Wandering and labyrinths are a part of many cultures. They're designed to throw you off balance. You can't help but focus on the twisting, bound path as the only reference point. It's hypnotizing. It really does feel like walking between worlds, a place of reflection and ultimately transformation.

As a bit of psychology, it's brilliant; only this is no mere mental workout.

Everything Foundation House showed us means something. Looking back at the spiral carved around Shiva's eye, I think I now understand what it was trying to say. Or rather what the PRF scientists—whom I believe are the real architects of this fantastic place and whose spirits we're dealing with—wanted to tell us.

The eye is our destination. Enlightenment and transformation. Wisdom gained and sacrifice given with the freedom to choose. This is what the Flicks designed and the scientists somehow built here, an occult machine intended to join our world with the world of the spirits. A place where there is nothing to separate us.

For better or worse, we are literally following in their footsteps.

Claire Kirklin's Journal
Claire's Sketch Depicting the Labyrinth

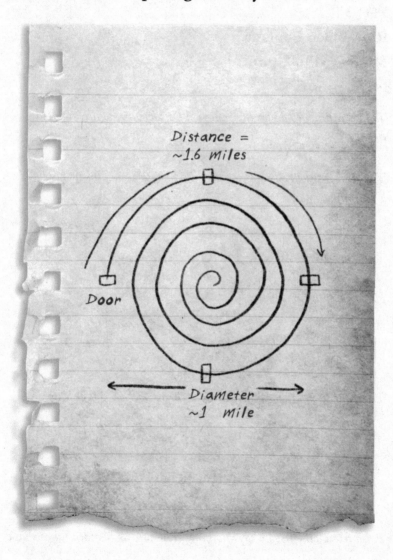

FADE TO BLACK
PROD: Ep. 13, "Paranormal Research Foundation, Part 3"
Raw Video Footage
Monday, 10:48 p.m.

The team trudges down the same old passageway, which suddenly stops.

The tunnel's walls disappear, and the investigators find themselves in a vast, open space.

   Kevin: I can't believe it.
   Jake: Oh, wow.

He lets out a disbelieving laugh.

   Matt: This is amazing.
   Jessica: Is this a room? This is a room, right?

The floor stretches to disappear in darkness so vast it is threatening.

   Matt: I think so. We have to check it out.
   Jessica (*gawking*): How did five people build this?
   Matt: I think we finally have the answer as to who actually made this place.

For a few moments, he says nothing, frowning as his idea takes shape in his mind. The rest of the team stares at him while he frames his thoughts.

> **Matt** (*murmurs as if talking to himself*): I'd thought it was the scientists too, but I was wrong. Dead wrong. The truth was in front of us the whole time. It was just too impossible to believe.
> **Claire:** That leaves only Jared Wright.
> **Matt** (*wags his head*): No. He didn't build it either.
> **Claire:** Then who?
> **Matt:** I think it's obvious now that it was the spirits they contacted.

The investigators respond with wide-eyed stares. Jessica looks up with a pained wince, as if she expects the roof to suddenly come crashing down.

> **Claire:** So people didn't build this to meet the entity...
> **Matt:** I think it was the other way around.

The team's eyes goggle even further as they try to comprehend they are standing inside a massive construction created by a paranormal entity.

Prior to this, they had accepted temporary aberrations in reality. Now they can no longer trust even the ground they are walking on.

> **Kevin:** You're kidding me. A ghost did all this.
> **Matt:** A spirit, yes. Or many spirits, possibly an elemental. Or maybe even some kind of god. (*shrugs in embarrassment*)
> **Claire:** For what it's worth, the scientists eventually used that word too.

Matt: All along, we thought we were chasing the ghosts of the PRF, who were chasing this entity. I think this entity is what we've been dealing with this entire time.

Kevin: So all the hippie talk and sixties music was just window dressing.

Matt: A way to communicate.

Jessica: Or a big, juicy worm for the hook.

Kevin: If it is, I'd say we've been caught. Fine by me. I'm ready to meet.

He takes out his handheld radio and mashes the talk button.

Kevin: Hello? We're here. Hello? Are you there?

He receives no answer.

Kevin: You invited us, and we came. Tell us what to do now. No more riddles.

Nothing.

Matt: What we do now is explore.

Claire walks off, the beam of her flashlight swinging impatiently to barely penetrate the thick darkness that seems to devour it.

Matt takes his time, methodically sweeping the floor, then the wall, and finally its upper slope that curves toward what is likely a domed ceiling.

The camera tilts up to catch the suggestion of one of the Foundation's occult symbols carved high on the wall. It is an ankh, at least five feet tall.

Jake (*to no one in particular*)**:** Seriously, can you believe this?

No one answers him. By now, everyone has asked the question or one like it at least several times, and the others replied each time that no, they cannot believe it. The question goes on being asked, however, more a coping mechanism than a serious inquiry at this point.

Kevin walks off toward the center of the room, still trying the radio. The camera follows, shooting at hip level.

Jake: Hey, if this is a dead end, then what?
Kevin: It's not a dead end.
Jake: How do you know? There's nobody home.
Kevin: You don't invite people to walk eight miles so you can ignore them.
Jake: Yeah, *I* wouldn't. But I'm not a—hey!

The camera swings away. We hear the alarming sounds of a physical struggle, men grunting.

Kevin (*pushes away from the lens*)**:** Get your hands off me.
Jake: Bro, look—
Kevin: What's the matter with you? I could have—
Jake: Look *down.*

The camera tilts to reveal that the two men are standing at the edge of a large circular hole cut into the stone floor. Kevin's flashlight beam splashes across stairs leading down.

And down and down, round and round. A vast, deep, spiral staircase that confronts the viewer like an invitation and a taunt.

Kevin: Holy hell.

Kevin Linscott's Journal

We just got here, and things are already starting to fall apart.

Jessica wants to turn back.

Nobody else does. Though looking down into that stairwell, so deep it gives you the weird sensation of falling, it's not like we want to keep going either.

"This isn't worth it anymore," she told us. "If we go down there, I don't know if we're coming back. I won't risk it."

Her gloom fell on fertile ground. This labyrinth rubbed our nerves raw to the bone. The lack of light, the eerie quiet that isn't quiet at all, the off-kilter feeling that all this was manufactured and we're not even on Earth anymore.

The ominous feeling that we're utterly alone here, cut off from the real world.

I decided to keep my mouth shut about it. If everybody wants to leave, I'll accept it.

Going down the stairs does not worry me in the least. Climbing back up is a whole other matter. I tossed a road flare down the hole, and it fell until it became a tiny red star. The stairwell has a bottom, but it's real deep. While I'm in good shape, I'm hardly a young man anymore.

On the other hand, if anybody wants to soldier on, I can't back out. The return trip will be hard—as in Mount Everest hard—but I'll do it. Matt's our leader, but only because we're still acting like this is a TV show. He can't handle this.

When he fails, somebody will have to step up, and it'll fall on me.

A role that I will of course accept. I am ready to take command when duty calls.

Then Claire said something I did not expect: "I think Jessica's right. If an entity did in fact build this, which is insanely plausible, it can rearrange matter however it likes. Which means there might be no end to this. We should leave."

I admit I found her theory worthwhile. Maybe this whole thing is a giant tease. The spirit lures you in and farther, ever farther, until curiosity kills the cat. Not out of malice, maybe, but by simply giving us what we want: a mystery.

Isn't that what this thing has been doing from the start? Giving us what we want while keeping us on the hook for more?

It's like handing a paranormal investigator a card designed to keep him occupied for hours. On one side, it says TURN OVER TO FIND THE GHOST!

And on the other... You guessed it. It says the same thing.

"We'd have come all this way for nothing," Matt said, all bitterness. "*Fade to Black*'s big finale is America watches us give up at the threshold."

"Not exactly the threshold," I pointed out.

"I'm not putting my life on the line for our fans," Jessica said. "If one of us trips on those stairs and sprains an ankle, how are we supposed to get them out?"

"It's a risk," Matt conceded.

"It could be a death sentence. Just one little fall."

"I'm with you, chief," I said, getting it on the record that I'm raring to go. "We should see this through to the end. Find out where these stairs take us, at a minimum. But if you all think we should leave, I'd be fine with it."

Matt turned to Jake. "What about you?"

"The stairs don't bother me. I have two days' provisions. I could keep going a little more. I'm curious about how far this clown car goes. It's you guys I'm worried about, though." He glanced at me, and I glared a warning back. He shrugged. "So I'll do whatever."

Yeah, I thought. *I'm sure you will.* It's practically the anthem of his generation.

"Safety first," Claire reminded us, as if that settled it. As a team, it's our biggest rule. "If anyone wants to come back, they can do it with the proper gear. A gurney, maybe, loaded with med kits, food, water, rope, stove, emergency flares, sleeping bags, portable lights—"

"Bicycles," I chimed in. "We could get around this top part real fast on bikes."

"All right," Matt said. "I'm getting the message everybody wants to turn back. We're all feeling wiped out. I know I certainly am. I say we sleep on it and see how we feel tomorrow. Okay?"

Nobody objected. We brushed our teeth, rolled out thin blankets, and settled in to sleep with our backpacks as pillows. Including yours truly, who believes his lumbar will have something to say about that in the morning.

And that's it, folks. It's over. A few hours and a wakeup from now, it looks like we'll be packing up and heading home, and *Fade to Black* will live up to its moniker. For all the talk about coming back better prepared, I doubt it will happen. This is the end of the line.

Which may seem like we failed, but look how much winning we accomplished to get here. When I walk out of this place, it will be with my head held high.

Jessica Valenza's Journal

Claire warned me how scary it would be, going underground.

The claustrophobia. How my hippocampus, my brain's spatial navigation system, would instantly balk at being forced to give up its familiar cues. How my circadian system would go out of wack as my body began to crave sunlight as if it were food. All of which turned out to be completely true.

But mostly, I was like: What if the walls suddenly collapse on us? What if the door closed behind us, and we're trapped and already running out of air?

This kind of disorientation is not terrific for a worrier like me. What was the word Dr. Flick used to describe me? Oh yeah: *neurotic*. Thanks a lot.

After a while, though, I got over it, and all said, the trip down wasn't so bad. I wasn't alone, and that made me feel safe, as we were following the safety-in-numbers horror movie rule. Everyone was excited, babbling in quick but respectful whispers, as if afraid they'd wake the dead.

Their excitement put me a little more at ease. It made the whole thing feel like an adventure. If they'd freaked out, I would have bolted straight home. In fact, in at least one major way, I actually felt pretty good. The second I got in here, my allergies finally let up.

Then after everyone stopped talking and settled into long silence, I fell into the same meditation the labyrinth inspired.

Deep in my head, I thought all sorts of things. How I act like a petulant teenager with Tameeka. How I go on fooling myself into believing my huge break is always around the next corner. How I can't wait to get home to my little man.

All in all, it was a weirdly therapeutic journey down the rabbit hole. And how's this for irony: It took me going in to realize how badly I wanted to be out.

I'll tell you what really did it for me. I had one good look at that staircase leading straight down into hell and thought, no way, no how am I going down there, not even to be the next Jennifer Lawrence.

I thought, here we are trying to puzzle out the meaning of every single thing the spirits are trying to tell us while ignoring Flick's assessment whether we'd *survive the vortex*, whatever that is.

Beware the Minotaur. Yeah, that too.

And then I thought about how none of us are even remotely qualified to be down here. The others actually still think they're paranormal investigators and that going down the stairs is an okay idea. They think they can handle whatever they're dealing with and have any control over how this game ends.

I mean, I'm the one who pretends for a living, yet I feel like I'm the only person on this team who's being realistic about all this. When the sole actor on your reality TV show is the only one who's no longer pretending, you know the show has jumped the shark.

Thank God they finally came to their senses and are coming back with me. Tomorrow, whatever that means in this place, we're out of here.

Out of this mirage and back to the real world.

Back to what is really important.

The others lie quietly around me on the ground, either asleep or somewhere deep in their own heads. I'm going to try to do the same, though this is the kind of place that wants you to sleep but makes you wonder if you'll wake up.

Sorry, everyone. I'm sorry if I'm letting you down. I know you wanted to go on playing. But Grady needs me more than you do. He needs a mama.

I guess Dr. Flick has me figured after all.

FADE TO BLACK
PROD: Ep. 13, "Paranormal Research Foundation, Part 3"
Raw Video Footage
Tuesday, 7:04 a.m.

Matt: Claire! CLAIRE.

Lights flick on across the camp. Acting on professional instinct, Jake nimbly gains his feet in a smooth motion, shooting the whole time.

Matt: CLAIRE!
Kevin: What's going on?
Matt: She's gone!
Kevin: Maybe—you know, the spirits—maybe they—
Jake: Maybe she just went to take a—
Matt: Her pack is gone too. She *left*.
Jessica: I found a note!
Matt: Thank God. (*grabs it and reads*) "I couldn't sleep, so I got an early start back. See you at Base Camp." What…?
Jake: Oh, good.
Jessica: She's safe. We can all head back.
Matt (*pulls out radio*)**:** Claire, it's Matt. Claire, come in.

No response.

Matt: Claire, honey, please answer me. I just want to know you're safe.

Again, there is no answer. Matt hooks the radio back onto his belt and crouches in front of his backpack, which he starts to reload with his provisions and gear.

Matt: She didn't go back to Base Camp.

Jessica: What do you mean?

Matt: She just wanted us to believe that so we'd leave.

Jessica: How do you know?

Matt (*with grim certainty*): Because I know my wife.

Jessica: Last night, she was all, "safety first," and—

Matt: I know my wife. She saw us arguing about whether to go back and wanted out of it. To her, it wasn't a group decision. She figured she would get us to return so she could keep going on her own without anybody stopping her. If she really wanted to turn back, she would have waited for us.

Kevin: My camera's missing.

Matt: That confirms it.

Jessica: Claire took his camera?

Jake: Why, though? Why is she doing this?

Matt (*pure bitterness*): Because she's not leaving here without solving her puzzle.

Kevin (*crosses his arms*): Okay. Tell me what the plan is, chief.

Matt: The plan is I'm going after her.

Kevin: You mean down the stairs.

Matt: That's my plan. Your plan is to do whatever you want.

Jake: I'll go with you, boss.

Matt: You don't have to do anything. The show's over. I hereby quit.

Jake: This isn't about the show. This is an emergency. I want to help.

Kevin (*with mounting incredulity*): It's hard to believe she did it. She made a damn mess.

Jake: You pointing that out is the opposite of helping.

Kevin: And you should be pissed off. I am. She put us all at risk.

Matt (*wags his head*): Not you. Just me.

Jake: The lady has balls. You have to give her that at least.

Kevin: I'd give her a...

Glancing at Matt's glowering expression, he decides not to finish the thought aloud. Matt zips his backpack closed. He scoops his GoPro from the ground and attaches it to its clip.

Matt: If you're coming with me, I'm leaving in five. If you're going back, you can leave anytime you want.

Jessica (*hopeful*): Kevin?

Kevin: I can't leave now either. I have to go too. Sorry about that.

Jessica: Why?

Kevin: I'm a former police officer. Somebody's life is at risk.

Jessica (*panicking*): So I'm going back by myself?

The prospect appears to make her physically sick.

Kevin: If you don't want to be alone, you should come with us.

Jessica: Are you kidding? Matt, you promised—

Matt: I'm sorry, Jess. You're a good person. I consider you a friend, I really do. But I'm going after my wife, and... you're either on the bus or off the bus.

Jessica: There's no way in hell I'm going down those stairs. It's stupid.

Matt: You'll be okay. All you have to do is follow the path straight back. When you get to the well, radio Donnelly. She'll help you get out. You can tell her what's going on here and call for help.

Jessica stares at him while he stands and hitches his backpack onto his shoulders. Her hair is matted, her clothes disheveled. Her eyes are wide and feral. Her lips pull back in a snarl.

Jessica: You know what? Fuck you, Matt.

He ignores her, adjusting his pack for a snug fit.

Kevin: Come on, Jess. Don't be—

She walks up to Kevin and gives him the finger right in his face.

Jessica: Fuck you too, Kevin. You don't even like Claire!
Kevin: Jess, please—

She shifts her aim toward the camera lens.

Jessica: Fuck you, Jake. (*flips the bird with both hands*) And fuck you, Claire!
Matt: Everybody ready?
Jessica: No! Please don't—
Kevin (*looks away, as if ashamed*): I'm good to go.
Jake: Yeah. Uh, ready.
Jessica: Please don't leave me here! Please!

Matt points at the exit.

Matt: All you have to do is walk straight back the way we

came. You literally cannot get lost. You'll be fine. You
should be back at the house by late afternoon.
Jessica: What if my flashlight goes dead? What if—
Matt: I'm going now. I'll see you back at the house.

*Gripping their cameras and lights, the men march toward the stairs.
They start down, keeping up a steady, clomping pace until Jessica's
curses and screams turn into a distant echo.*

THE MAZE

Jessica Valenza's Journal

If the trip down was horrible, the trip back is a nightmare.

I hate being alone here.

Not that I'm entirely alone. I feel watched, followed.

The first mile of my return flew by pretty easy. I was so pissed off that I forgot how scared I was. Then I remembered: Oh yeah, I'm practically crapping my pants.

For those of you who might judge me, *you* come down here and try it. The utter darkness barely held at bay by a flashlight, darkness that feels like it's alive, darkness that fills a labyrinth that itself may be alive and is watching your every step.

The dead stillness. The constant disorientation. The sense you're touring your own giant coffin, surrounded by millions of tons of earth, possibly in another dimension.

Every footfall sounds like a dinner bell for invisible predators. My field of view never changes. The walls constantly curve to the left, where the next stretch of tunnel always remains out of sight, shrouded in black. After a while, it becomes maddening.

What if my flashlight craps out?

I break into a run, but the view remains infuriatingly the same, as if I'm on a treadmill.

What if I round the bend and whatever's been following me is there, waiting for my beam of light as the signal to raise its head and smile?

For a place designed to inspire reflection and peace, it's goddamn nerve-shredding.

I reminded myself the ghosts come when you're alone and afraid. They're drawn to it like a mosquito is to the heat and scent of human flesh. That's not just a horror movie rule, by the way. Not just a scripted way to lose your plot armor in a film. It's accepted canon in ghost hunting.

"The light of protection I carry is strong," I say over and over.

I'm whistling through the graveyard.

When I ran into a wall of stink, I actually greeted it with relief. Kevin walked off during a quick rest stop in the inner spiral. I hope he brought toilet paper. Me, I haven't gone in three days. I may need an enema at the end of all this.

After walking and jogging for a few more minutes, I stopped for a break, huddling against the wall. I have to get a grip. I'm burning up with fever, pouring sweat. After four days in a haunted house, I'm running on panic and adrenaline.

Again, I tried the walkie-talkie. Again, no one responds to my calls.

I really wish I had a camera now.

There were only three, and when it came to divide them up, I said I didn't want one. Why would I, as we'd agreed to stay together? Safety first and all that, remember when that was important? I didn't need the extra weight.

Now I wish I had it.

Look at me. So dumb. Even now, I'm worried about getting enough screen time. But it's not that, not really.

The camera gives me something to be brave for. Something to play to. Namely you, fan, sitting on a couch after a long day, hoping to turn your brain off watching a hot girl run around scared in a haunted house.

Acting got me into this mess, it could have gotten me out. I'd play the tough, plucky final girl, hamming it up and narrating my feelings all the way out of here.

Instead, my last shot in *Fade to Black*'s Foundation House episodes that all America will watch might be me flipping everyone the bird and telling them to fuck themselves. I'll forever be "that chick who lost her shit and flamed out," the punchline to an internet meme.

On the left, a photo of Claire: I FOUND A CURE FOR CANCER.

On the right, me with fingers aloft: FUCK YOU, CLAIRE!

And other endless variations on the theme.

Kevin: NIETZSCHE SAID—

Me giving it with both barrels: FUCK YOU, KEVIN!

I'll have to somehow convince, beg, or bribe Jake to delete that footage. Offer him anything. Seriously, this could get ugly.

Not that the jerks didn't deserve every finger they got.

Yes, this is good. Journaling is good. Not as good as *Blair Witch*, runny-nose monologuing my way through this creepy, subterranean tunnel, but close.

By writing out my feelings, I can keep a grip on them. By writing about what happens after I get out of here, I can boost my confidence.

As long as I keep writing, the thing that's following me keeps its distance.

By writing as if the others are going to make it back—

Oh God.

I'm—

I just added vomit to the messes we all made coming down the tunnel, and I'm hoping "NO PIGS" wasn't a hygiene warning.

Sorry, spirits. Sorry, sorry, sorry.

I can barely handle worrying about myself right now without adding the stress of wondering if the others will make it back alive. It's too much. I don't want to be the final girl. I feel bad enough for leaving them.

They ditched *me*. But I can't shake the feeling I ditched them too.

Acting came to the rescue, or rather a breathing exercise I use to calm down before going on camera or stage. The 4-7-8 trick. Inhale through your nose for four seconds, hold your breath for seven, whoosh out through your mouth for eight.

It's working.

The light of protection I carry is strong.

The light of protection I carry is strong.

The light of protection I carry is strong.

Yes, that's good.

In fact, I'm feeling so good right now I'm actually thinking maybe I should turn back to catch up with the others.

Seeing this thing through to the—

No. Screw that.

I'm out.

FADE TO BLACK
PROD: Ep. 13, "Paranormal Research Foundation, Part 3"
Raw Video Footage
Tuesday, 7:33 a.m.

Matt and Kevin sit on the bottom step, their backpacks resting next to them. Matt takes a few deep breaths while Kevin massages his left knee. Their faces glisten with sweat.

> **Matt:** You wouldn't think going down the stairs would be that hard on the legs.
> **Kevin:** It's murder on my old knees.

The camera tilts to look up the ascending stairs, which disappear into impenetrable darkness.

> **Jake:** Unbelievable. Going back up is gonna suck the big one.
> **Kevin:** Like climbing to the top of a forty-story building. I counted the steps.
> **Jake:** How many did you count?

Already prickly from the pain in his knees, Kevin cocks an irritated eye at the camera shooter, no doubt trying to decide whether the man is messing with him. He apparently concludes Jake is not.

> **Kevin:** Around three hundred ninety.

Jake whistles.

    Matt: I see three exits over there.

The camera swings around to focus on where Matt aims his flashlight. We see yet another stone wall, though this one is constructed of large, thick blocks. The men do not seem to notice the mindboggling if utterly spare architecture; they have accepted the marvels of the labyrinth and now have more immediate concerns.

Cut into the wall, three black mouths mark separate corridors.

    Kevin: Three of us. Three doors. This place is just screwing with us now.

The camera pans back to frame the tech manager's sweating face.

    Jake: You thought it'd be easy?
    Kevin (*growls*)**:** I woke up in the dark, I haven't had my coffee, my back's bitching, and I'm already wiped out by those stairs. You do not want to mess with me.
    Jake: Sorry, bro. Jeez.
    Kevin: Good. Now get that camera out of my face.

The camera shifts to Matt.

    Jake: Which one should we take, boss?
    Matt (*stands*)**:** All of them.
    Kevin: You want us to split up, but I'm not sure why.
    Matt: How many chemlights did you bring?
    Kevin: I brought however many I was told to bring.
    Jake: Twenty.

Kevin: Then I have that, plus a few emergency flares.
Matt: Give me a chemlight. Please.

Kevin unzips a front pocket of his backpack, slides out a little plastic tube, and hands it over.

Matt bends it until it snaps and then shakes it. The chemlight flares a brilliant green. He holds it for a moment, his eyes appearing to drink in the precious light and color. Then he drops it to clatter onto the floor.

Matt: Each of these lasts twelve hours, which is plenty of time. We each take a separate exit. Every time we're just about out of eyeshot of our last chemlight, we drop another. We go as far as the light takes us. Got it?
Jake: Got it, boss.
Matt: I'm not your boss until this is over. You call your own shots. Kevin?
Kevin: Yeah, I—
Matt: If you find Claire, you come back here and you wait. If you don't find her, you come back. Anybody who is here at, let's say, two o'clock will go back together.
Jake: But if none of us find—
Matt (*shakes his head emphatically*)**:** If anybody doesn't show, you sure as hell don't go looking for them. Whoever is here should go straight back as fast as they can. Got it?
Jake: All right, but if you're not all waiting for me right here, I'm calling the cops when I get back to the house. I'll call the fire department. I'll call everybody. You feel me?
Matt: I'm counting on it. So if you somehow get hurt, know that help is coming.
Kevin: They'll take this place away from us.

Matt: It's not ours anymore. I don't think it ever was. But we discovered it.

Jake: We got our footage. So there's that.

Matt: All I care about now is finding Claire before she gets lost or hurt.

Kevin: Hang on a minute. I don't know if I like this whole "every man for himself." We should stay together.

Matt: Like I said, you do what you want. I'm taking the exit on the right.

Jake: We'll find her, boss.

Matt: Thank you, Jake. Kevin, you too, I mean it. Good luck, guys.

He shoulders his backpack and walks off toward the right corridor with a resolute gait. The other men watch him go, no doubt feeling far less certain.

Jake: If you want, we could explore both tunnels together.

Kevin (*glowers at him*): I don't need you babysitting me.

Jake: I just thought you didn't want to be alone.

Kevin stands on creaking knees, hitches up his belt, and sets his jaw. What he says next is what is known as a great sound bite, the kind that arrives destined to make it into Fade to Black's *first-season big finale.*

Kevin: It's time to man up, boy. Now let's go find our lost lady.

Claire Kirklin's Journal

Matt has his grail, I have mine.
   And I just found it.

FADE TO BLACK

PROD: Ep. 13, "Paranormal Research Foundation, Part 3"

Raw Video Footage

Tuesday, 9:20 a.m.

A chemlight flares in the distant dark like the last star in a dead universe.

>   **Matt:** This maze might be as big as the labyrinth.

He cracks a chemlight, shakes it, and drops it at his feet.

>   **Matt:** The only way to beat a maze is to always turn in the
>   same direction. In my case, right. It's easy to remember:
>   I'm going the *right way*. Remember this, gang, if you're
>   ever ghost hunting and end up in the spirit world.

Gone are the stately tunnels of the labyrinth. Here, the passageways are narrow, cramped corridors that seemingly go on forever.

>   **Matt:** Check this out.

The camera tilts down. He kicks at the floor. Bends to sweep his hand along it before holding it up for inspection.

>   **Matt:** For a little while up there in the labyrinth, I was
>   wondering if this might be some kind of lost civilization

thing that the PRF stumbled onto. But no dust? Not a single crumb? And listen...

In the ensuing silence, the microphone picks up a distant grinding, ghostly hum, which pulses rhythmically as if produced by some vast machine.

Matt: The farther I go, the louder it gets. The thicker the air feels.

He sighs and stands, ready to resume his journey.

Matt: You want to know what I think now? I think Claire is right and this place is building itself on the fly. The deeper we go, the bigger it gets...

He clears his throat.

Matt: It kind of makes me wonder if what's behind us is still there as we left it.

The camera aims down the narrow stone corridor as he starts forward.

Matt: But why? Why is it doing this? That's what I don't understand... If it wants to show us something, why not show it? If it wants to kill us, why not just get it over with? This is like hide-and-seek, but with entirely different rules.

He marches on for several minutes and turns around. The last chemlight he dropped glows like another green, dying star.

Matt: Screw this place.

Another chemlight snaps and falls to the floor.

Matt: Seven left.

He keeps walking.

Matt: I think the second we came down here, we placed ourselves entirely in this spirit's hands. It's the spirit's show now, not ours. We're now on its script.

Matt Kirklin's Journal

I'm not a very good husband.

I mean, I thought I was. I did everything you're supposed to do. I may not be super muscly, manly, or mysterious, but for the things I think truly count, I'm there each and every day.

Showing affection isn't something that scares me. In fact, it's one of my favorite drugs. That and making Claire laugh or at least getting her to raise her left eyebrow in amusement—her ability to do that being one of her superpowers.

I can't help myself; I dote on her. She completes me.

And I now see that's a problem.

We met at the big Barnes & Noble in Ralston. Some bookstores I've visited on my RIP travels, they put the New Age section right across from Faith and Spirituality. You're browsing titles on ghosts, crystals, Wicca, and lost civilizations, while next to you, some prim and proper lady is immersed in a book about the singular healing power of Jesus Christ.

Sometimes, it can get awkward. You might exchange a glance as you pass each other, wondering if you're on the same team.

The Ralston B&N has a real sense of humor. They set up the New Age shelves to face the Science section like some kind of metaphorical prizefight between mysticism and empirical reason. That's where I chanced upon the woman who would change my life.

Even then, Claire's style presented a feminine take on Victorian masculine, which just drove me wild. I appreciate nudity as much as any man does, but suggestion is my fetish. Leave something to my imagination, and I become very interested, curiosity being my main catnip.

Besides that, I've always had a thing for redheads and independent, smart introverts. I had no idea, but I was about to meet a woman who hit every box on the checklist. Not a perfect woman by any means, but perfect for me.

For a while, we faced opposite directions, eyeing our separate passions. I was trying to check out a new book on paranormal investigation techniques but found myself increasingly distracted by my growing awareness of her standing near me.

My radar pinged like crazy, and I questioned it. She steadily inched closer. Was she getting in my space on purpose, trying to signal something—maybe an invitation to start a chat?

My radar may have worked fine, but I was clueless about what came next. While I schemed and plotted and pictured scenarios, she broke the ice.

"What are you reading?"

I smiled and showed her the cover.

"Ghost hunting, huh?" she said.

"What about you?"

She blushed. "Oh, it's just a book about how quantum mechanics is challenging what we think we know about causality."

It was adorable how she thought *she* was the weird one for her reading choices.

I fell in love right then, which explains what I said next.

"I have an idea. I'll buy that book, and you buy mine, and we'll talk about them over dinner."

And now we're married. We like to tell people the story of how we met. Usually, I'm the one telling it, and the people I tell it to are my friends. That's the thing about extroverts and introverts. The extrovert usually sets the agenda.

All along, we've been on my trip. Claire always seemed to enjoy it, and a lot of our marriage's chemistry relies on me being the dreamer and her the curmudgeon. She appears to like the way I draw her out of her shell to pursue off-the-wall ideas and other things a scientific mind would consider forbidden fruit.

But it's always been my trip. It may give her a sugar high, but in the end, she can't live on it.

I'm only realizing this now, thanks to Dr. Flick, a trip through the labyrinth, and Claire taking off alone on her dangerous quest. I had no idea she wasn't happy with being on *Fade to Black*. Had no clue she'd stopped even trying at paranormal investigation and had been just debunking. Hadn't even imagined all this was intellectually stifling her and keeping her from dreaming her own dreams.

When I find you, Claire, I'll be the husband you need. I'll listen more closely and help you pursue your own dreams. You're everything to me, and I promise I'll do better to earn your love. When I find you, I'll take you back home if you want, or if you want to stay, we can keep going, all the way to the end.

I'll stand at your side, without expecting you to complete me anymore.

But first, I must reach you, and I won't quit until I do.

I don't want to lose you the moment I truly found you.

FADE TO BLACK

PROD: Ep. 13, "Paranormal Research Foundation, Part 3"

Raw Video Footage

Tuesday, 9:26 a.m.

Claire smiles down at the camera lens, her face filling the screen in extreme close-up. Her hair is a shambles. Overall, she looks exhausted but jubilant to a level where she is almost shining.

 Claire: Get ready to explode!

The camera spins around only to come right back to her manic leer.

 Claire: Seriously, you *might* want to sit down for this.

Another spin, settling on a wall covered in chalked graffiti, its bottom illuminated by scattered chemlights.

 Claire: Eureka.

As she moves closer, we see it is not graffiti but densely written symbols.

 Claire: At first, I thought they were runes. But they aren't. They're equations. *(she points to a section)* This is a solution to the sum of three cubes problem first posed in the third century.

The symbols, however, appear undecipherable in the footage, blurry and shifting. If Claire does in fact see equations, we cannot.

Claire: Pretty cool, huh? Now check this out.

The camera pans to show that the wall goes on to the left until disappearing in the darkness. Then it moves again to reveal the symbols sprawling in all directions.

Claire: A little ways down that way is Stephen Hawking's mathematical proof that black holes exist, reinforcing Einstein's theory of—

Radio (*Shawn Roebuck's calm, murmuring voice*): Everything we do is about freedom.

Claire: Shush...I wonder what Hawking would make of this place. There is a singularity here. Zero being divided by zero. A point in time and space where the laws of physics crash and burn and stop making sense. A physical paradox. (*laughs*) The one thing this wall can't explain is itself.

Radio: If you're free, you can be anything—

Claire: I said, shush—

Radio: You should live your life dancing as if nobody's watching. Even if your dance is to music only you can hear.

Claire lets out a loud sigh.

Radio: Your dance is not an idea but a process, a way of living. Freedom lives in the soul. You're always groovy because you pick the groove.

Claire: That's very interesting. Are you done now?

The radio does not answer.

> **Claire:** Good...If this wall ends anywhere, I haven't found
> it yet. (*with reverence*) All human knowledge is here, the
> answers to all our questions. This is it—
> **Radio:** Are *you* free, baby?
> **Claire:** Not with you bothering me, I'm not. Say one more
> word, and I guarantee I will break this radio. I will kick
> it into next week.

The radio goes silent again.

> **Claire:** And to answer your question, yes, I am free. It's
> why I'm here.
> **Radio** (*older man's voice*)**:** You show so much promise as a sci-
> entist, Claire.
> **Claire** (*startled*)**:** Dr. Godwin?

*It does appear to be the voice of Ramsay Godwin, the Virginia Tech physics
professor with whom she reportedly had the closest academic relationship.*

> **Radio:** Not only for your intellect, which is considerable,
> but for your grounded spirit. At a young age, you already
> think like a scientist.
> **Claire:** Okay, spirit. If you want to tell me something, just
> spell it out.

*She sounds angry, but she is obviously a little shaken by her old
professor's voice appearing on the radio. As far as she knows, Dr.
Godwin is very much alive.*

> **Radio:** You harness your imagination to reason.

No doubt she is wondering if this place is occupied by the dead or something else, something that mimics humanity to push its victims to either truth or madness. Or maybe both.

Claire: You know, you could actually be useful and help me figure out how I'm going to capture all the data before my batteries give out. There's so much here.

Radio: The world needs trailblazers like Einstein and Hawking, men and women who think outside the box and indeed redefine its very parameters. The true advance of science, however, depends on the hearty, dependable pioneers who cultivate and grow our knowledge a bit at a time.

Claire: What do you know?

She has seemingly decided it does not matter who is behind the voices. She is no longer shaken but entirely angry now.

Radio: Like grains of sand trickling through an hourglass—

Claire: You don't know me at all.

Radio: In every tiny grain, I see the march of progress.

Claire: I could be a trailblazer. I could think outside the box.

Radio: I see—

Claire smashes the radio against the floor. A shard of plastic spins away. She snarls and kicks at the rest.

Claire: I'm free.

FADE TO BLACK
PROD: Ep. 13, "Paranormal Research Foundation, Part 3"
Raw Video Footage
Tuesday, 9:49 a.m.

Jake stares into the camera lens. Even in the gray night vision, it is easy to see that his face is haggard, his eyes wide with fear.

> **Jake:** If anybody ever watches this, I want you to know I did everything right. It's not fair. I came down here to help a friend. I was doing the right thing.

He pauses in his whispered monologue to rub his face, which twists into a grimace.

> **Jake:** The floor just dropped out from under me. I literally walked right off a cliff. My own damn, stupid fault. When you're in a maze, you *keep your eye on the path*. But I thought I'd seen something move ahead of me. I thought it was Claire, started to—

His head jerks to the side, ear cocked as if listening. For a full minute, he says nothing before turning back. The camera's directional microphone picks up his heavy breathing and, behind it, the pulsing hum of the maze.

> **Jake:** I don't know how long the drop was. It probably

only lasted a second or two, but it felt like forever to me. I came down pretty hard. I'm okay, but my left foot hurts like hell, and it's swelling up. I think I sprained it. I can walk on it, kinda, but—

He twists his neck again to glare off-screen for several seconds.

Jake: But I can't go back the way I came. Nobody answers on the radio. In short, I might be good and truly screwed. It's so stupid. So goddamn stupid. I'm lost, and I broke my one rule, which is survival first. To make—

He stops again and frowns, muttering something inaudible. When this piece of raw footage became public and was bootlegged to YouTube, the large majority of commenters agreed with the speculation he said, "Can't be him, can't be, can't be."

Jake takes a shuddering breath and releases it in a long, wavering sigh.

Jake: To make things worse, somebody's in here with me. I keep hearing them stomping around like they're wearing heavy boots. I called out a couple times, but nobody answered. I'm—

A gunshot roars somewhere in the maze, impossibly loud. The sound rolls through the maze. Jake flinches.

Jake: Jesus. I can't believe this is happening.

More gunshots erupt in the distance.

Jake: That has to be Kevin.

He pauses to listen again, but silence has returned.

Jake: He sounds close. I'm going to try to find him. I never thought I'd be so happy to hear a gunshot.

Kevin Linscott's Journal

I wish I could show you where I am right now, because it's mind-bending. But Claire stole my camera, part of the aggravating mess she made. I really hope somebody finds her so I can throw her back down the goddamn stairs.

Since I can't show you, I'll describe what I'm seeing in writing while I wait for the thing to go away before I turn back. As long as I stay away from the mirrors, it leaves me alone. Either it's real, or I'm losing my marbles.

Either way, this isn't good. In fact, this is a crap sandwich.

I'm sitting in a mirrored maze. While walking through it, your image multiplies in all directions, smaller and smaller reflections that run off into infinity. On top of my other woes, it gave me a royal headache. It was creepy and disorienting as hell to see endless versions of me gaping back from a black void.

I ran into this stupid maze pretty soon after leaving the stairs. My first thought was only an idiot would try to navigate such a place, but I'd only just gotten started, so I gave it the college try so I could say I did. Using a black marker, I tagged the glass at each corner with a number in a circle and dropped chemlights in between, playing it smart and safe.

I made it up to nine when I spotted the thing in the mirror.

I don't know how to describe it. Most of it was wispy, like gray smoke, flickering in and out of perception. I had an impression of horns and teeth. Long stringy hair. I didn't notice much because all I could really see was its glowing eyes at the middle of that smoky whirlwind.

Little pools of red fire. Not red like real fire but a burning, bright, angry red. The eyes were "filled with hate," I'm tempted to say, but it was worse than that. They looked at me as if yanking me apart atom by atom was just something the thing had to do because it had been created for this one purpose.

Just for me.

For a moment, I could only stare at it, wondering if it was real or a trick of the tiny amount of light I'm carrying around with me. Pareidolia run amok and playing tricks on my eyes, showing me my own worst fears.

Then it growled.

You probably think that I'm tough. You have to be to work Philly's rougher beats as a police officer. You'd have to be to come down here into this black hole. When I looked in the mirror at all the copies of a big former cop in a golf shirt, utility vest, and *FTB* ballcap, I saw a guy I would not mess with for all the money.

I am not ashamed to say, though, I ran yelling my head off after seeing that thing and hearing its snarl. I didn't just run, I ran blindly, deeper into the maze, while the thing popped up over and over in the glass everywhere I looked.

Each time, it appeared closer to my reflection. I knew that if it reached one of the me's in the mirror, it'd pop into existence right next to the real me and get to tearing.

My training took over. My nine-millimeter appeared in my hand, safety off and already shooting. The gunshot sounded impossibly loud in my ears, which even now are still ringing. The mirror exploded. I wheeled and blew the next into pieces.

Now I sit in this hallway filled with broken glass, wondering when it will be safe to try to go back. Wondering if I've gotten myself lost, the one thing you don't want to be in a maze with a horned, hairy monster after you.

I thought Claire with her obsession had made every horror movie mistake. Now it's my turn, and despite all my street smarts and training, I made the one that really matters. Never go running off into unfamiliar territory without marking your way back.

But hey, I'm alive. Still in one piece. What the movies don't show, can't show, is how genuinely terrified a man can become at the prospect of being ripped to shreds by something that doesn't know mercy. All I could think about—if I'd been thinking at all, which, no, I hadn't been—was running like hell.

Because I know what the thing is. I knew it from the start.

The Philly demon finally caught up to me.

All these years, while I hunted ghosts, the thing hunted me. It watched and learned. Then it waited patiently for me to arrive at this house.

If it doesn't go away, the only way I'm getting out of here is through it.

Countless Jakes holding video cameras at hip level stare back at their own camera lens, alternating normal and reverse images in an endless, receding line.

An infinity of blond beards, muscled and tattooed arms, and FTB ballcaps. An infinity of black T-shirts tucked into an infinity of jeans, the shirts printed with "Updog Awareness Foundation."

A humorous invitation to ask, "What's updog?"

The Jakes shake their heads in unison.

> **Jake:** A hall of mirrors. (*utter sarcasm*) This just gets better and better.

A gunshot booms somewhere in the maze. The camera pivots toward the sound only to face its own lens again at the next mirrored corner. Jake stumbles a little on his sprain, hopping on his good foot.

> **Jake:** Kevin? (*shouts*) Yo, Kev!
> **Radio:** You got it coming, kid.
> **Jake:** Kev?

Radio: You got it coming.
Jake: It can't be—this isn't funny, bro. Where are you?

Another gunshot thuds through the air, farther away this time.

Radio: Do you know what time it is, Jacob?

Jake pulls the radio from his belt and holds it up for inspection.

Jake: Dad?
Radio: It's payback time.
Jake: Jesus.
Radio: Think how tall I'll be.
Jake: Can we not do this?
Radio: When I'm standing on your teeth.

Jake drops the radio and stomps it repeatedly until it shatters into pieces.

Jake: You know where *I'm* gonna stand, mother—? Jesus.
  I'm arguing with a dead man. It's not real. It's not real.
  It can't be real.
Voice: Come on over here, Jacob.

The camera pivots to face the far end of the mirrored corridor. Despite the Steadicam, the view trembles. Jake's body is shaking uncontrollably.

Just under his heavy breaths, we can hear the heavy stomp of boots, which stop just beyond the bend.

Voice: I want to show you something.

Jake sags, as if resigned.

Jake: You're never going to leave me alone, are you.
Voice: I ain't gonna hit you. It's good. You'll like it.

A utility knife with a three-inch blade flickers in the frame before disappearing.

Jake: Be right there, Dad.

Jake Wolfson's Journal

My past has come back to haunt me. Just in case: GOODBYE.

Dad keeps beckoning me forward, only to disappear each time. Like a dutiful son, I follow his voice deeper and deeper into the maze.

As always, the waiting is the worst part. I keep following because I just want to get it over with. The sucker punch.

I don't think I'm leaving this place.

There's nobody outside of here I want to say goodbye to, nobody who would really care to hear it. Nobody who will really miss me, which is good in one way as nobody will get hurt, but it's also a crappy thing to realize. Seriously crappy.

That just leaves Claire, Matt, Jessica, and Kevin. Maybe they'll miss me.

I hope they can all get out of here, even if I can't.

I really wish I'd done more. I wish I loved somebody. I just never could. Even after I escaped Dad, he still won. Still sucker punched me anytime I wanted to take a chance on having more. It's my own damn fault. I let him beat me even after I left him in the dust, even after they put him in the ground.

Just like those Flick assholes said.

Reading that brutal takedown of a personality I'd kept locked up safe and sound all these years, I thought, okay, maybe I'll try to open up more. Show Flick and the other Flick who's the real boss of me. Reach out to the people on this show and make myself more available. Try to get to know them better.

This time, I was a part of the story. We were all in it together, I thought.

When Claire disappeared, I thought: This is my chance to step up. Now look where that got me. The biggest sucker punch of all.

If anybody ever reads this, whoever you are, please consider me a friend. Wish me luck. Good luck to you too. And if you can, get the hell out of here right now.

He's calling again.

I have to go now. GOODBYE.

Matt Kirklin's Journal

The last time I tried Claire on the walkie-talkie, I heard a faint female voice hissing in the ether. I actually started sobbing.

I'm here, Claire... Come in, please... It's Matt, I'm here...

But it wasn't my wife.

Do you want to play with me, Matt?

Exactly how I remember Tammy's voice.

Let's play something.

Normally, I'd like that. I'd like it very much.

Finding Claire is all I care about right now, however. Sorry, spirits. You set up this whole labyrinth to force me to think about what's really important to me, and guess what, it's the living, not you. It's Claire.

I found the perfect spot, Matt!

I don't mind Tammy sticking around, though. I charged down here on pure anger and determination only to wind up far, far from where I started and with nothing to show for it. I'm starting to shake with helpless frustration, one second away from losing it. One second away from shutting down and giving up.

I twirl the wedding band around my ring finger again and again, trying to squeeze more hope from what it symbolizes for me.

I bet you can't find me.

Only two chemlights left, enough to search a little farther. I have enough battery power to keep searching after that, but it won't last forever, and I have a long, long way to go to get back, if the way back is still there.

By now, the others should have started their return. I pray they're okay.

As for me, I hope I have the energy to go on. Trail mix and water are keeping me going, but that's not what I'm talking about. I'm talking about mental energy. With each step I take deeper into the maze, I feel this crushing sense of despair and dread. I'm not utterly lost yet, but I might as well be.

You're not even trying, Matt!

Obviously, I'm stressed out about being here and worried sick about Claire, but on a hunch, I took out the EMF meter and did a reading.

I don't know if I like you anymore.

Sure enough, it's maxed out. My guess is the actual level is very, very high right now.

The presence of the spirits or something else here is acting as an electromagnetic field pump. Maybe it's part of that annoying background hum that only grows louder the farther I go. Some types of EMF can produce fear in people. They make you uneasy and feel like you're being watched. In extreme cases, you wind up paranoid, crying your eyes out, and absolutely terrified.

EMF can even make you hallucinate ghosts.

You were a lot more fun before you grew up!

That I can agree with. Back then, the spirit world was fun and friendly, something I'd spend a lifetime wanting to know better. They weren't entities that lured people underground only to set them loose in a maze, like rats.

"You're not the real Tammy anyway," I said. "You're just another trick."

I should get back on my feet, but I don't know where to look. I'm starting to worry that Claire might be gone forever, consumed by this horrible place. I twirl the wedding band around my finger, but this time it only feels like dead metal.

The tears have finally come, and they won't stop—

Wait.

Thank God.

Tammy just said... *I know where Claire is.*

She says that she'll take me to my wife. She says she feels sorry for me sitting here crying all by myself. She says she's going to help me.

I already know what you're going to say, so don't say it.

What choice do I have?

FADE TO BLACK

PROD: Ep. 13, "Paranormal Research Foundation, Part 3"

Raw Video Footage

Tuesday, 10:36 a.m.

Still shooting at hip level, the camera lurches with Jake's limping gait past infinities of himself reflected in mirrored glass. He does not care anymore about capturing footage, only using the camera as a flashlight.

> **Jake:** If you aren't gonna show yourself, I'm leaving. You win. I'm going home.

The voice of his father does not answer. Jake stops to lean on his knees, sucking air into his lungs.

> **Jake:** The fighting sucked, but I could handle it. What I hated was the waiting. The endless... You know what?

The maze is silent.

> **Jake:** I know you aren't my dad. Pretending you are is just mean. We came here to play, and we thought you were good with that. But you're cruel.

No answer.

> **Jake:** I don't get why you sat here all these years waiting to

be a dick. If the idea is to scare me, you win. I'm scared shitless. Good for you. Now let me go home.

Silence.

Jake: Thank—
Voice: I couldn't handle getting older.
Jake: What?
Voice: Getting older, son. You reminded me of every mistake I ever made. I wanted to be you. A clean slate. If I couldn't, I wanted you to end up like me.
Jake (*wearily*)**:** It's all good, Dad.
Voice: I'm trying to explain—
Jake: I forgive you, okay? You win. Just let me leave.
Voice: Let me finish, son. I'm trying to explain why I'm gonna wear your face.
Jake: PLEASE, JUST LET ME LEAVE.
Voice: I'll be alive and young again, wearing your pretty—

A gunshot booms close by.

Jake: Just stop. Please. Just stop.
Voice: It ain't like you're using it for anything worthwhile. You know what they say, youth is wasted on the—

A man's voice screams in the maze.

Jake: Kevin?

The scream turns into howls of terror.

Voice: I wouldn't go help him if I were you.

Jake: Kevin! Hang on!

The camera swims up and down as Jake limps down the corridor.

Jake: Yo, Kev! Where are you?

Loping around the corner, he hesitates. The mirrors here are funhouse mirrors, showing himself as fat, skinny, short, tall.

Jake looks back at himself with a grotesquely large head.

Jake: Fuck this place—

Kevin howls again. Another gunshot, even louder this time, followed by stomping feet. He is close. Just around the bend, in fact.

Jake: I'm coming, Kev!

He turns the corner and rears at an incredible scene, one of the most analyzed in all the Foundation House footage. Kevin stands at the end of a corridor surrounded by funhouse mirrors, two of which are shattered to expose plain stonework. His back to the camera, he shouts and waves his gun.

In the mirror he faces, an apparition swirls like intricate gusts of gray smoke against a window. Jake is recording the scene at 30 frames per second, which over the next four seconds is 120 frames. In each frame, the apparition completely changes.

A claw appears, reaching. Curved horns. Swishing tail. Hairy animal form. Long-toothed snarl. Clouds of gray smoke.

Rolling as continuous video, these images form a swirling, disjointed, nightmare vision broken only once to show, for a single frame only, a tall, skinny man wearing a hoodie that shrouds his face in shadow.

The only element that remains consistent in every frame is a pair of eyes, glowing red like coals.

Kevin is crying. The apparition snarls, a deafening staccato that sounds like the coughing muffler of a souped-up sports car.

The mirror explodes in a spray of glass as Kevin shoots it.

Jake (*barely audible over the noise*)**:** Kevin, it's me, I'm coming!

He lurches forward, closing the distance rapidly. He reaches out to grip Kevin's shoulder. Kevin wheels on him with a high-pitched scream. The gun fires with a blinding flash.

The camera falls with a burst of electronic noise and then nothing.

Jessica Valenza's Journal

NOT FAIR.

I went back all the way to the beginning, only it wasn't there.

When I reached the last door, I ran at it laughing.

Beyond it, though, the tunnel just kept going.

Right back to this door marked NO PIGS.

Somehow, I'd gotten turned around.

On the way back, the hippie messages, scrawled on opposite sides of the tunnel, seemed to mock me:

YOU'RE EITHER ON THE BUS OR OFF THE BUS!

!SUB EHT FFO RO SUB EHT NO REHTIE ER'UOY

Soon, I reached the door marked NO PIGS.

NOT FAIR.

NOT FAIR, NOT FAIR, NOT FAIR.

RIAF TON.

I don't know how long I've been walking. My watch stopped when I passed through the last door. It's like time itself stopped. Nothing moves here except me. Nothing makes sound. It's like I'm walking through a picture. A dead simulation.

When I get to the beginning, I start over. When I reach the end, I'm back at the beginning. Changing directions doesn't help. It's always the same. The wall curves to the left. Then it curves to the right.

Like a hamster on a wheel, huffing and puffing, thinking she's getting somewhere. I'm going out of my fucking mind.

For a while, I cursed every bad decision I made, from taking the contract for this dumb show right up to refusing to stay with the others. At some point, I started monologuing. I don't need a camera after all to perform. I no longer feel watched or followed, but I'm hoping the spirits are there if only for the sense of company. In horror movies, the ghost tortures the girl until the girl has some epiphany or unlocks some mystery, and finally the spirit can rest.

Oh, you poor ghost. You had such a sad life. I understand. I'll make sure your moldy bones are properly buried and your murderer is brought to justice. You can sleep now. And in helping you, I learned a valuable lesson about my own life. Thank you.

Roll credits.

Only this isn't a movie.

I tried everything. Ad-libbed monologues fueled by every phase of grief except acceptance. Nothing has worked.

I've done the loop six times, pausing only to rest here and there, maybe sleep a little. Strangely, I'm not hungry. I barely get tired. I don't seem to need water.

My flashlight, however, is dying.

Kevin Linscott's Journal

Officer-involved shooting. Here's my incident report.

This report is generated to notate the death by police of Jake Wolfson. I prepared it for the review authority investigating this incident.

During a foot pursuit, the demonic entity failed to comply with verbal commands. In the ensuing altercation, Jake Wolfson approached me from behind with a utility knife held in a threatening manner.

Fearing for my safety, I discharged my firearm, striking Wolfson. Without means to notify ambulatory services, I checked his vitals and pronounced him.

FADE TO BLACK
PROD: Ep. 13, "Paranormal Research Foundation, Part 3"
Raw Video Footage
Tuesday, 10:47 a.m.

In extreme close-up, Kevin's stubbled face stares blankly past the lens of the camera held in his lap.

    Kevin: I don't. I don't.

He frowns. It turns into a pained wince.

    Kevin: I don't...

He stares into empty space again for several minutes.

    Kevin: I don't know why I wrote all that. The whole thing was an accident.

He turns away, his face contorting with wracking sobs.

    Kevin: Why'd you have to sneak up on me like that? Running at me with a knife in your hand and grabbing me like that? Stupid idiot.

The sobbing gains steam until he can't control it. He buries his face in his hands.

Kevin: I'm sorry I gave you a hard time, kid.

He lies on his side with his back to the camera and curls into a tight ball, crying.

Kevin: I'm sorry, sorry, sorry, SORRY.

He lets it out for several minutes, his body heaving. Slowly, he pushes himself back to a sitting position. He wipes at his eyes and sniffs.

Kevin: If it's any consolation, I think I'll be joining you soon. I don't think any of us are getting out of here.

He closes his eyes and breathes deeply for another few minutes. The underground world's background hum appears to surge in volume.

His eyes flash open. Holding up his nine-millimeter handgun, he ejects the magazine, gives it a brief inspection, and tosses it aside.

This done, he reaches into his backpack and pulls out a fresh magazine. He slides it into the well.

Kevin: If I'm going down, I'll go down fighting.

Another gold sound bite, though this time, he is not playing to the camera. This is the real Kevin. He stands and takes the camera with him, which briefly sweeps over Jake's frozen, bullet-ridden corpse lying facedown on a bloody carpet of broken glass, one hand outstretched and one sightless eye open.

Then he chambers a round in the gun.

Kevin: If there's a way to kill these things, I'm going to do it.

FADE TO BLACK
PROD: Ep. 13, "Paranormal Research Foundation, Part 3"
Raw Video Footage
Tuesday, 12:18 p.m.

Matt walks down another narrow path bound in stone.
The camera swings on his hip. Ahead, in the distance,
we hear Tammy singing, her child's voice echoing down the
passageway.

>**Tammy:** Matt and Claire, sittin' in a tree, K-I-S-S-I-N-G.
>First comes love—
>**Matt:** Where is Claire? We've been walking a long time.
>**Tammy:** It's a really big ol' place, my good ol' buddy pal.
>**Matt:** Can I ask you something?
>**Tammy:** You're going to ask me something boring.
>**Matt:** What's this all for?

Tammy's laughter floats through the air, loud and close.

>**Matt:** What's the point?
>**Tammy** (*in mocking imitation*)**:** What's the point?
>**Matt:** I want to know why you're doing this to us.
>**Tammy:** I want to know why you're, uh, doing this to us.
>**Matt:** We just wanted to talk to you.
>**Tammy:** We just wanted to talk to *you*!
>**Matt:** Shut up. I'm sick of it.

Tammy's laughter fades away. Matt gasps, which turns into a single heartbreaking sob.

Twenty yards ahead, a shape sprawls on the floor.

Matt: Claire?

For a few moments, he does not move, as if too afraid of what he will discover.

Matt: CLAIRE!

The camera's view swims as he rushes forward.

The shape is a woman lying curled on her side, her long, dark hair splayed above her head, her face fixed in the rictus of a final scream.

Matt (*whispers*): Gloria Flick.

The camera lingers on her leathery, mummified features. The light flashes on her open eyes, which eternally gape into the dark, glassy and unseeing.

Matt: I'm close to the end now.

The grating hum is louder here, rising and falling as a steady background roar, like the tidal ebb and flow of a cosmic sea.

Claire (*a distant echo*): Matt?

He jumps, utterly startled.

Matt: Claire? Is that you?

Claire: I'm in here! Follow my voice.

*Shouting to each other, at last Matt enters a vast room, a
dizzying sight after so much time in the maze's claustrophobic
passageways.*

Claire waits for him there, smiling.

Matt (*sobbing*)**:** Claire!

*Before she can say a word, he rushes to envelop her in a crushing hug
while she laughs.*

Matt: I can't believe I found you.

Claire: You weren't supposed to come after me. You should
have gone back.

Matt: I couldn't leave you. Did you think I could just leave
you?

Claire: I'm glad you came.

*She chuckles, but he refuses to let go of her, as if he believes she will
disappear again if he does.*

Matt: You're real. God, you're so warm. I can't believe I
found you.

Claire: You're shaking.

Matt: We have to catch up with the others and get back.

Claire: I have something to show you, Matt. I found it, and
now I get to share it with you.

Matt: Found what?

Claire: Everything. Come look.

At last, reluctantly, he lets her go. She takes him by the hand and leads him to the vast wall, a section of it illuminated with chemlights.

The wall is covered in blurry, writhing symbols.

> **Claire:** You won't believe the knowledge I've discovered here.
> **Matt:** You can read this?
> **Claire** (*giggles*): Of course, silly. It's science. The language of the universe. And this is its encyclopedia.

Matt hesitates. Clearly, he cannot reconcile her manic giddiness with the precariousness of their situation. And the wall does not make sense to him.

> **Matt:** Honey? All I see are what look like Nordic runes.
> **Claire:** They're equations, darling. They're ...

In a daze, she stumbles to the wall.

> **Claire:** But ...

She plants her hands against the symbols, which smear at her touch.

> **Claire:** I don't understand.

Her voice has become like a small child's, a child who is alone and lost. Her head jerks in all directions as she frantically searches more of the wall. She emits a heartbreaking moan.

> **Matt:** Are you okay?

Claire: They were just here. (*cups her head in her hands as if trying to keep it from exploding*) No. No, no, NO.

Matt: This place...It was a trick.

Claire: They were *here*. I *saw* them. I was just looking at a beautiful solution to Erdős's sunflower conjecture. It was right here. It's *gone*.

Matt: I understand. I'm sorry.

Claire (*laughs bitterly*): Understand? I was holding the entirety of human knowledge in my fingers, and now it's gone! How can you *understand*?

Matt: I do—

Claire: You ruined it!

Matt: You know I didn't. It—

Claire: You showed up, and they took it all away!

Matt: Claire, listen to me. It was just another trick.

Facing the now empty wall, she raises trembling fists, and for several moments, it appears she is about to try to pound it down. Instead, her hands splay into claws—

And begin scratching at the stone with a nauseating scrabbling sound.

Claire: FUUUUUUUUCK.

Matt lunges forward, his voice wobbly with panic.

Matt: No! Stop!

She shrugs away his hands to stand alone, shaking. She gapes at her bloody fingers.

Her eyes glaze over.

Claire: All gone.

She slowly crumples to her knees and bends until her forehead touches the floor. Matt kneels next to her and places his hand gently atop her heaving back.

Matt: I'm sorry. We were wrong to come here. This place is trying to break us. The others have already started back for the house. We have to go too.

She remains on the ground for several minutes, taking long, shuddering breaths.

At last, she speaks.

Claire: We can still do it.
Matt: Do what? We've got to get out of here now.

She rises to her hands and knees, still struggling to control her breathing.

Claire: We have to finish what we started. It's what they want and what we want.
Matt: What I want is for us to get out of here safely.
Claire: It's not going to let us. Not until it gives us its message.
Matt: I tried. I asked it point-blank. The answer is there is no answer.

She rises to her feet, slowly, as if unsure of her legs, that the ground under her is substantial, or both. Matt rises with her.

Claire: There's always an answer. We have to find the source.

Matt: The source?

Claire: That noise. The background hum. It's louder here.

Matt: Yes.

Claire: We need to follow it.

Matt: To where? This place doesn't want to show us anything real, honey. It's all a trick. All of it. A lie. None of it means anything.

Eyes blazing with manic light, she approaches and slowly reaches to cup his cheek. He flinches back at first, but then he allows it. Claire offers him a weak, sympathetic smile.

Claire: Did they break you?

He hesitates, considering his answer.

Matt: I came close to losing hope I'd ever find you. I saw Gloria Flick's dead body in the maze and thought it was you.

Claire: . . .

Matt: Yeah. They broke me.

Claire (*glances back at the wall*)**:** Me too.

Matt: Why is that important?

Claire: Because everything in this place has a purpose. Because I think it means we're ready for what comes next.

Matt: What comes next is we lose our minds or it kills us. The EMF levels—

Claire: Darling. *Matt.* There is no going back.

Matt: No. No, that can't be right. You're saying it's hopeless.

Claire: "To the end or the beginning." A labyrinth often ends in an exit. To get out of here, we have to go all the way to the end.

Again, Matt hesitates as he processes all this. At last, he comes to a decision.

Matt: Is this what you really want?
Claire (*offering a sad smile*): It's what we need. There is no other way out.
Matt: Okay.
Claire: Okay?
Matt: Okay, we'll do it. We'll go all the way to the end.

Jessica Valenza's Journal

Jessica Valenza's entries become increasingly erratic and sloppily written as they progress to fill every inch of her journal.
Chronologically, her story continues here, as it is hinted it is occurring while the other investigators are down the stairwell, though it has already also clearly diverged, as if she experienced time differently from the others once they separated.

Walking, always walking.

Like that Greek myth about the guy who rolls a rock up a hill just so it can roll right back down, only I have no rock. Me, I'd love a rock right now. A rock sounds great. It would give me something to do.

The light of protection I carry is strong.

I feel like I've been here forever. I started to fill the margins of my notebook with little slashes marking every time I walked the loop, but I gave up counting, and then my flashlight died anyway. By then, my phone was also dead, filled with endless text messages to Tameeka that I can't send. After that, I wandered the dark in the green glow of chemlights.

Which then also died, one by one, until the dark closed in.

The light of protection I carry is strong.

Something funny: It took meeting the Flicks to realize who I am and the true nature of my relationships with everyone who loves me. All so the Flicks and their friends could take it away from me only a few hours afterward. Thanks a lot.

The light of protection I carry is strong. Only I forget what light looks like. Even my memories, which I replay in my mind's eye over and over like a private movie collection, have begun to lose their color. Only when I dream do I remember, and I worry the dark will one day take that from me as well. At that time, the dark will become a part of me, and I will disappear in it forever.

When I ran into Grady, I knew I'd finally lost my final grip on sanity.

These are what I believe are my last two blank pages, so I'll end my story with his. I've gotten good at writing with blindness. I only hope my pen still has ink in it.

Not that it matters, haha. No one's ever going to read this.

All this time, I've kept walking. Why? What was the point?

To have something to do, obviously. At first, it was out of the tiny hope this might be the loop where I get out of my own personal version of *Groundhog Day*. After a while, though, I kept going for the simple pleasure of finding the next door and marking it as progress. The feel of its rough texture instead of smooth, polished stone. I worried a piece of it off with my fingernails and started cutting my arms with it, just to feel something else, even if it's pain. Each cut marking another completion of the loop.

I considered digging it across my jugular, but I couldn't give up yet. I had to get home to my son, who is wondering where his mama is.

It was at this point—realizing I still clung to hope—that I understood I'd lost my mind.

While I plodded along, someone started walking next to me. The air felt cold, another sensation I welcomed. Sweet, delicious, painful cold.

Who are you? I asked, my voice raspy from disuse.

I'm Grady. He said it in a man's deep voice.

That's my son's name.

My mother's name is Rashida, but she went by another in her acting days.

My son is four years old.

I grew up while you were gone.

Are you...gone too?

He didn't answer, and I started to get pissed off.

So I missed your life, I said. *Wow, what a cutting metaphor. Nice trope, ghosts! I'm a single mom, and I work a lot of hours. It doesn't make me a bad parent. It makes me an adult living in the United States of America.*

I made out okay, the voice answered. *I hated you for a while, but I got over it.*

Yeah, well, it's not like I didn't try to get back to you. If I missed your life, you can blame these stupid ghosts. I tried my best. I've walked a lot of miles trying to get home.

You don't owe me anything, Mama. You're free to make your own choices.

HAHAHA.

Me having choices. What a hoot!

They wanted me to tell you the way is still open, the man claiming to be my son said. *To go down the stairs and finish what you started. You can join the others who have yet to complete their testing. All you have to do is want it. They'd like you to know they think you're interesting.*

They? Who is they?

No answer.

Interesting in what way? I asked next.

You're stronger than they thought. You haven't broken.

Another trick. If they were doing this to me, I didn't want to think about what they were doing to the others. This *testing.* I knew it would mean giving up on ever getting home. *Broken.*

Am I interesting enough to let me go home to my son?

Again, he didn't answer, but it didn't make me angry this time.

If I decide to just keep walking, will you stay with me?

I'll stay with you, Mama.

That's all I want, Grady. Hold my hand.

I said, *Because I choose you. All I want is you.*

I said, *I'll never leave you again.*

I said, *Tell me about your life. What have you been up to all these years?*

His hand is dry and smooth and cold.

Wherever he goes, I will follow.

Claire Kirklin's Journal

For the smartest girl in the room, I've acted like a total fool.

Matt lies next to me, his head warm on my lap, resting before we start again. The chemlights remain where I left them, illuminating the mocking, now-blank wall.

All along, the spirits baited and teased us by showing us things that can't be known. Each glimpse they gave us only hooked us further. I'm supposed to be the girl without delusions, and they hooked me worst of all.

When Matt and I married, I was finishing up grad school, utterly absorbed in my dissertation applying data from new telescopes to confirm old models. He'd listen patiently while I worked out kinks in my methodology and vented my anxiety over whether I'd impress the thesis committee.

Would they find my thesis publishable? If published, would people find it worthwhile? I was adding to the body of scientific knowledge, which carried enormous responsibility. My PhD rode on it. The pressure was unreal.

Matt would always listen wearing his little smile. Sometimes, I'd find it irritating. *He thinks I'm being cute!* Other times, I swelled. *He's proud of me.* That's when the tradition of his waking me up with a mug of coffee started, back when I burned the midnight oil dreaming cosmological dreams.

Looking back on those years, they were the best of my life.

Before ghost hunting ruined everything.

My wants became needs, and Matt became their obstacle, and this tension became a part of my mindset. Ever since the spirits manifested at Foundation House, I've been pushing him away to chase them almost single-handedly. When I left the team to explore the dark on my own, I made what I'd been doing all along official.

Not anymore.

I no longer want all the answers on a wall; I want to go back to searching for them. Matt is with me, and the end of the maze is our ticket home. We're going to get out of here, and we're going to do it together.

Matt has always given me what I want. Once I'm back, the rest will be up to me.

FADE TO BLACK

PROD: Ep. 13, "Paranormal Research Foundation, Part 3"

Raw Video Footage

Tuesday, 3:15 p.m.

Matt and Claire walk along another passageway. They travel slowly, using infrared lights on their cameras and navigating using their camera viewfinders. The background hum is even louder here, filling the air with white noise rich with the potential for apophenia.

Matt: Did you record any of the equations? Get them on video?

Claire: Plenty.

Matt: We could, you know...

Claire: I'm afraid to play it back. I don't know if I can face it again if the whole time I was getting off on runes.

She does not know this at the time, but none of the equations on the wall that she saw and recorded are decipherable in the footage.

Matt: I'm sorry it happened. I never saw you that sad before.

Claire: I was on the wrong mission. When we came down here, we were always following their agenda, not ours.

Matt: Does it matter if you bring back the science? You saw it. It's yours now. Do you know what I mean?

Claire: I know what you mean. I don't think it really matters. What hurt the most wasn't losing the knowledge, it was that I'd barely scratched the surface. I could have spent a lifetime staring at that wall, and even then, I wouldn't have learned everything.

Matt says nothing. The background noise fills the emptiness with its throbbing aerosol roar. They are close to the source now.

Claire: What about you? Was *Fade to Black* about proving to the world that Tammy was real?

Matt: No. But yes, in a way. Not proving, though. I wanted to share it. I wanted anybody who's ever lost somebody to know the comfort my mom felt when I gave her Tammy's message. But really it was about me wanting to talk to them.

Claire: You did both.

Matt: Not really. Being taunted isn't exactly a conversation, and it's nothing I'd want to share with the world. But yeah, even if we don't... we got enough footage out to prove the spirit world exists.

Claire: And even if we don't... maybe one scientist will believe what she sees in the footage and get to work figuring out how it all works.

Matt: So we won.

Claire: We won.

Matt: But it's not over yet. We—wow. Oh, wow.

The passageway ends at a vast, open space. If it is defined by walls or ceiling, these are not visible. In the distance, a round dais rises above a black plain. On it stands a large rectangular monolith pulsing light and sound in a slow rhythmic cycle, a glowing beacon in the eternal dark.

Claire: This is it.

The beating heart of the labyrinth.

Matt (*awestruck*)**:** It's incredible.

He holds out his hand, and Claire takes it.

Matt: Ready?

A flashlight flares to life on their right.

Kevin: Are you real?

Kevin Linscott's Journal

Nobody's laughing anymore.

Police departments take 911 calls about hauntings all the time. *I can hear somebody murmuring in the walls*, the operator writes down. *Footsteps in the attic. The piano in the living room started up, but when I got downstairs, I found the room empty.*

And always: *I think somebody is here, watching me.*

Police are public servants. Even when we think a call is funny, we take it seriously. We dutifully respond to every call, even ones we know are going to be weird or end with us pandering to somebody who's not all there in the head.

Every now and then, I'd catch a ghost call, and they'd always end the same.

The house is locked up good and tight, sir and/or ma'am. We see no signs of forced entry. We don't hear anything now. We think you are safe. No, we do not have the resources to station an officer here with you overnight.

But if anything happens, you know you can call us. We'll be close by.

When I worked for the department, I rarely laughed, even at the weird stuff. Policing is a high-stress job, and I probably should have laughed more for my health, but the things I saw that weren't funny—were, in fact, soul crushing and horrible—cast a long shadow over the rest of my day and all the days after that. Over time, it really added up.

After I shot the thrashing dude in the liquor store, I couldn't think of a single thing about my job that I'd find funny enough to laugh at.

So no, I didn't take the ghost calls seriously. In fact, I considered them dumb and a drag and time wasted babysitting somebody who's high-strung or lonely.

Then I met the demon in a Philly housing block.

I couldn't talk about that call for a while. Word had gotten around I'd caught some Jeffrey Dahmer shit, and the other guys at patrol all wanted to hear the story. Even Wexler, the rookie who went around showing off, trying to impress and imitate his seniors, ended up mum about it. He turned green every time it came up. We wrote up the incident report, and then we tried to forget all about it.

Only I couldn't. I'd become convinced I'd faced a real, bona fide demon.

And I knew it would kill again.

Lieutenant Clapper agreed to see me, wearing his usual expression that said he'd patiently hear me out but reserved the right to kick me out of his office at any moment if he thought I was wasting his time.

He finally did cut me off. *Fine, Linscott. What do you want me to do about it?*

I told him I wanted to put together a special unit that would investigate paranormal activity. Instead of wasting patrol resources responding to these calls or passing scared citizens off to local paranormal investigators, the new ghost unit would handle them.

The lieutenant found the whole thing hilarious. Soon, everybody did.

Now I'm sitting outside a maze staring at a glowing white monolith that appears to be the bull's-eye point in a huge underground world populated by spirits intent on destroying us, mind and body, one by one.

Anybody laughing now?

Anybody want to make a *Ghostbusters* joke about crossing the streams?

No? No haha? Not even a single chuckle?

I didn't think so. Yeah, now you believe me. Now you know I actually do understand my business.

I'm writing in my journal to kill time before I finally act. My hope is Matt and Claire will follow the same hum I did and find their way here. They'll see what I can do. They'll have their cameras with them, so everybody can see.

You'll see that I'll never be afraid again.

I'm sick of dancing to this demon's tune. No, I'm not afraid of it anymore. In fact, it should be very afraid of me. I'm alive, and what is that demon? Literally smoke and mirrors. I'm armed with the kind of weapons that can hurt its kind.

Get ready for real leadership, the kind we should have had from the beginning on this job. Cool, collected, and proactive. Unafraid to take the offensive.

You are all about to find out what I'm really made of.

FADE TO BLACK

PROD: Ep. 13, "Paranormal Research Foundation, Part 3"

Raw Video Footage

Tuesday, 3:20 p.m.

Kevin walks into the beams of Matt and Claire's IR lights and becomes visible on Matt's camera.

> **Kevin:** I asked if you're real.

He looks like a zombie version of himself, his face taut with stress, his eyes glimmering, deranged and hungry.

Matt replies with a relieved chuckle.

> **Matt:** I guess we should ask you the same thing.

Kevin's burning gaze shifts to Claire.

> **Kevin:** It looks like you found your lady. I'm happy to see it.
> **Claire:** I'm glad you're okay too.
> **Matt:** Have you seen Jake? Did he go back?

Kevin grimaces and looks away.

> **Kevin:** Jake ran into a big problem.
> **Matt:** What does that mean? Is he okay?

Kevin (*angrily*): No. He is not *okay*.

Matt: What happened?

Kevin shakes his head.

Kevin: We were seeing things. Bad things.

Matt: Me too. I mean, I heard them.

Kevin: You know how I told you about the demon I faced in Philly?

Matt: We know that story.

Kevin: Well, it followed us here.

Claire: Kevin, I don't understand what you're saying. What happened to Jake?

Kevin: He's dead. The demon tore him apart.

Matt: What?

Claire: Oh God.

No one speaks for some time. Matt starts to say something but cannot find the words. Claire bends with her hands on her hips, taking shuddering breaths, on the verge of being physically sick.

Kevin: I tried to help him, but I couldn't reach him in time.

Claire: It's just hard to believe he's dead. Really dead. This is *Jake* we're talking about. He's dead?

Matt: Even after everything, I thought this was all still a game of sorts.

Claire: I don't think it was ever a game.

Matt: Not a game. No. But I mean, I didn't think it would kill one of us.

Kevin sets his jaw in determination.

Kevin: Well, it did. As for me, I waited for you. Now I'm taking you back.

Claire: That's where we're headed. The door.

Kevin: Door? What door?

Claire (*points at the distant monolith*)**:** That. I think of it as a door. A portal.

Matt: Claire believes it may be the exit.

Claire: It's how we get home. Or maybe to the next level. Either way, it's our best shot at getting out of here.

Kevin responds with a condescending chuckle, like a father who is both amused by and fed up with his errant children.

Kevin: Yeah, that's a no go, lady. I'd say you and our great leader here screwed the pooch enough already thinking these fuckers play fair.

Claire: What's that supposed to mean?

Kevin: For one, if you hadn't run off, Jake would still be here.

Claire (*steps back as if struck*)**:** You were all supposed to go back.

Kevin: Thanks to your hubby here, we didn't.

Matt (*patiently*)**:** I made it perfectly clear I was all too happy to go it alone. I stopped being anybody's leader the second I got on those stairs.

Kevin: And that worked out so well for everybody. It worked out really well for Jake.

Matt: That's not fair, and you know it.

Kevin: You can't just walk away from leadership, chief. Anyway, there aren't gonna be any spirits, anyway. Not after I'm done with them.

Matt: What are you going to do?

Kevin: I'm going to kill them for what they did to Jake.
Claire: Look, you can do whatever you want. I'm going to the door.

Kevin pulls up his shirt and slowly draws his handgun from his waistband. Claire freezes at the sight of it.

Kevin: Yeah. I'm gonna have to ask you to stay put.
Matt: What the...?
Claire: Where the hell did you get a gun?
Kevin: Shut up and listen. You're staying put right here.
Claire: And you can go straight to hell, Kevin.

Kevin taps the gun against his thigh, as if itching to use it again.

Matt: Claire, please. Kev, what are you planning to do?
Kevin: Sit down and find out.
Matt: Fine. We'll sit.

The camera's viewpoint drops with him. For a moment, Claire glares in defiance, but her husband gives her hand a tug, and she sits as well.

Satisfied, Kevin crouches to unzip his backpack and pulls out a bundling stick.

Matt: Sage?
Kevin: Yup.

The sage used in bundling sticks is often of the California white variety. When burned, it produces a smell that calls to mind bitter herbs and woodsmoke.

Matt: Don't do this, Kev.
Kevin: Too bad. I'm going to kill your precious ghosts.

Thumbing a lighter until it flames, he lights one end of the bundle,
which begins to smoke.

Matt: I just think picking a fight we can't win is not a great
idea right now.
Kevin: What was it you said before? Oh yeah. You aren't
in charge anymore.

He stands with the smoking bundle, gun gripped tightly in his other
hand.

Claire: Matt's right. Smudging isn't going to work here.

Smudging is an ancient method of cleansing an area of negative spirits
and energies, connecting to the spirit world, and enhancing intuition.

Kevin: I think the last thing we need right now is your science.
Claire: All you're doing is shooting spitballs at it.
Kevin: Let's just say this ain't the only weapon in my
arsenal. And this ain't my first trip to the rodeo.

Waving the smoking bundle over his head, he marches around the
space.

Kevin: I am cleansing this place! All negative spirits must
leave! I am cleansing this place!

It seems pathetic, words and sage smoke against the radiant monolith
in the background and the vast world it created, but there is something

oddly heroic about it. Kevin is using these meager weapons because they are all he has.

Using them, he is fighting back. This is his stand.

Kevin: I order you to leave, negative spirits! I am cleansing—

A voice calls out from the distance.

Kevin: What was that?
Voice (*barely audible*): You SHOT me, bro!

Kevin blanches, shrinking back from the voice. When it speaks again, it is louder.

Voice: I'm dying over here! Why'd you shoot me?
Matt: Jake?
Kevin: It was an accident! You came at me with a goddamn knife!
Claire (*snarls in disgust*): You son of a bitch.
Voice: I was trying to *help* you! You shot me!
Kevin (*roaring*): It was self-defense!
Claire: You lying son of a—
Matt: Kev. *Kev.*

Kevin is breathing hard, almost hyperventilating at the edge of panic.

Matt: Kevin!
Kevin: What—what?
Matt: Is it at all possible that's the real Jake?
Kevin (*shakes his head*): It can't be.
Voice: Can somebody please help me?

Matt: You're in charge, Kevin. What now?

Kevin wags his head, breaking free of his panic. He sets his jaw again.

> **Kevin:** New plan. You're getting your wish. We're going to your spirit door.
> **Matt:** Okay, good—
> **Kevin:** I'm going to fuck it up.
> **Matt:** What? How—?
> **Kevin** (*with a menacing, gloating smile*): I'm gonna dump salt on the threshold, for starters. Then I'll sprinkle it with holy water. And then I'll deliver the coup de grâce when I nail a cross to it. Like a stake through a vampire's heart.
> **Claire:** Kevin, please. We're not in control here.
> **Kevin:** You're right about that. I'm in control.
> **Claire:** It brought us here—
> **Kevin** (*grins*): I don't need your lecture, professor. This isn't science, it's magic. Always has been. You're in my realm now. I know how to fight negative spirits.
> **Claire:** You're making this a story where you're the—
> **Matt:** Claire, please. Let's just go. We all want to go to the same place.

Kevin tosses aside the smoldering bundling stick and pulls another object from his pack. A roadside flare, which hisses to life with a vibrant, bright red flame.

> **Kevin:** Okay. Let's do it.

He hands Jake's camera to Matt, keeping his hands free to hold the gun and flare, and hoists his backpack onto one shoulder. Together, they walk toward the luminous monolith perched atop its dais like a lighthouse overlooking an endless empty, black sea. Minutes roll by as Matt's GoPro tracks it. The background roar is so thick now it is almost tangible.

The camera yanks to a halt.

Matt: STOP. Everybody, back up, now.

The camera tilts down to weakly penetrate a seemingly bottomless void. They are standing nearly at the edge of a vast chasm.

Kevin: Holy...

He tosses the flare over the side. It falls in a streaming arc until becoming a tiny, distant spark. Then it disappears in the thick black.

The chasm appears so deep that one might die of thirst before hitting the bottom.

Kevin: They're laughing at us.
Matt: There has to be a way.
Kevin (*shouts*): I'm coming for you! You think this can stop me?

Jake's laughter rings back across the chasm.

Claire: Jesus.
Matt: Should we take a look around, see if we can find a way across?

Kevin ignites another road flare, which burns bright against the surrounding darkness. Matt and Claire turn on their flashlights.

Kevin: I'm getting over there if I have to fly.

He swings his wild glare to fix on Claire.

Kevin: You. Don't go too far.
Claire: Where would I possibly go?
Kevin: I just want you where I can keep an eye on you.

The camera veers away to explore the edge of the artificial canyon. Matt's light passes over and then fixes on a strip of stone stretching into the black. The beam slowly traces the span until the darkness eats the light.

He takes a step and places his foot down, testing its strength.

Matt: I think I found a bridge!

Claire jogs over first.

Claire (*in a quiet voice*)**:** He's completely lost it. We have to get away from him.
Matt: I know. Don't antagonize him. Just play along for now. We're almost there.

Kevin approaches as if taking a leisurely stroll, bright in the reddish glow of his hissing road flare. He takes off his ballcap, wipes sweat from his brow, and then puts it back on as he inspects the bridge for himself. So close to the monolith, the pulsing hum crescendos and rolls over them with the force of thunder every ten seconds.

Kevin: That does not look sturdy.

Matt: Should we find another?

Kevin: It's time for a leap of faith, chief. You two can go first.

Claire: That's fine with me. I'll lead.

Kevin (*grins*): Look at you, professor. We made a true believer out of you after all.

Claire: I can't argue with that. Matt?

Matt: Let's do this. I love you, honey.

Claire (*smiles back*): I love you, darling.

With her leading, they start across the stony span in single file. The camera illuminates the back of her head and shoulders. She walks in slow, careful steps, as if treading thin ice. They only have a few feet of stone on each side of them. Past that, empty space. A single misstep could be fatal.

Kevin: When this is over and people see what I've done, I won't be following orders anymore. I'll write the book. I'll have my own show.

Matt: You can have this one if you'd like it.

Kevin: Are you really done?

Matt: If we get out of this, I'm never setting foot in a haunted house again.

Kevin: What about you, professor?

Claire: I think "getting out of this" is a very big *if* right now.

Kevin: I don't think you're leaving the paranormal field. I think it's in your blood now. It must be quite a feeling, finding out you were wrong all along. Now you're playing with the fire.

Matt: How does it look ahead of us?

Claire: It's still going.

Kevin: When we get over there, watch and learn, kids. (*chuckles*) I've never seen a negative spirit beat salt. Or a demon that could beat a cross and holy water.

Matt: Hey, Kev?

Kevin (*stops chuckling*): What.

Matt: I don't think we know anything. That's been the problem from the start.

Kevin: This is wisdom passed down by shamans for thousands of years. I think we know something. If you want to get out of here, you stick with me.

Matt: I'm all for that. I really am. I just hope we don't piss it off—

A voice cries out in the darkness.

Kevin: Shut up, already!

Claire: Is that—?

Matt: It's coming from behind us now.

Voice (*louder*): You shot me!

Matt: Christ, it's on the bridge with us—

Voice: Don't walk away from me, *bro*.

Kevin: I said, shut up!

Voice (*louder*): Why'd you shoot me?

Kevin: Stay away from me! Stay back or I'll—

Voice: Let me try again!

It is no longer Jake's voice. It sounds higher pitched, desperate.

Kevin: No. No—

Voice: Let me try again! I can do it!

Kevin: You're dead!

Voice: I can do it!
Kevin: Shut! The!

He fires his gun at whatever is behind them with deafening reports, the muzzle flashes strobing like lightning flashes in the darkness.

Kevin: Fuck! Up!

Ahead of Matt, Claire flinches and stops.

Matt: Keep going! Go!

Shoulders hunched, she dashes forward while Kevin blazes away at the pursuing spirit.

Voice: LET ME TRY AGAIN.
Kevin: Stay away from me!

His voice has become shrill with panic. The gun rapidly booms as he empties the last bullets in his nine-millimeter's magazine.

Matt: Go, Claire!
Voice: I CAN DO IT.

A bestial snarl fills the air. A horrible ripping sound.

Kevin screams.

Matt: Oh God—

He turns in time to catch the blurred spark of the flare disappearing into the black, taking its light with it. The camera glimpses Kevin's floating, writhing form being torn apart. Kevin bellows a bloodcurdling howl as Matt turns back to continue his dash across the bridge.

Matt: Run! Go!

The howl quickly fades as Kevin plummets into the chasm.

Matt: Go! Go!

Claire reaches the other side and falls gasping to her knees. Matt catches up and wheels again to gaze behind. The camera briefly reveals a tall man in a hooded sweatshirt gazing back from the span. An instant later, the man disappears.

Matt grips Claire's arm and hauls her to her feet. Pure white light flares around them as another roaring pulse bursts from the monolith, turning to distortion in the camera's flooded microphone. The monolith is close now.

Claire: Kevin—
Matt: He's gone! We have to keep moving!

The haloed air around the monolith throbs with cosmic energy, the slow, steady heartbeat of a god.

The view wobbles as Matt and Claire dash hand in hand across the final stretch.

Claire: The air…so heavy!
Matt: I feel it too! We can make it! Just a—

He cries out as the ground disappears from under him.

FADE TO BLACK

PROD: Ep. 13, "Paranormal Research Foundation, Part 3"

Raw Video Footage

Tuesday, 3:52 p.m.

The flaring light reveals square holes of various sizes randomly checkerboarding the stone around the monolith. These hazards are similar to the trap that snared Jake in the maze.

Claire drops her camera and backpack and scrambles on hands and knees to the edge to shine her flashlight down into the hole where Matt disappeared.

Claire: Matt! MATT.

We cannot hear him. Wobbling from the impact of being dropped, the camera flops onto its side, making the scene off-kilter.

Claire: I can see you! Matt, please talk to me!

The spirit door blazes with white fire, shedding waves of energy that strike Claire with physical force. Its roar again overwhelms the microphone, becoming groaning audio distortion. The camera's view boils with pulsing vibrations. The very air seems to tremble with psychic emanations.

Fighting this force, Claire slowly regains her feet to face the glare. She gazes down at the hole Matt fell into, her mouth moving.

*If in fact Claire says anything, or if Matt replies, we cannot hear
either of them, and the guesses as to what she says widely vary,
ranging from "I'm so sorry" to "I will, okay" to "I love you."*

*She takes a laborious step toward the monolith, followed by another,
but every bit of progress seems to increase the resistance confronting
her. She staggers under the crushing weight of invisible forces and
struggles upright again.*

Another step, another, each requiring enormous effort and will.

*As she reaches the dais, bits of her ballooning sweater disappear to
whirl into the dark. She turns from the raging light with a pained
wince. Hair flying, mouth opening wide in a soundless scream, she
steps onto the platform and buckles to her hands and knees.*

There, she crawls onward, her progress now marked in inches.

*The audio distortion becomes whirring and flat and discordant. The
lens cracks, blurring the scene until the camera autocorrects. When
it does, we see bits of Claire disappearing in puffs of black dust.
Particles at first, and then whole pieces, creating holes in her form
that the light shines through in blinding beams. Her body jerks and
spasms. Claire Kirklin is physically disintegrating, her very substance
bleeding into the cosmic wind. Impossibly, she still lives, fighting to
haul her splintering body back to its feet one final time.*

*At last, mere yards from the spirit door, she collapses under the
colossal gravity into crumbling shards that themselves fly apart in a
final black swirl.*

Claire Kirklin's Journal

As I suspected, finding the source unlocked the final mystery of the maze.

When I died, I learned everything.

Claire Kirklin's Journal

The Foundation's experiment didn't work. Whatever they believed, there never was any scientific or even occult sophistication at play.

Only simple intent.

The researchers wanted the spirits to appear, so they did.

This is how it has always worked, going back to the days when these entities were worshipped as gods and priests prayed to them in marble temples and at sacrifice stones in pastoral groves. The more intent, the stronger their response.

Before I died, I was not studying them. They were studying me, studying all of us. We were in *their* experiment. We were in *their* investigation.

In their collective mind, a simple test.

It starts with an invitation. Response to intent. Once you're here, once you're in this Hades world, the only way to go is forward. You either transcend or you die.

I alone proved worthy of transformation. The only way to learn about these spirits is to join them. I wanted to know them so badly that I became one of them.

Roebuck is here, and others, and now I am too. Of all humanity, we're among the few who know the secret of ghosts because we're ghosts. We know everything, in fact, though we no longer consider it important to know.

My new home is the dark dimension, which coats the dimensions of light like a thin layer of tendriled, fuzzy black mold. That was one thing Roebuck had right. Here, there is no light or time, only gravity and its primordial hum. The spirits ride these warm tidal currents as a multitude of pure frequencies, of which I am now one.

Though not yet, not quite.

For now, I remain in the bubbled construction the spirits built for us to explore, still clinging to the lower dimensions, unable to let go yet. Roaming the maze like a freezing wind, I witness the death and suffering my obsession caused.

Like a skipping record, I see Kevin shoot Jake again and again, watch Kevin plunge howling into the chasm, and witness the hole appearing under Matt. I observe these events while all around, the omnipresent spirits contort and pirouette and observe from the shadows.

It hurts to see my husband and friends suffer, but it won't hurt for much longer. Already, my sense of self is starting to fade away.

So much of what made me Claire was a projection of genetics, chemicals, and environment. Take them all away, and what are you?

Just a ghost.

Claire Kirklin's Journal

I reach into the maze to find my husband where he lies in the dark, haunted and broken and slowly dying.

When I stood before the monolith, I could not save him. If I'd tried, I would have ended up wandering in the dark looking for him until I too became doomed. I remember believing if I opened the spirit door, I'd be able to save him. I remember him yelling at me to keep going.

I don't know how much of this is real or how I choose to remember it. That part I refuse to replay. The moments before my destruction, when I gazed directly into Shiva's burning eye.

I remember that at the end, I realized the spirit door didn't offer a path home. It offered the final answer to Foundation House.

I fall upon Matt and swirl around him. He cannot see me, and he cannot touch me, but his body is a sensor, and it knows my presence. When I whirl too close to his broken form, he moans and shivers with cold instead of pain.

He calls out for me, and I reach down to stroke his stubbled cheek, leaving a patch of freezer burn.

Why didn't you just go back like I wanted you to? What I wanted was my own doing. You should never have suffered for it.

"I couldn't leave you," he answers.

It's time to go home.

"Can't move. It hurts too much. My ankle seems to be broken. My hand, some ribs—"

I'll take you. I can get you out.

"Will you come too? Home?"

I remember a study with back-to-back laptops on facing desks, nearby shelves loaded with books. A window glowing with blinding light. I remember pots and pans on a stove, food and spices cooking with savory smells. I remember a king-size bed in a bedroom furnished in blues and whites and grays. I remember its warmth in the morning, waking up to my smiling husband handing me a mug of coffee.

I remember how it was never enough.

It's too late for me, Matt. I can't leave now.

"You made it. You passed through."

I did.

He fosters a weak smile, proud and bitter in the dark. "It's what you wanted."

I didn't know what it would cost me. You. All of us.

"I want to be like you. We'll be together. Tell me how to do it."

You once told me that people who can't let go of the earth remain as ghosts, but that's not correct. The opposite is true. To join the spirits, you must let go of all earthly desires until the only thing you want is to know them. The journey is always taken alone. This is far more difficult than one might think.

"Earthly desires," he says. The pride is gone, leaving only bitterness. "Including me."

I say nothing. I needed him, but I also needed to know.

In the end, I couldn't have both.

"It doesn't matter. I love you, Claire. I'll always love you."

Which is precisely why he cannot join me.

You must go. If you don't, you'll die.

"I'll never leave you. Never."

My sweet, beautiful man. Where I saw the physical laws in action, Matt saw magic. He made everyone he met see magic. For a while, I did too.

And he was right. There is magic. There is magic and wonder all around us if you know how to look, with a child's eyes ready to see anything.

He was right all along.

I still loved him for this and everything else, though I have no heart. I only wish I could have loved him the way he loved me, with everything I had and seeing it as enough.

I stay with him in the dark a single moment or an eternity, it's all the same to the spirits. Even if he allowed me to take him out of the maze, I have no idea what year or even decade it would be back in his world, where time existed to create and destroy.

I remember our lives together, all our hopes and joy and sadness and dreams, and it all seems so meaningless and also piercingly beautiful, a single act in an endlessly repeating play in which the actors constantly change. A play in which the story doesn't matter but whose continuation is essential. A mystery that fascinates the spirit world, their version of reality TV.

I am already forgetting what love is, as it is only another projection of the physical. Neurochemicals. Dopamine, serotonin, and norepinephrine that make falling for someone new so exciting, compulsive, anxious, and even dangerous. Oxytocin and vasopressin that facilitate long-term bonding.

Without them, love is just another human construct. A chance meeting in a bookstore is just a meeting, and our lives take on a different direction and meaning. For me, love is fast becoming only a memory. A hint of sweet, like an aftertaste. Already, I feel the pull to shed the last dregs of Claire Kirklin and join the eternal choir.

To finally let go and become like the rest of the spirits.

Please go back, I beg him. *Do it for me. Please. I'll be okay. You will too. Let me go. Please don't suffer for me anymore. You can survive.*

He only moans and shivers from pain and cold. Without me, he cannot go on, but he's already without me. I'm already gone.

"Not without you, Claire."

Matt—

"NO." His final decision. "Never without you."

He does not need to suffer. Good intention draws good. Bad draws bad. A good man deserves good. If the spirits have a moral law, it is this simple sense of karma, no matter how harsh their tests may seem.

Intent—the core you, the real you, defined as your single driving desire—attracts result. We spirits are genies that deliver based on need instead of wishes, and our magic can be beautiful or harsh but is always transformative.

Before the last of my love for him bleeds away, I kiss my husband until his lips turn blue. I reach into his brain and trigger a vivid memory of a random meeting in a bookstore. I draw up another of our wedding day, me smiling at him in my wedding dress, both of us so hopeful about the future and what it'd bring us.

Then I reach into his heart and kill him the way Jessica once said I would.

I have no eyes to weep.

Claire Kirklin's Journal

Matt's energy releases as heat, which I consume. Now he will always be a part of me, just as he wanted. And he finally achieved another desire, which is to learn what comes after death. He learned that everyone lives forever in one form or another. Everyone receives immortality.

. We are just no longer ourselves. That is the great sadness of it.

In my case, I'm becoming a god.

Writing this without hands or eyes, I am almost out of words. More human constructs assigning meaning to instinct and chaos. Claire's journal is now complete and will be placed in the house along with the other artifacts, all of them combining to form an invitation to come closer.

A majority of humans will not believe it. Most who believe will experience wonder but not devotion. The spirits do not mind. Their world is only for the worthy, the ones brave enough to escape Plato's Cave and burn in the sun.

These few will believe and make their own wishes upon a star. The spirits will answer them, like moths drawn to the same light. Intent and response. Mystery and testing. Perhaps we will find another human willing to shed themselves to know us.

And, like me, gain eternal life.

Forever altering the song, which here is both pleasure and survival.

Its purpose served, the maze is already crumbling.

The song of the spirits calls to me, and I must go.

Like a butterfly freed from its cocoon, I will flutter to join the joyful celestial music, my frequency adding its crystal note to the eternal mantra.

But first, there is one more thing I must do to make things right. Like a freezing wind, I rush and swirl through the maze.

Jessica is still alive.

THREE YEARS LATER

VALLEYVIEW RESORT & SPA
Denton, Virginia
Website

Paranormal Tour

Valleyview Resort & Spa: the new haunted hotel built on the site of "Foundation House," made famous by *Fade to Black*'s terrifying thirteenth and subsequent final episodes.

Strange experiments in parapsychology by New Age scientists who vanished in 1972...incredible paranormal events captured on video by a reality TV crew's investigative team, who themselves vanished to become part of the legend.

Hear the incredible story of Foundation House and more tonight at 8:00 p.m. when you take our Paranormal Tour that concludes in the basement, where you can see the original uncovered well where the spirit door appeared.

Walking and stairs are required. Accessibility to all areas is ensured, but please request assistance in advance if you need it.

FOUR YEARS LATER

UNEXPLAINED AMERICA
SEASON 2, EPISODE 1, "*FADE TO BLACK*"
Episode Introduction, Transcript

Music flourish. A well-dressed woman looks past the camera.

> **Paisley Hirsh:** Our team's last message was they were going into what they called the "house under the house." Their footage and journals turned up, but they're gone. Where did they go?

White flash transition accompanied by Unexplained America*'s theme, punctuated by "breaking news" style music cues. A photo of Foundation House blurs into a* Fade to Black *publicity photo showing Matt, Claire, Jessica, and Kevin posing with arms crossed in front of their black van.*

> **Voice-over:** This time on *Unexplained America*, the video footage of a haunting that shocked America, and the vanishing of the TV crew that produced it.
> **Sheriff Hunter Gaines:** After questioning Donnelly and Wilder, we conducted a thorough search of the house. At the bottom of the well, we found a pile of cameras and journals. As for the door the TV crew allegedly went through, it doesn't exist.

Night vision video rolls of the spirit flaring to life in the Apparition Room. The trigger objects rise to become a swirling spiral.

Voice-over: Was it all an elaborate hoax that ultimately went wrong four years ago? Or did the veteran paranormal investigators of *Fade to Black* stumble onto something far bigger, far more dangerous than they imagined?

Captain Don Clapper: After the liquor store holdup, Kevin suffered a great deal of mental strain about the shooting. The murder at the Mattice Homes proved the last straw. We tried to help him, but he chose a different path. That was Kevin.

Montage of short video clips, showing the hand reaching from the well to offer itself to Claire, Matt standing in front of the door marked NO PIGS, and Matt, Claire, and Kevin rushing down the stairs to flee the house.

Voice-over: Backed by exclusive interviews and new theories supported by fresh, never-before-seen evidence, we're going to look at the incredible events caught on tape by the *Fade to Black* paranormal investigation program.

Ramsay Godwin: Claire Kirklin had seen things she could not explain. She struck me as a very intelligent, very rational woman trying to make sense of the irrational.

The tall woman apparition's jack-o'-lantern face grins from the doorway.

Voice-over: You'll be amazed by our analysis, which proves these events actually occurred, despite a massive effort to deny their authenticity.

Tameeka Brewer: I know Rashida wouldn't just abandon

her son. Her last text told me she thought she was in danger. Maybe she's alive, maybe she's gone, but we deserve to know the truth. We deserve it.

Claire fights for every step to the monolith, finally collapsing and disintegrating.

Voice-over: Watch as the shocking mystery of Foundation House is solved once and for all in *Unexplained America*.

Final musical flourish. Fade to black for commercial break.

FIVE YEARS LATER

PERSONAL VIDEO
Uploaded to YouTube User KidzRock7730

*Recorded on a personal digital camera, the video shows a large
swimming pool awash in bright sunshine. Several adults in swimsuits
stretch out in pool chairs while their children splash in the turquoise
water.*

> **Kid:** Marco!
> **Other kids:** Polo!

*On the other side, we see a small outdoor bar and, beyond, the
ground level of the Valleyview Resort & Spa, built on the former site
of Foundation House.*

*The camera jerks around the poolside and finally swings back to
frame a middle-aged woman rooting in a beach bag.*

> **Mom:** Are you sure you put it in here?

*The camera swings to the man sitting next to her under a beach
umbrella, zooming a little to capture the face of a man feeling uptight
when he wants to be relaxing.*

> **Dad:** No. I didn't have to. We never took it out after we
> were out here yesterday.
> **Mom:** We need suntan lotion. We're going to fry in this
> sun.

The camera ping-pongs between them as if capturing an athletic contest.

    Mom (*looks directly into the lens*): Davey. Why don't you jump in the pool and play Marco Polo?

    Davey: Somebody has to document this, Mom. It's a major unsolved mystery. Where did the lotion go? Where did it *go*?

    Mom: Well, guess what, it's not in the bag.

    Dad: Keep looking. That bag is like a black hole.

    Mom: Like your ears.

The kid chortles at this. He is enjoying the show. In the distance, behind his parents, a young woman shuffles toward the pool dressed in a black T-shirt and jeans and carrying a backpack, all of it worn out and threadbare and riddled with holes, her sneakers in scraps and practically falling off her feet. Scars cover her arms. She has an instantly unsettling appearance, utterly out of place.

    Dad: We don't really need it. We'll be okay.

    Mom: You might. I'm going to burn.

The woman in the background totters on uncertain legs, as if in a hypnotic trance. The camera jerks a little, drawn to her. Arms splayed at her sides, she stops and stares at the scene as if waking up to an incomprehensible reality.

    Mom: *Someone* is going to have to buy us some at the gift shop.

    Dad (*with a loud sigh*): Fine. Did we bring any money?

The camera zooms to get as close as possible to the woman's face.

She is Black and pretty, though utterly haggard and disheveled. Her watery eyes squint and blink at the bright sunlight as if she finds it physically painful. Her mouth wobbles open and closed, struggling to form speech. She does not appear to be saying anything, though some speculate she said, "It's not real, you're not real."

Mom: It's up in the room, but—

Dad (*rises with another loud sigh*): I'm tired of being responsible for what's in *your* bag.

Mom: But you don't need money, Phil.

Dad: What do you mean, I don't need money?

Davey: Mom?

Mom: You can just charge it to the room.

Davey: *Mom.*

Mom: What?

Davey: Is that lady a ghost?

His mother turns to stare at the strange woman, who is visibly shaking. Other people have noticed her as well. While the kids go on playing in the pool, the adult chatter fades to a tense, awkward silence.

Dad (*muttering under his breath*): God. This place really draws in the weirdos.

Jessica Valenza opens her mouth wide until clearly forming the words: "Where did you go?"

Then she falls to her knees and releases a long, piercing scream of utter anguish.

ACKNOWLEDGMENTS

A novel is the product of a journey rarely taken alone. Special thanks to my mom, Eileen DiLouie, and brother, Chris; to my partner and fellow horror author, Chris Marrs; and to my children who give my life supreme meaning—with a special shout-out to Alex, with whom I spent hours playing *Phasmophobia* to get in the mood for some fictional ghost hunting.

To the horror community, which is so friendly and welcoming, the great horror authors who inspire the rest of us, the readers I've befriended on social media, and all my colleagues at the HWA and IFWA—with special shout-outs to Charles Prepolec (who generously provided notes on an early draft), John Dixon, Peter Clines, David Moody, Ron Bender, Ella Beaumont, Rena Mason, Patrick Freivald, David Walton, and Timothy W. Long: Thank you.

Last but certainly not least, a big thanks to my agent, David Fugate, and to my amazing editor, Bradley Englert, conversations with whom about found-footage horror films inspired me to write an epistolary novel that attempted to bottle their fun and terror.

MEET THE AUTHOR

Jodi O

CRAIG DILOUIE is an American-Canadian author of horror, dark fantasy, and other speculative fiction. His most notable works include *The Children of Red Peak* (Redhook, 2020), *Our War* (Orbit, 2019), *One of Us* (Orbit, 2018), and *Suffer the Children* (Gallery Books, 2014). He is a member of the Horror Writers Association, International Thriller Writers, and Imaginative Fiction Writers Association. Learn more at CraigDiLouie.com.

if you enjoyed
EPISODE THIRTEEN
look out for

THE CHILDREN OF RED PEAK

by

Craig DiLouie

David Young, Deacon Price, and Beth Harris live with a dark secret. They grew up in an isolated religious community in the shadow of the mountain Red Peak—and they are among the few who survived its horrific last days.

Years later, the trauma of what they experienced never feels far behind. And when a fellow survivor dies by suicide, they reunite to confront their past and share their memories of that final night.

But discovering the terrifying truth might put them on a path back to Red Peak, and escaping a second time could be almost impossible....

1

REMEMBER

After years of outrunning the past, David Young now drove straight toward it.

His Toyota hummed south along the I-5 as the sun melted into the coastal horizon. The lemon trees flanking the road faded into dusk. Most nights, he enjoyed the solitude of driving. He'd roll down the window and disappear in the sound of his tires lapping the asphalt, soothing as a Tibetan chant.

Not this time. California was burning again.

The news blamed the wildfire on a lightning strike in the sequoias. Dried out by the changing climate, the forest went up like a match. Outside the car, the air was toxic. A crimson glow silhouetted the Sierra Nevadas like a mirror sunset.

Red Peak called to him from all that fire and ash.

David turned on the radio to drown out his memories. He'd spent years forgetting. In all that time, he hadn't kept in touch with the others. He hadn't even told his wife about the horrors he'd survived. Claire believed he was visiting a client and not on his way to the funeral of an old friend to whom he owed a debt.

He didn't want to go, but Emily was dead, and he had her letter.

I couldn't fight it anymore, she'd written in flowing cursive.

All those years ago, five children survived. Now there were four.

He found a parking space at the All Faiths Funeral Home and cut the engine. Cars filled the lot. A sizable crowd had come to attend Emily's wake, friends and family who wanted to say goodbye.

Whatever happiness she'd found hadn't been enough for her.

He turned on the overhead light to inspect his appearance in the rearview. People said he had both charisma and looks, a genetic gift from his mother. Under dark, wavy hair, his angular face was sensitive and inspired trust.

Tonight, wild eyes stared back at him, the eyes of a man he didn't know or had forgotten. The eyes of a scared little boy.

You have children you love more than anything, he told his reflection. *You have a job that allows you to help people escape the worst of what you suffered. You're alive. The past isn't real. It's dead and gone.*

"I'll be okay," he thought aloud and opened the car door.

The warm night air smelled like an old brick fireplace. The mountains burned in the east, bright and close.

David turned his back on the view and lit a cigarette, a crutch he revisited in times of stress. He took a long drag, but it tasted terrible and only made him fidget more. He ground it under his shoe and went into the funeral home.

Black-clad mourners filled the foyer and lobby, mingling in the air-conditioned atmosphere heavily scented with fresh-cut flowers and sharp cleaners and the acrid tinge of wood smoke. Organ music droned over the murmur.

Stomach rolling, David scanned the faces. There was nobody here he recognized. He stood in awkward tension on the thick carpet. He should visit Emily's body and say goodbye, but he wasn't ready for that, not yet.

Then he saw her. Emily, still a child, reaching to tuck her long blond hair behind her ear, a frequent gesture he remembered well.

His heart lurched. He was seeing a ghost.

A man sat on the folding chair next to the girl and stroked her hair while she frowned at a tablet resting on her lap. On her other side, a towheaded boy played with his own device.

Her children, he realized. Around the age of his own kids. The girl was about the same age as David when he first met Emily in 2002.

They slouched in their chairs, miserable and bored. They didn't understand how profoundly their world had changed, not yet. After his mother died, David had taken a long time to process as well. A stabbing pain of homesickness stuck in his chest. He missed his own children back in Fresno, safe in Claire's care, still naive to how cruel the world could be.

The man caught him staring and rose to his feet with a scowl.

David held out his hand. "You must be Emily's husband."

"Nick." His breath was thick with whiskey. "Who are you?"

"David Young. I'm sorry for your loss, Nick."

Still protective, distrustful. "How did you know Emily?"

"We grew up together."

The man's scowl softened until he wasn't looking at David at all. Emily's suicide had broken him. "Where did...?"

David waited until the silence became awkward, then said, "She was a very good friend. In fact, I was just thinking how much your daughter resembles her back when I knew her."

He and Emily used to talk about how all they had was each other, how they'd spend the rest of their lives protecting each other.

"She never mentioned you." Nick shambled back to his kids.

David released the breath he'd been holding and retreated as well. He found himself walking without direction among the black-clad mourners, who murmured in small groups and shot him curious glances as he passed. He'd always had a difficult time sitting still, but now he had a purpose for it. As long as he appeared he had somewhere to go, nobody could draw him into conversation, and the mourners would remain raw impressions instead of real people.

He reached into the pocket where he kept his phone. He thought about going outside to call Claire and tell her he'd arrived safe at his hotel. If he did, however, he might not come back inside. Instead, he edged closer to the viewing room.

On the far side, Emily's white casket lay surrounded by arrangements of lilies, carnations, roses, orchids, and hydrangeas. He glimpsed slender lifeless hands clasped over her breast. At the doorway, a large poster mounted on an easel displayed photos of her life. Emily smiling at the camera, holding a baby, hugging her children, posing with her family.

David found it jarring to see her grown-up. She was still so familiar, but the intervening years had turned her into a stranger. His breath left him in a gasp as nearly fifteen years rushed past in an instant.

Her smile was still the same, however. A smile that lit up the room. He leaned for a closer look at a photo of her on a windy beach at twilight.

How did you fool them all for so long? he thought.

Or maybe she'd fooled herself.

A familiar voice said: "I thought I was gonna find you hiding in a closet."

Again, a strange sense of vertigo. He wheeled to find a teenage boy wearing a comfortable grin. The boy morphed into a man.

David shook his head and smiled. "You're still an asshole, Deacon."

▲   ▲   ▲

Now in his late twenties, Deacon Price appeared much the same skinny kid with his boyish face and easy smirk. But he'd styled his shaggy hair into an emo swoop that shadowed one eye, and he wore a black T-shirt, leather wristbands, jeans, and Chucks. His shirt advertised he liked HOT WATER MUSIC. An odd choice for a funeral. Then again, Deacon's outfit struck David as some kind of uniform.

A long time ago, they'd been best friends.

"You dyed your hair black," David said after a tight hug. He didn't mention the tattoos that covered his friend's arms.

"And you got older."

"Okay, let me guess." He made a show of studying Deacon. "Stock broker."

"Nice try." Deacon chuckled. "Musician. My turn." He took in David's black suit, white dress shirt, black tie, and shiny shoes. "Bible salesman?"

David snorted. "Hardly."

"Then you must be a cult deprogrammer."

"Wow, how did you know?"

His friend rolled his eyes. "It's called Google, dude."

"Right." David flushed with a little embarrassment. He'd never checked up on his old friends. "I'm an exit counselor, though, not a deprogrammer."

Usually paid by the family of a cult member, deprogrammers retrained a person out of their belief system, and some used kidnapping and confinement. Exit counseling was voluntary, more like an addiction intervention.

"Whatever you say." Deacon shrugged, the difference lost on him. "Did you think I wasn't coming? I assume you got the same letter I did."

"I don't know what I was expecting." David thought about it. "Now that I've come all this way, I feel funny, like I don't belong here. Don't you? Whatever life Emily made for herself, I wasn't part of it."

Deacon's eyes roamed the room until settling on Nick. "On the other hand, these people weren't a part of her life with us. I don't think they even know."

"You talked to Nick, her husband?"

His friend ignored the question. "Which do you think was the real Emily?"

David shook his head, which hurt just thinking about it. He was having a hard time processing who he even was right now. "I need a smoke."

"Excellent idea."

They emerged in the dim parking lot.

Deacon lit a cigarette. "Is Angela coming?"

David leaned against the funeral home's brick wall and blew a stream of smoke. "I seriously doubt it."

"Why not?"

"She's angry."

Deacon snorted. "So some things don't change."

"Only she's a police detective now, so it's even scarier when she gets mad."

"I wonder what she made of Emily's letter."

"I know she's mad at Emily for doing what she did." David didn't want to talk about his big sister, with whom he rarely kept in touch. He gazed across the parking lot toward the distant red glow. "Jesus. Look at it. I hope it rains soon."

Deacon cast his own eyes toward the fire. "Two million acres going up this year, all thanks to climate change. The ol' Reverend was right. The world's coming to an end. Only it's happening so slowly, hardly anybody is noticing."

He didn't want to talk about the Reverend either. "So how are you, Deek? How's life been treating you?"

Deacon pursed his lips. "Uh, good, David. How about you?"

"I'm doing good. Real good."

They smoked in silence for a while, which suited David just fine. Nothing stirred among the cars parked in the dark lot. Deacon seemed to want to pick up where things left off years earlier. David was one bad vibe away from fleeing to his car. A little small talk wouldn't hurt. A little quiet.

His friend had never known how to take things slow. He seemed ready to talk everything out. He'd read Emily's letter and found some hidden meaning.

David gazed toward his car, which promised the safe routines of home.

A woman emerged from the gloom to pose with her hands on her hips. "You boys. I leave you alone for fifteen years, and look what you get up to."

Beth Harris was still petite, though she'd filled out in womanhood, and her long, straight, sandy hair was pulled back in a bun instead of flowing free around her shoulders. Otherwise, the years had done little to age her pixie face.

David hugged her. "It's really nice to see you."

She patted his shoulder. "You were brave to come."

He released her, and she and Deacon regarded each other with goofy grins. They stepped into an embrace that was far friendlier than the one she'd given David.

Get a room, David heard his twelve-year-old self say.

At last, they let go, though the tension between them hung in the air.

"Look at you." She appraised Deacon. "Rock 'n' roll star."

"You'd never guess what put me on this path."

"We're going to talk," she said and turned to David. "But we're going to take it slow." She reached into her purse and produced a silver flask. "I brought a little bottled courage to guide us on the path."

David smiled as Beth handed it over. The strong scent alone braced him. Rum. The alcohol burned down his throat with a warm, fuzzy aftermath. He passed the flask to Deacon, who tossed his head back in a long swallow.

Beth shot David a questioning glance. "No Angela, huh?"

"Nope."

Deacon stared at the distant fire. "God, look at it now." The fiery glow shimmered and pulsed in a natural light show. "It reminds me...Listen. Can I tell you guys something about the last night at the mountain?"

Beth raised her hand. "Going slow, remember?"

Deacon shuddered and took another long swig. "Okay."

"So. Have either of you visited Emily yet?"

They shook their heads.

"Then we should tear off that Band-Aid first." Her large brown eyes flickered between them. "We can visit her together."

David produced his box of Marlboros. "I need a quiet moment. You guys go ahead."

"We have to say goodbye." Beth rested her hand on his arm. "Once you do, you'll take all that weight off your shoulders."

He put away his cigarettes. "All right."

They entered the funeral home and threaded the crowd toward the viewing room. David's heart crashed like a rock flung at a brick wall.

Beth slipped her hand into his. "I'm right here with you."

He answered with a vague nod. There was no controlling his legs anymore. He simply floated toward the casket. Emily lay with her hands clasped as if to hide where she'd parted the flesh of her arms with a razor.

Memories flashed across his vision, which fragmented into

puzzle pieces. Emily sat next to him in a dark supply closet. Gripped his hand while his mother purified herself in the Temple. Said goodbye the day they left for separate foster homes and promised they'd be together again, as it was meant to be.

He groaned as Emily's corpse rematerialized before him. Sweat soaked through his dress shirt. He was shaking. Was going to be sick. The stress of revisiting the past. All the smoke in the atmosphere. Something he ate.

Beth guided him out the door into the open air. "You're having a panic attack."

David stood outside on trembling legs. His blood roared in his ears, his heart about to burst. His car seemed miles away. He spotted a row of camellias planted around the base of the funeral home and burrowed into them to sit on the mulch with his back against the rough wall.

"Look at me." Beth crouched to face him. "There's nothing to be afraid of. You're safe. Just breathe, okay? In through your nose for a few seconds, now out through your mouth, nice and slow. That's right. You've got it. It'll pass soon. I'll stay with you as long as you want me to."

David wiped cold sweat from his face. His tears were warm. "I'm stupid."

"No, you're not."

"I thought I was safe."

"You are safe."

He wagged his head. "All I did was find a bigger place to hide."